BURN
FOR
YOU

Also by J.T. Geissinger

Bad Habit Series

Sweet as Sin
Make Me Sin
Sin with Me

Wicked Games Series

Wicked Beautiful
Wicked Sexy
Wicked Intentions

Night Prowler Series

Shadow's Edge
Edge of Oblivion
Rapture's Edge
Edge of Darkness
Darkness Bound
Into Darkness

BURN
FOR
YOU

A
SLOW BURN
NOVEL

J.T. GEISSINGER

Montlake
Romance

Published by Montlake Romance, Seattle

www.apub.com

Amazon, the Amazon logo, and Montlake Romance are trademarks of Amazon.com, Inc., or its affiliates.

ISBN-13: 9781542047456
ISBN-10: 1542047455

Cover design by Letitia Hasser

Printed in the United States of America

For Jay, and twenty years of happily ever after.

ONE

BIANCA

The first time I laid eyes on the man known throughout the state of Louisiana as "the Beast," I thought he couldn't possibly be as bad as his reputation.

As it turned out, I was wrong.

He was worse.

Dressed all in black, standing a head taller than everyone else, his shoulders so broad they cast an ominous shadow over the polished wood floor, Jackson Boudreaux surveyed the bustling dining room of my restaurant with the expression of a king who'd stumbled upon a village of peasants infected with the plague.

His lip was curled. His eyes were narrowed. His nose was stuck so far up in the air, I wondered if he'd come in from the rain to avoid drowning.

"Hoo *Lawd*! We got ourselves a *loup-garou*! Get the garlic!"

Standing beside me at the stove in the kitchen, my sous chef, Ambrosine, made the sign of the cross over her ample chest as she peered through the glass wall at the man in black. Eeny, as she was affectionately called by everyone who knew her, was a retired voodoo priestess with a collection of superstitions almost as elaborate as her African tribal-print caftans.

"Garlic is for vampires, not werewolves, Eeny," I said, gazing past the tables of diners to the hostess stand at the front of the restaurant, where the man with the presence of thunderclouds stood glowering at the hostess, Pepper. The poor girl was visibly shrinking under the weight of his stare.

A flash of irritation made me frown.

It was the first, and mildest, of many such flashes I'd have tonight.

"That ain't no werewolf, or no vampire," grumbled a voice to my right.

I glanced at my pastry chef. Hoyt was a seventysomething Cajun with an accent thicker than bayou sludge, a grizzled white beard, and arthritic hands that still managed to make the best beignets in New Orleans. He jerked his chin toward the newcomer, then turned his attention back to the giant ball of dough on the floured wood board on the counter in front of him.

"I recognize his face from the papers," said Hoyt. "That there is the *boodoo tête de cabri*, Mr. Boudreaux Bourbon Jr. himself."

"Well butter my butt and call me a biscuit," I said, panicking.

My panic wasn't because Hoyt had called the mysterious new arrival a goat-headed bully. Hoyt had a way of describing people that was as colorful as the Mardi Gras parade. It was because that *particular* goat-headed bully was heir to the world's number one best-selling bourbon empire.

A bourbon I had created my entire spring menu around.

It was a menu that had been extremely well received by my guests and the cause for a surge in reservations. It was getting fantastic reviews from local food critics and had even just this month received a glowing mention in *Gourmet* magazine.

It was a menu, in all honesty, packed so full of love and soul and hope and sweat that it was like it was my own baby. I'd spent months preparing it, testing it, and fine-tuning it until it was perfect.

But having *Jackson Boudreaux himself* come in to dine was an event I was completely unprepared for.

I knew he lived in New Orleans—I read the papers, too, after all—but had heard so much talk of him being unsociable and hermitlike, I thought it unlikely he'd ever show up at my door, even if his family bourbon had inspired the menu.

Now here he was.

All six-foot-scowling-three of him.

Scaring the wits out of my hostess and sending an eerie hush through my dining room.

"How did I miss his name on the reservations list?" I cried. "If I'd known he was coming, I'd have made sure to give him the best table!"

Eeny said, "Pepper just seated a family of eight at the best table. It's an anniversary party, boo. They'll probably be there for hours."

I groaned. I was tempted to go out and find a table for him myself, but we were swamped in the kitchen. I'd just have to trust Pepper to do her best to fit him in somewhere as fast as she could.

"Y'all get back to work!" I instructed the rest of the kitchen staff, who had stopped what they were doing to stare at Jackson Boudreaux like everyone else in the place.

When no one moved, I clapped my hands. The staff jumped back into action, knowing that a clap meant business. I never raised my voice with them, even when I was angry, which was rare. I had a naturally sunny disposition.

It was about to be put to the test.

"Henri, I need more pepper jelly!" I called to one of my line cooks as I turned my attention back to the ramekins of duck étouffée I was plating. Every dish that left the kitchen did so only after a final inspection from me. As Henri rushed over with a container of the homemade spicy jelly, I pushed all thoughts of Jackson Boudreaux aside to concentrate on my task.

When finished, I quickly handed the plates off to a waiting server. Two more dishes needing final inspection instantly took their place from a server on my other side. The restaurant was filled to capacity, and at only six o'clock I knew I was in for a long night. I couldn't have been happier.

After all, this was my dream come true. I'd grown up in the kitchen of my mama's restaurant and had been saving and scrimping for years to open my own. Cooking was in my blood as much as jazz music and the Saints.

My happiness took its first hit when the hostess burst through the swinging metal kitchen doors in tears.

I looked up at her in surprise. "Pepper! What on earth—"

"That egg-suckin' son of a motherless goat can kiss my ass!" cried Pepper, swiping angrily at her watering eyes so her mascara smudged all over her cheeks.

Pepper swore like a sailor, wore too much makeup, had hair dyed an unholy shade of streetwalker red and skirts as short as her heels were tall, but she was a genuinely sweet girl who had a way with people. The regulars loved her.

Besides, this was the French Quarter. If I required a hostess who looked like a sexless nun, I'd be seating the tables myself.

I took Pepper by the arm and steered her through the kitchen to the back, near the walk-in freezer. The last thing I wanted was my guests getting a side of Pepper's notoriously salty mouth with their gumbo.

I handed Pepper a tissue. "What's going on?"

Pepper dabbed at her eyes and dramatically sniffled. "That man who just came in—"

My stomach dropped. "Mr. Boudreaux?"

Pepper nodded, then launched into an outraged rant.

"He said he wanted a table, and I told him unfortunately we were fully committed, and he said what the hell did that mean, and I tried to nicely explain that we didn't have any available tables, and then he said all snottylike, 'Don't you know who I am!' and demanded I *find* him a table, and I said I just *told* you there aren't any tables available, sir, and there's a waiting list a mile long, but he cut me off and said—really mean, too, he's like a crossbred dog!—that his name was all over our menu and if I didn't get him a table, he'd make sure *our* name was all over the papers, and not in a good way, either, because he knew all the press! So it was like he *threatened* me, and when I got upset, he growled at me to stop sniveling! *Sniveling!* Doesn't that just dill my pickle!"

Pepper ended her rant with a stamp of her stiletto heel.

I pinched the bridge of my nose between two fingers and sighed. So Mr. Boudreaux didn't have a reservation after all. And trusting Pepper to do her best hadn't exactly worked out as I'd hoped.

"All right, Pepper, first thing—calm down. Take a deep breath."

Grudgingly, she did.

"Good. Now go back out there and tell him—*nicely*, please—that the owner will be out to speak with him in a few minutes. Then show him to the bar and have Gilly give him a drink. On the house."

"But—"

"Pepper," I interrupted, my voice firm. "That is *Jackson Boudreaux.* Not only could the man buy and sell this town a hundred times over, he's no doubt connected with all kinds of highfalutin folks, which means that if he feels mistreated, all those people are gonna hear about it, which isn't good for business. I'm sorry he wasn't nice to you, but you need to learn how to handle peacocks like that without getting your own feathers ruffled."

Smiling to soften my words, I squeezed Pepper's shoulder. "And remember, the biggest bullies are the biggest babies inside. So just picture him in a nappy with a bottle stuck in his mouth, and don't let him intimidate you."

With a toss of her head, Pepper sniffled again. "I'd rather picture him with a bucket of crawdads shoved up his tight ass in place of that stick."

The loud cackle from the front of the kitchen was Eeny.

"Charming, Pepper," I said drily. "Now go."

With a final sniff, Pepper turned and flounced out.

It was ten minutes before I could steal time away from the kitchen. When I stepped out from behind the swinging metal doors, I saw Pepper had followed my instructions.

Jackson Boudreaux stood at the end of the bar, glaring into his drink like it had made a rude comment about his mother. Though the rest of the bar was crowded, around him there was a five-foot circle of space, as if his presence were repelling.

I wonder if he smells?

Judging by his appearance, it was a distinct possibility. The black leather jacket he wore was so creased and battered it could have been from another century. The thick scruff on his jaw made it obvious he didn't shave on anything resembling a regular basis, and his hair—as black as his expression—curled over the collar of his jacket and fell across his forehead in a way that suggested it hadn't seen a pair of scissors in years.

No wonder Eeny had called him a werewolf. The man had the look of something wild and dangerous you might run across if you were out for a midnight stroll in the woods.

He looked up and caught me staring.

From all the way across the room I felt the weight of his gaze, the sudden shocking force of it, as if he'd reached out and seized me around the throat.

My breath caught. I had to convince myself not to step back. I forced a smile. Then I made myself move forward, when all my instincts were telling me to turn around and find a vial of holy water and a gun loaded with silver bullets.

I stopped often to shake hands with the regulars and say hello as I made my way through the room, so it was another few minutes before I made it to the bar. When I finally found myself standing in front of my intended target, I was dismayed to see his expression had turned from merely unpleasant to downright murderous.

The first thing Jackson Boudreaux said to me was, "I don't like to be kept waiting."

And my oh my did the Beast have a beautiful voice.

Deep and rich, silky but with an edge like a purr, it was at total odds with his unkempt appearance. It oozed confidence, command, and raw sex appeal. It was the voice of a man secure of his place in the world—a voice that was as used to giving orders to employees as it was to women beneath him in bed.

A flush of heat crept up my neck. I wasn't sure if it was from annoyance, that voice, or his disturbing steely-blue eyes, which were now burning two holes in my head.

Before I could reply, he snapped, "Your hostess is incompetent. The music is too loud. And your drink menu is pretentious. 'Romeo and Julep?' 'The Last of the Mojitos?' Awful. If I were going on first impressions, I'd guess your food is awful, too."

The flush on my neck flooded into my cheeks. My mouth decided to answer before I did. "And if *I* were going on first impressions, I'd guess you were one of the homeless panhandlers who harass the tourists over on the boulevard, and throw you out of my restaurant."

Nostrils flared, he stared at me.

So much for unruffled feathers.

To cover my embarrassment, I stuck out my hand and introduced myself. "Bianca Hardwick. Pleased to meet you, Mr. Boudreaux."

There was a long, terrible moment during which I thought he'd start to shout, but he simply took my hand and shook it.

"Miss Hardwick. It's a pleasure to make your acquaintance."

Formal. So he wasn't born in a barn after all.

"Call me Bianca, please. I apologize for the wait."

Jackson dropped my hand, and with it, his brief civility. "If I wanted to call you Bianca, I would have. Where's my table?"

He glared at me, his hand wrapped so tightly around his drink his knuckles were white.

Pepper sure called this one. I owe that girl an apology.

Fighting the urge to kick him in the shin, I instead gave him my sweetest Southern-belle smile. I would *not* be intimidated, or bullied, or lose my cool on account of this arrogant jerk.

"Oh, it's here somewhere." Deliberately vague because I knew it would annoy him, I waved a hand in the air. "As soon as a table becomes available, we'll squeeze you in where we can. So nice of you to drop by. Now if you'll excuse me, I have to get back to—"

"Miss Hardwick," he hissed, stepping closer to loom over me. "Where. Is. My. *Table?*"

I felt a dozen pairs of eyes on us. In my peripheral vision, I saw the bartender, Gilly—almost an older brother to me—red-faced in anger at how I was being treated. And was it my imagination, or had the restaurant gone quiet again?

One thing definitely wasn't in my imagination. Jackson Boudreaux *didn't* smell. At least not bad. Standing so close, I caught his scent: a delicious whiff of exotic musk and warm, clean skin that would have been extremely sexy on anyone else.

But it wasn't anyone else. It was Prince A-hole, heir to an international bourbon dynasty, devoid of affection for shaving, haircuts, new clothes, or, it appeared, the human race.

Nappy! Picture him in a nappy with a binkie in his big fat mouth!

I lifted my chin and looked up into his eyes. I said calmly, "Maybe you were right about the music being too loud. It must have obstructed your hearing, because I just told you that we'd get you a table as soon as one becomes available. Or perhaps you'd prefer I throw someone out? Maybe that nice elderly couple by the piano? They look much less deserving of enjoying their meal than you do, am I right?"

His lips flattened. A muscle in his jaw flexed. Through his nose, he slowly drew in a breath.

I wondered if he was restraining himself from smashing his glass against the wall. Though my heart was hammering, I stood my ground and didn't blink.

Finally, he dragged a hand through the thick mess of his hair and exhaled, an exasperated sound that clearly telegraphed how much he enjoyed interacting with the peasants.

Especially ones who dared to get lippy.

He snapped, "How long?"

By this time my smile had died a painful death. "You made my hostess cry. How long of a wait do you think that's worth?"

Through gritted teeth, he replied, "I'm not a man to be toyed with, Miss Hardwick. As I told your hysterical hostess, I know all the prominent food critics—"

I snorted. "How lucky for them!"

"—and as my name is featured prominently on most of the dishes on your menu, I'd expect you'd be more accommodating—"

"Technically, Boudreaux is your *family's* name, correct?"

"—because I make it my business to protect anything with my name on it—"

"Excuse me, how did *my* menu suddenly become *your* property?"

"—and if your food is as bad as everything else I've experienced so far, including your attitude, I won't hesitate to speak with my industry contacts, along with my attorneys about your infringement on my *family's* trademark."

My mouth dropped open. I stared at him in horror. "You're threatening to *sue* me? You can't possibly be serious!"

For an answer, he narrowed his eyes at me. A low, dangerous growl rumbled through his chest.

Oh, no. Oh, no, he did *not* just try to scare *me* with that wild animal act!

I closed the final foot between us, looked straight into his cold blue eyes, and said, "I don't care who you are, Mr. Boudreaux, or how much bad press you can bring me, or how many overpaid attorneys you have. Your manners are atrocious. Growl at me again and I *will* throw you out."

I stepped back and met his burning stare with a level one of my own. "You'll get the next available table. In the meantime, have another drink on me. Maybe the alcohol will turn you back into a human being."

Fuming, I spun around and walked away, convinced Jackson Boudreaux was the most arrogant, stuck-up, bad-tempered man I'd ever had the misfortune to cross paths with. The only thing I could ever feel for him was disgust.

As it turned out, I was wrong about that, too.

TWO

BIANCA

Jackson stayed for four hours, straight through the third seating, sampling almost every damn dish on the menu, right down to two servings of blackberry-and-bourbon cobbler for dessert.

He ate the same way he talked. Mechanically, as if he took no pleasure in it, like it was a nuisance, one more thing to endure in the long, joyless span of his day. Still aggravated by our interaction, I watched from the kitchen as he sat alone and wolfed down plate after plate of food, eyes lowered, ignoring all the curious looks sent his way.

Stopping beside me to follow my gaze, Eeny exclaimed, "Looks like that boy hasn't eaten in a year!"

I sourly harrumphed. "Only the souls of all who've displeased him."

She chuckled. "I see LaDonna Quinn would like to give him somethin' else to chew on besides your spicy baby back ribs. Lawd, that dress she's wearin' is so tight you can almost see her religion."

For the third time, the newly divorced brunette sashayed by Jackson's table, hips swaying, toying with her hair and fluttering her lashes. She might as well have been invisible for all the attention it got her.

"Ooh—and here comes Marybeth Lee struttin' her stuff!" exclaimed Eeny gleefully, pointing to the bombshell Marybeth, man-eater extraordinaire, whose glossy blonde locks and hourglass figure never failed to turn heads. She emerged from the ladies' room and took the long way back to her table, gliding by Jackson's table with a sultry smile directed his way.

He sent her a withering glance and went back to his dinner.

I mused, "Maybe he's gay. I've never seen a man immune to Marybeth's double Ds."

Eeny cackled. "Judgin' by the way his eyes were glued to your behind when you were stormin' away from him at the bar, I'd say that boy is definitely *not* gay."

Outraged, I gasped. "He was looking at my *ass?*"

Eeny looked me up and down, her brows lifted. "What, you need to introduce a man to your mama before he's allowed to get an eyeful of your booty?"

I sputtered, "No, that's not—he's just—what a jerk!"

Eeny does this thing when someone isn't making sense where she squints one eye and looks at you sideways. She did it to me now, crossing her arms over her chest. "Don't tell me you don't think he's handsome."

I grimaced. "Handsome? How could I tell? It's impossible to see past the forked tongue and the horns!"

Eeny pursed her lips. "Mm-hmm."

"Don't you have some work to be doing, Eeny?" I said, exasperated by the turn in the conversation.

She shrugged. "I'm just sayin', if LaDonna and that scandalmonger Marybeth are spendin' so much time throwin' their hussy selves in his direction, it ain't because he's ugly."

"No, it's because he's stinking rich. And besides, you called him a werewolf. *You* can't think he's handsome!"

She clucked like a hen. "Oh, honey. I think all this time you've been without a man has made you blind."

From across the kitchen, Hoyt let out a hoot of laughter.

I looked at the ceiling and sighed. "Lord, why do I even employ these people?"

Hoyt hooted again. "I'm guessin' that's one of them 'moot' questions, 'cause we both know you wouldn't have a dessert menu worth eatin' if it wasn't for me—"

"Oh, shut your pie hole and get back to work, Hoyt!" bossed Eeny, propping her hands on her wide hips. "I swear, if I have to hear one more time about your mad skills with pastry dough, I'll keel over and die!"

Hoyt, who'd been in love with Eeny for going on sixty years and had been getting rejected for just as long, sent her a lazy grin and a wink. "Aw, c'mon now dawlin'. You know it ain't my dough-kneadin' skills that make you weak in the knees."

"Ack," said Eeny, rolling her eyes. "You're delusional, old man."

Hoyt grinned wider. "And you, suggie bee, are a sassy li'l blackberry. C'mon over here and give old Hoyt a kiss."

"Pffft! Don't hold your breath!" said Eeny with a flip of her hand.

Then Pepper breathlessly burst through the kitchen doors.

"Bianca! He's asking for you!"

My stomach turned. I didn't have to ask who she meant.

I peered out to Jackson Boudreaux's table, expecting to see him throttling one of the busboys, but he was just sitting there with his arms crossed over his chest, glaring daggers at nothing in particular.

The man gave the term *resting bitch face* a whole new meaning. He looked like his face had caught on fire and someone had tried to put it out with a fork.

I said, "What does he want? Did Marlene already bring him the check?"

"Yes! And then he called me over and gave me this!" Pepper triumphantly held up a crisp hundred-dollar bill. "And when I asked what it was for, he said all meanlike, 'I don't like to see a woman cry.' Can you believe that?" She giggled in delight. "If I'd known I'd get a Benjamin as a tip if I cried, I would've been bawling on the customers from day one!"

I ground my teeth together. The nerve of that man, trying to buy Pepper off for him being an overbearing prick!

Unfortunately, it was working.

But *I* wasn't about to let him start throwing his money around as payment for his terrible behavior. I might not be rich like him, but I had my pride. Nobody was buying *me* off. All his wealth didn't impress me one bit.

In fact, he could take his money and shove it right up there with Pepper's bucket of crawdads!

"Eeny," I said firmly, pointing to the cobblers I was plating, "make sure these get out to table six. I'll be back in two shakes."

"Uh-oh," she said, warily eying my expression. "Somebody get the fire extinguisher. I think poor Mr. Boudreaux is about to go up in flames."

I muttered, "Poor my patootie," and pushed through the kitchen doors.

I made a beeline to his table, stopped beside it, and didn't smile when he looked up. Cool as an iceberg, I said, "You asked to see me?"

I'd be professional, but I wasn't going to kiss his uppity butt, even if he could sue me and get me bad reviews. I didn't like being disrespected and spoken down to, and liked being threatened even less. Had he simply been polite, this evening would have gone differently, but here we were.

Staring with open hostility at each other.

Neither of us said anything. The moment stretched out until it became uncomfortable, and then intolerable. Staring into his eyes was like being physically attacked.

Finally he broke the awful silence by saying, "There's an error on my check."

"No there isn't."

His brows, thick and black, badly in need of manscaping, lifted. "There must be. It shows nothing due."

"Correct."

His cold blue gaze burned into mine. "I've been sitting here eating for hours—"

"Believe me, I'm perfectly aware how long you've been here and how much you've eaten."

He leaned back against the leather booth, spread his hands flat against the tabletop, and examined me the way a scientist might examine a germ under a microscope. It was horrible, but I gave no outward indication how much it rattled me.

I wondered if that muscle jumping in his jaw was a sign of an oncoming murder spree.

Then he had the audacity to say—with dripping condescension— "My opinion of you and your restaurant can't be swayed with freebies, Miss Hardwick."

Sweet baby Jesus, I wanted to pick up the steak knife on the table next to his empty plate and stab him in the eye with it.

Instead I said, "I'm not interested in your opinion, Mr. Boudreaux. Your meal is on the house because I love your family's bourbon and it inspired me to create this menu, which I happen to be very proud of, and which has made a lot of people happy. I would've comped you even if you *didn't* act like the sun comes up just to hear you crow."

For the first time I saw something other than steel in his eyes. It was only a moment, a flash of emotion that warmed his gaze, and then it was gone.

He said stiffly, "I insist on paying—"

"I'm not taking your money."

A flush of color crept over his cheeks. I supposed he wasn't used to hearing *no*. That gave me an enormous sense of satisfaction, even if I did just give away four hundred bucks' worth of food and couldn't afford to.

Then he stood. It was abrupt and startlingly smooth for a man so large—one swift unbending of limbs that had him on his feet and looming over me.

Again.

Looking up at him, I swallowed. It wasn't fear I felt, but he was definitely unnerving. And hot *damn*, why did this crabby, beastly bastard have to smell so good? If I didn't know better that my mouth was watering from the scent of bourbon-spiced gumbo wafting through the air, I might have almost thought it was because of him.

"Miss Hardwick," he said, the edge in his voice rougher, his eyes burning blue fire, "You. Are being. *Unreasonable.*"

Boy, did he like to punctuate his words with a hammer! A laugh escaped me.

"And you, Mr. Boudreaux, are the reason the gene pool needs a lifeguard. Have yourself a nice evening."

For the second time tonight, I turned my back on Jackson Boudreaux and walked away. Only this time I was painfully aware he might be staring at my ass.

Thanks a million, Eeny.

THREE

JACKSON

Rayford was already waiting at the curb with the car door open when I left the restaurant. That was a good thing, because in my current mood I might have torn the fucking door right off its hinges.

Seething, I climbed into the back of the Bentley. Rayford shut the door behind me without a word. When he started the car and we drove away, I couldn't tell if I was relieved or disappointed.

I'd never met such an irritating woman in my entire life. The mouth on her! The attitude!

The incredible heart-shaped ass.

I clenched my teeth and stared out into the rainy night. I hadn't wanted a woman in a long time. Cricket had seen to that. After that disaster, all I could see when a woman looked at me were the dollar signs in her eyes.

But this firecracker Bianca Hardwick. *Christ.* I wasn't sure if I wanted to kiss that smart mouth or put a gag in it.

"How was the food, sir?" asked Rayford, peering at me in the rear-view mirror.

Still boiling with anger, I snapped, "Adequate."

Well accustomed to my moods and knowing that was the highest praise I'd ever give anything, Rayford nodded. "Her mama was a great cook, too. Davina's restaurant was around for, oh, twenty years I think before Hurricane Katrina blew through and wiped it out." He chuckled. "I had many a meal there back in the day. Every time I came to visit my baby brother, I made sure to stop by. Never forgot Davina's jambalaya. It was like havin' a mouthful of heaven. And it wasn't only the food that kept me comin' back. Miss Davina Hardwick was one of the finest-lookin' women I ever seen."

The apple doesn't fall far from the tree.

Even with no makeup, her dark hair scraped back into a severe bun, wearing a pair of hideous clogs, a stained apron, and a sexless white chef's coat that covered her from neck to wrists, Bianca Hardwick was stunning. All flashing black eyes and glowing brown skin and ferocious self-confidence, she was a dead ringer for a young Halle Berry.

A young, aggravating Halle Berry.

I dragged a hand through my hair and exhaled.

It wasn't all her fault I was on edge. I'd been on edge before I even set foot in the place. My personal chef—the fourth in six months—had left in a snit after I'd said the eggs were runny at breakfast, I was hosting a charity benefit for three hundred people in two weeks and would have to try to find a caterer since I didn't have a chef, and Cody's good-for-nothing junkie mother had just gotten thrown in jail on possession charges.

Again.

But it was the phone call from my father that had really put the cherry on top. The same phone call I'd been getting every week for going on four years.

When are you coming back to Kentucky? When are you going to stop this foolishness and take over your responsibilities? Boudreaux Bourbon hasn't had a Master Distiller who wasn't a family member in over two hundred years! You're breaking your mother's heart!

And on and on, until my fucking ears bled. It didn't matter how much he begged, though. I was never going back.

Returning to Kentucky meant returning to that world of privilege and power I wanted nothing to do with, that viper's den of genteel, well-mannered people who smiled and shook your hand, then started sharpening the knives as soon as your back was turned. There wasn't a single person in my social circle aside from my parents I could trust.

Money makes people greedy. A lot of money makes them ruthless. I'd learned that the hard way.

Liars, schemers, and snakes, all of them. It was safer in New Orleans. I didn't have to fend off as many bullshitters trying to befriend me so they could get their hands on my bank account.

Bianca Hardwick definitely didn't care about befriending me. And judging by the free dinner, she didn't give a damn about my bank account. The only thing she seemed to care about was insulting me.

You're the reason the gene pool needs a lifeguard.

Sassy goddamn woman. No one *ever* spoke to me like that.

My mouth was doing something strange. It took me a moment to realize my lips were curving up, another moment to remember that meant I was smiling.

"You feelin' all right, sir?" asked Rayford, watching me in the rear-view mirror with concern.

"Of course. Why?"

"Because you look a little funny. Sick, maybe."

When I scowled, Rayford looked relieved.

How fucking depressing. I'd better never think about Bianca Hardwick's smart mouth or perfect ass again, or Rayford might think I was dying.

FOUR

BIANCA

Whoever coined the phrase *beauty sleep* had obviously never seen me in the morning.

"Damn, girl," I said to my haggard reflection in the bathroom mirror. "Those aren't bags under your eyes, that's a full set of luggage."

I splashed cold water on my face, pressed a wet washcloth to my lids, and held it there for a minute, to no effect. When I opened my eyes, I looked just as bad as I did before.

Serves me right for staying up into the wee hours of the morning working on a new menu.

But if Jackson Boudreaux was serious about his threat to sue, I'd have to revamp everything, fast. Then I supposed I'd have to hire myself a lawyer.

Stuck-up son of a lazy-eyed catfish!

What little sleep I'd had was filled with nightmares about being chased from the restaurant by a pack of wolves, led by one particularly large and nasty specimen that was all sharp teeth and vicious growls, his black fur bristling as he snapped at my heels. I woke with my heart pounding, the sheets drenched in sweat. And now I looked like I'd been chewed up and spit out by an ornery gator.

I pinned my hair into a bun, then smoothed a dollop of pomade over all the rebellious little flyaways staging a protest around my hairline. Then I brushed my teeth and got dressed, not bothering with makeup. There was no concealer on earth that could tackle my undereye bags today, and I'd never quite mastered the art of applying mascara. Or lipstick, for that matter. The last time I wore it was at Christmas, and by the time mass was over at church it had smeared all over my teeth. I looked like I'd eaten a box of red crayons.

So it was barefaced that I appeared at my mother's door to check on her on my way to the restaurant, as I did every morning. She took one look at me and raised her brows.

"Well," she said, "I know you don't look so rough because of a man, *chère*, so come on in and tell me the story."

"Actually it is because of a man."

I gave my mother a hug, then stepped past her into the small but beautiful front parlor of her home. Perfumed with vases of flowers and the scent of her Shalimar, with the low, throaty voice of Ella Fitzgerald crooning from the hidden speakers in the walls, it was a little oasis of elegance and style amid the gentle decay of Tremé.

The oldest African American neighborhood in the United States, Tremé was the musical heart of New Orleans, going all the way back to the seventeen hundreds, when slaves were allowed to gather in Congo Square on Sundays to dance and play music. Jazz was invented here. The civil rights movement started here. We have brass bands, incredible cuisine, cultural history museums, more festivals than days of the week, and famous historical sites galore.

But it's a bad idea for tourists to take a stroll after dark. Drugs are a problem, and jobs are in short supply. And all those boarded-up houses that were abandoned after the flood still stand, flowering with toxic black mold, a daily reminder of the heartbreak of Hurricane Katrina.

Life can be good in Tremé, but it's never been easy.

At the mention of a man, my mother got excited. "Well let me put on my glasses so I can hear you better!"

She often said nonsensical things like that. It was part of her charm. That, and her gift of making you feel welcome.

She slid her glasses up her nose and peered at me through them. Worn on a silver chain around her neck, they were her one concession to the fact that she was aging.

"It's a long story, Mama," I said with a sigh. "And not worth retelling."

She squinted. Her big brown eyes were magnified even bigger through the lenses of her glasses. "No saucy bits?"

"Not even one."

Instantly losing interest, she removed the dreaded glasses and let them dangle from the chain once more. "Did you have breakfast, *chère?*"

I shrugged. "Coffee and some aspirin."

"That's not breakfast, silly child!" she scolded. "Get your skinny behind in this house and eat!"

She turned and floated away to the kitchen in a cloud of perfume and motherly disappointment, her flowing purple robe billowing around her ankles as she moved. Barefoot and nimble, she still had her beauty queen's graceful, gliding gait, even at sixty-four years old.

Excuse me. Thirty-nine. For a second there I forgot what year it was that she'd stopped aging.

"I made collard greens, shrimp and grits, and Cajun benedict," she called over her shoulder. "And I've got okra gumbo and my famous jambalaya simmerin' on the stove for later."

That would've been a lot of food for a single woman living alone, but my mother had a steady stream of callers throughout the day, from brunch straight through to cocktail hour and beyond. There was nothing she enjoyed more than visiting. Or "holding court," as I liked to call it.

And speaking of callers . . .

"Good morning, Colonel!" I called down the hall toward my mother's closed bedroom door.

There was a pause, and then a muffled reply. "Mornin', sugar!"

There was only one reason my mother's bedroom door was closed in the morning, and the Colonel was it. Trying not to picture what might go on behind that door, I smiled.

"Leave him be, Bianca," said my mother from the kitchen. "C'mon now, I'm making you up a plate."

I strolled into the kitchen, dropped my knapsack on the floor next to the square wood table where I ate every meal as a child, and sat down, watching my mother put together a plate of food for me: a scoop from one pot, a ladle from another. She was more at home in front of a stove than anywhere else in the world.

I asked, "Another sleepover? Is this getting serious with you two?"

My mother looked over her shoulder and smiled. Her eyes danced with mischief. "No man could ever compete with your father, *chère*, God bless his soul, but that doesn't mean I'll stop them from trying." She fanned herself. "And my *word*, the Colonel is certainly trying."

"Ugh. It's depressing that you get more action than I do. I can already feel the emotional scars forming."

"Please, child, you're not that fragile. And how many times do I have to tell you to get back out there? Don't let that fool boy put a hex on your love life. He isn't worth it!"

The "fool boy" in question was my ex, Trace. I'd been head over heels for him, sure we'd get married, until I discovered his definition of monogamy meant he'd only cheat on me with one girl at a time. I'd been happily single for almost two years now, much to Mama's dismay. As an only child, I was her sole hope for the grandbabies she so desperately wanted.

Avoiding that minefield, I quickly steered the conversation into safer, and more important, waters. "So what did Doc Halloran say?"

Mama turned back to the stove. There was a brief, almost-unnoticeable pause before she answered. "Just what I told you he'd say, baby. I'm right as rain."

I frowned. "But you've had that cough for months now, Mama."

Smiling brightly, she turned around again and faced me. I was struck by how beautiful she still was, her face unlined in the bright morning light spilling through the kitchen windows. I got my complexion from her—"toasted chestnuts" my milk-pale father called it—and hoped I'd age as well as she was.

Though if the bags under my eyes were any indication, I was out of luck.

"It's nothing to worry about." She placed the plate of food on the table in front of me. "Just a side effect of getting old."

I laughed out loud. "Am I hearing things, or did the fabulous Miss Davina Hardwick just say the word *old*? I didn't think it was even in your vocabulary!"

"Hush, you!" My mother gave me a light, loving slap on my shoulder. "Or the whole neighborhood will hear!"

"Hear what?" said a booming baritone behind me.

I turned to find the Colonel in the doorway, grinning and pulling his suspenders over his shoulders. Trimly built and of below average height, he nonetheless had a big presence, fashioned in part from that booming voice, but mostly from twenty-five years leading soldiers in the army. As always, he was dressed in impeccable white, right down to his patent leather shoes. His eyes were an unusual, gunmetal gray, pale and arresting against the dark canvas of his skin.

My mother laughed and waved her hand at the table. "Nothing for you to be worrying about, just girl talk. Sit yourself down and eat."

Grinning wider, he propped his hands on his hips. "I've already got a belly full of sweetness from spending the night with you, woman."

My eye roll was so loud it could probably be heard from space.

Coy as a debutante, my mother pursed her lips and batted her lashes at him. "Why you silver-tongued devil. Whatever will I do with you?"

Faster than you'd think a seventy-year-old man could move, the Colonel had crossed the room and embraced my mother. He swung her around, lifting her so her feet cleared the floor, laughing in delight when she girlishly squealed.

"I can think of one or two things!" he boomed, rattling the windows. Then he set her on her feet and gave her such a passionate kiss my cheeks went red.

"Only one or two?" she said breathlessly when the kiss was over. "I thought you had more imagination than that, *tahyo!*"

Tahyo is Cajun French for a big, hungry dog.

I dropped my face into my hands and groaned. "Someone please kill me. Just kill me now."

"I told you not to talk to yourself, child, you sound like one of the hobos over on the boulevard!" Mama scolded.

Into my head popped a vivid image of Jackson Boudreaux's shocked expression after I'd told him he looked like one of the homeless panhandlers on the boulevard. It made me feel much better.

"You look a little tired this mornin', sugar." Finished slobbering all over Mama, the Colonel sat down beside me at the table and eyed me with concern. "Everything all right?"

Mama said, "Says it's a man that gave her that face, but she isn't saying who."

With a wink, she made another plate of food and set it in front of the Colonel. She gave us forks, and we dug in.

"I just had a late night is all," I said around a mouthful of succulent eggs.

The Colonel drawled, "This wouldn't have anything to do with your visit from a certain Mr. Jackson Boudreaux, would it?"

"Jackson Boudreaux!" Eyes wide, my mother whirled around and stared at me. "Good Lord in heaven, what were you doing with *him*? I hear that boy's meaner than a wet panther!"

I shot a sour glance at the Colonel, who lifted a shoulder unapologetically.

He said, "Word gets around this town fast, sugar, 'specially when it has to do with the most eligible bachelor in the state gettin' a tongue-lashin' in public from the owner of the hottest new restaurant in the French Quarter." He chuckled, shaking his head. "Rumor has it you nearly snapped that boy's head clean off."

I winced at the memory. "Not my best moment, for sure. But he deserved it. I've never met a more asinine, self-important, son of a—"

"Keep it up and I'll cancel your birth certificate!" my mother warned.

"—rabid crawdad in my life," I finished, smiling.

Even at thirty-one, I wasn't allowed to curse in her presence. Some things never changed.

The Colonel chuckled. "You didn't think the boy got the nickname 'the Beast' by bein' all rainbows and butterflies, did you?"

A beast he is, but a boy he most certainly is not. I remembered the breadth of Jackson's shoulders, the deep rumble of his voice, that hard, burning stare. The thought of it made me squirm in my seat.

Because I hated him, not because I found him attractive. Obviously.

My cheeks burning again, I stuffed another forkful of eggs into my mouth.

"Snapped his head off?" Mama pushed her glasses up her nose, took a seat opposite me, and leaned over the table, all ears.

I told a shortened version of the events at the restaurant last night. When I was finished, she took her glasses off, *tsk*ed, and patted my hand.

"Just goes to show that money is no substitute for class, *chère*. The true measure of a man is how he treats those less fortunate than him, make no mistake."

That was a reference to my late father, a Harvard-educated attorney who disappointed his wealthy parents when he decided to dedicate his life to helping minorities in the poorest communities of Louisiana instead of following in his father's footsteps and pursuing corporate law, and then a spot on the judicial bench. His parents' disappointment turned to outrage when he married my mother. Marrying "down" simply wasn't done by a Hardwick, especially when "down" included brown.

My mother was the first woman of color to marry into the Hardwick family tree.

Soon after I was born, my father was cut from his parents' wills. I'd never met my paternal grandparents, and God help them if I ever did. The tongue-lashing I gave Jackson Boudreaux would sound like a love song in comparison.

"Anyway it doesn't matter because I'll never see him again," I said, finishing my food. "Now I really need to get a move on or I'll be late for the produce shipment—"

Mama started to cough. Violent, dry, hacking coughs that racked her body and made her eyes water and her face turn scarlet.

"Mama!" I jumped to my feet and went to her. Gripping her shoulder, I was surprised by how frail the bones felt under my hand.

"I'm fine," she rasped, waving me away. "I'm just a little dry, *chère*, I need a glass of—"

A second round of coughing stole her words and bent her in half at the waist.

As I started to panic, the Colonel went to her other side and gently rubbed her back. "Easy, now, Davina, just take it easy, girl," he said softly. He glanced up and met my gaze.

I knew from his look that this coughing fit wasn't the first she'd had today. My body went cold. What was she hiding from me?

I rushed to the sink and poured water from the tap into a glass. My hand shook when I offered it to her.

"Thank you, baby," she said weakly after she'd swallowed it. "That's better."

I sat across from her again. Her skin had taken on an unhealthy ashen hue, and little beads of perspiration glistened at her hairline. Like mine, her hands were trembling.

I might not be the sharpest tool in the shed, but something about this smelled bad enough to gag a maggot.

I looked my mother straight in the eye and said firmly, "Mama. You better spit out the truth right now or I'm gonna cream your corn, as Daddy used to say. What did Doc Halloran *really* tell you about that cough?"

Something crossed her face. It was an expression I'd never seen my vibrant, carefree, and confident mother wear—an awful mix of resignation, sadness, and, worst of all, fear.

When she said quietly, "Owen, would you please give us a moment?" all the tiny hairs on the back of my neck stood on end.

The Colonel gently kissed my mother's head. "Of course, Davina." He squeezed her shoulders, shot me a worried look, and left, quiet as a kitchen mouse.

Then my mother gathered my hands in hers and started to talk, but I only heard a single word. A word that made my heart stop beating and my soul bleed.

Cancer.

CREOLE SHRIMP AND GRITS

Makes 4 servings

- 4 cups water
- 1 cup stone-ground grits
- 3 tablespoons butter
- 2 cups shredded sharp cheddar cheese
- 1 pound raw shrimp, peeled and deveined
- 6 slices bacon, chopped
- 4 teaspoons lemon juice
- 2 tablespoons fresh parsley, chopped
- 1 cup scallions, sliced
- 1 clove garlic, minced
- kosher salt
- freshly ground pepper

Preparation

1. In stockpot, bring water to a boil. Reduce heat to simmer, add grits, salt, and pepper, and cook until water is absorbed, about 20 minutes.
2. Remove from heat and stir in butter and cheese.

3. Fry the bacon in a large skillet until browned. Remove to paper towels, drain well, and chop.

4. Rinse shrimp and pat dry. Add into bacon grease and cook until shrimp turn pink. Do not overcook.

5. Add lemon juice, chopped bacon, parsley, scallions, and garlic, and sauté for 3 minutes.

6. Spoon cooked grits into serving bowls. Add shrimp mixture on top. Serve immediately.

FIVE

JACKSON

The feel of her warm, full lips around the head of my cock made me moan.

"Fuck yes," I whispered, looking down at her. "Don't stop."

Beautiful, dark eyes stared up at me as she opened her lips wider and took me down her throat. My pelvis flexed of its own will, sending my hard cock even deeper into the wet heat of her mouth.

So fucking good. Christ. So good.

Naked, on her knees between my legs on the bed, she wrapped one hand around my shaft while the other gently fondled my balls.

I was out of my mind with pleasure.

Moaning again, I cupped her head in my hands and started to slowly fuck her mouth, careful not to go too fast, timing my thrusts with the stroke of her hand, the bob of her head. When she squeezed just under the engorged crown and lingered there, sucking and licking like a kitten with a bowl of cream, a shudder ran through my body.

"Oh, you like that," she whispered playfully. "Let's find out what else you like."

Releasing my cock, she rose and straddled my hips, smiling down at me. My hands encircled her small waist. She reached down and grabbed my stiff cock again, and then began to slide it slowly between her legs, over and around her wet folds, rolling her hips, teasing me. I let her play and slid my hands up to her breasts.

She gasped when I pinched her nipples.

She had perfect tits, round and full but not too big, the weight of them lush and feminine in my hands. I sat up and sucked a rosebud nipple into my mouth, loving the sound of her soft groan as my tongue circled the hard bud. She arched into my mouth, her fingers still lazily stroking my erection.

I bit down gently on her nipple, and she gasped again.

Something about that sound made me feel like an animal. Like a powerful, hungry animal. Suddenly I desperately needed to be inside her.

With a low snarl, I flipped her onto her back. She lay there, blinking up at me with wide eyes, her lips parted, panting softly, a beautiful flush all over her chest. Her dark hair spread wild over the pillow. Her bare skin gleamed in the low light, a rich golden hue like poured honey.

I'd never seen anything as fucking perfect in my entire life.

"Jax," she breathed.

Her thighs were clasped around my hips, slightly trembling. I pressed forward, flexing my pelvis, finding her soft and open, ready for me. She arched her back and slid her arms around my shoulders. Her eyelids drifted closed as I pushed slowly into the heaven of her tight, wet pussy.

I gave her my weight. With one hand under her incredible heart-shaped ass and the other fisted in her hair, I started to fuck her, kissing her neck, instinctively biting her when she cried out in pleasure as I thrust deeper inside. She met my every thrust with an upward cant of her hips, her breasts bouncing against my chest, her soft moans of pleasure ringing in my ears.

"Oh God," she moaned. "God, yes. Please—Jax—"

"You're so beautiful," I said hoarsely, staring down at her. A shock-wave of heat surged outward from my spine, engulfing my pelvis and cock, making me throb deep inside her.

Her moans turned broken. On the edge of orgasm, she stiffened beneath me.

With the first hard clench of her pussy around my pulsing dick, I lost myself. I was a man no more. I was only blood and bone and sinew, a mindless thing striving toward the end that ached inside me. I became the thing I'd heard people call me behind my back, the nickname whispered as I passed them on the street.

I became a beast, fucking this beautiful woman with a savagery that terrified me.

"Bianca!" I shouted, my entire body jerking as I spilled inside her.

She clawed her fingernails into my back and, with her thighs and hands and whispered words of love, urged me on.

My own moans and the jerking of my body woke me from the dream.

Panting, sweating, my aching cock gripped in my fist, I stared up at the ceiling, blood roaring through my veins. For a long, disoriented moment, I lay in bed, trying to get my bearings. Finally I began to weakly laugh.

I hadn't had a wet dream since I was a teenager.

I sat up. The sticky sheets pooled around my waist. "Jesus, Jackson," I muttered, looking at the mess I'd made all over my hand, stomach, and poor, unsuspecting bedsheets. "You need to get out more."

I rose and padded into the bathroom, the marble floor cold as a mausoleum's under my bare feet. Why the hell I'd done the entire house in marble was a question I'd asked myself many times since moving into this echoing maze of a mansion four years ago. Every footstep could be heard throughout the place. Every pin drop sounded like a gunshot.

Even acres of Turkish rugs did little to muffle the echoes. It was like living inside the loudest tomb in the world.

Still distracted by thoughts of the dream, I quickly showered and dressed.

It was so unlike me to have that kind of vivid, visceral dream. I found it unsettling. I never remembered my dreams. Sleep for me was always like stepping off a cliff and falling into an endless black hole of nothingness.

Thanks to Bianca Hardwick, last night was *not* a black hole of nothingness. She was as snappy as an alligator, but damn that woman was hot. In fact, that smart mouth of hers only added to her heat.

Looking at myself in the mirror above the dresser, I ran a hand over my face. *I wonder if she likes beards.*

A rap on the doorframe pulled me abruptly out of my thoughts.

"Mornin', sir," said Rayford, standing in the doorway.

As usual, he was dressed impeccably in black suit and tie, his jaw freshly shaved, his bearing upright and elegant despite his age.

Not that I actually knew his age. That was a carefully guarded secret, something perhaps my own parents didn't know. He'd worked for them for over forty years as their butler, among other things, before relocating with me to New Orleans. At the time he'd said he wanted to be closer to his family, as he grew up here, but we both knew the truth.

He was afraid what would happen if he left me alone.

"Rayford," I said, nodding. "Good morning. Is he up?"

"Yes, sir, Charlie's just gettin' him cleaned up now. They should both be down for breakfast in a few minutes. Will you be dinin' at home this mornin'?"

His benign expression revealed nothing, but I knew he was wondering how the hell I was going to manage without a chef. Thanks to an upbringing that included an army of cooks, housekeepers, and other household staff, I couldn't boil an egg to save my life.

"I don't know yet." I paused. "Does Charlie—?"

"She does, sir," he said, knowing I'd been about to ask if the nanny could cook. "I asked her yesterday if she'd be able to fill in for a day or two until we could find a new chef. I already rang the service, so we should have a few applicants to interview by tomorrow." A hint of a smile crossed his face. "I doubt Charlie has Bianca Hardwick's talent, but she can probably make a sandwich for you and somethin' appropriate for Cody."

He disappeared with a murmured good-bye, leaving me wondering just what he meant by bringing up Bianca Hardwick.

Oh fuck. Did I yell out her name in my sleep?

Picturing my orgasmic shout echoing all over the house, I went red in the face.

When my cell phone rang, I answered it more abruptly than usual. "What?" I snapped, cheeks burning.

"Good morning, Mr. Boudreaux!" chirped a young male voice.

It was Matthew Clark, the event coordinator from the Wounded Warrior Project. He'd been working with me for months on the upcoming benefit dinner and fortunately was one of those people who took nothing personally. I could've told him I thought there was a tree stump in a Louisiana swamp that had a higher IQ than he did, and he would've heartily laughed and agreed.

He said, "I'm just calling to go over some last-minute details for the event on the fifteenth. Most importantly, I'd like to speak with your chef so we can finalize the menu and have the menu cards printed up. Is now a good time?"

Shit. The menu. *My chef.*

"No," I growled, "it isn't. I'll . . ." *Think of something, genius!* "I'll fax the menu over to you no later than tomorrow night."

"Oh, *great!*" said Matthew, with the enthusiasm of a man with zero interests outside of work. "Looking forward to it! The donors are always so keen to see what's on the menu. You wouldn't *believe* how seriously this group takes food. The better the food, the better the donations!" He gasped. "Oh—and the wine list! I completely forgot!"

Wine list? There's supposed to be a fucking wine list? I was really beginning to regret that comment about the runny eggs.

"I'll have it all over to you tomorrow!" I barked, and hung up the phone.

I strode from my bedroom, took the elevator to the first floor, and found Rayford in the kitchen, drinking a cup of coffee and reading the newspaper at the big white marble island.

I said, "Where do you think Gregory would've left his notes about the benefit dinner?"

Ever tranquil, Rayford calmly sipped his coffee and looked at me over the rims of his reading glasses. "He didn't leave any notes, sir," he said. "He packed up everything he had—recipe books, notebooks, them fancy Japanese knives—and cleared outta here like a scalded cat. Don't expect he'll be takin' your calls, either," Rayford added serenely, "seein' as how he said you were colder than a penguin's balls and he wouldn't piss on you if you were on fire."

Wonderful.

I had three hundred people arriving for a benefit dinner at my home in two weeks, and I had no menu, no wine list, and no one to put any of it together.

"Fuck," I said, making Rayford snort with laughter.

Then I had a brilliant idea.

SIX

BIANCA

The rest of the day passed with all my senses dulled like I was underwater. Shock, I suppose. And denial. I just couldn't believe things were as bad as they apparently were.

Stage three. It sounded more like a movie set than a diagnosis.

"You all right, boo?" asked Eeny with concern when she caught me staring into space over a big pot bubbling with jambalaya at the stove. It was my mother's recipe, the comfort food I always turned to in times of stress. The waitstaff had just eaten, as usual before the restaurant opened for dinner, and first service would soon begin, but I had no idea how I was going to make it through tonight.

"I'm . . ."

What? What was I? There wasn't a word. Finally I settled on, "Fine. Just tired is all. Couldn't sleep last night."

Chuckling, Eeny patted me on the shoulder. "That explains those bags under your eyes."

From across the kitchen, Hoyt called, "Looks like you been et by a wolf and shit over a cliff, dawlin'."

When I turned to glare at him, Eeny said, "Somebody had to say it!"

I threw my hands in the air. "Really? Somebody *had* to say I look like I was eaten by a wolf and shit over a cliff? That's something someone really *needed* to tell me?"

My aggravated tone made Hoyt whistle. "Aw, now c'mon, Miss Bianca, I'm only teasin'." He paused, squinting in my direction. "Y'all actually look like somebody died."

My throat closed. I turned back to the pot and stared down into it, stirring furiously with the wooden spoon while blinking back tears.

"I'm just tired," I repeated forcefully, feeling Eeny's gaze on my face. "Now could everyone please get to work?"

For a moment her colorful bulk didn't move from my peripheral vision. Then she walked off, the skirts of her yellow-and-orange-striped caftan swinging. "Make you a gris-gris," she said as she went, "for protection against whatever's ailin' you."

Eeny was always making someone one of her good luck voodoo amulets for whatever was ailing them. She had at least ten of her own hidden in small burlap bags in her pockets or strung around her neck at any time. You always knew when she was approaching by the tinkling.

But it wasn't me who needed protection. It was Mama. Mama who had stage three lung cancer, no health insurance, and no savings, because like me she'd plowed all her money into the restaurant. We were both so broke we didn't have two nickels to rub together. Though the restaurant was busy, we'd only been open six months, and I was up to my neck in debt and operating expenses. She wouldn't qualify for Medicare until she turned sixty-five next year, and by then she might be—

No, I thought, inhaling sharply. *Not going there.*

"You mad at that jambalaya, Bianca?"

I glanced up from the pot. Pepper stood beside me, watching me with arched brows and a worried look, like I might start throwing things.

I sighed. "No, and please don't say anything about how bad I look, I already—"

I stopped short, dumbfounded by Pepper's outfit.

Her neon pink blouse was cut so low her hoo-has were on display like buns at a bake sale. Her zebra-print leather skirt was so short it was almost a belt. Under the skirt she wore fishnet stockings and a pair of sky-high, red-and-black heels that screamed *Fuck me!* at the top of their cheap snakeskin lungs.

She asked brightly, "Hey, what do you think of these earrings?" and lifted her hair away from her face to display an enormous pair of gold hoops with little gold hearts dangling from the bottoms.

Hoyt called out, "Ain't nobody lookin' at ya earrings, *couillon.* And pull down that skirt, I kin see clear to the promised land!"

"They're lovely, Pepper," I said, to distract her from whatever insult she was about to toss back Hoyt's way. You had to have tough skin to work in a kitchen, but all the hazing was done with a generous dose of love.

Pepper smiled. "I bought them with the tip I got last night from Mr. Boudreaux. The heels, too."

And the rest of the outfit, most likely. Judging by the looks of things, she probably had enough left over from that hundred bucks to buy another ensemble of the same quality, with money to spare.

"How nice for you," I said. "Now tell me why you're in the kitchen and not up front at the desk."

"Oh yeah! That's what I came to tell you. It's about Mr. Boudreaux."

I stared at her with a bad feeling in the pit of my stomach. "What about him?"

Pepper beamed. "He's here. And he wants to talk to you."

I groaned. *Dear Lord, not today. Not him, today.* "Tell him I'm busy. I can't get away now." *Besides, I hate his stuck-up guts.*

Pepper blinked. Her brows pulled together. "Um. He sort of . . . you know. *Demanded* to see you. Like he does."

I narrowed my eyes at her. "Today you don't seem quite as inclined to shove a bucket of crawdads where the sun doesn't shine like you did yesterday, Pepper."

She admitted sheepishly, "He might have given me another tip."

Funny how some people's opinions can be changed with a simple thing like money. At least she had the decency to look embarrassed about it.

"What does he want?"

Pepper shrugged. "All he said was, and I'm quoting, 'Bring the owner to me. Now.'"

The owner. I bet that bastard didn't even remember my name, even though it was right over the damn front door! And he expected me to drop everything and come running when he called like I was some kind of servant? Like I was a *dog*?

Steam began to pour from my ears. I shouted, "That man could give the baby Jesus hemorrhoids!"

Eeny cackled. Pepper took a step back. Shaking his head, Hoyt let out another whistle. Everyone in the kitchen stopped what they were doing and turned to stare at me.

Flustered, I smoothed a hand over my hair and tried to compose myself. In a lower voice, I told Pepper, "You go tell Mr. Boudreaux that the owner is as busy as a one-legged cat in a sandbox. I won't be coming out to see him, now or ever. If he's got something to say to me, he can have his blasted lawyer write me a letter."

Pepper didn't look convinced. "Um . . . I don't think that'll go over, Bianca."

"Good, let him be the one to lose sleep for a change," I muttered, battering the jambalaya with a wooden spoon. If I kept this up, I'd be serving a finely blended soup instead of the chunky seafood-and-sausage stew, so I forced myself to breathe and slow down.

"All right." Pepper sighed, turning to go. "But I don't think he's gonna like it."

I grunted. *God forbid Prince A-hole doesn't get his way!*

I went back to work, as did everyone else. For a full sixty seconds, at least, until Jackson Boudreaux crashed through the swinging kitchen doors like a gale-force wind.

Hurrying in behind him, Pepper looked at me, her hands held up in surrender. "I tried to tell you!"

But I was having none of Jackson's nonsense today. I propped my hands on my hips and leveled him with The Look.

The Look was a Southern female specialty, handed down over generations. Every family of women had their own particular version. Some said The Look could even go through walls and be heard over the phone. It was an art form among genteel womenfolk, and its effect was always the same.

Jackson took one more step into the kitchen and stopped dead in his tracks when he spotted me.

"*You,*" I said, attitude set to bitch level ten, "are not welcome in my kitchen. Now turn your uppity butt around and get out."

And what did that ornery bastard do in response?

He smiled.

I wouldn't have thought it possible if I didn't see it for myself, but there it was, a cocky little smirk that lifted the corners of his lips just enough to let me know he found me amusing.

Then—just to make me mad enough to cuss out the pope—he ordered all *my* employees out of *my* kitchen.

"Everybody out!" he commanded without looking away from me, that deep voice rolling like thunder through the room.

When those turncoats had the audacity to start hustling their butts out, I almost lost my mind.

"Everybody stay put!" I said. "The next person who moves is fired!"

Cue the sound of screeching brakes. Then I had twelve employees looking back and forth between Jackson and me, waiting breathlessly to see what would happen next.

Standing by Hoyt, Eeny was busily fondling one of her trinket necklaces, muttering something under her breath. I hoped it was a voodoo curse that would make all Jackson's hair fall out and shrink his balls to the size of peanuts.

"Miss *Hardwick*," Jackson began, snarly as a grizzly bear, but I cut him off.

"Where's your attorney? Or are you serving me the papers yourself?"

He blinked, his thick brows drawing together. "Attorney?" Then his look cleared. "Oh. No, I'm not suing you."

Not trusting myself to speak, I spread my hands wide and stood there, like *What then?*

He said, "I have a job for you."

Mother Mary, the man was offering me a *job*? Like this restaurant thing I'd been planning and saving toward for years was just a little side hobby, something I did in my spare time to make a few extra dollars toward my rent? And judging by his smug, aren't-you-lucky delivery, he had every assumption that I'd be champing at the bit to come work for him. Because what a dream *that* would be.

I had to bite my tongue and count to ten before I was calm enough to string a coherent sentence together. Well, it wasn't actually an entire sentence. It was just a word.

"No."

I had to give it to him, he had extremely expressive eyebrows. Those thick black caterpillars perched over his steely-blue peepers had an entire language of their own. Right now they were drawn together in a glower that told me I was a rebellious little nitwit that he was fully prepared to have drawn and quartered and fed to his dogs.

My staff looked on in fascinated silence.

Through gritted teeth, he said, "This is an incredible opportunity for you—"

My sharp laugh made two of the line cooks jump. "How thoughtful of you to think of little ol' *me* for your precious opportunity! I've been waiting so *long* for such a tantalizing offer! Whatever would I do *without* you?"

That growl of his came on, low and dangerous. Even Eeny started to look nervous.

Deadly quiet, he said, "Everyone. Out. *Now.* If she fires you, I'll pay you each a year's salary and find you other jobs."

That offer proved to be too much for my employees to resist. I watched in red-faced fury as one by one they silently filed out in a single line, avoiding my gaze. At the end of the line, Eeny shrugged and mouthed, *Sorry, boo.* Hoyt sent me a wink.

I'd just gotten a painful lesson in the power of men with money, and I didn't like it one bit.

Swallowing back the string of vile curses boiling on my tongue, I folded my arms over my chest and stared at him.

He stared right back at me. Boy, did he ever. The Beast had a Look of his own. Truth be told, it would give mine a run for its money.

I said, "We open in ten minutes. I have two hundred reservations tonight."

He said, "You look tired."

I had to close my eyes and count to ten again. When I opened them, I hoped death rays were shooting out of my head. If I'd had a machete handy, I couldn't say for sure that I wouldn't lunge at him with it.

"And you look like you were raised in the woods by a tribe of cannibals. All you're missing is a bone in your beard."

That smirk appeared briefly again, there then gone. He ran a hand over his face, staring at me with such sudden strange intensity I thought I might spontaneously combust.

Unnerved, I asked, "Am I going to have to call the police to get you to leave?"

"The chief of police and I serve together on the board of the Peace Officers Association. I'm sure Gavin would be happy to take your call."

At my sides, my hands curled to fists. "You enjoy this, don't you?"

"What?"

"Throwing your weight around."

He took several slow steps toward me. I stood my ground as he approached, even when he got so close I could smell that masculine scent of his again, the hint of warm musk my traitorous nose found so intriguing.

Looking down at me, he said roughly, "About as much as you enjoy being told what to do, I think."

"I don't take orders."

"Neither do I. And for the record, I don't enjoy throwing my weight around, but every once in a while it's the most convenient way to get what I want. And I want you." His pause burned, and so did his eyes. "To come to work for me."

I found it impossible to speak for a moment. His closeness was disorienting, and that look in his eyes . . .

"I don't want to work for you. I don't *need* to work for you. And even if I did, I couldn't. Look around—*I'm busy.*"

He ignored that and started explaining in a patronizing, irritated voice, like he was a judge and I'd just violated my parole.

"It's a catering job. A onetime thing. I'm having a benefit dinner and auction at my home for a charity, and I need someone to create the menu and oversee the food and wine for the event. And cook, of course. You'd be in charge of the entire thing. You can bring in whatever staff you need to assist you. There will be press. A lot of press. I'd give you and your restaurant full credit in the event materials."

Oh. Well then.

Catering was an area I wanted to get into, not only because the money was good, but because it was fun. At a restaurant, the menu stayed fairly static, usually changing only with the seasons or the arrival of a new chef, but catering opened up a whole new world of creative possibilities. Each event was unique, an opportunity for a chef to stretch himself. To show off his skills, really.

And an event at Jackson Boudreaux's home would no doubt be filled with the crème de la crème of Louisiana society. I could reach a whole new clientele, one that didn't come to dine in the touristy French Quarter. I'd be a liar if I didn't admit I found that appealing.

My brain started impatiently tapping its foot.

I was forgetting who I was dealing with. If he aggravated me as much as he had over the course of one day, I couldn't imagine how bad it'd be through the time it would take to plan an entire event. I could end up with a stroke.

I said, "I'm flattered you'd think of me, but the answer is no."

Without missing a beat he replied, "Your fee would be twenty thousand dollars."

I almost dropped the spoon in my hand. I slow blinked more times than was probably necessary. "Tw . . . twenty . . ."

"Thousand dollars," he finished, carefully watching my face.

Though he was standing right in front of me, I wasn't even seeing him anymore. I was seeing my mother getting the chemotherapy she desperately needed. I was seeing her at the best hospital in the state, getting the highest level of care, being tended to by the best doctors.

I was picturing her *surviving*, when only this morning I'd been convinced she already had one foot in the grave.

When I didn't say anything, Jackson condescendingly added, "I'm sure you can find a use for that kind of money. Right?"

Think of Mama. Think of Mama and not how much you'd enjoy driving a stake through his cold, black heart.

I closed my eyes, drew in a slow breath, and grimly nodded.

As if he'd just won a bet with himself, the Beast said, "Right. The event's in two weeks. I'm having three hundred guests. I need a full menu with wine pairings by this time tomorrow."

My eyes flew open. "Three hundred people? Two weeks? Are you kidding me? That's impossible!"

The smirk I was beginning to hate appeared again. "No, it's twenty thousand dollars."

"Wait a minute—"

"I'll pay you up front."

Fresh out of arguments, I stood staring up at him with my mouth open like I was trying to catch fireflies.

His gaze dropped to my lips. The smirk disappeared. A muscle flexed in his jaw. With a sudden gruffness, like I'd done something to make him mad, he snapped, "I'll send a car for you at ten o'clock tomorrow morning so you can familiarize yourself with the kitchen."

Without waiting for a reply, he turned around and walked out the door.

SEVEN

BIANCA

At promptly ten o'clock the next morning, a sleek black sedan pulled up in front of my restaurant and glided to a stop at the curb.

I had no idea what kind of car it was, but I knew it was fancy-schmancy. Only really expensive, snobby-rich-people show-off cars had those stupid silver ornaments sticking out of the front of the hood like a middle finger to everyone who looked at them as they drove down the street.

Standing next to me at the window, Eeny said, "Your chariot awaits, boo." Then she burst into hysterical cackles.

I sighed. At Mama's insistence, I'd told no one about her illness. Her pride wouldn't allow her to publicly admit she was sick. Or maybe it was vanity. Either way, I'd been sworn to silence. She hadn't even told the Colonel. So no one at the restaurant knew the real reason I accepted a job from the Beast, but they were all getting a kick out of it. Hoyt had told me yesterday that one of the line cooks had started a pool to see how long it took before I quit.

But I couldn't quit, no matter how bad it got. Mama's life depended on that money.

I said, "Please don't forget to process the shellfish and get it on ice. And the Nieman Ranch delivery should be here no later than noon."

Eeny snorted. "Expectin' Carl to be on time with the meat is like expectin' to see a gorilla ridin' a tricycle down the sidewalk. That boy is slower than a Sunday afternoon."

And dumber than a box of rocks, I thought. He could throw himself on the ground and miss. He'd been delivering meat to me every day for months and still called at least once a week to get directions.

"Well off you go, Cinderella," said Eeny, bumping me with her shoulder. "Don't want your chariot to turn into a pumpkin!"

"I'm glad this is so amusing to you, Eeny," I said, giving her a stinky side-eye look.

Grinning, she patted me on the arm. "It's good for you to get out with a man every once in a while. Keeps the juices flowin', if you know what I mean."

My stink eye grew stinkier. "This isn't a *date*, Eeny."

"Oh, I know," she said airily. "But judgin' by the way Jackson Boudreaux looks at you like you turn his brain to scrambled eggs, it ain't all business, either. At least for him. Lawd!" she cried suddenly, pointing out the window. "Who's *that* tall drink o' water?"

Emerging from the driver's side of the sleek black sedan was an equally sleek black man. Dressed in a smart suit, his salt-and-pepper hair short and tidy, he stood looking at the front door, smoothing his tie. He was tall, elegant, and quite good-looking. I judged him to be somewhere north of sixty-five in age.

Immediately I thought of my mother. She'd be all over this one like white on rice.

"Must be Jackson's driver." I watched him come toward the door. "Wonder if he's as mean as his boss."

"Mm-*mmm!*" said Eeny, smacking her lips. "He could be meaner'n a drawer of snakes and I'd still take him for a roll."

I formed a terrible mental image of all three hundred pounds of Eeny rolling around naked in bed, chicken feathers and voodoo charms flying, getting her freak on with the well-dressed driver.

I grumbled, "Thanks for sharing," just as the gentleman in question came through the door.

"Mornin', ladies," he said, smiling. "Don't you two look prettier than a picture standin' there by the window!"

He flashed a set of pearly whites and an adorable pair of dimples, and Eeny nearly fainted.

"Good morning." I stepped forward with my hand extended. "I'm Bianca, and this is Ambrosine."

"Call me Eeny," she drawled, flagrantly flirting. "How *do* you do?"

"It's a pleasure to meet you both," he said, shaking my hand and nodding warmly at Eeny. "I must admit, I've been dyin' to come in and get a taste of your cookin' since you opened, Miss Bianca, but I just haven't found the time. I was a real big fan of your mama's restaurant. And might I say you bear a striking resemblance to your mama, too. Those beautiful cheekbones."

Eeny and I shared a look. This man could charm the birds right out of the trees. What on God's green earth he was doing working for the Beast was anyone's guess.

"Thank you, that's a lovely thing to say. Mr. . . . . ?"

"Where are my manners! I'm Rayford Hayes, Mr. Boudreaux's majordomo." He gave a short bow. "At your service."

He must be a new hire. No way someone this pleasant could work with Beastie for more than a week without losing his mind.

Wanting to get this meeting over with as quickly as possible so I could get back to the restaurant and prep for dinner, I said, "Shall we go?"

"Yes, ma'am. Eeny." He turned his warm gaze to her and lifted two curved fingers to his forehead in a little salute. "Have yourself a wonderful day."

Her soft sigh and furiously batting lashes had me pulling my lips between my teeth so I didn't smile.

"You do the same, Mr. Hayes," she said, waving at him with her fingertips. "Toodle-oo!"

Shaking my head, I followed Rayford out the door. He opened the car door for me. When I hesitated, he asked, "Everything all right, Miss Bianca?"

"Yes, but . . . would it be all right if I rode up front with you?"

He looked surprised. "With me?"

I was beginning to feel a little silly for having asked. "It's just that I'm not accustomed to being chauffeured. It seems a little . . . well, let's just say it's not my style."

Rayford's dimples flashed in his cheeks again. "Why of course. Whatever makes you most comfortable." He closed the rear door, opened the passenger door, and held out his hand. "Right this way."

Smiling gratefully at Rayford, I settled myself into the passenger seat. He closed the door, rounded the car, and got in on the driver's side. He started the engine, and we pulled away from the curb.

"This is a very nice car," I said, looking around at miles of supple leather and acres of gleaming wood. There was enough technology on the dashboard to make an astronaut dizzy.

Rayford chuckled. "You don't sound too impressed."

I wasn't impressed, but I did feel a bit embarrassed. "I don't even own a car. I live six blocks from the restaurant and walk to work every day. I couldn't tell you what kind of car this is if you held a gun to my head."

Rayford's chuckle was louder this time. "I'll be sure not to tell that to Mr. Boudreaux. It might break his heart."

He has a heart? Who knew?

"Have you worked for him long?" I was trying to make casual conversation, but I was curious, too.

"I've worked for his family for most of my life. Known Jackson since he was born."

Startled by that, I glanced at Rayford's handsome profile. "Really?"

He nodded. "Went to work for Clemmy and Brig before I even had hair on my chin. Started out in the stables, muckin' stalls, worked my way into the laundry, eventually got promoted to the kitchens."

Stables? Laundry? Kitchens, plural? Sounded like he'd been working at a castle. Fascinated, I listened as he continued.

"From there I learned everything there was to know about runnin' a grand house. Though Jackson's estate is much smaller than his parents', it's still an awful lot of work."

I bet. Just trying to keep your sanity living with him must be murder.

"So how did you come to be with him in New Orleans?"

A pause followed in which Rayford thoughtfully looked out the windshield before saying gently, "That's not my story to tell, Miss."

Oh boy. I just stepped in a big, steaming pile of none-of-your-damn-business.

"Got it. Sorry. My mama's always telling me I talk too much. Says my gift of the gab is a shade closer to a curse."

He sent me a smile and smoothly changed the subject. "How is your mama, anyway? I didn't know her well, just an occasional customer like I said, but I was real sorry to hear about what happened to her restaurant during Katrina."

My stomach did a slow roll. I glanced out the window and watched the road speeding by. "She's fine, thank you for asking. I just saw her this morning. We only live a few blocks apart so I like to stop by on my way to the restaurant."

I felt his look and wondered if he heard the change in my voice. If he did, he was too well mannered to mention it.

The rest of the drive was spent in pleasant chitchat. By the time we pulled up to an elaborate scrolled iron gate surrounded by a high stone wall, I'd almost forgotten to worry about my mother.

"Here we are," said Rayford. Like magic, the iron gates parted and swung slowly open, and I got my first look at the Beast's home.

I'm ashamed to admit I actually gasped.

Rayford chuckled. "Beautiful, isn't she?"

I stared in awe at the palatial estate at the end of a long gravel driveway. Flanked by ancient weeping willows and set against the glittering backdrop of Lake Pontchartrain, it looked like something a president might use on his weekends away from the White House.

Rayford said with pride, "Rivendell's got ten bedrooms, twelve bathrooms, and over fifteen thousand square feet on a five-acre lot. Jackson bought up the property on both sides and tore down the houses so he could have more privacy."

I looked at Rayford in surprise. "Rivendell? The house is named after the elven realm in *The Hobbit*?"

Rayford's brows climbed his forehead. "You a Tolkien fan?"

I shrugged. "A book fan in general. I'm a little obsessed, really. I read everything."

"Do you now," Rayford mused, sliding me a glance.

He wore a secret smile I found a little odd.

"My father used to always read to me before bed when I was little. I guess I fell in love with books way back then, and it's been an ongoing affair ever since."

"You'll be wantin' to see the library, then," Rayford said. "I swear we've got more books than the Library of Congress."

That gave me pause. The Beast loves books, too?

I decided he'd probably instructed his interior designer to buy a bunch of first editions so he could show off to his rich friends. Odds were he had an expensive wine collection he knew nothing about, too. A man who devoured food as joylessly as Jackson Boudreaux did wouldn't have the soul to appreciate literature or fine wine, either.

As we drove closer to the house, I grew more nervous. The scope of what I'd gotten myself into was starting to hit me. If the event didn't go off without a hitch, I suspected I'd be blamed for it. And I had no doubt Jackson wouldn't hesitate to give me a piece of his mind in front of three hundred guests if he wasn't entirely satisfied with the food.

"You're lookin' a little spooked over there, Miss Bianca." Rayford smiled at me. "You okay?"

"Fine as frog's hair!" I answered brightly. I'd rather chew off my own arm than admit I was feeling intimidated.

Rayford chuckled. "Good. He's lookin' forward to seein' you, too."

Wait. *What?*

Before I could gather my wits enough to respond, Rayford said, "Ah! Speak of the devil!"

When I followed his gaze, my heart sank.

Standing in front of the massive front door with his legs braced wide and his arms crossed over his chest stood Jackson, in regulation black everything, wearing an expression like he was about to launch a nuclear war.

The devil indeed, I thought, stifling a sigh. I'd assumed I'd be getting a tour of the house and kitchen from Rayford, but apparently the Beast had other ideas.

He probably thought I'd try to steal something.

As soon as we pulled to a stop, Jackson yanked my door open. He stood peering in at me with narrowed eyes, his head cocked. He snapped, "Why are you sitting in front?"

Right. I shouldn't be bucking protocol because I'm *the help*.

Heat crawled up my neck and suffused my cheeks. *Lord, grant me the serenity not to take off my shoe and hurl it at his balls.*

"And a fine good morning to you, *too*, Mr. Boudreaux," I said sweetly. "I see you're in your usual sunshine-and-rainbows mood. Did you misplace your human pills again?"

His lips tightened.

On my other side, I felt Rayford trying to stifle a laugh.

Jackson stepped back and swung the door wide, a silent command to exit.

I kept my expression neutral when he surprised me by offering me his hand. I grasped it gingerly, half expecting him to crush my fingers in his giant fist. His grip was firm and steadying, not crushing at all, though my fingers were swallowed by the sheer size of his rough paw.

As soon as I'd gotten on my feet, he dropped my hand like it had burned him. Then he turned and disappeared into the house without a word.

Exasperated, I said to Rayford, "Is he always this charming?"

Rayford smiled at me. He looked a little sad. "Not everyone has the gift of the gab, Miss." Looking at the empty doorway, he added, "And if you're treated like a stray dog long enough, you start to believe it and act like one."

With that mysterious statement, he turned and followed his employer into the house, leaving me standing in the driveway wondering exactly what I'd gotten myself into.

EIGHT

BIANCA

If I thought the exterior of Rivendell was something, the interior literally had me gaping.

Huge marble sculptures scattered everywhere: check.

Priceless oil paintings from French and Italian masters: check.

Ballroom, billiard room, indoor theatre: check, check, and check.

I'd never seen anything like it. Or been inside a house so bone-chillingly cold.

"I should've brought a sweater," I said to Rayford as I walked beside him, shivering. Our every footstep echoed off the walls before dying into ghostly silence. I had the oddest feeling of being inside a crypt.

"You get used to it," said Rayford. "The heat's always on, but marble's real stubborn about warmin' up, and this time of year we get a cold breeze comin' off the water, which doesn't help. The kitchen's better."

We passed another enormous room that appeared to be a formal dining room, with a polished oak table the length of a landing strip. Then we arrived at the library, and I almost wet myself in excitement.

"Holy Christmas!" I said, stopping short to stare.

Rayford chuckled. "Told you we had a lot of books."

A lot didn't even begin to cover it. The library was three stories tall, capped with a vaulted ceiling painted with reproductions of the frescoes of the Sistine Chapel. Chandeliers sparkled overhead. A huge marble fireplace yawned wide at one end of the room. A comfy-looking overstuffed sofa and chairs beckoned from a corner. And everywhere I looked, there were books. Stuffed into cases that scaled the walls, stacked in piles on enormous coffee tables, leather-bound spines glinting with gold script. Every one looked like a first edition. My fingers itched to touch them all.

From behind me a voice said, "Do you read?"

Of course it was Jackson. No one else could make that sound as if my literacy were in question.

"I've been known to," I replied, unable to tear my gaze away from all the treats calling me so bewitchingly. Distracted and in awe, I added, "Just before he died, my father asked me what I thought heaven was like. I told him heaven was a library that had a lot of comfortable chairs, good lighting, and every book ever written. If I lived here, I'd spend all my time in this room."

There was a short pause, then Jackson slowly moved into my peripheral vision. Thick scruff on his jaw, thick hair in need of a barber, thick head probably full of the howls of his woodland kin.

"That explains your interesting cocktail menu," he said, his voice gruff.

I turned my head to look at him. "Interesting? Not pretentious?"

He met my gaze. His blue eyes didn't look quite as steely as usual. In fact, they could almost be described as warm.

He said, "It's only pretentious if you're faking it." He considered me in silence for a moment, his gaze piercing. "So the classics are your favorite?"

He was referring to my cocktail menu again, which, in addition to Romeo and Julep and The Last of the Mojitos, included other literary-inspired libations like Tequila Mockingbird and Huckleberry Sin. And yes, they were all inspired by classic books.

"The classics were my father's favorites," I said quietly. "I created the cocktail menu in honor of him."

Because I was looking right into his eyes, I saw the brief flicker of regret there.

"I'm sorry," he said stiffly. "I didn't know."

"That's because you didn't bother to ask."

Jackson and I stared at each other in silence until Rayford discreetly cleared his throat. "Ahem. Should we proceed to the kitchen, sir?"

Jackson gave a curt nod and turned on his heel, giving me a view of his broad back again. He strode away down the echoing hallway, turned a corner, and went out of sight.

"Well," said Rayford, sounding a little dazed. "I think you'd best go buy yourself a lottery ticket, Miss Bianca."

When I looked at him with my brows raised, he chuckled.

"Mr. Boudreaux hasn't apologized to anyone in as long as I can remember. Today must be your lucky day."

"Rayford," I said, taking his arm. "Please don't make me curse. My mama doesn't like it."

His chuckles echoing off the marble, he led me away from the library and down the hall.

". . . and all the pans are in these drawers," said Jackson, opening yet another enormous drawer to reveal an array of expensive pots and pans, neatly arranged.

He'd shown me through the entire kitchen, stalking from the pantry to the professional-grade range to the cabinets above the sink, and finally the wall of pullout drawers below the row of ovens. The kitchen was almost as big as the library, with its own fireplace at one end and a flat-screen TV on the opposite wall. Everything was gleaming, top-of-the-line perfection.

And Rayford had been right. The kitchen was far warmer than the rest of the house. With the fire snapping and popping in the hearth and the television tuned to a morning news show, it was almost cozy.

"The side patio will be used for a staging area," Jackson continued, pointing to the French doors that opened onto a wide brick patio shaded by an arbor of wisteria vine. "The south lawn will be tented and set up with the dining tables. The silent auction is scheduled to begin at four with cocktails and passed hors d'oeuvres, and the dinner seating begins at six."

"Which event coordinator are you working with?"

Jackson mentioned the name of a well-known local coordinator who specialized in large events. I nodded, pleased by the choice.

He said, "She's got all the rentals already covered, including china, glassware, linens, tables, all of it. Everything will be set the day before, so there should be no one in your way when you get started."

That sounded good. Things were looking more together than I'd dared hope.

"I'll need to talk to her about the buffet setup—"

"It's not a buffet," he interrupted. "Dinner will be served."

Starting to sweat, I repeated, "Served?"

One side of Jackson's mouth tilted up. "I've hired waitstaff. And bartenders. All you have to worry about is making the food."

Oh sure. What a cinch. Easy peasy. Making enough food for three hundred people, keeping it hot without drying it out, and coordinating the simultaneous service of three hundred appetizers, entrees, and desserts—all while managing and directing a large waitstaff I'd only meet a few hours in advance—was absolutely no problemo.

Easiest twenty grand I'd ever earned.

My smile was much more confident than I felt. "Great. I'd like to talk to the coordinator today, if possible."

"I'll have Rayford give you her contact information before you leave. And the coordinator from the Wounded Warrior Project wants to speak with you, too."

So the charity gala was to raise money for wounded veterans. I was surprised it wasn't for something more superficial, like Billionaires Without Trophy Wives or the Southern Selfish Jerk Fund.

My ex would've been a founding member of that last one.

I said, "Oh, you were in the military?"

Jackson ambled over to the big marble island in the center of the kitchen, pulled out a stool, and sat down. He folded his hands and looked at me with his brows pulled together. "About the menu."

I'd obviously stepped in another steaming pile of none-of-your-damn-business.

Determined not to make the mistake of asking any more personal questions, I joined him at the island, taking a stool on the opposite side. From my pocketbook I removed the menu I'd been working on until two o'clock this morning. I handed him the pages and watched, chewing my lip, as he began to read.

After a few nerve-wracking minutes of silence, he said, "This will do. Wine pairings?"

I said, "No."

Jackson's head snapped up. Unblinking, he glared at me. *"No?"*

"Bourbon pairings. Specifically, Boudreaux Bourbon pairings."

He stared at me for a long time, his eyes hard. I had the feeling he was about to start growling again, but all he said was a curt, "Explain."

My heart picking up tempo, I said, "When I told you I loved your family's bourbon, it was the truth. There's a good reason it's the world's bestselling spirit—"

"Yes. Millions of dollars of marketing," Jackson said.

I was taken aback by the bitterness in his tone. "No. It's because it's the best bourbon money can buy."

Grinding his teeth together, he looked away. "You already have the job, Miss Hardwick. You don't have to blow smoke up my ass."

Face flaming, I retorted, "I never blow smoke into anyone's orifices, Mr. Boudreaux. Your bourbon is the best, or I wouldn't put it in my food and serve it to my blasted customers!"

His gaze cut back to mine. We stared at each other, tension crackling like a live wire between us. I got the feeling he didn't quite know what to do with me, the feisty little nobody with the big mouth. And I certainly didn't know what to do with him.

I inhaled a steadying breath. Though this man could start an argument in an empty house, bickering with him wouldn't get me anywhere. And I couldn't risk him getting teed off enough to fire me. I needed the money too much.

"Look. All this food I've proposed"—I pointed at the pages in his hands—"was chosen specifically because it would pair well with and highlight the unique aspects of the various lines of bourbon that you sell."

"That my *family* sells," he corrected acidly.

Well fry my bacon. Talking to this man about bourbon was like navigating my way through a minefield. Whatever the story was behind his attitude toward his family business, it was a doozy.

"Excuse me," I said primly. "That your family sells. My idea was that since *you* were putting on this event, as opposed to Joe Billionaire whose family makes urinal cakes, it would be nice to showcase the artistry and craftsmanship of your family's products. I think it would be a real treat for your guests, make it more personal. I mean, if you're going to all this trouble to make this event special, why not dazzle them with all the bells and whistles? Show them what the Boudreaux family name stands for. Show them what two hundred years of perfecting the craft of distilling tastes like. Give 'em the *steak*, not just the sizzle!"

He looked at me, looked down at the menu, heaved a sigh that sounded like he was deflating, and then raked both hands through his hair.

"Christ," he muttered, lacing his hands behind his head, "would my father love you."

That sounded distinctly like an insult, but I sensed a chink in his armor, so I forged ahead. "With the passed hors d'oeuvres, we'll start with a sparkling prosecco-based cocktail featuring the silver-label bourbon. It's called an Old Cuban . . . you'll love it."

When his brows lowered, indicating he doubted very much that he would love it, I hurried on.

"And we'll have a classic mojito using Boudreaux Special Select white rum, which will pair wonderfully with the first course. The main course features braised beef, which will be *delicious* with the black label—all that smoky, muscular character will really bring out the flavors in the meat—and for dessert we can make a Honey-Hattan with the honey bourbon to pair with the ginger-orange cheesecake. My mouth is watering just thinking of it!"

Jackson stared at me for so long I thought I might have fallen asleep and missed something. Then he said, "You actually do love my family's bourbon, don't you?"

He said it like that made me really strange, which was confusing. "Don't you?"

That angry muscle in his jaw made its reappearance, flexing like mad. "Sure, the same way I love getting a root canal."

The amount of family drama contained in that sentence could choke an elephant.

I noticed that sometime during our meeting, Rayford had disappeared.

"Mr. Boudreaux, I know what I'm doing. It's really difficult to pair cocktails with food, especially through an entire meal, which is another thing that's going to make it so special. I'll bet good money that none of your guests has ever had a curated bourbon pairing with a four-course dinner. Trust me. It's going to be fantastic. And the better they think it is, the bigger they'll open their wallets. Which is really the whole point, right?"

His look was intense and unwavering, with that gripping sense of concentrated attention that was so heavy and intimate it was almost like a touch.

It was almost sexual.

"Call me Jackson," he said abruptly.

Gently, with a smile, I replied, "If I wanted to call you Jackson, I would have, Mr. Boudreaux."

His intense look turned burning. "I suppose I deserve that," he said gruffly. "In my defense, I'd had a terrible day when we first met. I might have been a little more blunt than usual."

I laughed. "Blunt? Try tactless! Try rude! And by the way, other people have bad days all the time and don't turn into high-and-mighty mood monsters and start insulting everyone in sight. It's called common courtesy."

He didn't move. He didn't so much as bat a lash. He simply said, "If you were mine, I'd take you over my knee for that little speech."

I nearly fell off the stool.

Before I could recover my wits, a towheaded child about three or four years old burst into the kitchen, singing "Jingle Bells" at the top of his lungs.

And then a miracle occurred. Jackson "the Beast" Boudreaux's face split into a huge, genuine smile.

"Cody!" He leapt from the stool and picked up the child in a bear hug.

I watched in six different kinds of shock as the child put his little arms around Jackson's neck and screamed in glee while Jackson spun him around and around, that happy grin still plastered on his face.

"I'm so sorry, Mr. Boudreaux, he just got away from me!"

A harried, fiftyish blonde woman ran into the kitchen, panting. She had food stains on her blouse, hair escaping in every direction from her ponytail, and looked as if she hadn't slept in about a year. Immediately I felt sorry for her.

"It's all right, Charlie. Have a seat. I'll take him."

Jackson kissed Cody on the cheek and then lifted him straight up in the air, making the boy scream in delight again.

Not that I was about to ask, but the boy's fair coloring indicated Jackson was most likely not his father. And his distinctive facial features indicated he had Down syndrome.

Charlie, who I guessed was Cody's nanny, glanced at me. "Oh, no, sir, I can see you're busy."

Jackson growled, "I said sit."

Without further argument, Charlie gratefully collapsed onto the stool next to mine. "Good morning," she said, brushing a few stray blonde wisps from her face. "I'm Charlotte Harris."

I shook her extended hand. "Bianca Hardwick. It's a pleasure to meet you."

Charlie's face brightened. "You're the new chef! Oh, thank heavens. I'm afraid my repertoire goes about as far as scrambled eggs and toast. Poor Mr. Boudreaux has been surviving on scraps since Gregory quit, and I—"

"She's only helping with the benefit, Charlie," said Jackson, casually tossing Cody over his shoulder. He stood holding him with one strong arm wound around the boy's back and one hand propped on his hip, like a proud lumberjack bringing in his haul of wood.

It was adorable.

A word I never in a million years would've thought I'd use to describe Jackson Boudreaux.

For his part, Cody loved it. He hadn't stopped singing, laughing, or screaming happily since he'd come into the room. He bubbled with energy. I could see why Charlie was so tired.

I said, "Well, since I'm here, would you like me to make something for lunch?"

Charlie looked like I'd just told her she'd won a million dollars. "Oh, no, I *couldn't* ask you to do that," she said, her eyes begging me to contradict her.

I smiled and squeezed her shoulder. "Sure you could. Sit a spell and let me see what's in that airplane hangar of a refrigerator."

I stood. Jackson and I locked eyes, and something deep in my belly fluttered. *Is he angry? What's that look he's giving me?*

I froze, uncertain if I'd just crossed a line. "I mean . . . unless you'd rather I didn't."

Jackson carefully set Cody on his feet. As soon as his little shoes touched the ground, he launched himself at me, arms held out, fingers grasping.

"Lady!" he shouted. "Hi, lady!"

He slammed into my leg, hooked his chubby arms around it, tilted his head back, and smiled up at me. I smiled back at him.

"Hi, Cody. I'm Bianca." I reached down and ruffled his hair, fine as chick fluff.

Cody shouted, "Jingle bells!" and laughed.

Jackson said quietly, "Yes, Miss Hardwick. I think we would all like that very much."

I realized he'd just let Cody decide whether or not I should stay and make them lunch. Whoever this boy was to him, Jackson obviously loved him.

Why that affected me I don't know, but it did, deeply. I looked up at Jackson and said impulsively, "Please, call me Bianca."

His lips twitched. His eyes burned. He sent me a small, curt nod. I turned away before he could see how my face flamed with heat.

Then I set about making lunch, trying all the while not to recall the way his eyes had looked when he'd said *If you were mine.*

BIANCA'S OLD CUBAN

Makes 1 serving

- 2 ounces prosecco
- 1½ ounces bourbon
- 1 ounce simple syrup
- ¾ ounce fresh lime juice
- 2 dashes Angostura bitters
- fresh mint leaves to garnish

Preparation

1. Combine all ingredients except prosecco in a shaker and fill with ice.
2. Shake vigorously to chill.
3. Strain into a chilled coupe glass.
4. Top with prosecco and garnish with mint.

Simple Syrup Preparation

Combine 1 cup sugar and 1 cup water in saucepan and bring to a boil, stirring until sugar is dissolved. Remove from heat. Store leftovers in airtight container in the refrigerator for up to two weeks.

NINE

JACKSON

My father once told me the only difference between a woman and a man-eating shark was the size of their teeth.

At the time I'd agreed with him. I'd had good reason to. But watching Bianca Hardwick move gracefully around my kitchen, making us lunch while chatting animatedly with Charlie and interacting with Cody as if she'd known him since birth, made me think that might have been too harsh a judgment.

And no shark on earth had an ass like Bianca's.

Besides being a fucking masterpiece of design, the damn thing was an eyeball magnet. I'd already caught myself half a dozen times ogling it, my dick twitching under my zipper like some horny teenager's. Even those hideous brown work pants she favored that looked like they were made from old potato sacks couldn't diminish its appeal.

It was so round, like an apple. So taut and smooth. I wanted to bend her over the stool, yank those pants down her hips, and sink my teeth into it. I wanted to squeeze it and kiss it and stroke it and—

Christ, what was the matter with me?

Get a grip on yourself, Jackson!

"—like some pepper?"

I snapped back to myself just as Bianca was asking me a question. Something about pepper. I couldn't quite remember because all the blood in my head had gone south.

"What? What did you say?"

Bianca tilted her head and gazed quizzically at me from under a pair of long, curving black lashes. "I said would you like some fresh-ground pepper with your pasta?"

She held my pepper mill in her hands. In front of me was a bowl of something that smelled delicious. I had no idea how long I'd been zoned out in Pert Ass Land, but I felt like I'd been caught red-handed. So I answered more forcefully than I probably should have.

"No!"

Bianca blinked. Her brows arched. She said, "Allrighty then. No need to alert the entire state."

She turned to Charlie and asked the same question and received a far more polite response.

"I'd love some pepper, thank you! This smells amazing, Bianca."

"There wasn't much left in the fridge," said Bianca, smiling, "but pasta and a few sautéed veggies always makes for a quick and tasty meal."

"Sweet of you to make Cody mac and cheese," said Charlie, nodding in Cody's direction. He sat across from me at the island, happily slurping up cheese-covered pasta from a spoon and banging his feet against the metal legs of his stool.

"In my experience, kids will always go for a bowl of mac and cheese, no matter how much of a picky eater they are."

"Do you have little ones?" asked Charlie.

The question startled me.

I guessed Bianca wasn't married because she didn't wear a ring, but that didn't mean she was childless. She could be divorced. She could be a single mom. She could be all kinds of things my inner caveman instantly decided needed protecting.

Bianca laughed. "I don't, much to my mama's disappointment."

Then her laughter died. Her face did something strange. Her eyes registered pain for a moment, but then she squared her shoulders and smiled.

It looked forced.

I resisted the urge to ask what was wrong, because clearly something was. But I knew she wouldn't tell me. And besides, she was my employee now. I needed to stop thinking about her glorious ass and fixing whatever problems she might have and keep it professional.

Someone needed to tell that to my cock, because he wasn't listening to me. Pert Ass Land was too much of a temptation.

Bianca said, "Someday, though, hopefully. I love kids."

She loves kids. She looks like that and she loves to read and she cooks like a three-Michelin-star chef and she loves kids.

And she's made it perfectly clear she can't stand me.

I shoveled pasta into my mouth to stifle the groan breaking from my chest.

Bianca walked over to Cody and ruffled his hair. He grinned at her, cheese smeared all over his chin and most of his hands. Then she rinsed the dishes in the sink and loaded them into the dishwasher, like she'd been preparing meals in my kitchen for years.

I stared at her for a moment, surprised by how much I liked having her in this space. And it wasn't just her spectacular ass that made me feel that way. It was her.

Mouthy, bossy, yet surprisingly non-shark-like her.

Who can't stand me.

Who was now in my employ.

Goddamnit.

"And now I really need to get back to the restaurant. I'll give both coordinators a call this afternoon," she said, turning to me, "and let you know if I have any other questions."

"Fine," I growled into my bowl of delicious pasta. Then, because my dick was throbbing and she was leaving when I wanted her to stay and I fucking hate feeling confused and I'm shit with good-byes, I snapped, "Rayford will give you the check for your fee on your way out."

Even with a solid slab of marble separating us, I felt Bianca's anger flare at the sharp, dismissive tone I'd used. I glanced up to find her staring at me with fire burning in those beautiful, dark eyes.

"It's always a pleasure, Mr. Boudreaux," she said with quiet sarcasm.

And we're back to Mr. Boudreaux. Fuck.

She exchanged good-byes with Charlie and then turned and walked out.

I swear I tried not to stare at her ass as she went, but even Achilles had a weakness.

TEN

BIANCA

The first thing I did after Rayford dropped me off at the restaurant was hustle over to the bank to deposit Jackson's check into my mama's account. We'd scheduled her initial round of chemo for a few days away, and I didn't want to take any chances that Jackson, in one of his inexplicable beastie moods, would put a stop payment on the check.

With that done, I felt better.

Until I ran smack into my ex in the bank's parking lot. Literally *into* him.

The noise I made when I collided with his chest was something so unladylike my mama would've pitched a hissy fit if she'd heard it. It was part grunt, part groan, and part something that sounded like it shot out of my butthole on a hot burst of air, excuse my French. Hands flailing, I dropped my pocketbook on the ground and stumbled back in surprise.

"Whoa!" A pair of strong hands gripped my upper arms to steady me. "Easy, girl. I know I'm handsome as sin, but there's no need to throw yourself at me."

I looked up—and there he was. The Devil himself. Beautiful as a sculpture and just as soulless.

"Don't flatter yourself." I shrugged off Trace's hands. "I just wasn't watching where I was going."

Looking me up and down, Trace smiled.

Let me put that in perspective.

Trace looks like Denzel Washington, Dwayne Johnson, Jason Momoa, and a hot Tahitian swimsuit model had a wild orgy and nine months later he popped out, with equal parts of all their perfect genes. When he smiles at you, it feels like the clouds suddenly opened up on a rainy day and a sunbeam illuminated your head in a brilliant, heavenly glow.

You feel special. You feel like a special little snowflake twinkling in the sun, until you realize he smiles that way at *every single woman* he comes into contact with, and then you just feel like a dope.

He said, "Where you going in such a hurry, bumble bee?"

Hearing him call me by my old nickname made me grind my back teeth together. "Away from you," I said, and picked up my purse. When I straightened and moved to go around him, Trace stepped in my way.

"Wait," he said, suddenly serious. "I want to talk to you."

"No." I tried to move past him again, but he didn't let me.

"Bianca, please," he said in a low, pleading tone I'd never heard. "I really want to talk to you."

I looked him right in his eyes. In his gorgeous, caramel-flecked-with-gold eyes that used to be able to coerce me into anything. Not anymore.

I said, "I know you're not really clear on this, Trace, so let me break it down for you. When a woman says *no*, she doesn't mean yes. She doesn't mean maybe. She doesn't mean please try to talk me out of it because I really don't mean it, but I just want you to work a little harder. She means no. N. O. Now get out of my way."

"But you never gave me a chance to explain—"

"*Explain!*" Astonished by his nerve, I laughed. "Explain what? That you tripped and fell and your penis accidentally landed inside my best friend? And the checkout girl at Halley's Market? And the waitress at Dooley's? And whoever the bimbo was who kept texting you for a booty call at two a.m.? That's a lot of tripping, Romeo. You need to see a doctor for your balance problem."

At least he had the sense to look ashamed of himself. "I know I was an idiot, but I swear I've changed."

My brows lifted. "Really? Got a brain transplant, did you?"

Very solemnly, Trace said. "No. I found God."

After a beat of shocked silence, I threw my head back and laughed. "Well good for you! Hallelujah! Now get your slutty butt out of my face before I lose my temper and send you off to meet Him!"

I had to give him credit. The old Trace would've been pissed about that remark. Probably would've made a rude comment about *my* butt, which he used to tell me could be "fixed" by a visit to a lipo doctor. But this Trace—whoever he was—only looked sad.

"It's been two years, Bianca. I swear, I'm a different man. Please, I just want to talk to you."

I folded my arms across my chest. "I get it. This is like a thirteen-step program, right? You have to apologize to me or else you won't get past the pearly gates?"

He winced. "I think you mean twelve step. And no, that's not it. I just . . . You cut me off and never took any of my calls again—"

"I'd rather talk to a bill collector," I interrupted angrily. "At least I know it'd be an honest conversation."

Then—hand to heaven, I could not make this up—the man got a tear in his eye. A big ol' crocodile tear that sat there and glimmered and trembled like a makeup artist had just run over with a bottle of glycerin in between film takes.

He said roughly, "I'm sorry. That's all I wanted to say. I treated you badly, and you didn't deserve it. I didn't want to stalk you after we broke up, but I kept hoping I'd run into you somewhere. And here you are.

So . . . I'm sorry. I really did love you, even though I did what I did. It just took losing you to make me realize it."

He looked at his shoes, took a breath, and then met my gaze again. Very quietly, he said, "Actually, I *still* love you, bumble bee. I think I always will."

I admit it. My heart did a major flip-flop. I got a serious case of butterflies in the stomach. Who doesn't want the ex she was madly in love with to do a bit of groveling after he treated her like a disposable napkin?

Unfortunately for him, the girl I was then and the girl I am now are two different Biancas altogether.

I took a breath, squared my shoulders, and lifted my chin. "I can't say it was nice to see you, Trace, but it was definitely interesting. Good luck to you."

My head held high, I walked briskly past him. I didn't look back. I kept walking—my gait was almost a power walk it was so fast—until I got to the restaurant. Then I threw open the front door and ran inside to hide because I wasn't 100 percent sure he wasn't following me.

"Um, whatchya doin', boo?"

Eeny's confused voice came from behind me.

"Making sure I wasn't followed," I said, peering out to the street through the blinds on the windows.

"Followed?" She chuckled. "Your meetin' with the werewolf went that bad, huh?"

Satisfied Trace wasn't about to burst through my front door, I let the blinds fall back into place and turned to look at Eeny with a sigh. "Ugh. That was a whole other disaster. Remind me to have a shot of liquor before I talk to Jackson Boudreaux again. Maybe he'll make sense if I'm tipsy. But I wasn't talking about him. I was talking about Trace."

At the mention of his name, Eeny made the sign of the cross over her chest.

I'm not even sure she's a Christian, but she likes to keep all her bases covered.

"Trace! *Lawd!* What on earth you doin' talkin' to him?"

"Believe me, it wasn't my idea." I walked past Eeny on my way to the kitchen. Huffing and excited, she followed right on my heels.

"Well what did he say? More importantly, how did he look? Does he still have all those big ol' muscles in all the right places, or did he let himself go?"

I snorted. "The day Trace Adams lets himself go is the day the earth stops spinning."

"So he looked good? What was he wearin'?"

I stopped and turned to look at her. "Eeny. Focus. The man is a liar and a cheater. It doesn't matter how good he looks."

She pursed her lips. "Can you just tell me if he was wearin' those tight jeans like he always used to that accentuated his nice big package and tight butt?"

I sighed and turned away, headed for the kitchen. "No. He was wearing a pair of sweatpants."

Hello, white lie. Trace *had* actually been wearing jeans that accentuated his bulge and tight butt, but I wasn't about to tell Eeny that. She'd get nothing done for the rest of the day. And I wasn't admitting to myself that I'd noticed, anyway.

Only I had, which was pathetic. Trace was the last man I'd had sex with, and he knew what he was doing in bed. I wasn't sure if my lack of attraction to anyone since was due to how badly he broke my heart or a terrible suspicion that no other man would be able to make me scream the way he had.

Either way, my dry spell had gone on so long the inside of my vagina probably looked like one of those old Western ghost towns, all tumbleweeds and abandoned buildings, mean-looking vultures picking over dried-up bones.

"Sweatpants!" exclaimed Eeny. She made a clucking sound, like a hen. "Lawd, what a waste. That's like hangin' curtains on the statue of David."

Even though I wanted to, I couldn't disagree. Trace might be all kinds of wrong, but I'd never seen another man as beautiful.

If only the inside matched the outside. But, as Mama always told me, beauty is as beauty does. Some of the prettiest faces hide the meanest hearts, and smooth talk is no substitute for good character. The only way to judge a person is by his deeds.

Like caring for a special needs child who isn't your own, I thought pensively.

Then I pushed the thought aside and got to work.

Three days later I was sitting in a hospital room that smelled like antiseptic and desperation, holding my mother's hand as poisonous chemicals dripped into her veins from a clear plastic bag elevated on a metal pole.

My mother treated the whole thing like it was an outing in the park, chatting with the nurses, flirting with the doctor, reading gossip rags, and laughing.

I, on the other hand, was on the verge of a nervous breakdown. *Mama was being filled with poison!*

Cancer-killing poison, but poison nonetheless.

"Buck up, child, you look like you're at a funeral!" Mama scolded, smacking me on the arm with a rolled-up magazine.

"I'm sorry." I sniffled and sat up straighter in my chair. "You're right. What can I do for you? Can I get you anything? Water? A snack? Something else to read?"

A male nurse came over, silently checked the catheter inserted into Mama's arm, then nodded and left. Watching him go, Mama muttered, "Hoo! There's my snack right there. You think he likes older women?"

I had to laugh. "I think those chemicals are going to your head."

She pretended to be offended. "Are you saying you don't think I could hit that?"

I grimaced. "Hit that? Are you a rapper now?"

Mama went all practical. "If I were, I'd want to be Jay Z. Married to Beyoncé, can you imagine? That boy has *no* idea how lucky he is!" She tapped me on the arm with her gossip rag. "And if he doesn't watch out, Kanye West is gonna get all up in there and steal his woman."

I blinked at her. "I'd ask if you've been drinking, but I'm afraid of the answer."

"Speaking of drinking," she said, watching me from under her lashes like she does when she has something scandalous to reveal, "I got a real interesting phone call the other day."

"Oh?" I said, watching an old man with a walker shuffle by the door. His blue hospital gown was open in the back, exposing his wrinkled, white butt. I looked away, embarrassed for him.

Lord, hospitals were depressing.

"Mmm-hmm," said Mama. "From Trace."

My head snapped around so fast it almost flew clear off my neck. "Trace! You're joking!"

"I'm serious as a car crash, *chère*." She pursed her lips, tilting her head to look more closely at me. "Why didn't you mention you saw him?"

"Because I was trying to forget, obviously," I grumbled. "And what business did he have calling you? The nerve!"

"Oh, don't you worry, I gave him a good piece of my mind." She paused for a moment, thinking. "Funny, he agreed with everything I said about him. And then he apologized."

I rolled my eyes. "Oh, Mama, you know better than to listen to that snake oil salesman. You should've hung up the second you recognized his voice."

"I did," she said, nodding. "Until he called me back and told me that losing you was the biggest mistake he'd ever made."

"Gag," I said.

"And that he'd do anything to get you back."

"Oh, for the love of God."

"Which was his other point."

I glared at Mama. "Please don't tell me you *believe* his whole 'I've been saved by Jesus' spiel!"

She looked at me for a long time, not saying a word. Then she lifted a shoulder. "For some people, hitting rock bottom is the only way they can start a new journey toward the top."

"Rock bottom! He's a *ho*, Mama, not an alcoholic! Land's sake, he slept with my best friend! *In my bed!*"

That last part might have been a little loud, judging by the way the nurse walking by the open door snorted.

Mama patted my hand. "I know he did, baby, and that was an awful thing to do. All I'm saying is . . . occasionally good people make stupid mistakes." Her eyes grew misty. "And honestly, lately I've been thinking a lot about all the mistakes I've made in my life. Sometimes it takes something really bad to put all the good in perspective."

"Sweet Jesus," I said, staring at her. "He's put a spell on you."

She waved a dismissive hand in the air. "Nobody's put a spell on me. I'm too thick-headed for it to work." She sighed, toying with the glasses on a chain around her neck. "But after sixty-four years on this earth, I know when a man's lying, and I know when a man's telling the truth. And when Trace said he still loved you and would do anything to get you back, he was telling the truth."

I shook my head in disbelief. "I can't believe we're having this conversation. You saw how devastated I was after we broke up. You remember how much weight I lost and how I cried every day and how I couldn't get out of bed for weeks, right?"

"I remember," she said quietly. "But I also know you haven't even looked at another man since him. Which makes me think all those feelings you had for him might still be there."

Something awful occurred to me. "Oh, no. Please tell me you didn't tell him that."

She pulled a face, like, *Oops.*

I shot up from my chair and stared down at her. "*Mama!* You *didn't!*"

She leveled me with her own version of The Look. "Don't you raise your voice to me, young lady. I am *not* gonna leave this earth without seeing you settled, you hear?"

"You're not going anywhere!" I said, horrified she was talking about dying.

She ignored my interruption. "And I'm gonna tell you something else—your own daddy wasn't the saint you think he was. Before we were married that man chased every skirt he saw, and when I found out, I left him flat as a penny run over by a freight train. But he begged me to forgive him, and I'm glad I did because we were happily married for more than thirty years and he gave me the best gift I've ever gotten—*you.*"

I stared at her with my mouth hanging open.

She continued. "Men aren't like us, baby. They're dumb as doughnut holes when it comes to love. But once they decide to commit—not *say* they're committing, but deep in their heart actually *make* the commitment—they never waver. Your father didn't waver for thirty years, even when his own parents cut him off without a cent because he married me. He didn't waver when we found out I couldn't have any more babies, even though he wanted a big family. He didn't waver through good times or bad, sickness or health, for all the years after he took a vow to love and cherish me. In the end the only thing powerful enough to put us apart was death."

Her voice grew quiet. "And sometimes I'm not sure that did it, either. I can still feel him when I'm low. Every once in a while I smell his cologne, even when I'm in a room all by myself. Just this morning I rolled over in bed and felt a hand on my forehead, but when I opened my eyes there was no one there. I don't know what that means, but I do know this. If your father, God rest his soul, could turn out to be the honest man and true friend and loyal husband he was for all those years, *chère*, there's hope for anyone. Even a scallywag like Trace."

Rattled to my core, knees shaking, I sank back into my chair. I whispered, "You never told me any of that before."

She smiled and leaned over and brushed a lock of hair off my cheek. "I've never been dying before."

"You're *not* dying," I insisted, gripping her hand.

"We're all dying, baby. It's just a matter of when." She lifted my hand and pressed it to her lips. "I've had a wonderful life. Maybe better than I deserve. I'm not afraid to go, so don't you be afraid, either."

I teared up, hard. "How can you not be afraid? I'm so afraid for you."

This time her smile was truly beautiful. "Because your daddy's waiting for me on the other side, baby," she said gently. "Finally we'll be together again. Being afraid of that would just be plain stupid."

My lip quavered. My throat closed.

Then I burst into tears.

"Oh, come on now, *chère*," she said, opening her arms. I buried my face into her chest and cried. She patted me on the back and kissed the top of my head, chuckling softly. "You always were such a sentimental little thing. Crying over dead goldfish and those Morris the Cat commercials where he's lost and his owner's looking for him in the rain."

My reply came out muffled. "You're not a goldfish!"

Her sigh sounded philosophical. "Might as well be. We're all just here for a blip in time, riding on a rock that's flying through space at a million miles a day in a galaxy that has a hundred billion stars. Me, Jay Z, the president, a goldfish . . . in the end there's not much difference, *chère*. We come and go. We live and die. If we're lucky, we love and are loved."

She tilted my head up with a finger under my chin and smiled at me. "And I've been incredibly lucky, so don't you waste your tears on me, you hear?"

I wiped my face with the back of my hand. "Yes, ma'am."

"Good girl." She looked over my shoulder. Her voice turned brisk. "Now where the heck is that male nurse? I feel in need of some mouth-to-mouth resuscitation!"

There was nothing else to do but laugh. I laughed until the doctor pulled me into the hallway and told me in a solemn voice that Mama was going to need chemo for the next seven days straight, have a break for a week, and then another seven days, and so on for the next month . . . and each round would cost almost $3,000.

Which didn't include lab tests, imaging tests, radiation, or the antinausea and other drugs she'd need in addition to the intravenous chemo.

I was going to need a lot more than twenty grand.

ELEVEN

BIANCA

By the time Jackson's charity benefit rolled around, I was jumpy as a cat on a hot tin roof.

Doc Halloran had told us what to expect in the way of side effects of the chemo, but neither Mama nor I was prepared for the reality of it. She felt fine for the first few days, and then everything kicked in with one big wallop.

The nausea and vomiting were the least of it. She also had massive headaches, frightful mouth sores, and fatigue so bad she could hardly get out of bed.

I went with her every day to the hospital for the first week, then helped out at the house during the second, trying to get her to eat and fielding all her callers, turning them away with excuses that she had the flu. Even the poor Colonel wasn't allowed inside. Mama didn't have the energy to put on her face and pretend, so away he went, shoulders slumped.

I didn't think it was right she didn't tell him what was really going on, but it wasn't my place to make that decision.

But most of all, I dreaded what would happen when she had to go back for the next round of chemo. The first was so bad it seemed likely to kill her before the cancer did.

"Perfectly normal," said Doc Halloran every time I called him in a panic. "It's a sign the medicine is working, Bianca. Just let it take its course."

It's so irritating when someone stays calm while the world is ending.

In between all that I worked in a frenzy to get ready for Jackson's charity benefit. I met with the coordinators, ordered all the meat, produce, and alcohol, and added extra shifts at the restaurant to start the food prep.

And I avoided Trace's calls.

Twice he called the house. Both times I saw the number and let it ring, flipping the bird at the phone. When the answering machine came on, he hung up with a heavy sigh, like I was being unreasonable.

I gave Mama a pass on account of her being sick, but there was no way *I* was gonna listen to a single word he had to say. I knew for a fact he was only calling because I'd given him the brush-off. Our time together had proven to me in a hundred ways that Trace was the kind of man who only wanted what he couldn't have. Rejection heightened his interest. His appetite was whetted by the chase. If I'd shown the least bit of tenderness when we'd run into each other on the street, he would've gone on with his life without giving me a second thought, as he'd been doing for the past two years.

In hindsight, I should've told him I was still madly in love with him and watched the smoke rise from the rubber burns the soles of his shoes left on the sidewalk as he fled. But my heart was still too bruised to play that game. Instead I started carrying pepper spray in my pocketbook in case I saw him again. I had enough on my plate. I didn't need a lying, cheating, born-again BS artist to contend with.

"So we're all set with the canapés and cocktails," said Claudia, briskly ticking off a box on the list on the clipboard she held in her perfectly manicured hands. "The musicians are warming up on the lawn. In thirty minutes I'll light all the candles, and fifteen minutes after that the guests are scheduled to start arriving."

She looked up at me and adjusted her stylish black eyeglasses. "Do you need anything from me at this point?"

I shook my head. "No, thanks. I'm all set here."

"Good." Claudia looked at her watch. "I'll check in with you again in fifty minutes. If you need me, I'm on my headset. The number's—"

"On the schedule," I finished. "I know."

The coordinator Jackson had hired to oversee the event was a sleek-haired brunette, lanky as a giraffe and the most efficient person I'd ever met. She had everyone running around like chickens with their heads cut off, trying to keep to her exacting schedule, which counted time in precise five-minute increments. Though she was perfectly pleasant, I got the impression she'd turn into a screaming meemie if her schedule wasn't followed.

As of now we were two minutes behind, and her left eyelid had already begun to twitch.

"Ladies. How're we doing?"

Jackson stood in the doorway of the kitchen, looking at Claudia and me. It was the first time I'd seen him since I'd arrived at his house early this morning to start the setup.

"Everything's under control," I said. "Claudia's doing a great job."

She smiled tightly and adjusted her glasses again. I felt her gratitude for my small show of support. It was obvious how intimidated she was by Jackson. She could barely look him in the eye, probably because he was wearing a scowl as black as his outfit.

But I was used to that by now. I didn't let it alarm me.

I asked him, "Is that what you're going to wear?"

Jackson looked down at himself, then looked up at me with his brows drawn down over his eyes.

Seeing his murderous expression, Claudia ran out of the kitchen like her pants were on fire. "Fifty minutes, Bianca!" she called over her shoulder, then disappeared through the French doors.

Jackson didn't seem to notice she'd left. He demanded, "What's wrong with what I'm wearing?"

I shrugged. "Nothing, if you want people to think you've been living under a bridge."

He crossed his arms over his chest. I tried to ignore how that made the muscles in his biceps bulge.

He said, "You must be mistaking me for someone who cares what people think."

Propping my hands on my hips, I examined his untucked T-shirt, wrinkled jeans, and scuffed boots, his unshaven jaw, and his hair that appeared to have last seen a comb when he walked by one that had fallen out of someone's pocket into the street.

I said, "Lord knows I'm no style maven, and I dress for comfort more than anything else, but your guests deserve the best version of you, Mr. Boudreaux. I'm sorry to say this isn't it."

His glower was so searing it could have melted a weaker woman. But after the past few days I'd had, I was in an ornery mood. An ornery *truth-telling* mood, because I'd recently decided life was too short to beat around the bush.

Plus, his check had already cleared the bank.

"Oh, really?" said Jackson, his voice acidic.

"Yes, really." We stared at each other. It must have been my imagination, but it felt like the temperature in the room jumped several degrees.

He snapped, "So what would you recommend I wear, then?"

"Do you own a suit?"

His expression turned even darker. "I *hate* suits."

"But do you have one?"

When he didn't answer and just stood there glaring at me like he hoped a stray asteroid would smash through the ceiling and land on my head, I said, "That's what you should wear. With a tie." I looked at his boots. "And dress shoes."

He ran a hand over his face—probably deciding whether he was going to pick up the toaster from the counter and throw it at me—and I added, "Also, a shave wouldn't kill you."

He looked at me with a strange new expression. "You don't like beards."

He said it flatly. It wasn't a question.

"Beards are fine. But that thing carpeting your jaw? Honestly, I've seen tidier jungles."

For a moment I thought he would let loose a string of expletives so loud it would deafen me. But then his lips twitched, and I realized he was trying not to smile.

He said, "You're in fine form today, Bianca."

It was the first time he'd used my given name. I nearly fainted in surprise but managed to control myself. "I'm sorry," I said, looking down at the schedule I still held in my hands. "You're right. It's just . . ." I cleared my throat. "It's just been a rough few weeks."

There was silence for a moment, then he walked closer. "What's wrong?" he demanded, gruff and growly as a bear.

I glanced up at him and was surprised again. I could've sworn he was looking at me with concern in his eyes.

Concern and something else a little hotter.

My heart decided it was time to run a sprint. It took off like a jackrabbit chased by a pack of hounds. I said, "Just some personal stuff. My mother . . ."

I trailed off, dazed for a moment by his eyes. I hadn't noticed before, but they weren't only blue. He had tiny flecks of green and gold around his irises, warming those steely-blue depths.

And by God, the man smelled delicious. If that was his natural scent, he could make a few more billion by bottling it and selling it to men with less scrumptious—

Wait. What am I doing? Why am I mooning at him? Am I out of my ever-loving mind?

"Your mother?" he prompted, but I quickly stepped away, smoothing a hand over my hair.

"It's nothing. I'm so sorry, I'm being unprofessional. If you don't mind, Mr. Boudreaux, I'll just get back to work now—"

"Jackson," he said. He gazed down at me, eyes burning. His voice dropped an octave. "I want you to call me Jackson, Bianca."

My sprinting heart tripped all over itself and fell flat on its face inside my chest. Heat rose into my cheeks. I said haltingly, "Um . . . okay."

His gaze dropped to my lips.

Every muscle in my body tensed.

When he abruptly turned around and left, my knees shook so badly I had to lean against the counter for support.

What on earth just happened?

The next few hours passed in a blur. In between directing a setup and serving staff of almost one hundred people and ensuring the food was kept at the right temperature until ready to be served, was plated properly before it left the staging area, and that there was enough of it, I didn't have a moment to catch my breath, let alone reflect on what had happened between me and Jackson in the kitchen. It was nothing, really . . .

But it sure felt like something. I had all sorts of tingling girly bits telling me so.

"Bianca!"

At the sound of my name being shouted, I jumped. I whirled around to see Claudia headed toward me across the lawn at a pace just short of a run, gripping her clipboard against her chest, her face pale as a bedsheet.

I said, "What? What's happening?"

She hustled up next to me and blurted, "Mr. Boudreaux asked for you. He's in the tent. You'd better hurry."

I frowned, handing off two plates of cheesecake to a waiting server, who turned around and sprinted away with them. We'd gone through almost three hundred pieces of my ginger-orange cheesecake already, and though typically not every guest would have dessert, this crowd seemed especially ravenous.

Thank Jesus I'd made plenty extra, because the last thing I wanted was Jackson hearing complaints that there hadn't been enough.

I said, "In the tent? Why would he want me in the tent? Isn't the auction supposed to be starting now?"

Claudia—whose hair gel had failed so her coiffure was now frizzed out into a cloudy brown halo around her face—said, "Six minutes ago! Which is why you need to hurry! Go! *Now!*" She gave me a little shove toward the direction of the tent.

I was perplexed. "Well hold your horses, I'm going!"

"Quickly!" she said, flapping her hands and panting.

Figuring it must be some kind of culinary disaster, I went as fast as I could, my heart in my throat. I trotted over the lush green grass toward the enormous tent set up on the back lawn. It was all white and looked like something from a Cirque du Soleil show. Three tall, flagged peaks reached like ghostly fingers toward the twilight sky. Servers streamed in and out from open flaps around the perimeter, clearing plates and bringing drinks. At one flap near the front stood a young female server, waving madly.

At me.

Fried chicken, this doesn't look good.

I stopped beside her and peered inside the tent. I didn't see anyone puking, didn't hear any shouts of distress, could detect nothing out of sorts in the murmuring, well-dressed crowd of hundreds seated at candlelit rounds.

I asked, "What's going on?"

"Get up to the stage."

She pointed to the raised dais at the rear of the tent, where a wooden podium and microphone stood, illuminated by a spotlight. Behind the stage were three large white screens with a backdrop of a shirred black-fabric cloth hung to hide wires and audiovisual equipment.

"The stage?" I repeated. "Why?"

The server threw her hands in the air. "Like anybody tells me anything! All I know is you're supposed to get up there right now."

I protested, "But the schedule—"

She turned and walked off before I could get anything more out of her. Then it didn't matter if she'd left because at that moment Jackson walked out onto the stage and into the spotlight, and I was rendered speechless.

It wasn't him. It couldn't be.

Then he strolled up to the microphone and started to speak, and that smooth, rich-like-molasses voice proved that it was.

"Good evening, ladies and gentlemen," he said. "I'm Jackson Boudreaux."

The place went wild. Three hundred people jumped from their chairs and clapped and hollered and whistled, making such a racket it could probably be heard for miles.

I stared around at all the clamoring people, wondering if someone had spiked their drinks with cocaine. All this excitement for the Beast?

"Thank you so much for coming," Jackson said over the noise. "I'm honored to welcome you to my home."

Who is this person? I thought, stunned. *This polite, charming person?*
Standing there onstage, in a tuxedo that fit his large, muscular
frame so perfectly it had to be custom-made, with his dark hair slicked
back and his face freshly shaved, was a stranger. A smiling stranger who
sounded like Jackson and called himself Jackson, but looked nothing
like the man I knew.

The Jackson Boudreaux *I* knew made Chewbacca look well groomed.

The Jackson Boudreaux *I* knew made King Kong seem civilized.

The Jackson Boudreaux *I* knew didn't look like Superman and dress
like James Bond and have a crowd of three hundred people on their feet,
showering him in adoration.

Maybe I was hallucinating. I put the back of my hand to my forehead, testing for fever, but it was cool and dry.

New and Improved Jackson said, "As you may know, I first became
involved with the Wounded Warrior Project after my best friend,
Christian LeFevre, was wounded while serving in the Marines in
Afghanistan."

So this is why Jackson's involved with the charity. How tragic. I listened
with my hand over my mouth as he went on.

"A roadside bomb took Christian's legs but not his love of his country, his joy for life, or his dedication to serving others. Though compli-
cations from his amputations ultimately claimed his life, the Wounded
Warrior Project was there for him in his final months the way no other
organization could have been."

Jackson's voice broke. He stopped speaking abruptly, ran a hand
through his hair, and drew a slow breath.

I watched, enthralled. He had feelings. The Beast *had feelings.*

I'd seen his irritation before, of course, and had also seen firsthand
his devotion for Cody. But this was something else altogether. This was
raw. This was powerful.

This was *vulnerable.*

GINGER-ORANGE CHEESECAKE

Makes 8 servings

- 1½ cups graham cracker crumbs
- ⅓ cup butter, melted
- ⅓ cup white sugar
- 32 ounces cream cheese, softened
- ⅔ cup white sugar, plus 2 tablespoons
- 1 cup sour cream, divided
- 1 tablespoon grated orange peel
- 4 eggs
- 2 cups clementine wedges
- ½ cup finely chopped crystallized ginger

Preparation

1. Preheat oven to 325 degrees. Mix graham cracker crumbs, butter, and ⅓ cup sugar together. Press on bottom of 9^2 x 3^2 springform pan and just enough up sides to seal bottom.
2. Place cream cheese, ⅔ cup sugar, ½ cup sour cream, and orange peel in food processor. Cover and process about 3 minutes or until smooth. Add eggs. Cover and process until

well blended. Spread over crust.

3. Bake 1 hour 20 minutes, or until center is set. Cool on wire rack for 15 minutes. Using spatula around edges to loosen, remove side of pan.

4. Refrigerate uncovered 3 hours or until chilled, then cover and continue refrigerating at least 4 hours, but not longer than 48 hours.

5. Mix ½ cup sour cream and 2 tablespoons sugar and spread over top of cheesecake. Top with fresh fruit and crystallized ginger. Store uneaten portion covered with foil in fridge.

TWELVE

BIANCA

Though I wanted to turn and bolt, I didn't. The man had paid me an obscene amount of money for this job, after all. And I was a professional. I wouldn't embarrass him in front of all his guests by refusing his request.

Also, I was intrigued by this new Jackson, this well-dressed stranger who spoke so eloquently about honor and selflessness and used words like *please*.

I didn't think that word was in his vocabulary.

So it was with curiosity—and a healthy dose of embarrassment—that I walked around the perimeter of the tables and climbed the few stairs to the stage.

Then shock took over as Jackson wound his arm around my shoulders, pulled me against his side, and smiled down at me. I was too busy trying not to keel over in surprise to pay much attention to how perfectly I fit under his arm, how snugly I nestled against the solid bulk of his body.

How hard he was, all over.

I'm definitely hallucinating. Or Jackson Boudreaux has a twin no one knows about.

A twin that had three long, thin, mysterious scars on the right side of his face that his beard had been hiding.

"Pretend like you don't hate me, and smile," he said, his jaw barely moving, his lips stretched tight over his teeth. "Please."

There's that word again. I'm as lost as last year's Easter egg. Am I on camera? Expecting to see myself on a prank video sometime in the near future, I smiled.

Satisfied, Jackson turned back to the audience. "I discovered the magic of Bianca Hardwick's cuisine when I visited her restaurant in the French Quarter. The food was so good I stayed all night and tried everything on the menu—"

"Maybe it wasn't the food you stayed for!" shouted someone from the audience, then whistled, one of those catcalls boys lean out of car windows to deliver as you walk down the street.

Three hundred people laughed. My face went molten hot.

Jackson chuckled. His arm squeezed tighter around my shoulders. He said, "Well. Maybe for the first hour it was for the food."

Who is this chuckler? I thought wildly, my heart galloping but the rest of me frozen stiff. *This crowd pleaser? This . . . flirt?*

At that moment, he tilted his head and sent me a sly wink.

He *winked*.

From my peripheral vision, I saw several camera flashes. Sweet Georgia Brown, I was being photographed grinning at Jackson Boudreaux like the village idiot.

I looked back out at the faceless crowd. Cold sweat trickled down between my shoulder blades. My smile stayed plastered firmly in place.

Jackson said, "I want y'all to visit Bianca's in the Quarter before month's end. Will you do that for me?"

The crowd made more noise. Jackson nodded, and then he said some other things I was too discombobulated to recall. Then a man came onstage and shook Jackson's hand, and Jackson led me off by the arm, smiling and waving good-bye to the crowd.

The moment we were out of earshot of any guests, he dropped my arm and snapped, "You can stop smiling now, for Christ's sake!"

"Oh thank heavens," I said sarcastically. "For a minute there I thought I was living in an alternate universe where you actually had a good side."

He swung around and stood in front of me. We were outside the tent, off to the side of one of the openings where waiters were still coming and going, glaring at each other in cold semidarkness while the auction began inside.

He snapped, "You're right. I *don't* have a good side. The person I was in there is a fabrication, the Jackson Boudreaux who *likes* people and *enjoys* the spotlight and feels right at home in a fucking *penguin suit*." He ripped off his bowtie and threw it to the ground. "But *that* guy knows how to work a crowd and raise money by the fuckload for a charity that helps a *lot* of soldiers in need."

He stepped closer and growled, "And *that* guy is willing to do whatever's necessary to keep his end of a bargain with you and promote your restaurant and act like we're on good terms, even when it's painfully fucking obvious you'd rather be pushed off a building than have my arm around your shoulders!"

Normally this was the part where I'd lose my temper and tell him to kiss my grits or some other silliness. But I realized like a slap across the face that the reason he was so angry was because he was hurt.

He was hurt because he thought I hated him.

That he actually cared what I thought about him left me breathless.

After a moment I said, "Just to be clear, I would rather have your arm around me than be pushed off a building. That is definitely preferable to death."

He stood there staring at me, breathing heavily, blue eyes glittering, the pulse pounding hard in his neck. The scars on his lower jaw moved as a muscle flexed beneath them.

I said, "Also to be clear, I don't hate you. You said that earlier, but it's not true. What I feel when I'm around you is usually irritation, I admit that, but only because you're always acting like you just escaped from a zoo."

Aside from his chest, which rose and fell in irregular bursts, he didn't move. He stayed still as a statue as I continued to speak, his intense gaze never leaving my face.

"And even if that was an act in there, I admire that you would do all this"—I made a gesture encompassing the tent, the scurrying servers, the side of the house with all its rented ovens and equipment—"in memory of your friend who passed away. And to raise money to help others like him."

My gaze fell to his jaw, to those mysterious white lines that almost looked like claw marks. What had it taken for him to shave off his beard and put those on display?

What had made them in the first place?

And why would he have taken *my* advice?

My voice softer, I said, "And to shave and wear a penguin suit and say such nice things about my restaurant, even if you didn't mean it."

He said flatly, "If I didn't mean it, you wouldn't be standing here."

And the other part? I wanted to ask. *The part about only staying the first hour for the food, suggesting you'd stayed the rest of the time for me?*

But that was too dangerous. I wasn't sure I really wanted to know the answer.

Instead I said, "I'm not comfortable in front of large crowds. That's why I was stiff. I was surprised that you put your arm around me and that you were acting so differently, so that contributed to my general weirdness, too, but to be honest I was also very moved by what you said about your friend and hadn't quite recovered when you called me up."

Hoping the answer was no, I asked, "That part wasn't an act, was it?"

Jackson swallowed. He shook his head. "I loved Christian like a brother. We went to college together. That's why I adopted Cody. He's Christian's son."

So I'd been right about Cody not being Jackson's biological son. What a beautiful thing that he'd adopted his dead friend's child. I didn't dare ask where Cody's mother was, so instead I studied Jackson's face.

There were so many layers to this man—compassionate, complex layers beneath that thorny exterior. He was quick to snap and snarl, but just as quick to get his feelings hurt.

Maybe he had to grow that thorny skin to protect a tender heart? Maybe whatever happened to his face and whatever made him talk with such bitterness about his family business changed him?

Or maybe I had a vivid imagination.

Either way, his delicious smell was teasing my nose, he was standing a little too close, and he was looking at me in that odd way he did, the way that made my heart pump faster and my palms sweat. I had to go somewhere else, fast, so I could think about what the Fanny Hill was happening to me, because I was pretty sure it wasn't only the cold that had my nipples hardening.

In a crisp, businesslike tone, I said, "Well if you'll excuse me, I have to get back to work before Claudia discovers I'm still gone and has a stroke."

Then I hurried away over the lawn toward the house, telling myself I really *couldn't* feel Jackson's gaze on me as I went.

Only I could.

And it was fire.

By midnight, the auction was over, the guests had left, and a team from the rental company had arrived to strike the tent and tables. Claudia was so relieved the event had gone well—and only deviated from her schedule by twelve minutes—that she hugged me. All that was left for me to do was find Rayford, who had promised to drive me home.

But I hadn't seen Rayford in hours.

I didn't feel comfortable skulking around the house in search of him, so for a while I lingered in the kitchen, assisting the strike team with loading the plates and glasses back into their crates and packing up the rest of the kitchen equipment. When that was done, I decided to give the kitchen counters a good scrubbing because I couldn't stand leaving a kitchen a mess at the end of the night.

It was while I was in the middle of scraping burned food off the stove that I felt someone watching me. I turned to find Jackson standing in the doorway, a bottle in one hand and two highball glasses in the other.

He said, "Since you like Boudreaux Bourbon so much, I thought you might want to try something special."

He lifted the bottle, a beautiful piece of cut crystal filled with an amber liquid so dark it was nearly brown. The gold label read, "Heritage 30 Year."

My eyes widened. "I thought that stuff was an urban legend!"

Jackson moved from the doorway to the large marble island in the middle of the kitchen and set the bottle and glasses down. He'd removed his jacket and rolled up the sleeves of his white dress shirt. I still couldn't get over how different he looked, though his hair was trying its hardest to return to its former state of disarray. Several unruly dark locks flopped over his forehead in an appealing, boyish way.

He said, "It's an orphan from one of only a few dozen barrels made with this particular mash bill. An experiment that was ended when my father opened the barrels after ten years and declared it shit. The rest of the barrels were sold to a competitor for blending, but one was misplaced, found in the back of the rickhouse a few years ago. Turns out the mash bill was perfect, but it needed a lot longer to age than the other recipes."

I heard my mother's voice telling me, *Some caterpillars need more time to turn into butterflies than others* when I asked her why, at fifteen, I didn't have boobs like all my friends. Like the Heritage 30 Year, I was a late bloomer.

It was both strange and strangely comforting to find I had something in common with a rare, expensive liquor.

Jackson uncorked the bottle, poured a precise measure into each glass, and put the corked cap back on. He picked up one glass, swirled the bourbon, sniffed it, and then held it out to me.

"Tell me what you smell."

Unsure if this was a test of some kind, I set down the sponge I was holding, walked over to him, took the glass, held it to my nose, and inhaled. Aromas of caramel, toasted oak, vanilla, maple, dried apricots and lemon zest filled my nostrils. My eyes drifted shut in bliss. I said, "I smell heaven."

Jackson chuckled. When I opened my eyes he was smiling. "I thought heaven was a library filled with every book ever written."

Surprised he'd remembered that comment, I smiled back at him. "You have to have something good to drink while you're reading a good book, Mr. Boudreaux."

His smile slowly faded. He took up his own glass and lifted it to his mouth. He kept his gaze on me as he took a sip, swallowed, then set the glass back down. He slowly licked his lips and then said huskily, "Jackson."

Hell's bells, the man should work as a phone-sex operator! That voice!
I cleared my throat. "Right. Jackson. Sorry."

"Have I said something to offend you again?" he asked.

I blinked. "No. Why?"

His gaze dropped to my cheeks. "Because your face gets flushed when you're mad."

"Or embarrassed," I corrected. "I get it from my father's side. You could always tell when he was feeling something strong because his cheeks would go red as Rudolph's nose."

Jackson let that bizarre admission hang between us for a moment, watching as the flush spread from my cheeks and down my neck. Then in a low voice, he asked, "Why would you be embarrassed that I told you to call me by my first name?"

Gee, let's see, it could be that your porn actor's voice could induce spontaneous orgasms in women who remember what sex was like, or that you have this dominant way of giving orders that I'm starting to find less annoying and more interesting, or that watching you lick your lips has set off a nuclear detonation between my legs.

Instead of saying any of those insane thoughts aloud, I simply threw my head back and chugged the bourbon in my glass. "Whew!" I exclaimed when I was finished. "That possum's on the stump!"

Jackson slowly raised his brows.

"It means it doesn't get any better than that," I said hastily, feeling like a class A idiot.

Jackson said, "I know what it means. I'm just wondering what's got you so riled up." Then he stared at me, his eyes burning like blue blazes.

I stammered, "I—I'm uh . . . tired. I get kinda loopy when I'm tired."

Dear God, if you will please help me out and grant me the power of invisibility or cause my sudden death from something quick and painless, I'd be much obliged.

But God was probably having much too good a time watching me squirm to grant my wish. I stood there looking at Jackson while he looked back at me, neither of us saying anything.

He tipped his head back, exposing the strong column of his throat, and drank his bourbon. I watched his Adam's apple bob up and down as he swallowed, and imagined God was a teenage girl giggling madly as I felt the heat in my face and neck spread all the way down to my chest.

I reached for the bottle and poured myself another glass. I downed that one, too, coughing at the end because, although the bourbon was hands down the best I'd ever had, it was meant to be sipped slowly, not inhaled. Fumes seared my throat.

"Smooth," I said, eyes watering, and laughed.

Jackson cocked his head and stared at me. He asked, "Do I make you uncomfortable?"

Maybe I should just fill the sink with water and stick my head in it, I thought, desperate for some way to escape. At the moment, suicide wasn't out of the question.

I looked over Jackson's shoulder. "Have you seen Rayford anywhere? He said he'd drive me home."

"No. And that was the worst segue I've ever heard. So I have to assume the answer to the question you avoided is yes. My next question is, why?"

Lord, he was direct!

I blurted, "You've made me uncomfortable since the first moment I met you," and instantly wanted to punch myself in the face.

When his face darkened, I added, "But tonight's the first time that it's not a bad kind of uncomfortable."

Unblinking, he stared at me. *Thump, thump, thump* went my heart.

His voice thick, he asked, "What kind of uncomfortable is it, Bianca?"

Oh dear.

Have you ever stood at the edge of a high cliff and looked over?

When I was little, my father took us to see the Grand Canyon. Being the curious child I was, I wanted to get as close to the precipice as I could. So when my mother turned her attention away for a split second, I scurried under the wood barricades, ran right up to the rocky lip of the canyon, and stared down.

With wind whipping my hair away from my face and dirt shifting uneasily under my feet, I was terrified. And exhilarated. And strangely certain that if I leapt off and spread my arms, I'd be able to fly. There was something magical about my terror, something that made my heart soar even as it stole my breath and froze my blood to ice.

That's the exact sensation I had gazing into Jackson's blue eyes as he waited for me to answer his question.

He must have seen it in my expression, because he carefully set his glass down and stepped toward me.

THIRTEEN

JACKSON

"I should be going," Bianca said abruptly, sounding like she just remembered she'd left the stove on at home.

I stopped dead in my tracks, disappointment cutting through me like knives. I'd mistaken her look for one of lust. I'd obviously been projecting my own feelings onto her, because judging by her wide-eyed, panicked look at my approach, I'd seriously miscalculated what was happening here.

She was just being nice, while I was being a creepy, pervy, wildly inappropriate douchebag who couldn't keep his boner in his pants.

What a fucking idiot.

"Of course," I said, mortified. "It's late. I won't keep you."

Blood pounded in my temples. I stepped back quickly, dragged a hand through my hair, and took a steadying breath.

Bianca said, "Rayford was supposed to drive me home, but I haven't—"

"I'll take you!"

It was out before I could stop it, a barked declaration that made her blink in surprise at its force.

"Oh," she said. "Um . . . I don't want to bother you."

"It's not a bother," I answered through gritted teeth, gutted by her obvious dismay at the thought of sharing a car ride with me. But I couldn't let her leave like this, with all this tension and awkwardness. I'd have to make it up to her on the ride somehow, say something suave or charming that would bring on that laugh of hers and ease the steel band tightening around my chest.

Yeah, good luck with that, dickhead.

"This way," I snapped, and turned on my heel and left the kitchen.

I didn't look back to see if she was following me as I made my way to the garage, partly because I could hear her footsteps echoing on the marble and partly because I was too busy beating myself up for acting like such a fool. Also, my face was flaming red in embarrassment. I didn't want her to see how horrified I was by my own stupidity.

I should've known that a woman like Bianca Hardwick would never be interested in a man like me. The only women who wanted me were mercenaries.

I'd been alone so long I'd forgotten.

You're only worth the balance in your checking account! Cricket had screamed at me all those years ago, yanking her engagement ring off and throwing it at my chest. *Did you really think I could love you? That anyone could love you?*

Then she'd made a few choice comments about my prowess in bed, and that was the last time I trusted another human being.

I slammed the door of the garage open, flicked on the light switch, grabbed a set of keys from the hook on the wall, and stalked over to the Porsche. Rounding the passenger side, I yanked open the door and stood in seething silence, watching as Bianca hesitantly approached.

Avoiding my eyes, she slid into the passenger seat and folded her hands in her lap.

I growled, "Seatbelt."

Without glancing at me, she slid the safety belt across her body and clicked it into place. Then she sat looking straight ahead, with an expression on her face like she was going to a funeral.

I closed the door and tried not to pound my fists on the roof of the car.

I got in, started the engine, pulled up to the garage door, and waited for it to open.

Bianca said politely, "That's quite a car collection you've got. I counted twelve?"

"I have to spend my money on something," I said bitterly.

She glanced at me. When the garage door was up, I gunned the Porsche. The car leapt forward, slamming us both back against our seats.

We drove in silence until we'd passed the gate of my property. Then Bianca said, "Why are you mad right now?"

It startled me. I didn't know how to answer, so I stayed silent, concentrating on the road.

She said, "You're driving like a crazy person, and I'm not ready to die yet, so maybe if you told me why you're so angry, we could talk about it and you'd slow down."

I snapped, "I'm not angry!" but eased my foot off the gas pedal so the car immediately dropped speed. The last thing I wanted was for her to feel unsafe with me.

After a long moment, she sighed. "Okay."

I muttered, "Fuck." Then I cleared my throat and looked at her. "I'm sorry."

She turned her head and met my gaze. In the dark interior of the car she had an otherworldly look, like something out of a dream, all glittering eyes and burnished skin, electrifying beauty.

I admitted, "I'm not very good with people."

Her lips curved up. "You are when you want to be."

Again she'd surprised me. Was that a compliment?

I turned my attention back to the road, because looking at her was dangerous. I couldn't trust myself not to say something stupid when our eyes held.

I asked, "Where am I going?"

"Tremé. Saint Ann Street."

We drove in silence for several minutes, long enough for it to be uncomfortable, almost long enough for it to be weird. Then she broke the silence with another surprise.

"I want to thank you."

"For what?"

"For overpaying me. It came at exactly the right time."

I couldn't help myself. I looked at her again. "You weren't overpaid. You saved my ass. No one else could've pulled tonight off on such short notice. And the food was incredible. You were right, people opened their wallets. It looks like the auction will be the most successful the Project has had."

She looked out the window at the passing night and slowly shook her head. "Well, anyway. Thank you."

She sounded so melancholy. It brought me out of the pity party I was throwing for myself, and suddenly all I could focus on was her. I said, "What do you mean it came at the right time?"

She lifted a shoulder. "Nothing, just . . . it's appreciated. You were very generous. It really helped."

My mind went a million miles an hour, trying to figure out what she could mean. She'd mentioned her mother before . . .

"Is this about your mother?"

Her head snapped around. She stared at me with big, shocked eyes. "How did you know about my mother?"

So my guess was correct. "You mentioned her earlier. You said it had been a rough few weeks."

Bianca turned stiffly away.

I asked gently, "Is she sick?"

She inhaled a slow breath, then blew it out silently. "She would literally kill me if she knew I told you, so I'm not telling you. But yes. But you didn't hear that from me, and please don't share it with anyone."

She looked over at me again, her eyes pleading, and I nearly drove off the road from the explosion of emotion in my chest.

I said gruffly, "You have my word I won't tell a soul."

She nodded, swallowing hard, then whispered, "Thank you. It's been really hard not having anyone to talk to about it."

I stared at her, my heart starting to pound, amazed how easily she could make me feel like I was melting and flying and having a heart attack, all at once.

Holy fucking yellow submarines, this woman is my kryptonite.

I looked back at the road, gripped my hands around the steering wheel, and tried to breathe. I said, "My mother's been sick for a long time."

Bianca sucked in a breath. "Really? Oh, no! Is it . . . is it bad?"

Why yes it is, I didn't say, *and it's all my fault.* "She had a stroke several years ago. She mainly stays in bed now. Has trouble speaking, needs constant care."

That's pretty much all I got out before my throat closed and I stopped talking.

"Oh, Jackson," said Bianca. "I'm so sorry to hear that. How hard it must be for you!"

When I didn't respond to that, she said hesitantly, "Or are you two not close?"

I briefly closed my eyes. This was something I hadn't spoken about to anyone, ever, but Bianca had just shared something very personal with me, and it felt like the right thing to do to share in kind.

"We used to be. But that was before I became such a disappointment."

"A disappointment? You? But you're so . . ."

Expecting a nasty joke about my character, I looked over sharply. But Bianca was looking back at me seriously with her brows pulled together, searching for a word.

Finally she declared, "Well I don't know what the right word is, but anyone who adopts a special-needs child and raises money for charity and keeps his end of the deals he makes isn't a disappointment in my book." With a smile she added, "Even if you are stuck-up higher than a light pole."

"Stuck up! I am *not* stuck up!" I exclaimed, pleased as fuck by what she'd said, even if it did end with a jab.

Bianca waved a hand in the air. "Oh please, Jackson, you're so highfalutin, you think your shit tastes like sherbet."

Then she slapped her hand over her mouth and stared at me in horror.

I threw my head back and laughed.

"Oh my goodness, I'm so sorry," she breathed. "That was just classless and rude."

I kept on laughing, so hard tears formed in my eyes. Her expression was classic. Had anyone else said that to me, I'd have exploded in fury.

She begged, "Please tell me you're not going to put a retroactive stop payment on your check!"

"That's not even a thing," I said between gasps of air.

She buried her face in her hands and groaned. "If my mother knew I'd said something like that, she'd knock me into next week."

Unthinking, grinning like a lunatic, I reached out and squeezed her shoulder. "Don't worry about it. You've been giving me grief since the minute we met. I think I'm starting to like it."

She raised her head and looked at me. Then she looked at my hand on her shoulder.

I snatched my hand away so fast it was a blur. "Sorry," I said gruffly, my face reddening again.

After a minute of excruciating silence, she said, "Turn here."

Wishing for a time machine so I could undo my colossal mistake of touching a woman who hadn't invited me to do so, I turned the corner into Bianca's neighborhood. A few more turns and I found her street.

"The white one on the left with the red door," she said, pointing to a house.

As I pulled to a stop at the curb, Bianca cried softly, "Oh!"

I followed her gaze out the window. A man sat in a chair on the front porch of her house. When he saw her, he rose and stood next to the door, waiting.

At one o'clock in the morning, there was a man waiting for her to come home. A young, handsome man by the looks of it. Though the porch light was dim, it was bright enough to see that.

Shit.

Crushed by disappointment and an irrational, unwarranted jealousy, I said stiffly, "Your boyfriend?"

Bianca's head shake was violent. She recoiled from the window. "Ex-boyfriend. So very, very *ex.*"

Her disgusted tone revealed exactly how she felt about the man on the porch. Obviously whatever had happened between them had left her angry, bitter, and with zero desire to see him again. My jealousy was replaced by outrage and a need to protect her that was so strong I almost snapped the steering wheel in half.

"I'll get rid of him," I growled. I reached for the door, but Bianca stopped me.

"No." She turned to me with an intensity I'd never seen in her before. She laid her hand on my forearm. "I have a better idea."

Then her gaze dropped to my mouth, she leaned toward me, and my heart stopped dead in my chest.

FOURTEEN

BIANCA

Before you judge me, let me just say in my defense that my brain wasn't firing on all cylinders on account of the sexual tension between Jackson and me in the kitchen, fright over how erratically he'd been driving, making him laugh (a beautiful, unexpected sound), having his big, warm hand settle on my shoulder in a gentle yet distinctly possessive grip, and seeing Trace standing on my front porch in the middle of the night.

So yes. I kissed Jackson.

Hard.

That wasn't the bad part. His lips were soft, his face was smooth, and he smelled even better up close. The bad part was that he *didn't kiss me back.*

When it became clear after several long moments that he wasn't opening his mouth, and had in fact frozen stiff as a corpse left out in the snow, I withdrew a few inches and sheepishly looked at him.

He said, "Did you just kiss me to try to make him jealous?"

I said, "Um."

We stared at each other. I felt like every one of my nerve endings had been dipped in lighter fluid and set on fire.

He lifted his hand and slowly brushed his thumb over my lower lip. His voice an octave lower, he said, "You caught me off guard. Let's try it again. And this time put your hand on my chest so it looks more authentic."

I grumbled, "Lord, you're bossy—"

But then I shut up because Jackson took my mouth and I couldn't think, let alone speak.

He tasted like bourbon and secrets and frustrated desire and kissed like he was starving. It started out slow, his tongue gently parting my lips, his big hands cradling my head, but quickly turned hot and greedy. When I curled my hand into his hair and pulled him closer, he made a low, masculine sound deep in his throat that might have been the sexiest noise I'd heard in my entire life.

After what felt like forever, he pulled away first. We were both breathing hard.

I opened my eyes and looked at him and became concerned that my panties might spontaneously combust from the look he was giving me.

He whispered, "God, I hope you have a lot of exes you want to make jealous."

Intensely aroused and equally shocked by my behavior—I don't have a habit of randomly attack-kissing men—I sat back and smoothed my hands over my hair. I said, "Only the one, unfortunately."

He jumped on that faster than a hot knife goes through butter. "Unfortunately?"

Face flaming, I groaned.

Then there was a sharp knock on my window.

Trace leaned over and looked into the car. "Uh, Bianca? You gonna sit out here all night or are you coming in?"

I should've guessed Trace wouldn't be threatened by the sight of me kissing another man. His ego was bigger than the state of Louisiana. I said, "It's none of your business what I do, Trace Adams!"

Trace pouted. "I need to talk to you, bumble bee."

Jackson asked me, "Do you want to talk to him, Bianca?"

"No! Not now, not ever!"

Trace said, "Of course you do. You're just being stubborn."

Jackson growled, opened his door, and exited the car.

I said to no one in particular, "Uh-oh."

Across the top of the car, Jackson said to Trace, "You have ten seconds to get the fuck away from that window before I make you a fist sandwich and shove it down your throat, my friend."

Slowly Trace straightened. All I could see on either side of me was half a man's body, torsos and legs and muscular arms, hands curled to fists.

Trace said to Jackson, "I don't know who you are, asshole, but nobody talks to me like that."

Jackson said, "And nobody calls me 'asshole.'"

"Oh," said Trace, "ain't you an asshole? Because from where I'm standing, you sure look like one."

Deadly soft, Jackson replied, "And from where I'm standing, you're looking like you're one dumb remark away from a visit to the emergency room."

Okay, I thought. *Time to intervene before we're on the morning news.*

I unlocked my door and popped out of the car, missing Trace's crotch by a hair as I swung the door open. I looked up at him and said crossly, "Excuse me, person who claims to have found God, but your ratty old soul is showing!"

Trace said cajolingly, "Bumble bee—"

"Don't you 'bumble bee' me! I told you the last time I saw you to leave me alone! I never want to see you again!"

Trace folded his arms across his chest and looked down at me with a smug expression. Before he even said it, I knew what was going to come out of his mouth.

He drawled, "Your mama told me different."

I'm not a violent person, but my palm sure did itch to make contact with the side of his pretty, self-satisfied face. I said, "Just because trash can be recycled doesn't mean you deserve another chance."

Behind me, Jackson snorted.

Trace flicked his gaze to Jackson, glared at him for a moment, then turned his attention back to me. "Fine," he said. "I can see you're not going to be reasonable in front the asshole. So why don't you give me a call when he isn't around."

Then he dismissively jerked his chin at Jackson and turned around and sauntered away down the sidewalk.

Jackson watched him go with a tense, coiled readiness, dangerous as a cobra about to strike.

Trace hopped on a motorcycle parked at the curb two houses down, gunned it to life, then burned rubber and roared off down the street.

"Ooh," I said, watching him go. "How *manly*." I made a retching noise and headed for the house.

I retrieved my spare key from the hide-a-key that looked like a rock hidden under a shrub next to the patio, then climbed the steps and unlocked the front door. When I turned around, Jackson was slowly climbing the porch steps, flexing his hands like he was trying to release tension from them.

I said, "I'm sorry. That was embarrassing."

Jackson stopped a few feet from the open door. He looked down the street in the direction Trace had gone, his gaze dark. "Don't apologize. You have nothing to be sorry for. Do you want me to sit out here awhile, make sure he doesn't come back?"

That threw me for a loop. Jackson Boudreaux was willing to sit on my front porch in the middle of the night like my own personal watchdog?

Maybe he liked that kiss as much as I did.

"Thank you for offering, but Trace won't come back tonight. He'll need to go lick his wounds in some woman's bed for a night or two before he works up the nerve to show his face to me again."

I sighed, suddenly bone-tired. "Believe me, I've seen it a million times. It's just too bad I didn't bring my pocketbook with me today, because I've got a little present for him in it that will definitely keep him away longer."

Jackson leaned against the doorjamb and looked down at me. "A present?"

"Pepper spray."

A shade of tension eased from Jackson's body. He even managed a small smile. "Remind me never to get on your bad side."

I rubbed my temples. I had a nasty headache coming on. "I don't know about a bad side, but I do know that a man has to choose me or lose me. I'm not a backup plan."

Jackson was silent. When I glanced at him, he was giving me that burning look again, the one that made me feel like I might ignite.

He murmured, "He's an idiot. But he's a lucky idiot."

"Why do you say that?"

"Because for a while, he had you."

Heat rose in my cheeks. Flustered by the unexpected compliment, I changed the subject. "Can I ask a personal question?"

Without hesitating, he said, "Yes."

I gestured to his arm. "Why do you have a semicolon tattooed on your wrist? I noticed it when we were in the kitchen."

Jackson turned his left hand up and gazed down at the simple black tattoo on the inside of his wrist. He was silent for a long time, then looked up and met my eyes.

He said, "You're an avid reader. You know the meaning of a semicolon."

I frowned. "It's when the author could have ended a sentence but chose not to."

"Exactly."

"I don't understand."

Jackson looked deep into my eyes. His smile might have been the saddest thing I'd ever seen. He said softly, "I'm the author, and the sentence is my life."

Oh my God.

My heart fell at my feet. I whispered, "Jackson . . ."

He pushed away from the doorframe, dragged a hand through his hair, then looked at his car. "It's been a long day. I'll let you get some rest."

He seemed distant now. Depressed, too, like my question had brought back all kinds of bad memories and now he couldn't wait to get away from me, and them.

Feeling like a fool and not knowing how to erase this new awkwardness, I said, "Thank you for the Heritage Thirty Year. That was a treat."

The sad little smile still hovered around the corners of Jackson's lips. I didn't know what he was thinking, and he didn't enlighten me. All he did was tip his head and turn to leave.

When he got to the curb I called out, "Jackson?"

He turned to look at me.

I said, "I'm sorry about the kiss."

He stared at me with a look of such longing and loneliness it took my breath away. He said, "I'm not. It's going to get me through the next four years."

Then he got in his Porsche and drove away, leaving me standing in my open front door wondering why he'd put an emphasis on the word *next*.

And what had made him get that semicolon tattoo.

And why I suddenly wanted to know everything about him.

I didn't sleep a wink that night. I didn't toss and turn, either. I just lay on my back in the dark staring up at my bedroom ceiling, my mind a merry-go-round that wouldn't stop spinning.

Who was the real Jackson Boudreaux? The Beast that snarled and snapped? The suave sophisticate at ease in front of crowds? Or the sad, lonely man with a mysterious tattoo and eyes full of bad memories?

He was a puzzle. A puzzle I ached to figure out, but the charity benefit was over. And with all that had happened last night, I doubted Jackson had any desire to see me again.

I wanted to kick myself for using him to try to make Trace jealous. It was a selfish, childish thing to do. Though it seemed we'd both enjoyed that kiss, if the tables were turned and *I'd* been the one being used for revenge, I wouldn't have been happy about it.

Whatever Jackson's opinion of me had been before, after last night it must be lower than a snake's belly in a wagon rut.

In the morning, I stopped by Mama's as usual. I found her in bed, drenched in sweat, miserable with nausea.

Her pillow was covered in hair, which had started to fall out of her head in clumps.

"How did the event go, *chère?*" she whispered, wincing when I turned on the bedroom light.

Fighting back tears at how bad she looked, I sat on the bed next to her and held her hand. It felt clammy and frail. "It went fine, Mama. Great, in fact. Everyone loved the food."

She closed her eyes and nodded. "Of course they did. You're the best cook in Louisiana."

"Next to you."

Her smile was faint. "And how did you get along with the infamous Mr. Boudreaux? Was he as ornery as usual?"

I thought about how to answer that, about how Rayford had said of Jackson *If you're treated like a stray dog long enough, you start to believe it and act like one.* And something my father had once told me that had stuck with me for years. *Fate is just the sum of all our bad decisions.* And something Jackson himself had told me.

That was before I became such a disappointment.

I said, "I think sometimes it's easier for a man to be the worst version of himself than to let the world keep breaking his heart."

Mama cracked open an eye. "You been hittin' the sauce this morning, baby?"

I sighed deeply, fighting exhaustion. "I wish. A nice little soul-numbing habit would go a long way on a day like this. But never mind me, what can I get you to eat?"

At the mention of food, her complexion turned faintly green. "Lord, please don't talk to me about food."

"You have to eat something, Mama," I insisted. "You need your strength. How about some applesauce or white rice? A bit of boiled chicken?"

Mama weakly waved me away. "Nothing. I couldn't keep it down, baby. Just let me sleep for a bit, I'll feel better later."

But I knew she wouldn't. I knew this was going to be one of the bad days, the days when she'd never even make it out of bed.

I put a fresh pillow under her head, kissed her cheek, and turned off the light on my way out of the room. I knew I couldn't leave her alone all day. I'd have to come back before first seating at the restaurant to check on her. Her doctor had mentioned the possibility of having a home health-care nurse stop by a few times a week during the day to help out, and that was looking like a good idea.

I'd thought I could take care of everything myself—running the restaurant and whatever Mama needed in terms of support and daily care—but I was beginning to have my doubts.

The second round of chemo started in a few days. If it was anywhere near as bad as the first, I was going to need an army of help.

I boiled a chicken breast and some plain white rice and left it in the fridge with a note in case she felt a little better later. When I was about to leave, an envelope on the kitchen table caught my eye.

It was from the hospital. It hadn't been opened.

I slid my finger under the glued flap, removed the folded piece of paper, and all the blood drained from my face.

INVOICE. Big, blocky letters screamed from the upper right-hand corner.

When I read the amount due at the bottom, I sank into the kitchen chair.

Then I had myself a good, long cry.

BIANCA'S BLACKBERRY & BOURBON COBBLER

Makes 8–10 servings

- 12 cups fresh blackberries
- ¾ cup raw sugar
- ¼ cup high-quality bourbon
- cooking spray
- ½ vanilla bean
- 1 cup granulated sugar
- 2 cups all-purpose flour
- 1 tablespoon plus 2 teaspoons baking powder
- ½ teaspoon table salt
- 1 teaspoon lemon zest
- 1½ cups milk
- 1 egg
- ¾ teaspoon vanilla extract
- 6 tablespoons butter, melted

Preparation

1. Preheat oven to 350 degrees. Combine blackberries, raw sugar, and bourbon in a large bowl. Transfer mixture to a 13^2 x 9^2 baking dish lightly greased with cooking spray.

2. Split vanilla bean, and scrape seeds into granulated sugar, making sure vanilla bean seeds are distributed evenly.

3. Sift together flour, baking powder, salt, and granulated sugar mixture into a large bowl. Stir in lemon zest. Whisk together milk, egg, and vanilla extract, and then stir into dry ingredients. Add melted butter and stir.

4. Pour batter evenly over fruit. Place dish on a baking sheet.

5. Bake at 350 degrees for 1 hour and 10 minutes or until crust is deep golden brown.

FIFTEEN

JACKSON

I was barely listening to my father prattling into my ear as I stared out the window of the library into the sunny spring morning outside. My attention was preoccupied with thoughts of Bianca Hardwick.

Sweet, sassy, fascinating Bianca, who spoke her mind and worried about her sick mother and knew how to make a man feel like a king with her kiss.

No wonder her idiot ex was still sniffing around.

In the four days since the benefit, I hadn't been able to get her out of my mind. Even when I was sleeping. I'd woken up with a stiff cock every morning, tortured by dreams of her sweet mouth, how soft her eyes had looked after she kissed me, how her hand had curled so tightly into my hair. Every night I'd decided to go into her restaurant, only to change my mind on the drive there and turn around and go home.

I'd said too much, acted too strangely, even threatened her ex with bodily injury. She must think I'm a lunatic. An unstable, depressed, hotheaded lunatic who'd be better off—

"—married," said my father.

My attention snapped back to the present. "Sorry? Who's getting married?"

"You are, son."

After I got my bearings, I said flatly, "I think we both know that's never going to happen."

The following pause wasn't long, but it was cavernous, and echoed with his disappointment. "You haven't been listening to a word I've said, have you?"

My pulse quickening, I tightened my hand around the phone. "What are you talking about?"

My father's deep sigh echoed over the line. "I'm talking about your obligations to this family. I'm talking about your mother's broken heart. I'm *talking* about your trust, Jackson."

"My trust?" I repeated, confused. I'd heard the family obligations and broken heart themes a million times before, but my father had never mentioned my trust.

He'd set it up for me when I was born. When I turned twenty-one, I started to get monthly distributions from it. Monthly distributions in seven figures, which allowed me to live . . . well, like I did.

Without my trust, I'd be penniless.

Ironically, without my trust I also wouldn't be the people-hating hermit I was today. *Thank you, Cricket.*

My father said, "Yes. Your trust. Which, as you'd know if you'd ever bothered to read the thing, stipulates that you must be involved in the day-to-day operation of Boudreaux Bourbon to continue to receive. In lieu of that, you must marry by thirty-five."

I opened my mouth and found myself unable to speak.

My father said, "I put that last one in place so you didn't piss away every dime on strippers and blow, like Harvey Culligan's son did. And thirty-five is generous, you have to admit! I could've made it twenty-five, but I figured a man deserves a few good years to sow his wild oats before he gets hitched. Hoein' around builds character. To a point."

I would've laughed, convinced he was joking, but one thing my father never joked about was money.

Into my astonished silence he said, "Your mother and I have been very, very patient with you, son. This conversation never needed to happen at all if you'd just married Cricket and taken over as Master Distiller like you were supposed to. But after what you did to that poor girl, well . . ."

Oh my God. This isn't happening. This can't be happening.

My father's voice turned brisk. "We don't need to go over all that mess again. My point here, Jackson, is that you're my only son. You're the heir to this whole thing the Boudreaux family has built over eight generations. If you continue to shirk your obligations and refuse to at least settle down and give your mother the grandbabies she wants, then I'm sorry to say, but you're gonna be cut off without a red cent to your name."

I made a little strangled sound, which my father took as his cue to end the conversation.

"I've been beatin' around the bush about this for years because I felt bad about the state you've been in, but now I'll put it to you straight. You have until your birthday to get your ass back to Kentucky and take over as Master Distiller, or get married. To a decent girl, mind you. I'm not welcomin' a hoochie mama into this family! And before you think about bein' tricky and gettin' a quickie divorce, you should know that any marriage you enter into needs to last *at least* five years for you to continue to get your money. The decision's yours."

He hung up without saying good-bye. I stared at the phone in my hand.

My thirty-fifth birthday was next month.

This wasn't real. He was just trying to scare me. It was all empty threats.

Right?

With my heart in my throat, I dialed my family's longtime attorney. Then I listened with my eyes closed as he told me the bad news.

"So your daddy finally threw down the gauntlet," said Rayford, calmly reading a newspaper as he sat across from me in the library. "Well, you gotta give Brig some credit. At least he gave you a choice."

"A *choice*?" I leapt from my chair and started to pace. I felt like a caged animal. "He didn't give me a choice, he gave me an ultimatum!"

Undisturbed by my outburst, Rayford turned a page. "No such thing as a free lunch, Mr. Boudreaux. You know that better'n anybody."

I stopped pacing and glared at him. "You know if I'm poor, you're out of a job, right?"

Rayford lowered the paper and peered at me over his eyeglasses. "Don't be foolish. You've got Cody to think about. His care, his education, everything he needs. Besides, you don't know the first thing about bein' poor." He snapped the paper up and started reading again.

I folded my arms over my chest and stood with my legs braced apart, like I was preparing for a group of suits from the bank to knock down the front door and I'd have to fight them to the death for possession of the house. "Maybe not, but you know as well as I do that I'm never going back to Kentucky."

Rayford smiled. It looked a little mysterious. "So that leaves marriage. Who's the lucky girl?"

I wanted to tear out my hair. Instead I took up pacing again. "Gimme a break, Rayford! Even if I wanted to get married—which I *don't*—I couldn't find a wife in thirty days! I haven't even been on a date in four years! There's not a sane woman in the entire state who'd agree to marry a complete stranger and stay married to him for half a decade!"

"So find an *in*sane one. Seems to me there's lots of 'em."

"Jesus Christ. You're no help at all."

Rayford made a noncommittal noise that was neither agreement nor disagreement, then crossed his legs. His gaze still on the paper, he mused, "Funny, I thought I was plenty helpful the other night."

I stopped pacing and stared at him. "Please don't be cryptic. I can't handle cryptic right now."

Rayford looked up at me. His mysterious little smile grew wider. "When I was nowhere to be found at the end of the night of the charity event and *you* had to drive Miss Bianca Hardwick home."

For a minute I was speechless. "You're kidding me. You did that on purpose?"

Now his smile positively beamed. "Lovely girl, isn't she? Lots of moxie, as my mama used to say. And speakin' of mamas, did I overhear her tell you her own mama was havin' some troubles? Somethin' about it bein' a rough couple of weeks?"

My eyebrows flew up my forehead. "Were you *eavesdropping* on us?"

He shrugged. "Just passin' by the kitchen. I've got a pair of workin' ears, no need to get all excited."

I said sternly, "Rayford."

He said, "You know she likes you, don't you?"

After I came back to my senses, I decided my legs weren't feeling quite normal and sat back down in my chair. I cleared my throat, buying time to let the frog jump out of it before I had to speak again. "What makes you say that?"

Rayford ruefully shook his head. "If I might be so bold, sir, for a smart man you can sometimes be awful stupid."

Then he folded the newspaper in half and turned the side he'd been reading toward me.

Charity Benefit Raises Millions for Wounded Vets, the headline read. Directly beneath it was a large, color photo of Bianca and me onstage. She was tucked tight under my arm, smiling up at me like an angel.

I said, "I told her to smile at me. She was just following orders."

Rayford rolled his eyes. "No woman smiles at a man like *that* because of an order." He tapped his finger on Bianca's face, inviting me to look closer.

I opened my mouth to protest but closed it again.

Because he was right. Bianca's smile wasn't only on her mouth. It was in her eyes, in her face, in her entire body. She was leaning into me, her arm around my waist, staring up at me like the sun was shining out of the top of my head.

She looked . . . bedazzled.

I was looking at her the exact same way. In fact, if I'd seen this picture anywhere else and I didn't know the people, I'd have assumed it was an engagement announcement.

I sat back against the chair. A breath left my chest in a noisy rush.

"Mm-*hmm*," said Rayford, full of himself. "So there you go."

"There I go what?"

"Lord, do I have to do *all* the heavy lifting?" he muttered. Then he waggled the paper impatiently at me. "Hello, future Mrs. Jackson Walker Boudreaux?"

I blanched. "You're . . . that's . . ."

Rayford said, "You already know each other, it's clear that she likes you and you like her—"

"I never said I liked her."

"Oh, be quiet, now you're just talkin' trash," said Rayford, then continued on with his ridiculous explanation. "And there's a very good chance that if you sweeten the deal a little bit, she'd say yes."

I was starting to get a bad feeling about this. "Sweeten the deal?"

Rayford sat back in the sofa and crossed his legs again. Smoothing a hand down the lapel of his suit jacket, he carefully said, "Everybody's got a price. You didn't know that last time you got engaged, but now you do."

I said quietly, "Ouch."

"I know. I'm sorry. But it seems to me that if you go into it with your eyes open, with all your cards on the table, it might work out for both of you."

He let me process that, then added, "She doesn't even own a car."

I closed my eyes and rested my head on the back of the chair. "I can't believe we're having this conversation."

Rayford said, "You told me Cody likes her."

I groaned.

"She's smart, she's got her feet on the ground, and she comes from good stock."

"Rayford! What century is this? We're talking about a woman, not a cow!"

"And she isn't too hard on the eyes, either."

That made me pause. I had a vivid, fleeting image of Bianca prancing naked around my bedroom and had to shake my head to clear it.

"It's not gonna happen. What would I do, mosey into her restaurant and say, 'Oh, hi there, I was just thinking since you're poor and I need a wife that we should get married'? How romantic! I'm sure that's the proposal of her dreams!"

Rayford said, "Maybe if you prefaced it with the mention of a million dollars, it would be."

I jerked my head up and stared at him in outrage. I sputtered, "*A million dollars?*"

He didn't even blink. "Oh, I'm sorry, are you not a billionaire? With a *b*?"

"No! My *father* is a billionaire!"

"And who's his only son who's gonna inherit all that money?"

I threw my hands in the air. "This is completely insane."

But Rayford wasn't giving up so easily. He said, "And *who* gets an annual trust stipend in the gazillions every year before his father dies?"

"Gazillions aren't units of currency."

"I'm takin' poetic license here, sir, cut me some slack."

A sensible man would've withered under the stare I sent Rayford. Obviously he wasn't sensible.

Being annoyingly reasonable, he said, "You don't want to go back to Kentucky. You also don't want to be dead-ass broke, because you've never had a job in your entire life, and you don't know how to do anything except collect overpriced automobiles and mope around in your big ol' mansion. You wouldn't last an hour as a poor man. So your only other option is marriage. Ideally you'da had a girlfriend you could ask, but your antisocial self doesn't have one of those, so we gotta be practical and determine who you could stand livin' with for the next few years before you get divorced and go your separate ways, and everybody's happy because everybody's rich."

He smiled at me. "And from where I'm sittin', only one woman in the world fits that bill."

I had to admit it. The man made some very good points.

Shit.

SIXTEEN

BIANCA

Four days had passed since the benefit, and though I kept hoping Jackson would walk through the front door of my restaurant, he never did.

Now I'm as liberated as the next girl, but one thing I will never, *ever* do is chase after a man. No matter how much of a fascinating puzzle he is. My mama always said the minute you make a move on a man is the minute you lose control, because then he knows he's got you.

"A woman worth her salt should be the hardest thing a man has to work for in his life, because then she's a prize, not a gift," she'd told me. "Anything you get for free is worth exactly what you paid for it: nothing."

I wasn't looking for control in a relationship, but I knew she had a point because I'd thrown myself at Trace like I'd been shot from a cannon, and look where that got me.

So I put Jackson Boudreaux out of my mind and focused my energy into taking care of Mama, running the restaurant, and trying to think of ways to make more money.

Unfortunately I was coming up short on all three counts.

"Boo, what's *happenin'* with you?" said Eeny, hands propped on her hips. "I've never seen you lookin' so raggedy!"

We were in the kitchen. It was a weeknight, and the restaurant was full. Mama was in her second round of chemo and was sick as a dog. I'd started spending the night at her place because I was afraid to leave her alone. When I'd looked into the cost of a home health-care worker to help out, I'd nearly fainted.

I should've gone into health care instead of the restaurant business.

"I'm fine, Eeny," I said, rubbing my eyes. They were grainy and bloodshot from lack of sleep, and swollen from crying.

Watching someone you love being slowly poisoned to death is not much fun.

"Girl, you are *not* fine!" said Eeny, folding her arms over her chest. "I've known you since I was cookin' in your mama's restaurant and you were knee-high to a grasshopper, and never once have I seen you in such a state! I think you should tell me what's goin' on before I pay a visit to Miss Davina and get the truth!"

I stopped stirring the big pot of jambalaya on the stove in front of me and turned a tired eye to Eeny. She stood there glaring at me, searing my eyes with the canary-yellow caftan she was wearing, which had turquoise-blue stripes and a matching turban. All she needed was some fruit in it, and she'd look exactly like the Chiquita Banana lady.

"Where's your apron?" I asked. "You're blinding me with that getup."

She said, "I'm not coverin' up this beautiful frock I special ordered with one of those dingy ol' kitchen aprons! And don't change the subject!"

I loved that she was worried about me, but if I told her the truth, the news would spread around the city faster than the speed of light. Eeny was many wonderful things, but circumspect wasn't one of them. She loved gossip as much as she loved loud frocks and fried plantains.

So I said, "I'm fighting a bug."

That wasn't exactly a lie. I *was* fighting a bug. The depression/insomnia/so-broke-I-can't-afford-to-pay-attention bug.

Eeny narrowed her eyes at me. She opened her mouth, but before she could get anything out, Pepper ran through the kitchen doors.

"He's here again!" she shouted gleefully. "It's him!"

There was only one person in the world who could get Pepper so excited. I wondered how much Jackson had given her this time.

My heart beating faster, I said, "He'll have to wait for a table, unless you can move some of those reservations around."

Pepper, in a tight, shiny gold dress so short it looked like a skirt she'd hiked up over her boobs, jumped up and down, grinning like mad and clapping her hands.

"He doesn't want a table! He wants to see *you!*"

Eeny muttered, "Get the poor man a pair of sunglasses and a stiff drink."

Over on the other side of the kitchen, Hoyt started to whistle the theme to *Jaws*.

I said, "Pepper, please tell him I'll be out in a min—"

Jackson burst through the kitchen doors. He spotted me standing frozen at the stove and said loudly, "Everyone out."

The entire kitchen staff turned to look at me.

Oh Lord. Not this again.

Smoothing my hands over the flyaways from my bun, I said, "Jackson, we're so busy right now. I'm sorry, but I can't have my employees—"

"We're getting married," he pronounced, and stared at me.

Pepper gasped. Eeny did a comical double take. Hoyt started coughing and couldn't stop. Everyone else stood stock-still, their eyes wide and their mouths hanging open.

Most of me was convinced he was joking. It was in terrible taste, but that was really the only option that made any kind of sense.

There was a tiny part of me, however, that noted the determined look in his eyes and wasn't so sure.

"How nice for us," I said sarcastically. "And when will the blessed event take place?"

When he looked relieved, I started to panic.

He said, "As soon as possible. Tonight, if you want. We can go to the courthouse right now."

Pepper squealed in glee. No one else made a peep, except for Eeny, who threw her head back and started to laugh.

That's when my panic turned to anger.

I marched over to Jackson, grabbed hold of the front of his shirt, and dragged him out of the kitchen and into the alley behind the restaurant, kicking the back door open in front of me. When the door slammed shut behind us, I whirled on him and let him have it.

"What the Sam hell is the matter with you? This is my *place of business*! Some of us have to *work* for a living! You can't just barge in here and start telling stupid jokes—"

"It's not a joke," he interrupted, his voice hard. "And if you marry me, you'll never have to work again."

I stared at him in disbelief. "You've lost it. You've seriously lost your mind."

"Just hear me out—"

"*No*, I won't hear you out! I don't know who you think you are, but I don't find this funny! And I don't have time to listen to whatever stupidity this is! I swear I oughta just call the loony bin and have them pick you up—"

"I'll give you a million dollars."

He obviously thought that was a good direction to take this conversation, but I felt like he'd just punched me right in the gut.

It was painfully obvious now that he wasn't joking. He was serious as a heart attack. He'd walked into my restaurant and announced we were getting married—not asked, *announced*—and then told me how much he was paying me to do it.

The man thought he could buy me. He thought I was for sale.

He thought I was a *whore*.

Heat flooded my face. In a raw, shaking voice, I said, "How *dare* you."

"I know you need the money—"

That's all he got out because I stepped up and slapped him across the face.

The *crack* of my open palm hitting his cheek seemed unnaturally loud. But maybe face slaps were always that loud. I had no idea, because I'd never done it before.

His head snapped around. He lifted a hand to his cheek and stared at me with his lips slightly parted, his eyes dazed. Bewildered, he asked, "What the hell did you do that for?"

What an idiot.

I hissed, "I'm not a whore, Jackson Boudreaux. Whatever your opinion is of me, I'm setting you straight right here and now. *You can't buy me.*"

"I don't think you're a whore! Jesus Christ, hold on a minute—"

"No, *you* hold on, you rich, dumb, arrogant *ass*! I took the catering job because I needed the money, yes, but not for myself, and not so I could get sold into prostitution later on!"

"What the fucking hell—"

"You should be ashamed of yourself! What would your mother say if she could see you right now, offering money to a girl to sleep with you?"

"Holy fuck, Bianca!"

"Stop cursing at me!"

He took two steps toward me and shouted right back, "I never said anything about sleeping with me! I'm talking about marriage!"

We stood nose to nose, glaring murder at each other, breathing hard, our hands clenched to fists.

"Oh, I see," I said through gritted teeth. "You're gay. You need a beard."

Jackson closed his eyes and muttered an oath under his breath. "No. I am *not* gay." He opened his eyes. "And you know it, because that kiss we had was hotter than the sidewalk in July."

We continued to glare at each other. I said, "Your metaphors need work."

"Excuse me. Hotter than a billy goat with a blowtorch."

"That doesn't even make sense. And comparing a lady's kiss to anything to do with a goat is just bad manners."

His eyes glimmered with laughter, but his face stayed straight. "You're right. I'll try it again. That kiss was hotter than a housewife reading *Fifty Shades of Grey* at the *Magic Mike* premiere."

My lips twitched. "Better," I said, and turned my back on him, folded my arms over my chest, and blew out a hard, frustrated breath.

He let me settle for a minute, then walked slowly around and stood in front of me. "Obviously I came at this in the wrong way—"

"You think?"

He sighed. "Can I just get a word in edgewise, please? Let me say my piece, and then you can send me on my way. Deal?"

He was standing in the exact right position for me to give him a good, swift kick in the balls, but now my curiosity was getting the better of me, so I gave him a surly look and a shrug.

"Thank you," he said. "Okay. A little backstory. I have a trust. It's . . . big."

I rolled my eyes.

Jackson sighed again. "As I was saying, I have a big trust. And no, that's not a metaphor. I found out today that to keep my trust and inherit my fortune once my father dies, I need to either work for the family company or get married. By my thirty-fifth birthday." His look turned sheepish. "Which is next month."

I made a face. "So go work for the company, dummy!"

He didn't appear to appreciate being called a dummy, but he restrained himself from whatever smart remark he wanted to say and instead said, "I can't. I'll never go back to Kentucky. Never."

"Why not?"

He looked away. That muscle in his jaw started jumping. "There's nothing for me there but ghosts."

His voice was tight, his spine was stiff, and he looked miserable at just the mention of Kentucky. I looked down at his wrist, hunting for the semicolon tattoo, and caught a glimpse of it in the shadows.

If he was trying to get me to feel sorry for him . . . it was working a little.

"Uh-huh," I said. "So marry some debutante and have your two point five perfect babies and live happily ever after with your country club membership and your polo ponies. I'm sorry, but I don't see the problem here."

Jackson turned his head and looked at me. The expression in his eyes stole my breath.

He said, "The problem is that you're the only woman I've liked in a long time."

He let that sink in, then added, "And I don't want to be poor. I'd be exceedingly bad at it. For one thing, I'm not nice enough."

"How ridiculous. Not all poor people are nice."

He frowned. "Really? Every poor person I've ever met has been extremely nice to me. Well . . . except you."

I threw my hands up. "God, you're hopeless. They're nice to you because you're rich! They want your money!"

"Oh." He looked disappointed. "I thought only rich people were like that."

I stared at him in amazement. "You're right. You couldn't be poor. You have no idea what real life is like."

"Exactly!" he said. "So you understand my predicament!"

"What I understand is that I have a restaurant full of guests and I'm standing in a dark alley talking to a delusional rich man about his imaginary problems. You need a bride, run an ad in the paper. You'd have five thousand responses the first day."

"I told you. You're the only woman I've liked in a long time. I don't like strangers. I don't trust people. Women in particular."

Whew, I wasn't touching that one with a ten-foot pole. "You just told me I wasn't nice to you. Why would you like me?"

His eyes started to burn. "You're honest. And real. And you don't care about my money—"

"Ha! So you offer me a million dollars of it?"

"I wasn't finished. You don't care about my money, and you're kind, and responsible, and you're not afraid to call me on my shit, and you're so fucking beautiful it sometimes hurts to look at you, like I'm gazing into the sun and could go blind if I stare too long."

He stopped talking abruptly, as if he'd shocked himself with what came out of his mouth.

He wasn't the only one.

Beautiful. He called me beautiful. That right there was worth more than the money he'd offered.

In a spectacular display of intelligence, I said, "Oh."

He shifted his weight uncomfortably from one foot to the other. He looked at the ground. He squinted up at the stars sparkling in the night sky. Finally when he couldn't find anywhere else to look, he glanced gingerly sideways at me, like maybe he was expecting another smack across his face.

I closed my eyes and counted to ten. Then I said, "Let me get this straight. You want me to marry you."

"Yes."

"But I don't have to have sex with you."

"Right."

"If I don't marry you, you won't marry anyone else."

"Correct."

"And there's no chance of you going to work for your family's company."

He shook his head emphatically. "None."

"So what you're basically telling me is that if I don't agree to marry you, I'll be responsible for you losing all your money and becoming a pauper and ruining the rest of your life."

He blinked. "Well . . . yes."

I snorted. "Gee, no pressure."

He lifted his hands, palms out, in a surrendering gesture. "It wouldn't have to be forever. Just five years and then we could get divorced."

"Five years!" I exclaimed, freshly horrified. "I'm thirty-one years old, Jackson; that puts me close to forty by the time you're finished with me!"

He looked pained by my choice of words. "I think your math is a little off there, Bianca."

"What if I want kids? Have you considered that? By the time we get divorced, I'd be an old maid!"

He said, "Hardly. And you could always do IVF. I mean, you'd have enough money. Or get a surrogate. Or adopt . . . why are you looking at me like that?"

"Because I'm having an out-of-body experience. Somehow I've been transported to an alternate universe where a psychotic billionaire is trying to convince me to enter into a sham marriage, give up five years of my life, and forego the possibility of actually falling in love and sharing a future with someone. Someone *who loves me for who I am*, not what I can do for him. Do you really think any amount of money could convince me to do something so—so—*wrong*?"

For a moment, he looked agonized. Really, truly pained, like I'd stabbed him in the heart.

Then he said in a gravelly voice, "You're right." He swallowed and backed away a step. "You're absolutely right. I'm so sorry. This was . . . stupid. Reckless. I shouldn't have thought you'd . . . you're not the kind of . . . fuck. Please forgive me."

He turned around and walked away at a pace that was close to a run.

SEVENTEEN

BIANCA

Astonished, I watched Jackson go until finally he disappeared into the night, melting into the darkness like a phantom.

I went back into the restaurant in a daze, avoiding Eeny's and Pepper's excited questions with an order to get back to work that must have sounded appropriately sharp because they did what I asked, lickety-split.

The rest of the night was a fog. I kept seeing Jackson's face when he told me I was beautiful. I kept going over everything he said.

I kept trying not to think about how a million dollars would change my life. And Mama's.

I kept wondering what woman would take him up on his offer.

Because one would, I was certain of that. Somehow he'd find a woman who would be more than happy to take his money and give five years of her life in return. Lord, I could think of half a dozen off the top of my head. And then she'd be living in that icebox of a mansion and interacting with that sweet boy Cody and getting to see Jackson every day.

Maybe even getting to kiss him.

Or share his bed.

That was the part that really tripped me up. No sex. We could be married, and he wouldn't expect sex. For heaven's sake, what man in his right mind would offer that?

One who wasn't in his right mind, that's who.

Or one who was desperate.

I supposed Jackson Boudreaux was a little bit of both.

I didn't know it then, but after another few weeks went by, I'd find myself both of those things, too.

The doctor's office was like every other doctor's office in the world. At least that's what I thought, sitting with Mama in uncomfortable plastic chairs across from a desk in a room that was small and starkly bare except for a half-dead plant in one corner and a few framed diplomas on the walls.

"You okay?" I asked my mother gently, holding her hand.

She nodded, though I wasn't buying it. She'd lost almost twenty pounds, her skin was ashen, and all her hair had fallen out, so she'd taken to wearing head wraps that reminded me of Eeny's colorful turbans. Only there was nothing colorful about Mama now, in her clothes, skin, or spirit. Chemo had washed the once-vibrant woman into a sickly shade of gray.

"Mrs. Hardwick."

Doc Halloran entered the room, manila folder in hand. He was bearded, stout, and red cheeked, and bore more than a passing resemblance to Santa Claus. He shook Mama's hand, then mine, then settled himself behind his desk and opened the manila file.

"So?" I asked, impatient for an update on Mama's condition. That's why we were here after all.

Doc Halloran looked up at me. He turned his gaze to Mama and smiled. He said, "Good news."

I just about fainted. Mama raised a shaking hand to her mouth.

He continued talking. "The scan shows the tumor has shrunk about fifty percent, which is where we needed it to be before we could do surgery. Your body has reacted very well to the chemotherapy drugs, Mrs. Hardwick. How are you feeling?"

Mama said softly, "Like I went twelve rounds with Muhammad Ali."

The doctor nodded. "Once chemo is stopped, you'll start to feel a whole lot better."

My whole body was shaking. Water pooled in my eyes. I couldn't catch my breath. I said, "So does this mean she's going to be okay?"

Doc Halloran flipped the folder shut, leaned back in his chair, and folded his hands over his belly. "It means the treatment is working. Which is excellent, mind you. Many times we have to try several different drugs before we see a result. But I don't want to sugarcoat anything. After we remove the tumor, we're looking at an additional five to fifteen weeks of chemo to get any stray cancer cells that might have been left behind in the lung or chest wall. We also need to consider radiation, depending on the outcome of the surgery. The lymph nodes are only marginally involved, which is good, but we won't really know if the cancer has been contained, or eradicated, for several months."

He kept speaking, but all I could hear were the words *five to fifteen weeks of chemo*. My heart beat fast and furious as a hummingbird's inside my chest.

We didn't have the money for that. We didn't have the money for surgery or radiation, either. I'd already applied for assistance from the local social services department and been told it could take months to get a response, and even if we were approved it wouldn't cover much. I'd applied for online grants but knew those were a shot in the dark. I'd done everything I could think of to search for financial help and was amazed to discover that if you had lung cancer and no health insurance, you were basically up shit's creek without a paddle.

"I'd like to schedule the surgery for the week after next," said Doc Halloran, looking at me.

What could I say? No? It's too expensive? I don't have the cash to save my mother's life?

Suddenly all my self-righteous arguments about why I couldn't marry Jackson Boudreaux for money seemed as flimsy as a fart in the wind.

So I squeezed my mother's hand and forced a smile. "Do it."

When I got home that afternoon, I picked up the phone, called Jackson, and asked him if his offer was still on the table.

EIGHTEEN

JACKSON

"Sir," said Rayford, "you're gonna wear out the rug."

"I'll buy another one," I growled, turning around and pacing back the direction I came. I couldn't keep still, and Rayford nagging me about it wasn't helping.

The two of us were waiting inside the foyer for Bianca to arrive. Rayford was his usual tranquil self. I, however, felt like a nuclear reactor on the edge of a meltdown.

I was going to get married.

Bianca Hardwick was going to *be my wife*.

At least that's what it appeared would happen. She had called me yesterday and asked me if my offer was still on the table, and I nearly fell out of my chair. We'd agreed to meet today to discuss it further.

I slept all of fifteen minutes last night. I spent an hour getting ready, showering, taming my hair, and obsessing over which clothes to wear. I even shaved again because I knew she liked it, even though the sight of those fucking scars on my face made me want to punch the mirror. She was due to arrive any minute, and the possibility that Rayford would open the door and I'd drop dead of a massive heart attack the moment I spotted her was pretty solid.

I hadn't been this nervous in . . . ever.

"Maybe you should have a drink," Rayford suggested, watching me pace. "So you don't scare the poor girl off with all this"—he waved a disapproving hand in the air—"energy."

"My energy's fine," I snapped, flexing my hands.

Rayford snorted. "Sure, if you're gearin' up to ride into battle on your war horse and lop off some heads with an axe."

I shot him a murderous glare, which made him smile.

He said, "Have it your way. But don't say I didn't warn you when I open the door and Miss Bianca sees the state you're in and turns around and runs off."

"She's not the running-off type," I said. "She's more the light-you-on-fire-and-walk-calmly-away-while-you-burn-to-ashes type."

Rayford chuckled. "This is gonna be fun."

I stopped pacing and stared at him. "Fun? This is the most bizarre and unbelievably serious thing I've done in my life, and you're talking about it being *fun*?"

He smiled. "I meant for me, sir."

Before I could reply, the doorbell rang.

Rayford said brightly, "And here's the fire starter now!" and opened the door.

Bianca stood on the marble front step of my home wearing a red dress and a grim, resolute expression like she was arriving for an audit with the IRS. In spite of her obvious discomfort, she was breathtaking.

This was the first time I'd seen her out of her chef's clothes, and my eyes greedily drank her in. The term *hourglass figure* was invented for women like her. Her waist was narrow, her hips were generous, and her legs were long and bare. And her breasts . . . I almost groaned out loud.

The dress had a neckline obviously designed to devastate men. It was cut low enough to give a glimpse of cleavage while still being classy, wide enough to reveal the upper swell of a pair of breasts that appeared to have been molded by God himself.

If she wore that with a mind to negotiate for more money, she'd won. I'd willingly hand over my entire trust if I'd be allowed to look at her wearing that dress for more than five minutes.

My God, her skin was flawless. Fucking flawless, like—

"Are you going to invite me in, or would you prefer we talked in the front yard?" asked Bianca tartly.

My gaze snapped up to her face.

Rayford coughed into his fist to hide his laugh.

And I went red to the roots of my hair.

"Yes," I said too loudly, flustered. "Come in." Then I turned around and stalked toward the library, mortified I'd been caught ogling her chest like the enamored, sexually frustrated Neanderthal that I was.

Over the roar in my ears, I heard her sigh, heard Rayford's murmured words of hello, heard the front door close. I decided to take Rayford's advice and pour myself a drink to take the edge off, so as soon as I entered the library I made a beeline for the crystal decanter on the sideboard and poured myself a glass.

Rayford ushered Bianca into the library and asked her if he could get her anything.

"A three-legged stool and a whip," she said.

When I turned to look at her, she sent me a tight smile. "Isn't that what every lion tamer needs?"

Rayford snorted. He was enjoying this *way* too much.

"Thank you, Rayford," I said, gripping my glass so hard it was in danger of shattering in my hand. "That will be all."

"Yes, sir," he said pleasantly, and soundlessly slid the library doors shut, leaving Bianca and me alone.

Unless he was standing outside with his ear pressed to the wood, which was definitely possible.

Bianca looked at me. "So, Mr. Boudreaux, are you ready for a Mrs.?"

I downed the entire glass of scotch in one gulp.

Her laugh was as grim as her expression. "That makes two of us. And if you don't mind, I'll have whatever it is you're having. My stomach is pitching the kind of dying duck fit only hard liquor can help." She crossed to the sofa and perched on the edge of it, knees together, back ramrod straight, hands clasped tightly around the small white handbag she carried.

So she was nervous, too. That eased some of the tension between my shoulders. I didn't like the idea of her feeling uncomfortable, but knowing she took this as seriously as I did was heartening.

I poured her a scotch and gave it to her. She took it, avoiding my eyes, and tossed it back like I had. Then she blew out a hard breath and looked up at me.

"Please sit down," she said. "You're intimidating when you hover."

"I can't believe you'd find anything intimidating," I said, but did as she asked and sat opposite her in a chair, the coffee table between us.

"I suppose you'll soon be finding out all kinds of things about me," she murmured, looking at her glass.

A painful silence followed. I decided to break it with an admission of truth. "I'm worried."

Surprised, she blinked up at me. "Worried?"

I nodded.

"About what?"

My voice came out rougher than I intended. "About this. About what we're about to do, if we agree to do it. But mostly . . . about fucking things up and making you hate me."

One of her hands trembled around the purse. She clenched it even tighter to stop it. "Thank you. I don't know why, but that makes me feel better."

I sat slowly back in the chair and gazed down at my empty glass, giving her space. I wanted her to start when she was ready, to ask whatever questions she wanted to ask, to feel that she was in control of this exercise in insanity. I might not know much, but I knew that any small chance of success we had at even being friendly in the future hinged on her, and her alone.

I was already all in. It was Bianca who still hadn't placed a bet or shown me her hand.

Finally she said, "You shaved."

I glanced up and met her gaze. "I know you prefer it."

She pulled her lower lip between her teeth and chewed it. I'd never seen her do that before, and found it devastatingly sexy.

She said, "And you're wearing a suit. With a tie."

My smile was faint. "I never said I didn't own any suits. I just said I hate them."

"But you're wearing one."

"The occasion seemed to call for it."

We stared at each other for a while, until Bianca tossed aside her handbag and leapt to her feet. "Oh *God* this is weird!" she said, and started to pace.

"I know."

She dragged her hands through her hair. It was down, falling in gentle waves around her shoulders, a dark mass of soft curls made for running through my fingers.

I closed my eyes and pinched the bridge of my nose. *Jackson, shut the fuck up.*

"My mother has lung cancer. Stage three."

Startled, I opened my eyes. Bianca was still pacing restlessly, her arms now folded over her chest.

Without stopping, she said, "We're broke. She doesn't have insurance. Her doctor wants to do surgery. Chemo has shrunk her tumor, but she needs surgery and possibly radiation, and definitely more chemo after the surgery. All that stuff costs money. A lot of money. I've already burned through the twenty grand you gave me for the charity event, and that was only for the initial rounds of chemo and some prescriptions."

She turned back and paced the other way, the hem of her dress flaring out around her knees. "There's no guarantee the surgery will work, of course, but without the surgery she's dead. That's it. Finito. Over. Done. Sixty-four years of running a business and raising a child and being a wonderful wife and mother and friend and good citizen and God-fearing churchgoer and taking care of everyone else without a thought to her own needs, and this is what she gets in repayment. *Cancer.* Like that's fair? Like that's how it should be?"

When she turned around to face me, I saw how upset she was. The color was high in her cheeks. Her chest rose and fell in rapid bursts. Not knowing what else to do, I set my empty glass on the coffee table and stood.

Bianca said, "My mother is my closest friend. She's the best person I've ever known. I'd do anything for her, you understand?" She looked at me with wild eyes.

"Yes," I said quietly. "I understand. You'll marry a man you don't love and give up five years of your own life so you can have the money to save hers."

She swallowed hard, her eyes filling with tears.

I said, "That doesn't make you a whore, forgive me for saying that word. It makes you selfless."

She quickly swiped at her eyes, then turned around and started pacing again. "I don't know what it makes me, but I've decided it doesn't matter. I'm willing to do whatever it takes."

As I watched her move across my floor, spilling her heart, fighting tears, sacrificing herself for someone she loved, I was gripped by an almost overpowering urge to take her in my arms. I wanted to kiss her and comfort her and tell her I was going to make it all right, that I'd take care of everything.

Instead I said gruffly, "Tell me what will make this easier for you."

Her steps faltered. She looked over her shoulder at me, chewing her lip again, her brows pulled together in a frown. Then she came back to the sofa and sat down, so I sat down, too.

Looking at the floor, she said, "Knowing what to expect will help." Then she lifted her chin and met my stare with a direct, unwavering gaze. I knew exactly what she meant.

I said, "Sex isn't part of the contract."

Faint color rose in her cheeks, but she didn't back down from her frank stare. She said, "So we'll have a contract?"

I nodded. "My attorney will draw it up based on whatever agreement we make, and you can have your attorney review it. The only nonnegotiables are the five-year time period prior to a divorce, a nondisclosure, and that you have to live here for the entirety of the marriage."

Her brows lifted.

"Married people live together," I said gently, leaving out that my father's attorney had told me in no uncertain terms that was part of the bargain.

She turned her gaze to the rows of books lining the library walls. When she didn't say anything for a while, I added, "There are eight guest bedrooms here, besides the master bedroom and Cody's room. You can have your pick."

She flattened her hands over her lap and moistened her lips. The pulse was going gangbusters in the hollow of her throat. I wanted to gently press my finger to it, to whisper something reassuring in her ear, but I kept my ass parked firmly in the chair and waited.

Later on I'd deal with the question of how I was going to live with her under the same roof as me for the next five years without my balls exploding, but right now wasn't the time for that.

She said, "I don't want a million dollars," and my heart skipped a beat.

Here came the negotiation. Damn that red dress of hers, because I already knew I was going to say yes to whatever she wanted.

I sat back, crossed my legs, and kept my expression neutral.

"What I want," she said, "is for you to pay for all my mother's medical bills, prescriptions, any hospitalizations and surgeries, and whatever other necessary care she needs, until she beats the cancer or . . ."

She paused and looked at me, leaving the word *dies* unspoken.

I said, "Keep talking."

She shook her head. "That's it."

After staring at her in silence for what was probably much too long, I said slowly, "What do you mean, that's it?"

She made a face. "Anything else and I'll feel dirty. This isn't about greed or getting rich. I love my life, if you want to know the truth. And if I'm being perfectly honest, all your money doesn't seem to have made *you* very happy."

She had me there.

"The only problem I have is that I can't pay for my mother's cancer treatments. We could run up a huge bill and let the hospital come after us, but then we're looking at bankruptcy court and debt collectors and maybe even having what few assets she owns being seized. And my mama is too proud to even tell her friends she's sick—she'd rather die than go bankrupt or be a burden on anyone. If she lost her house and had to move in with me, she'd stick her head in the oven the first chance she got."

I was beginning to see where Bianca got her moxie, as Rayford called it. I said, "There must be something you want for yourself. Something for the restaurant, or your future—"

"My future is my concern," she said softly but with steel beneath it. "You're buying a five-year pretend wife, and I'm buying a chance for my mother to live. That's it. That's the deal, or we don't have one."

My chest ached. This woman was in a position to get almost anything she wanted from me, and all she wanted was for her mother to be well.

For the first time in years, I had hope for humanity.

"How about this," I said. "I'll put the money in a trust and name you the sole trustee. That way it will be protected, and you can have access to the money whenever you need it, instead of having to rely on me. I think it would be . . . awkward for you to have to come to me with every bill. Then whatever is left over when your mother gets better, you can do with as you choose. Buy your mother a bigger house, give it to charity, whatever you want."

When she opened her mouth to protest, I said firmly, "That's the deal, or we don't have one."

She pressed her lips together. We looked at each other in silence as the clock ticked on the wall and my heart pounded like a jungle drum.

She said quietly, "All right, Mr. Boudreaux. You have a deal."

She stood and held out her hand. I rose, crossed to her, and took it. Staring down into her beautiful brown eyes, I said, "How many times do I have to tell you to call me Jackson."

Holding my hand and gazing up at me, she sighed. "I suppose if I'm going to be your wife, I ought to have a nickname for you. Does anyone call you Jax?"

Oh God, she moaned. God, yes. Please—Jax—

With a gargantuan effort of will, I pushed aside the memory of the intensely sexual dream I'd had about her after the first time we met.

"No," I said, my voice rough. "No one calls me Jax. No one but you."

When her lips curved up at the corners, I felt like I'd been living my life up to then at the bottom of a dark well filled with trash and slimy water, and someone had just lifted the lid and lowered me a ladder.

FRENCH QUARTER BEIGNETS

Makes about 3 dozen

- 1½ cups warm water
- ½ cup white sugar
- 1 envelope active dry yeast
- 2 eggs
- 1¼ teaspoon salt
- 1 cup evaporated milk
- 7 cups all-purpose flour
- ¼ cup shortening
- 1 quart vegetable oil
- 3 cups confectioners' sugar

Preparation

1. Mix water, sugar, and yeast in large bowl and let sit for 10 minutes.
2. In another bowl, beat the eggs, salt, and evaporated milk together. Stir egg mixture into yeast mixture.
3. Add 3 cups of the flour to the egg/yeast mixture. Stir to combine.

4. Add the shortening and mix. Continue to stir while slowly adding the remaining flour until all ingredients are well combined.

5. Place dough on lightly floured surface and knead until smooth.

6. Cover dough with plastic wrap or towel. Let rise at room temperature for 2–3 hours.

7. Preheat oil in a deep fryer to 350 degrees.

8. Roll the dough out to $\frac{1}{4}^2$ thickness and cut into 2^2 squares. Deep fry in batches, flipping constantly, until golden. (If beignets don't pop up, oil isn't hot enough.)

9. Drain on paper towels.

10. Shake confectioners' sugar onto hot beignets. Serve warm.

NINETEEN

BIANCA

I left the same way I arrived: in a cab, by myself, fraught with anxiety.

If my mother knew what I'd just agreed to, she'd slap me silly.

She knew I'd gotten the twenty thousand from Jackson for the catering event, but admitting I'd be getting a million for marrying myself off to him so I could try to save her life was another situation altogether.

Knowing there would be a nondisclosure in our contract was actually a relief. It meant I had a legal obligation to keep my mouth shut about my real reason for marrying the Beast.

Now I just had to figure out what *fake* reason I was going to try to sell.

"He's so charming I couldn't *help* but fall in love with him, Mama!" I muttered sarcastically to myself. The cabbie shot me a strange look in the rearview mirror, but I had more important things to worry about than his opinion. Before I left, Jackson told me that we had to be married and living together by his birthday, which was in just over two weeks.

Two weeks. I had to think fast.

"Unplanned pregnancy?" I mused, garnering another stare from the cabbie. I thought about it a moment, then shook my head. "Not unless you want to pretend you've been sleeping with a man everyone thinks you hate and then fake a miscarriage in a few months." I sighed, watching sunlight glitter off the lake as we sped by. "Temporary insanity? Hmm. Probably the most reasonable explanation, other than suffering a recent head injury. Lord, this is bad. How am I gonna get *anyone* to believe I married him for love when all we do is fight?"

The cabbie, a young black man wearing a New Orleans Saints cap backward, said, "Slap, slap, kiss."

Startled, I looked at him. "Excuse me?"

He grinned, exposing an impressive set of gleaming white teeth. "It's a popular film and TV trope where the writers put two characters who can't stand each other in close quarters and let them verbally spar, until one of them suddenly kisses the other, and they both realize they've had mad sexual chemistry all along and the fighting was just a cover for it."

I stared at him with my mouth open.

He shrugged. "Just brainstorming with you. I'm a writer. Or trying to be. I spend lots of time studying this trope stuff. It's actually how stories are told. Even Shakespeare is filled with tropes."

I said drily, "You don't say."

"Oh yeah," he replied vigorously, warming to the subject. "For instance, *Much Ado About Nothing*? That play is stuffed so full of tropes you could choke on them! But the bottom line is that two of the main characters, Beatrice and Benedick, have this history of seriously hating on each other, but everyone else can see they're perfectly matched. I mean, the opposite of love isn't hate. It's indifference. They wouldn't fight so much if they didn't care so much, right?"

I said, "It sounds like a really dysfunctional relationship, if you ask me."

The cabbie's grin grew wider. "Yeah, but all the best ones are. It's not true love if you don't want to kick his teeth in every once in a while."

According to that definition, Jackson and I were a match made in heaven.

I was silent for the rest of the ride home, grateful for the time to think. When I got home, I changed into my work clothes and headed over to Mama's to check in on her before I went to the restaurant.

And nearly had a stroke when I saw the motorcycle parked at the curb outside her house.

"Why that low-down, dirty dog!" I said, staring in outrage at Trace's bike. Then I marched up the stairs and barged into the house.

Mama and Trace were sitting in the front parlor drinking tea, smiling and chatting, thick as thieves. They broke off when I came in.

"Well here she is now!" said Mama, setting her teacup on the table beside her chair, which had a huge bouquet of fresh flowers on it that Trace had obviously brought. "Your ears must've been burning, *chère*, we were just talking about you!"

I glared at Trace. "I don't know about my ears, but my ass is certainly on fire!"

"*Bianca!*" Mama exclaimed, scandalized. She lifted a hand to her throat. "I did *not* raise you to speak like that! You apologize right this minute!"

"It's all right, Mrs. Hardwick. It's probably just the new influence in her life," drawled Trace, rising from his chair. He smirked at me. "I hear that Jackson Boudreaux fella Bianca's been spending time with has really earned his nickname."

"One more word, Trace," I said, "and I'm gonna get my daddy's gun out of the garage and turn you from a rooster to a hen with one shot."

"Now stop it, Bianca, I won't have this kind of behavior in my home!"

Mama's voice was loud, but wavered. When I looked at her, she appeared to be struggling for breath. She tried to rise from her chair but swayed unsteadily. I rushed over and helped her ease back down.

"What are you doing out of bed, Mama?" I said crossly, kneeling in front of her.

She was indignant at being treated like a baby. "I'm sick of being in bed, Bianca, and I'm feeling a little better today, so I got up and had breakfast. Then Trace called and asked if he could come by, and I was in the mood for a little visiting, so I said yes."

"It's real nice you're taking such good care of your mama, Bianca," said Trace.

I froze. "What?"

"Since she's been so sick," he explained. "You know, with the flu?"

My mother and I shared a look, and my shoulders sagged in relief. The last person on the planet I wanted to know about Mama's illness was Trace. Obviously she'd fed him the same line she'd been feeding everyone else.

Though I doubted anyone had ever heard of any flu that made all your hair fall out.

I said, "Right. The flu. It's been going around." I stood, holding onto Mama's hand, and stared at Trace. "So you were just leaving, right?"

Trace crossed his arms over his chest and smiled at me. With his tight jeans and his perfect face and his biceps popping out from under the sleeves of his painted-on T-shirt, he looked like he should be on the cover of a romance novel. I wanted to take off my shoe and smack a dent in the middle of his forehead.

He said, "Actually I was just telling your mama about the new business I started."

I looked at the ceiling, praying to God for restraint.

In the three years Trace and I had spent together, he'd started—and abandoned—a dozen businesses or more. A mobile car wash. A vitamin line. A motorcycle courier service. A new energy drink, because God knew the market didn't have enough of those. Inevitably his new pursuits required an influx of cash, and guess who the lucky "investor" was?

Yes. Me. Gullible, stupid-in-love, working-three-jobs-to-save-for-a-restaurant me.

I said flatly, "Another new business. How *thrilling* for you."

Trace's smile grew wider. He said, "It is, actually. It's the one we always talked about starting together. You remember, bumble bee?"

My whole body went cold. "No," I said, but my voice sounded dead.

He nodded, pleased as punch with himself. "Sure you do! A *restaurant*. Got a few investors with some serious cheese, just signed the lease on the space. We'll be opening up next month. Right down the street from your place, as a matter of fact. We'll be neighbors!"

Shocked into silence, I stared at him.

Mama said, "Why that's wonderful, Trace!" She squeezed my hand, trying to get me to look at her, but all I could do was stare in disbelief at the Benedict Arnold who used to be my man.

Who, in a few short weeks, was going to be my *competition*.

Because I'd already put Mama through her paces by saying my ass was on fire, I didn't want to make a stink in front of her about this awful piece of news. So I put a smile on and said pleasantly to Trace, "Isn't that nice. Would you mind if I talked to you outside for a minute?"

My invitation brought a smug look to his eyes, like he knew it was only a matter of time before I came to my senses.

He wouldn't be so smug if he knew I was picturing severing his genitals from his body with a pair of pruning shears, but Trace never was very good at reading people. He always assumed everyone had the same high opinion of him that he had of himself. Right now he was probably thinking I wanted to get him outside so I could throw myself at his feet and beg to be part of his new endeavor.

"Of course," he said with a twinkle in his eye. He turned to Mama and said, "Always a pleasure to see you, Mrs. Hardwick."

"And you, Trace," she said, shooting me a glance that said *be nice*.

He might not know what was in store for him, but Mama obviously did.

Trace held the door open for me on the way out. He walked behind me down the porch steps. When I stopped at the sidewalk, he stopped, too. Then he looked down at me and smiled his heartbreaker smile and proved exactly how dumb he was.

"I was just about to ask your mama for some of her recipes when you came in."

If the top of my head were a volcano, it would've exploded with a fountain of flaming orange magma so huge the entire southern United States would be wiped from the map.

My voice shaking with fury, I said, "If you ever come near her again, I'll break into your house when you're not home and replace all your shampoo with hair remover."

Trace blinked. His sculpted eyebrows pulled together.

I pointed my finger in his face. "You're a *liar*. And a *cheater*. And I don't care how much you screech about finding God, a leopard doesn't change his spots. I know all your tricks, Trace Adams. I know all your tells. And I know that you getting into the restaurant business has nothing to do with new investors and everything to do with trying to outdo me and prove that I made a mistake when I kicked your sorry behind to the curb."

Trace shrugged. "Well, you did."

I made a sound of astonishment. "You're unbelievable."

He reached up to tuck a stray lock of hair behind my ear, but I swatted his hand away. He said, "I know I made my mistakes, too, but I want to put all that behind us." His voice grew stroking. "C'mon, bumble bee. I *know* you still have feelings for me, or you never would've kissed that asshole in the car the other night. That's not your style."

Blood pounded in my face, in my ears, through every vein in my body.

I shouted, "That *asshole* is my fiancé!"

I wished I had a camera. His look of shock was worth preserving for posterity.

"The fuck you say?" He stepped closer, eyes narrowed, but I stood my ground.

"You heard me. We're engaged. We're getting married."

His nostrils flared in outrage. He stared down at me in jaw-clenched fury until finally he said, "Huh. Never thought I'd see the day that Miss High and Mighty turned into a gold-digging whore."

That hurt. It hurt like getting all my skin peeled off and taking a saltwater bath, but I didn't want him to see it. So I smiled, even though the effort felt like it would split my face in two. "There he is. *There's* the Trace I know. Welcome back, player. Now get lost!"

I turned on my heel to leave, but Trace caught me by the arm and jerked me against his chest. He put his nose up to mine and hissed, "How much he payin' you, Bianca? How much does it cost to get you to suck a dick?"

I yanked my arm from his grip and backed away, so angry I could scream. "If you come near me or my mama again, I'll call the police. And then I'll call my future husband. And believe me, Trace, you'll want the police to get to you first."

I strode away and didn't look back, not even when I heard him call me the c-word and spit on the sidewalk.

TWENTY

Bianca

The next afternoon, Jackson kept to his usual MO and arrived unannounced at the restaurant.

It was five o'clock, an hour before the first reservations, five hours after the meat delivery was supposed to have arrived. The staff was eating their preservice meal together at the long table in the glassed-in private dining room. Meanwhile I was pacing, my new favorite form of exercise. When the door opened and I saw the long shadow fall across the dining room floor, I knew who it was without even turning around.

Pepper's excited squeal only confirmed it.

I turned and found Jackson standing inside the door, staring at me. He was wearing faded jeans and his battered motorcycle jacket, with a white cotton shirt molded to his body so his abdomen muscles were on display like an ad for stacked bricks.

He was not altogether unfortunate looking.

I said, "Oh. Hello."

His brows quirked. He glanced at the gathering in the private dining room, fifteen people staring at us in open curiosity from behind a sparkling sheet of glass. "Is this a bad time?"

Is there a good time to sign away five years of your life?

I said, "It's fine. They're contained for now." I made my employees sound like a nasty viral outbreak, which wasn't too far from the truth. "Let's go into my office."

I led him through the restaurant, past the private dining room with its gaping menagerie, and through the kitchen. My office was down a hallway in the back. It was a cramped, messy space where I regularly collapsed into exhausted comas at the end of the night or cried over the mountain of unpaid bills strewn on my desk while I examined my life choices.

I opened the door, he closed it behind him. He looked around with a critical eye. "Looks like a bomb went off." Then his gaze fell on the bouquet of red roses on the edge of my desk, and he went stone-still. His tone was acidic. "From an admirer?"

I snorted. "If you can call Satan's spawn an admirer."

In two long, jerking strides, he was in front of the bouquet. He snatched the little white enclosure card off the plastic stick. He read it aloud while his free hand curled to a fist. "I'm sorry, bumble bee. I didn't mean what I said yesterday. Please call me, we need to talk. Trace."

Jackson pronounced Trace's name as a hiss. When he cut his gaze to me, all the air left the room.

He growled, "What happened?"

I dropped into my ratty captain's chair and sighed. "We had a little run-in at my mother's house."

"A run-in?" he repeated slowly. His eyes had turned an unnerving serial killer shade of black.

"Long story short, I stopped by Mama's on my way to the restaurant, and he was there. I told him we were getting married, and he called me the c-word."

Jackson turned the little white enclosure card to dust with a single crushing flex of his fist.

I said, "That's not the worst part."

His eyes were seriously weirding me out. I expected laser beams to shoot out of them at any second and blow the place apart.

"He's opening a *restaurant*," I said, unable to hide the quaver of fury in my voice. "Down the street. As a big f-you to me and all the plans we made to do it together."

Suddenly my office wasn't big enough to contain Jackson. Hulklike, his entire body expanded with his angry inhalation. I wasn't sure the seams of his clothing would be able to hold him.

I said, "It's just another one of his childish games. There's nothing he can't stand as much as being ignored, and he knew this would get my attention. He *wants* me to obsess over it. Which is why the only thing I can do is act like it doesn't get to me."

Jackson said darkly, "We'll see."

The implied threat made the little hairs on my arms stand on end. "I'm not condoning violence, Jackson."

"Who said anything about violence? There are ways to deal with this kind of situation that don't involve shedding blood." His serial killer eyes burned. "Even though I'd very much like to rip his head off and shove it up his own ass for what he said to you."

I allowed myself to enjoy the mental image of that for a moment. What a beautiful thing. Then I waved a hand at the chair across from my desk. "Sit. Please. You're making the room seem smaller than it already is."

He sat in the chair. His bulk appeared to reduce it to the size of a piece of child's furniture. He seemed to be getting bigger every time I saw him, all legs and arms and towering strength, potent masculinity. I felt dainty in comparison, which was impressive considering what the bathroom scale had read this morning.

"I brought the contract," he said, still bristling.

I blew out a tremulous breath.

"Bianca. Your face just went white."

The laugh I produced sounded a little crazy. "That would certainly be a feat."

We stared at each other. He said, "Do you want to see it?"

I held out my hand. From his coat pocket he brought out several folded pages and handed them to me. I flattened them over my desk and reached for a pen.

"You need to have your attorney review it before you sign," he said sternly.

"I don't have an attorney."

"Then get one."

"I can't *afford* an attorney, Jax."

He swallowed at the mention of his nickname. Moistened his lips, shifted his weight in the chair. Intrigued by his response, I momentarily forgot about the contract. "Do I make you uncomfortable?"

"Don't change the subject."

"It's a legitimate question. If we're going to be married, I should probably know these kinds of things."

He glowered for a while, then said, "You've made me uncomfortable since the moment we met."

I smiled in spite of myself. He was throwing my own words back at me and avoiding the question, all at once. He liked avoiding questions, which of course made me more curious than I otherwise would have been.

I said, "I've been thinking about the rings."

He leaned back, crossed his legs, and blasted me with his baby blues. Then he said, "I can't concentrate with these fucking roses staring down at me like a dozen bloody middle fingers."

Was he mad that I didn't throw them away? "I was going to toss them in the garbage as soon as they arrived this morning, but Eeny said she'd take them. Something about a ritual involving rose petals and goat blood. I didn't ask for details."

Jackson stood. He grabbed the vase of roses, opened the office door, set the vase outside in the hallway, closed the door, and sat back down, looking slightly less inclined to engage in a murder spree.

"Better," he said. "The rings. Shoot."

Amused, I shook my head. "I want a five-carat flawless Tiffany brilliant-cut center stone with a pair of flawless one-carat stones flanking it, set in a platinum band."

One of his eyebrows slowly lifted.

I smiled. "You got me. A simple gold band will do. What should I get you?"

He cocked his head and stared at me with new interest. "You want to get me a ring?"

"I'm not marrying a man who refuses to wear my ring. If we're doing this, we're doing it right. Jewelry included."

"Why does it matter?"

Good question. I didn't think I could tell him I wanted every other female who looked at him to see that small gold "off-limits" sign on his ring finger, because that would make no sense. Other than legally, I'd have no claim on him. In fact, since sex wasn't part of the contract, as he'd so kindly pointed out, I had no reason to believe he'd be faithful to our pretend marriage.

Interesting that it hadn't occurred to me to ask. Or to ask myself if *I* would be.

He said, "Whatever conversation you're having with yourself, I'd love to join in. It looks fascinating."

I chewed on my lower lip. It made his eyes flare, so I stopped. "I was just . . . wondering . . . about the sex stuff."

How can someone go from blistering anger to amusement to whatever this molten, dark energy thing was that he was doing now? However he managed it, I found myself squirming a little in my seat under the heat of his stare.

"What about it?" he asked in a neutral tone that didn't match his eyes or the tension in his body.

Feeling shy, I looked down and fiddled with the pen. "Um. What if you get a girlfriend? How do we—"

"I won't."

Startled by the finality of that pronouncement, I glanced up. "You can't know that. You could meet someone the day after we get married and fall madly in love with her. We should talk about what will happen in that scenario. Would she come live with us?"

In a move I was beginning to recognize as his tell for whenever he was really agitated, he raked a hand through his hair. He sat forward, propped his elbows on his knees, and pinned me in his gaze.

"There won't be any girlfriends," he said. "There won't be anyone else while I'm married to you."

The air was sucked out of the room again. I really needed to take a look at the ventilation. "So the 'no sex' clause is actually like a 'celibacy' clause?"

He leaned back in his chair, none of the high-tension electricity leaving him. "You should go over it with your attorney."

"I want to go over it with *you*."

One of his fingers started a restless staccato beat against his thigh. "It clarifies that there's no expectation of sex between *us*. It's not a requirement to fulfill the contract."

I mulled that over for a while. "So, then, it's voluntary."

He'd been looking at a print on the wall of a kitten hanging from the branch of a tree by one paw that read, HANG IN THERE! but his head snapped front and center, and he stared at me with such intensity I almost thought he was angry.

I said, "I mean, it's not *against* the rules."

I can't describe his expression. It hovered somewhere between serial killer and starving animal.

He said softly, "Why, Future Mrs. Boudreaux, are you proposition-ing me?"

And here came the blood flow from my neck straight up to my hairline like my head was dipped in a bucket of red paint. I looked down at the contract, hiding.

"Sorry," I said. "This is just all very strange. I suppose I'm nervous. Forget I even asked."

"Oh, no. You're not getting off that easily. Look at me."

I peeked up at him from under my lashes.

He asked, "When was the last time you had sex?" and I swear I almost fainted.

"That's none of your business," I said primly, and sat up straighter in my chair.

He said, "The last time I had sex was more than four years ago." His chuckle was wry. "I mean, with anyone other than myself."

Wow. And I thought *my* dry spell was bad. "No! Really?"

"Really."

"Are you a monk?"

He got that burning look again, the one I expected would ignite me. "Do you get the impression I'm a monk?"

Something unhealthy was happening to my heart. Being around him was causing a terrible arrhythmia that might eventually kill me. I decided to ignore his question and hazarded a tentative, "Did you . . . go through . . . um, a time when you weren't sure . . ."

Jackson looked in aggravation at the ceiling. "I already told you I'm not gay, Bianca."

I said, "So . . ."

He snapped, "I'm not bisexual, either, if that's where you're heading! I'm not confused about which sex I prefer, and I don't have a disease I'm trying not to spread! I just haven't had a girlfriend for a while, for Christ's sake!"

I had to backtrack before he exploded into full Hulk mode and his clothes were ripped to shreds. "Okay, I hear you, you're not confused, you're not diseased, you're just unusually . . . nonsexual."

That was the wrong thing to say. I sensed the change in him the way you sense a change in the weather. The electricity that crackles dangerously in the air before a thunderstorm, the spike of pressure in the barometer. If his eyes had been black before, now they were the pitch of the deepest pit of hell.

He rose, stood over me, and lifted me to my feet with his hands under my armpits like I was a doll. He said, "Tell me if this feels nonsexual to you."

Then he took my face in his hands and kissed me.

TWENTY-ONE

BIANCA

This time it was me who froze in shock when our lips came together. It took him several long moments of gentle coercion with his tongue before I finally opened my mouth. When I did, it was on a soft groan that he stole when he inhaled.

He was so big, and warm, and hard everywhere, except for his mouth, which was like cotton candy. I melted into it. He slid his thumb under my ear, and I shivered. His fingers pressed into my scalp. When he sank his teeth gently into my lower lip, lightning flashed through me.

I fisted my hand into the scruff of his neck and pulled him closer.

Suck, slide, nip, repeat, feel your pulse in all the hidden places in your body. This kiss was cashmere. It was luxuriant. It was decadent, unhurried, sweetly delicious, like stretching out on warm sand and drinking a mai tai. His scent was in my nose: pine and musk and something earthy and fresh, the way the woods smell after it rains.

He made that masculine sound deep in his throat that I found weirdly thrilling and pressed his hand into the small of my back. It brought our lower bodies together and provided me with impressive evidence that Jackson Boudreaux was anything but nonsexual.

"Oh," I breathed.

His laugh was soft and dark. "Yes, oh. Stop talking."

I couldn't catch my breath, but it didn't matter because his lips were on mine again. Little puffs of air through my nose would have to sustain me.

His hand in the small of my back became the iron band of his arm around my waist. My nipples tightened. His heartbeat crashed against my chest. The kiss turned from slow and sweet to hard and hot, first melting me and then lighting me on fire.

He tangled his hand into my hair, pulled the clip loose that held it all in place, and let it fall to the floor. He made that sexy, manly noise again when my hair spilled into his fingers. I fought the urge to press my hips against his, then softly moaned in relief when he did it for me, one big paw cupped under my bottom. *Yes, yes, yes,* thrummed my heart, aching for more.

He broke away, breathing heavily. My eyes drifted open. He stared down at me with a look like he might devour me.

Good thing I was in the mood to be devoured.

"We're not done yet," I whispered. I stood on my toes and wound my arms around his neck.

The kiss changed again. Desperation took over. Need took over. There was no more gentle exploration, no more unhurried pace. Now everything was white-hot and burning, clutching hands and greedy mouths, bodies straining to get closer. His fingers tightened in my hair. His hips rocked against mine. A new heaviness settled between my legs, and I wanted to violently rip off all his clothes and—

Someone knocked on my office door.

"Boss? Sorry to interrupt. Meat delivery finally arrived."

It was Hoyt.

I was going to kill Hoyt. Probably with my bare hands.

"Thank you," I called, sounding like I'd swallowed a handful of gravel. "I'll be right out." I glanced at Jackson and thought I might go up in a puff of smoke.

His eyes were heavy lidded, dazed and lust filled, glittering silver like the flash of a cat's eyes in the dark.

I said, "I have to . . ."

"I know. Give me a second." His voice was raw. He blinked slowly, combing his hand through my hair, watching the strands flow over his fingers.

Without thinking, I touched the scars on his jaw. He closed his eyes and made a soft noise like he was in pain.

"What are these scars from?"

My question broke whatever spell he'd been under. He dragged in a deep breath and reluctantly released me. With a cruel twist to his lips, he muttered, "A man-eating shark."

He turned away and raked both hands through his hair, and I knew that mysterious response was as good as I was getting.

Flustered and unsteady, I hastily scooped my hair clip from the floor. I had all my hair stuffed into it in record-setting time, though I probably looked like an escapee from the mental asylum, goggle-eyed, wild haired, shaking and sweating. I smoothed a hand down the front of my white chef's coat, which did absolutely nothing to calm me, but at least wicked the moisture from my palm.

I said, "Well. That was . . ."

My mind was as blank as a fresh sheet of paper.

Without turning around, Jackson blew out a hard, shuddering breath. Over his shoulder he said, "Get the contract reviewed by an attorney as soon as possible. Send the invoice to me. And I need to meet your mother."

He opened the door and was gone.

I sank slowly into my chair and allowed my knees to stop knocking and my heart to slow down before I went out to see about the meat.

The next day I visited an attorney in town who looked at Jackson's contract for a long time while the wrinkles on his forehead multiplied faster than rabbits. More than once he glanced up at me across from him as I nervously twisted my fingers together, aiming for nonchalant and missing by a continent.

Judging strictly from his expression, he thought I might be wearing a hidden camera.

"Miss Hardwick," he began carefully, pushing the contract toward me across his desk as if he thought it might burst into flames. "This is . . . unusual."

My laugh was closer to a donkey's bray. "You don't say!"

"I've never seen anything quite like this before," he said, disturbed. Under the fluorescent lights, his bald head glowed like a streetlamp. "I assume that you're entering into this agreement due to . . ." he coughed politely into his hand. "Financial problems?"

"Bingo. So give me the bad news."

He looked startled. "You're marrying a man solely for his money. What other bad news do you need?"

He was lucky this was on Jackson's dime, because that little zinger would have made me get up and walk out before he could dispense whatever sage advice he'd be dispensing.

"I'm talking about the contract. What's bad in there for me?"

He gave me a look like I'd completely failed to listen to his first question.

I sighed. "I know. You can stop judging me now, okay? Just tell me if there's anything in the contract we should counter. For instance, the part where it talks about me not having to have sex with him. Is that in order?"

It was obvious I was shortening the poor attorney's life span. No one blinked that rapidly who was long for this earth.

"Yes," he said after a rough throat clearing. "But we should counter for more money. One million dollars for five years is only two hundred thousand dollars per year. That works out to"—he did a mental calculation faster than I could stand up—"five hundred fifty-five dollars per day. Give or take. In my professional opinion, that's not nearly enough compensation for the length of time involved. You should be asking for five million at least, ideally double that."

I waved an impatient hand in the air. "The amount stays the same. That's not the important part."

He leaned back in his chair in slow motion, his liver-spotted hands spread flat over his desk. I imagined he was trying not to fall over in shock. "I don't concur, Miss Hardwick. When you're marrying for money, money is the *only* important part."

I said, "It's complicated."

"Uncomplicate it for me."

When my lips twisted, he sorrowfully shook his head. "I'm sorry, Miss Hardwick, but my advice to you is not to sign this document. It isn't in your best interest. You could conceivably make one million dollars in five years with the income from your restaurant."

Not in my wildest dreams, sir. And I don't have that much time.

I drummed my fingers impatiently on the arm of the chair. "Aside from the money, is there anything *else* in there I should worry about? Any language you want to tweak? Any offensive codicils we should remove? Anything?"

After examining my face in silence for what was definitely longer than polite, he said, "A few minor points. It's very straightforward, actually, and fair, if such a word could be applied to this situation."

"Good," I said, standing. I couldn't wait to leave. "Can you have the changes to me by tomorrow?"

He squinted up at me from behind his eyeglasses. "May I say something?"

"No."

I could tell right away he was going to anyway, which he did.

"You're an attractive young woman, Miss Hardwick. You also seem intelligent and pragmatic, a combination that in my experience is rarer than a unicorn sighting. There's no need for someone like you to sell yourself short."

I winced at his choice of words. He had the grace to look apologetic.

I said tightly, "Just have the changes to me by tomorrow," and left, slamming the door behind me.

I had to lean against the wall in the corridor outside for a long time before my stomach settled enough to keep walking.

A few days later I had the finalized contract in hand. I decided to celebrate by having a mental breakdown.

I was facedown on my desk when the phone rang. Inconveniently, it kept on ringing, even when I ignored it and let it go to voice mail twice. After a short pause it started to ring again. I had the sense it was shouting at me, and I knew who was on the other end of the line before I even picked up.

"Hello?"

"Bianca. It's Jackson."

He sounded agitated. What a surprise. "As if I couldn't tell from the growl."

"Why weren't you answering? I called the front desk and Pepper insisted you were in your office."

I added Pepper to the list of my employees I was going to kill. "I am in my office. I'm just . . . thinking."

There was a short pause. "That sounds ominous."

"I had an attorney review the contract."

Another pause, then his voice, dry as bone, "Please contain your excitement. I don't think my ego can handle such enthusiasm."

I sighed, flopped back into my chair, and propped my feet up on my desk.

He demanded, "Talk to me."

I fought a childish urge to stick my tongue out at the phone. "Just prewedding jitters, dear, nothing to worry about."

His voice changed to the soft, stroking murmur he so rarely used. "Getting cold feet, are we?"

The intimacy in his voice raised gooseflesh on my arms, which I defiantly credited to the air-conditioning. "Are you deliberately talking about me in first-person plural pronoun to irritate me?"

"I only have to breathe in your presence to irritate you. Now tell me what's wrong."

I closed my eyes and spent a few seconds deciding where to start. "It's a little overwhelming, this whole thing we're doing. I never imagined getting married would be like applying for a line of credit."

"It's always like that," he replied instantly. "What else is wrong?"

My eyes snapped open. He sounded a little too sure of himself there. "Are you speaking from experience?"

His silence was fraught. I bolted upright in the chair. "You've been married before?" I attributed my unnecessary shout to my breakdown and gave myself a pass.

"No. I have. *Not.*" He punctuated his words with a hammer like he did when especially miffed, but I sensed something more behind this denial than his usual pissiness, so I decided to poke the bear.

"Are you lying to me?"

Over the phone came a bristling animal noise which, had I heard it while walking outdoors in the dark, would have made me wet myself.

"I. Will. Never. Lie to you. *Never.* Do you understand?"

Oh dear. Poking the bear produced unpleasant results. "Sorry. It just sounded like there was more to what you said."

I don't know how silence can vibrate with emotion, but his did. Finally after a few incoherent growls and grumbles, he muttered, "I was engaged once."

That was like dangling a brand-new, catnip-filled feather toy in front of a cat. My ears perked up, my eyes narrowed, my tail started twitching. "What happened?"

"She didn't love me is what happened," he thundered. "She was only after my money!"

After a few moments I realized that sound in my ears was the pounding of my pulse. I breathed out slowly, feeling sick.

"It's different with us," he said more gently, guessing why I couldn't speak.

"How, exactly?"

His voice turned vulnerable, almost boyish. "This time I know."

Shot through the heart. Bullet to the brain. Fall from a forty-story building. With that one sentence, he killed me in a dozen different ways.

"Jax," I breathed, trembling. "Oh God."

"It's ancient history, Bianca. I'm over it. I wouldn't have even mentioned it if you hadn't asked." His voice took on a brisk, brittle quality. "And *I'm* the one who offered this deal, remember? This was my idea. So don't blame yourself for anything."

Oh, but I could. And I did. I blamed myself for ever thinking this would work, and for being a cold-hearted, cash-hungry mercenary.

For a moment I hated myself with the blinding fury I usually reserved for people who walk too slow and block the sidewalk.

"This is crazy," I whispered, so full of guilt that if someone falsely accused me of murder, I'd confess and demand the electric chair. "We can't do this."

"Is that what you're going to tell your mother? That you *can't* get the money for her surgery?"

I went from anguished guilty person to outraged shouty person in two seconds flat. "That is so not fair!" I hollered, slamming my hand on the desk.

"Life isn't fair," he countered bitingly. "This is a business deal, Bianca. A good one for both of us. We're not doing favors for each other. No one is getting taken advantage of here. We're going into it with our eyes open, fully informed and consenting, with an exit strategy that's painless and precise. Which is a hell of a lot more than most people can say about their marriages."

God, the bleakness of that. Whoever she was, the woman he'd been engaged to had certainly done a number on him. That . . . man-eater.

It dawned on me that those scars on his jaw he said had been caused by a man-eating shark were from his ex-fiancée. What did she do, hit him with a pitchfork?

Pushing aside the knowledge that I myself had wanted to do that very thing to him when we first met, I threw myself headfirst back onto the desk.

Sounding worried, Jackson said, "What was that noise?"

"My head and the desk getting better acquainted."

A low chuckle, and he'd officially cycled through every emotion a human can have in the course of a three-minute phone conversation. "Funny, I never pictured you as a drama queen."

I never pictured myself as the bride of hot Frankenstein, either, but here we were. "So what's the next step?" I said, recovering enough to attempt rational conversation.

"Do you own or rent your home?"

I wrinkled my nose at the phone. Now he was a Realtor? "Rent."

"Give notice. We need to have you transferred to Rivendell by my birthday on the sixteenth."

He made it sound like a women's prison. "What about my things? Furniture, clothes, books?"

"Pack what you want to keep, and leave the rest. I'll send over moving boxes and arrange for a storage unit. If your landlord charges removal fees for anything you leave behind, I'll take care of it."

My lip chewing must have been audible, because Jackson prompted, "Spit it out, Bianca."

"And the wedding itself? When will that happen?"

"As soon as you meet my parents. Ideally we'll go this weekend, but if you need to arrange—"

"Wait. Meet your parents? *Go?*"

His voice turned dark. "We need to make a quick trip to Kentucky before we get married."

The realization of what he meant made me suck in a horrified breath. "Oh Lord. Your parents have to *approve* me, don't they?"

His silence was my answer. I hollered, "I have to audition for the role of your fake wife?"

"It's just a formality. They're going to love you."

I groaned and covered my eyes with my hand. I could picture it now: Jackson pulling up to his boyhood home—in my mind it looked like the plantation Tara from *Gone With the Wind*—and introducing me to his rich, conservative, and very white parents.

His mother would get a pinched look. His father would turn purple with anger. All the servants who'd lined up to greet us like they did on *Downton Abbey* would titter behind their hands at Jackson's audacity for bringing home a colored girl.

Mercy! Is that his maid?

"I know you're thinking again because I can smell something burning," said Jackson drily.

Think of Mama. Think of Mama. Think of Mama.

"I can have Eeny cover for me for a few days," I said weakly. She'd have to cover for me forever after I died of humiliation when Jackson's parents had their dogs chase us off the plantation, anyway; might as well get her up to speed.

"Good. We'll leave Friday, then. When can I meet your mother?"

Feeling like I was in a dream, I said, "I'll find out."

DAVINA'S FAMOUS CREOLE JAMBALAYA

Makes 8 servings

- ½ pound raw bacon, diced
- ½ pound fresh pork sausage, casings removed
- ½ pound andouille sausage, sliced
- 3 tablespoons butter
- 4 boneless chicken breasts, cut into 1-inch cubes
- 1 large yellow onion, diced
- 1 green bell pepper, diced
- 3 celery ribs, diced
- 3 garlic cloves, minced
- 2 cups long-grain white rice
- 1 teaspoon dried thyme
- 2 bay leaves
- ½ tablespoon chili powder
- 1½ tablespoons paprika
- 1 teaspoon ground cayenne pepper
- 1 teaspoon celery salt
- 1 can diced tomatoes
- 2 cups homemade (or organic) chicken stock
- 1 cup good-quality red wine

- 1½ pounds wild-caught raw shrimp, peeled and deveined
- 8 scallions, chopped
- fresh parsley

Preparation

1. In a large Dutch oven or high-sided pot, melt butter. Cook bacon and sausages for three to five minutes or until lightly browned, stirring frequently. Season chicken breasts with salt and pepper, add to pot, and cook additional 5 minutes or until browned.

2. Add onion, bell pepper, celery, and garlic and cook until soft and fragrant, about 10 minutes. If pot seems dry, drizzle lightly with olive oil.

3. Add rice, thyme, bay leaves, paprika, cayenne pepper, and celery salt and stir to mix. Increase heat to high. Add tomatoes, red wine, and chicken stock. Bring to a boil, reduce heat to medium/low, cover pot, and simmer for 15 minutes or until rice is tender.

4. When rice is done, add shrimp and green onions. Cook on low for additional 10 minutes or until shrimp is pink and cooked through. Remove bay leaves, fluff jambalaya, and serve, garnishing with fresh parsley.

TWENTY-TWO

BIANCA

After I hung up with Jackson, it took a solid fifteen minutes of dithering before I worked up the nerve to call my mother. She answered on the first ring.

"Hi, Mama. How are you?"

The gentle laugh that came over the line was reassuring. "I told you this morning I'm feeling good today, *chère*. You worry about me too much."

"That's good."

After listening to the cavernous silence that followed, her mother-bear instincts kicked in. She said sharply, "Bianca? What's the matter?"

I stared at the kitten poster on the wall of my office until it blurred. "Uh . . ." *Be brave. You've got this.* Terrified, I cleared my throat. "There's someone I'd like you to meet."

She didn't even miss a beat. "Who, Jackson Boudreaux?"

My jaw hit the desk. When I recovered my wits, I said, "How did you know?"

"Sweetheart, I've known Eeny for going on fifty years. Did you think she *wouldn't* call me when a man barged into your kitchen and announced you were getting married like you'd just won the Publishers Clearing House sweepstakes?"

Eeny! I should've known she'd blab! The air leaked from my lungs like a punctured balloon.

Mama said, "Well, he might have a reputation for being too big for his britches, but the man must have some sense in his head to fall in love with you."

Love? I almost slipped into a coma. But what could I say? *No, actually we're only getting married to save his inheritance and your life?*

That would so not go over.

Her tone became businesslike. "Bring him by tomorrow at ten o'clock. And be prepared to leave for a few minutes so I can give him the business. He doesn't get to marry into this family unless he's good enough for you."

She hung up, leaving me staring in bewilderment at the phone. The dreamlike feeling intensified.

Body snatchers, I thought. That was the only rational explanation for her nonchalance. Aliens had stolen my mother and replaced her with a robot look-alike. Right now the robot was sitting blank eyed in Mama's armchair downloading instructions from the mother ship.

Or maybe the chemo had unraveled something inside her brain.

Or I'd been involved in a serious car accident and was lying in a hospital bed somewhere, doped up to the gills, my opiate-soaked brain manufacturing this whole thing.

"Only one way to find out," I said aloud to the empty room and then cackled like a lunatic.

I was taking the Beast home to meet my mother. The world had officially come to an end.

At five minutes to ten o'clock the next morning, I sat on the edge of the sofa in Mama's living room, pretending I wasn't having a brain embolism while I waited for Jackson Boudreaux to knock on the front door.

Regal in purple, Mama sat in her big white armchair, openly studying me. "Doc Halloran's office called yesterday to confirm the surgery," she said suddenly.

"Next Wednesday at nine," I said, nodding. "I remember." I glanced at the clock on the wall. Four minutes to ten. T minus four minutes. Three. Two. My knee started to bounce.

"In case anything goes wrong—"

My head snapped around. "Nothing will go wrong!" I said too loudly.

She smiled at me, amused. "As I was saying. In case anything goes wrong, I've gathered all my important documents and put them in a binder. It's blue. I'll leave it on the kitchen table before we go to the hospital."

I swallowed around the lump in my throat. "Documents?"

"My will. The title to the house. Copies of insurance policies and bank statements. You know, documents."

I pressed my cold fingertips to my closed eyelids and breathed deeply.

"Oh, *chère*," said Mama softly. "Dying isn't the worst thing that's ever happened to me. It's just the only thing I won't live through."

"How many times do I have to tell you?" I said, my voice breaking. "You're *not* dying!"

She waved a hand impatiently as if to swat away a fly.

A knock like a boom of thunder on the front door made me leap from my seat. "It's him!" I cried, then stuffed my knuckles into my mouth and stared at the door as if the boogeyman were about to burst through it.

"Well go answer it, child," Mama chided, shaking her head.

I smoothed my trembling hands down the waist of my dress and gulped in a few brimming lungfuls of air. Then I wobbled to the front door and gracelessly yanked it open.

Jackson stood on my mother's front porch in a beautiful navy-blue suit and an ice-blue tie that exactly matched the color of his eyes. His dark hair was tamed. There wasn't a whisper of stubble on his square jaw. In his hands he held a tiny, perfect African violet plant, the pot wrapped in cellophane and lilac tissue paper.

He said solemnly, "Bianca. Good morning."

I wasn't sure if the house was sinking or I was floating, but somehow my feet had left the ground. "Jax," I whispered, completely out of breath.

His eyes flashed with warmth, there then gone. "May I come in?"

I realized I was standing there staring at him stupidly, my mouth hanging open in what was most likely a highly unattractive way. I snapped my jaw shut and nodded. "Of course. Please enter."

Dear Lord. I sounded like an uptight butler.

Then Jackson was standing in Mama's living room, a burst of living color and electricity, taking up all the space as he always did.

"Mrs. Hardwick," he said to my mother. "It's a pleasure to meet you, ma'am. Thank you for inviting me to your home."

Mama flicked me a look. It said: *He's got manners.* She held out her hands to him. "Forgive me for not standing, Mr. Boudreaux, but I've recently been ill and I'm a little loosey-goosey on my feet, if you know what I mean."

Jackson crossed to Mama and extended his hand. She clasped it in both of hers, like she was praying. She looked up at him—all the way up—and said, "Goodness! The air must be thin up there, son. Please, take a seat."

Son? I sank into the nearest chair and concentrated hard on staying upright.

"This is for you, ma'am," said Jackson politely, parking himself next to Mama in a chair that was woefully undersized for his sprawl. He held out the plant.

The flowers Trace brought the other day had mysteriously vanished.

"Oh." Mama touched a hand to her throat. She stared at the violets in amazement. "Why, African violets are my favorite! I haven't seen these in years!" She turned her gaze to me. It was glittering. "Bianca, did you think of this?"

Before I could answer, Jackson said smoothly, "Your daughter is always thinking of you, ma'am." When his gaze slid to mine, I wanted to cry.

Why was he doing this, coming here to meet my mother? He didn't have to do this. I'd already agreed to sign the contract. This was unnecessary.

Mama held the plant in her hands and beamed at it. "What a lovely surprise. You've just made my day." Cradling the violets in her lap like a small, treasured dog, she turned her beam onto Jackson. "What can I offer you to drink, Mr. Boudreaux? Coffee? Water? Something stronger, maybe, an Absinthe Suissesse?"

"Nothing for me, thank you, ma'am. And please, call me Jackson."

The two of them grinned at each other while I looked on, utterly confused.

Jackson said, "I understand Bianca gets her talent in the kitchen from you, Mrs. Hardwick."

Mama batted her eyes, coy as sin. "Oh, I taught her a thing or two, but she's got talents I never had. Creativity, that's the mark of a true artist! Like the spring menu she put together for her restaurant, for example." She shot me a proud glance. "Wouldn't you say that was a stroke of genius, Jackson, all those recipes featuring Boudreaux Bourbon?"

Very gravely, Jackson replied, "The menu is incredible, but I think her true genius is actually with people." His eyes found mine. His voice changed. "She knows how to make them feel like they matter."

With his intense gaze burning into mine, I lost the power of language. My tongue sat in my mouth like a lump of soft cheese. I was going to have to take sign language classes to communicate from here on out.

Mama looked back and forth between us for a moment, then sighed.

It was a satisfied sound, filled with relief and pleasure, like when you find something precious you've been searching all over for that you thought you'd lost.

Flustered, I looked down at my hands twisting together in my lap.

"Bianca," said Mama. I looked up to find her giving me *make yourself scarce* eyes. "Would you mind putting these in my bathroom and giving them a drink?" She held out the violets. "And see if you can find that old photo album from your school days; I want to show Jackson those pictures from when you won the spelling bee in the fifth grade." Her smile was conspiratorial. "You might have to rummage around in those bookcases in the office for a while, I can't remember exactly where I put it."

Stifling the groan that I knew would gain me nothing but a rebuke, I stood and dutifully took the violets. I left them chatting, their voices becoming indistinct as I made my way down the hall into Mama's bedroom.

I dribbled water into the plant from the bathroom faucet. I set it on the sink and fussed with the tissue paper, smoothing out any stray wrinkles, pursing my lips in consternation. I'd grill Jackson later about how he'd known these were Mama's favorite flowers, but for now I was still in a mild state of shock that he was even here.

I'd been dreading this. I didn't want to tell Mama I really *was* getting married, it wasn't just some bad joke Eeny had witnessed. Mama's nose was sharper than a bloodhound's. She'd guess right away something smelled funny.

But maybe I could put it off until after her surgery. Yes, that's what I'd do, I decided. No need to run headlong toward disaster. I could ease her into it a little bit.

Then I remembered I'd be living with Jackson before I even got my next period. There was no easing anything at this point.

"Slap, slap, kiss," I said to the mirror. "And make it sound believable, Bianca!"

My reflection didn't look very convinced it would work.

I dawdled as long as I could without being obvious, then reentered the parlor with a warning cough. Mama and Jackson were leaning toward each other, deep in conversation, but broke off when I appeared.

Like an old-fashioned gentleman, Jackson stood as I walked into the room.

It made me flush. Mama's slight, approving head nod made me flush even more.

"Couldn't find the photo album," I lied, sitting on the sofa. "It's probably in the garage."

"Hmm," said Mama. "Well, perhaps another time."

She smiled at me with her eyes. We both knew exactly where all the photo albums were. Stacked in bookcases in what used to be my bedroom.

Jackson abandoned the chair he'd been sitting in before and lowered himself to the couch beside me. His weight made the cushions dip and rolled me slightly toward him. I tried to be casual as I straightened myself, but Jackson draped his arm around my shoulders and pulled me against his side, like he'd done it a million times before.

Blushing furiously, I made a peep of surprise.

Mama said to Jackson, "She gets it from her father, that flush. That and her stubborn streak."

Jackson chuckled. "She's stubborn? Gosh, ma'am, I hadn't noticed."

They both laughed. I wondered if a person could die of embarrassment.

They talked for a while, easy in each other's company, while I sat stiff and uncomfortable beside the man who would soon be my husband and watched the woman who raised me charm the pants off him.

He charmed the pants off her, too. The housecoat, I mean.

Finally after what seemed an interminable period I spent examining a crack on the opposite wall, my mother said, "Well. It's been so lovely visiting with you, Jackson, but I'm afraid I'm feeling a little tired now."

I snapped back to attention like a dog at the end of a yanked leash. "Are you okay? What can I get you?" I rose, filled with anxiety, but Mama waved me off.

"Nothing at all, *chère*, nothing at all. I'm just going to go back to bed for a spell. Rest these old bones. Would you lend me a hand?"

I helped her stand, wincing at her fragility. But she pulled herself upright and smiled like she didn't have a care in the world, and I breathed a little easier.

"It's been wonderful to meet you," said Jackson, solemn again. He came forward and gently took my mother's outstretched hand. "I can see where Bianca gets her beauty and brains."

"And I can see why she likes you so much," Mama said warmly. "You remind me an awful lot of her daddy. Crème brûlée, I always called him. Hard as nails on the outside, but inside all soft and gooey sweet."

I almost dropped dead. "Mama!"

"Oh hush, child, you embarrass too easily." To Jackson she said, "I can trust you to take care of my baby, now, can't I, Jackson Boudreaux?"

She was smiling, her tone playful, but there was a steeliness behind her eyes that left no doubt she wasn't asking a question. She was giving a command, and God help him if he answered the wrong way.

But Jackson rose to the challenge with a quiet grace that surprised me. He said softly, "You can trust me with her life, ma'am."

It was a simple statement, breathtaking in its honesty. There wasn't a doubt in my mind he meant exactly what he'd said.

Mama felt the same way. She nodded, the steeliness in her eyes slowly replaced by that strange relief that had echoed in her sigh. Her hand relaxed in mine.

"Would you just help me to the bedroom, *chère?*" Mama asked.

"Of course."

"I'll wait for you outside, Bianca. Mrs. Hardwick." Jackson slightly bowed his head, managing to look royal, elegant, humble, sophisticated, and sincere, all at once. "I hope to see you soon."

He made his way to the front door and quietly let himself out.

When the door shut behind him, a huge breath left my chest in a rush. I felt like I might collapse into a heap, all my bones made of rubber.

Mama patted my hand. "I owe you an apology, Bianca."

"What are you talking about?" I said, truly confused.

She searched my eyes. "I overheard what Trace said to you the other day, out on the sidewalk after you both left. I was wrong about him."

"Oh, Mama," I breathed, sorry she'd had to hear that wretched skirt chaser call me a terrible name.

Then she said, "I heard what you told him, too," and all the blood drained from my face.

That asshole is my fiancé! I'd shouted into his face, loud enough for the whole block to hear.

"I thought you were just being spiteful, which he deserved, don't get me wrong. But Jackson Boudreaux just asked for my permission to marry you."

My whole body went numb. So that's why he wanted to meet my mother. He wanted to ask her for my hand.

I wasn't sure which would happen first, the fainting or the vomiting.

She smiled. "Don't look so traumatized, baby, I said yes. It seems awful fast, but who am I to judge? It was the same way for me and your daddy. And you've always had your head screwed on straight. I know you wouldn't want to marry him unless you were in love, even if you have been tight-lipped about it." Her eyes narrowed slightly as she dared me to contradict her.

Like a deer in the headlights, I froze. I blurted, "Slap, slap, kiss."

She looked confused for a moment, then her face cleared. "You mean the old romance trope where two total opposites fight like cats and dogs until they suddenly realize they're crazy about each other?"

After a second of shock so profound it felt like a cannonball had blown through me, I started to laugh. I laughed so hard I started crying. "Exactly!" I howled.

She shrugged. "Makes perfect sense to me."

And just like that, it was done.

TWENTY-THREE

JACKSON

Though she only lived a few blocks away from her mother, Bianca was in no shape to walk home. I wouldn't have let her walk anyway, not when I had a car, but she had a blank, stunned look when she came out of the house that made me think she'd stumble aimlessly around the neighborhood for hours before finally realizing she was lost and lying down in the gutter for a nap.

I've seen someone hit in the head with a shovel who had more presence of mind than she was displaying.

I held the car door open for her. She inserted herself into the seat with the grace of a zombie, all jerking legs and stiff arms, the opposite of the way she normally moved.

"I didn't think having me meet your mother would be so traumatizing for you," I said once I was seated behind the wheel.

Bianca laughed. It was the noise a dog made when you stepped on its tail. "You asked my mother for permission to marry me," she said.

"I did."

She looked at me with eyes so wide the whites showed all around her irises. "What would you have done if she'd said no?"

I answered truthfully. "Become one of those panhandlers on the boulevard you said I reminded you of."

"We wouldn't get married?"

I wanted to attribute her horrified tone to desperate disappointment that I wouldn't be her husband, but I knew what she was thinking. And it wasn't about me.

"I would've paid for your mother's surgery, and then I would've found a nice, comfortable bridge to live under." I started the car and drove off, feeling her eyes on me like laser beams.

After a long time, she asked, "Why?"

Because I'd do anything to have you look at me the way you looked at me when I kissed you, even if it was only for one more time.

Aloud I said, "No one should have to die because they're broke."

She studied me in silence as we drove. I liked it, having her attention focused on me like that. It felt natural to have her riding beside me, sharing the same air. I wanted to reach out and take her hand, but didn't want to push my luck. Instead I turned on the radio.

A song came on. "Like A Virgin." Madonna crooned, "Feels so good inside."

I turned the radio off.

"Wait." Bianca looked out the window in confusion. "We're going the wrong way."

"No. We're going home."

"But my home is—"

"We're going to *our* home," I said. "I want you to pick out your room before we leave this weekend. We need to get you settled. And I don't want to have to lie to my parents when they ask if we're living together."

She made a small, strangled noise in her throat, then rested her head on the back of the seat and closed her eyes.

"You're terrible for my ego," I said drily.

"I'm sorry. This is all just so . . . surreal."

Her voice was muted. When I sent her a surreptitious glance, I saw that her face was pale and her knee was bouncing up and down. She really *was* traumatized.

Had I been a less selfish man, I would've turned around, driven her home, paid for her mother's surgery, and ripped up our contract. But now—aside from the fact that I dearly loved my house and my car collection and all the things my father's money bought me—I had to admit that the thought of us living under the same roof had me as excited as a five-year-old on Christmas morning.

I'd get to see those long-lashed doe eyes *every day*. I'd get to hear that voice, a jazz singer's honeyed, husky timbre. I'd get the indescribable pleasure of watching her move among my things, warming all the cold marble surfaces with her fire and her laugh and her vibrancy.

In short, I'd be the luckiest fucking man on earth. I wasn't giving that up over a simple thing like decency.

"I know," I said. "I'm sorry."

After a moment, she sat up straighter and blew out a breath. "You have nothing to apologize for. It's me who's acting silly. You were right, this is a business deal that we're both benefiting from." She sent me a weak smile. "I'm grateful to you."

Now I really felt like a louse.

We drove the rest of the way in silence, lost in our thoughts. When I stopped in front of the house, Rayford opened the door and bounded out, smiling from ear to ear. I wondered how long he'd been standing inside waiting for us to show up, peering out the windows like an anxious mother.

"Miss Bianca!" he said, opening the passenger door. He grinned at her with his entire body. "So good to see you again!"

For once I was glad of Rayford's indestructible cheer. It visibly lifted Bianca's spirits.

"Rayford." She took his extended hand and allowed him to help her out of the car. Then she hugged him.

He looked as surprised as I felt.

"Why, Miss Bianca," he said, chuckling and patting her back. "You'll make an old man blush."

She said something to him that I didn't catch, then pulled away. I got out of the car as fast as I could, convinced I'd miss something important, but Rayford simply took her hand and put it into the crook of his arm and led her into the house.

I frowned at his back. The old goat just usurped me!

"So tell me how it went with your mama and Mr. Boudreaux," said Rayford, gazing down at Bianca affectionately as they walked down the hall and I followed behind like an obedient dog, trying not to sniff too closely at her heels.

"It went great," Bianca said, wonder in her voice. "She really liked him."

Rayford threw a glance at me over his shoulder that said, *Maybe she's got a screw loose.*

I made a face at him. He turned back to Bianca, suppressing a smile. "Of course she did. What's not to like about Mr. Frownypants?"

I almost choked on my tongue, until Bianca laughed so heartily that I instantly forgave him. "Let's take the elevator," I said when Rayford headed for the spiral staircase to the second floor.

Bianca looked startled. "Elevator?"

"The master of the house enjoys installing unnecessary technology," said Rayford, like I wasn't two feet behind him. He patted her hand. "But now that you'll be staying here, maybe you can talk him into finding a more useful hobby."

"Disposing of dead bodies," I muttered under my breath.

"Here we are!" Rayford stopped in front of the sleek brushed silver elevator doors, pretending like he hadn't heard me. He couldn't miss the glower I sent in his direction, however, or the *Leave us alone!* I transmitted directly into his brain.

After almost thirty-five years of knowing someone, telepathy is a given.

In one of the most unfortunate turns of phrases I'd ever heard, he said, "I'll leave you two rabbits to it!"

He pressed the "Call" button on the elevator and went on his way down the hall, his footsteps and jaunty whistle echoing off the marble.

We got into the elevator. When the doors slid shut, Bianca said doubtfully, "Rabbits?"

I sighed. "I'd fire him, but he's my only friend."

"I'm your friend, too," she said.

When I looked down at her, she glanced away and started to chew the inside of her cheek.

Friends. That should have made me happy, but it didn't. It made me want to break something. Which is how I realized this lie of convenience was much more to me than just a business deal. I raked a hand through my hair and blew out a breath.

Bianca said quietly, "Was that the wrong thing to say?"

"No. Of course not. Why do you ask?"

"Because when you get really aggravated, you stab your hands through your hair."

"I do?"

She nodded. "And you bristle. You literally get larger somehow. It's freakish. Also you make some very unnerving animal sounds and have serial killer eyes."

"What a charmer," I muttered, crushed.

"It's not all bad," she said, looking at the ceiling.

My ears perked up, but I didn't want to sound too eager, so I said with utmost disinterest, "Do tell."

"Well. Um. You smell amazing. After you stopped murdering me with your eyes and I got past all the hair and your generally disheveled, hobolike appearance, it was the first thing I noticed about you."

What a strange tingle that was, skittering over my skin. I didn't dare speak and prayed for the elevator to go slower.

My silence prompted her to add, "And you have a really beautiful voice. If you ever decided not to be a layabout rich person, you could have an incredible career as a phone sex operator."

Holy fuck. She thought I had a sexy voice.

For a second I stopped breathing. After my lungs remembered what their normal function was, I said, *"Layabout?"*

The elevator doors opened. Neither of us moved.

She said, "You're right. That was rude. What's an inoffensive word for idle?"

I wasn't at all offended, because *layabout* and *idle* were both pretty accurate descriptions for how I spent my days, but I was enjoying the compliments too much to let this conversation get steered off topic. "Maybe you could tell me a few more things you like about me to make up for your horrible manners."

The elevator doors began to slide shut, but I put out a hand, and they opened again. I looked at Bianca, my brows raised, waiting.

Under my stare, her cheeks faintly colored.

Christ, how I liked that.

She said, "You'll get a big head."

A smile broke over my face. "There's just so many things, eh?"

With typical sass, she lifted her chin and flounced past me. "Actually I ran out of things already. I'm just trying to buy time to make up something else."

Watching her walk past me, her dress swaying around her knees, I felt like a snorting, ground-pawing bull when a toreador flares his red cape.

Then Cody came tearing around the corner. He stopped short when he saw Bianca, his face lighting up. "Lady!" he hollered, and made a beeline for her legs.

Before he could slam into her, I scooped him up and tossed him into the air. He screamed like a banshee, his usual response to being delighted. He was easily delighted, so I lived with a lot of banshee screaming in my house.

"Oh! You've got him, sir, thank goodness!"

Panting and wheezing, Charlie staggered around the corner, her hair disheveled, one hand holding her side like she had a stitch. I wondered how long she'd been chasing him.

"Morning, Charlie." I tossed Cody over my shoulders and held onto his ankles so he dangled down my back. "Is he wearing you out already?"

She passed a hand over her perspiring brow. "I don't know where he gets his energy, sir. I swear it's like Sunkist puts cocaine in their orange juice. Every day after breakfast he just starts bouncing off the walls and doesn't stop until he falls asleep at night."

Cody banged his little fists against my butt, laughing like it was the greatest game in the world. Bianca looked on in amusement, shaking her head.

In a quick move, I flipped him upright and set him on his feet. Then I knelt in front of him and gave him a hug, which instantly calmed him. He loves hugs more than anything else in the world.

Rubbing his back, I said, "What do you think about having Charlie read you a book, buddy?"

His head resting on my shoulder and his arms wrapped tight around my neck, he gurgled a laugh. "Book buddy book buddy!"

That was a yes. Charlie sighed in gratitude. I gave Cody a kiss on the top of his head. I murmured into his hair, "Love you, buddy."

Cody looked at me and grinned, his pale, chick-fluff hair standing on end from static electricity. He pronounced, "Cody loves Daddy, too."

I kissed his chubby cheek. "Now I have to talk to Bianca for a while, but I'll come and read with you and Charlie when we're done, okay?"

Cody placed his warm, sticky hands on my cheeks and squealed in happiness.

When I glanced up, I caught Bianca watching us with a strange, pained look on her face, like she might be about to cry. She looked away quickly and said a muted hello to Charlie.

"Nice to see you again, Bianca," said Charlie, smiling warmly.

I stood, holding Cody's hand. "Buddy, can you say hello to Bianca without tackling her?"

Looking like a miniature soldier, Cody stood up straight and put his hand to his forehead. He shouted, "Lady!" then grinned.

Bianca laughed softly. "Hello, Cody."

"Book buddy book buddy!"

Bianca smiled at him. "Do you have a favorite book?"

Cody jumped up and down, laughing and stamping his feet.

"That means he likes them all," explained Charlie, taking Cody's other hand. He released mine, deciding it was time to make like a barnacle and attach himself to Charlie's left leg. She gently peeled him off, then lifted him up and settled him on her hip. She gave him an affectionate peck on his forehead. "Ready to go read, Cody?"

His answering shriek in the affirmative was almost deafening. All three of us laughed.

"Okay, then. I'll see you later, sir. Bianca." Charlie nodded at Bianca then turned around and went back around the corner toward the nursery, Cody chattering away on her hip.

"You're very good with him," said Bianca quietly once they were gone.

I looked at her sharply. Why did she seem so disturbed? "He won't be a bother to you, if that's what you're thinking. Charlie keeps him busy, and he'll start preschool next year—"

"Jackson! That's not what I was thinking at all!" Bianca looked appalled. "I just meant that you're very . . . *good* with him. A natural. You seem like you were born to be a father."

That floored me.

I loved Cody with all my heart, like he was my own flesh and blood, but I was always convinced I was doing something wrong or could be doing things better. I'd gone to boarding school as a kid, and when I was home my father was always working, so I didn't have much in the way of day-to-day role modeling from a father figure. I was basically just winging it with Cody, praying my best was good enough for him.

So for Bianca to tell me I was a natural at fatherhood made me feel fifty feet tall.

"Thank you," I said gruffly. Then I noticed that her nostrils were flaring and her face was red, and I went from flattered to confused. "Are you angry?"

She said stiffly, "I'm not the kind of woman who's *bothered* by children."

My confusion was growing like a tumor in my stomach. "Of course you're not. I didn't mean—"

"Yes, you did," she cut in, eyes glittering, "or you wouldn't have said it."

I was beginning to get the sense I'd done something extremely stupid and should proceed with utmost caution, assuming live munitions were buried every few feet under the floor. I said slowly, "Whatever I've said to offend you, I'm sorry."

She stared at me with those glittering eyes for a while. Then she turned away stiffly and shook her head. "Forget it. Let's just get on with this."

Her bitter tone wasn't easing my mind. In fact, it was driving me crazy. Before she could take two steps away, I curled my hand around her arm and gently turned her back to me. She refused to look at me, so I put my hand under her chin and tilted her head up.

"What is it?" I said softly.

For a moment her expression seemed to convey her answer would be two stiff fingers poked into my eyes. But then her look softened, and she sighed.

"Ignore me. I'm premenstrual."

She tried to pull away, which I was having none of. "Bianca," I said, pulling her closer. "What. *Is* it?"

When she looked into my eyes, everything else disappeared.

She said, "I'm not the girl you need to think the worst of, Jax. I'm not the girl whose motives you need to suspect. You said you wouldn't lie to me, and I believed you, so I'll extend you the same courtesy." She inhaled, her lower lip trembling. "When you say something thoughtless, my feelings are going to get hurt. That child is the sweetest little boy I've ever met. He won't be a *bother*. He won't be a *burden*. I don't know how much interaction you'd like me to have with him, but I would very much like to become his friend, and for you to insinuate that I'm that heartless that I'd be *put out* by living in the same house as him, well . . ." She sniffled and looked away. Her voice got high. "That really makes me want to smack you again."

With my slow exhalation, my final, futile shreds of resistance slipped away. My lips said, "I'm an idiot. Please forgive me."

But my heart said, *I'm yours.*

TWENTY-FOUR

BIANCA

I chose a corner bedroom that had windows on two walls and a built-in bookcase on a third that reached all the way to the vaulted ceiling. The room was about the same size as my entire house.

"If you need to change the temperature, close the drapes, or turn the lights on and off, everything is operated from this screen." Jackson made spokesmodel hands at a square touch screen on the wall by the door. "And if you're not near the door, you can just speak your command aloud and Alexa will execute it."

"Who's Alexa?" I asked, worried someone was about to burst out from under the bed.

He pointed to a small black cylinder lurking on the bedside table. "It's a voice assistant. It can also read your audiobooks, check the weather, and let you buy things online just by using your voice. The whole house is wired."

Rayford wasn't kidding about Jackson's technology obsession. I looked at the black cylinder with trepidation. "Will it watch me sleep?"

Jackson chuckled. "No. But there is a video option on the touch pad so you can FaceTime with anyone in any room in the house."

When I looked alarmed, he chuckled again. "You have to accept the incoming call before the video feed activates. No spying."

I smiled and said, "Of course not," but the first thing I was going to do was tack up a piece of black cloth over that contraption. And Alexa was getting unplugged.

Jackson looked around the room. It was large and beautifully furnished, done in shades of cream and celadon with an elaborate four-poster bed that would have looked at home in Buckingham Palace. He frowned at the bed.

"We can change out any of this stuff you don't like," he began, but stopped when I laughed.

"What?"

"Everything's perfect," I said. "This makes the bedroom at my house look like a homeless shelter. I love it."

I'd never spent time or money decorating my house because I had so little of either. I was always working, at Mama's, or asleep. In comparison, this was the Taj Mahal.

Maybe living here for a few years wasn't going to be *all* bad.

"Good," said Jackson, obviously pleased but acting businesslike and nonchalant. I tried not to notice how adorable that was.

"I do have a lot of books, though," I warned, looking pointedly at the bookshelves, which were only half-full.

"Bring them. I want you to be comfortable here. Bring anything that makes you feel at home."

He smiled at me. A flutter started deep in my stomach. I looked away. "So. What's next?"

He moved across the room, headed for the soaring windows, his hands shoved into the front pockets of his jeans. Gazing out into the bright morning sky, he said, "Packing. Moving in. Kentucky." He turned his head and looked at me, his face now serious. "We fly out tomorrow."

The flutter in my stomach turned into a sick feeling, like I was being marched to the gallows. "Oh. But I don't have a ticket yet—"

"My father's sending his private jet."

His private jet. Of course. I blew out a nervous little breath, trying to quell the hysterical laugh lurking behind my teeth. "I see. What time are we leaving?"

"Five o'clock."

Exactly when I would normally be getting ready for the first guests to arrive at the restaurant. My heart did a dying-fish flop under my sternum. "When will we get back?"

"Sunday night."

"Okay," I squeaked, praying to God that Eeny and Pepper could manage for three days without me.

Jackson said, "I've hired a home health-care firm for your mother. They're going to send someone to her house tomorrow to help out while you're gone for the weekend. If you like the girl, you can keep her on indefinitely, but you can also interview other candidates next week . . ."

He stopped when he saw my expression. "Was that wrong?"

I sank into the nearest chair, overwhelmed. "No. That's wonderful. Thank you. I asked Eeny if she could check in on Mama while I was gone, but this is . . . better." I cleared my throat, determined to get a grip on myself. Today was turning out to be a strangely emotional one for me.

Jackson said quietly, "Would you like a moment to yourself?"

I passed a hand over my face. Then I looked up at him and forced a smile. "No. I've brought the contract. I suppose we should sign it now. And a bourbon wouldn't go unappreciated."

Jackson looked concerned. "It's not even noon."

"It's five o'clock somewhere. And you know how I love your family's bourbon."

Jackson crossed to me and held out his hand. "Since you're marrying into the family," he murmured, gazing down at me with burning eyes, "bourbon it is."

We signed our marriage contract over snifters of Boudreaux Black Label at the formal dining room table. Rayford witnessed and then beat a hasty retreat. Then we put aside the fountain pens and raised our glasses in a toast.

"To five years of wedded bliss," said Jackson solemnly.

"To not killing each other in our sleep," I said, and guzzled the bourbon.

When I finished, Jackson was staring at me with a cocked eyebrow and a sour twist to his lips. "You're a true romantic, you know that?"

"To the marrow of my bones. What kind of clothes should I bring for this weekend?"

Jackson smirked. "Ones that cover your lady bits?"

"Ha. I need to know if I'm expected to go horseback riding or ballroom dancing or whatever it is rich people do on weekends."

His brow crept up another inch. "I see. And you have jodhpurs and ball gowns in your wardrobe?"

I said airily, "Oh, tons. Doesn't every girl?"

I was amusing him. He pressed the smile from his lips and swallowed his bourbon. "Naturally. But don't worry about what clothes to bring. I'm taking care of it. Just pack a small bag with your toiletries and underwear."

I stared at him with a furrow forming between my brows. "I have no idea what that means, but it sounds vaguely worrisome."

He leaned back in his chair, crossed his legs, swirled his bourbon around in his glass, and leveled me with a smoldering stare that probably ignited the silk flower arrangement on the credenza behind me. He drawled, "Don't trust me, hmm?"

This felt like dangerous territory. But the contract was already signed, so of course I jumped right in.

"Well, you do have a reputation." I matched his droll tone and leaned back in my chair as he had. I crossed my legs so our positions were mirrored. I wanted to swirl my bourbon, too, but I'd look ridiculous swirling an empty glass, so I left it on the table.

He stared at me for a long time, studying my face, his expression growing darker by the moment. "Yes," he said softly. "I certainly do."

I grew uncomfortable under the dark intensity of his gaze. "Why do I get the impression I just stuck my foot in my mouth?"

He inhaled, restlessly tapped his finger on the side of the snifter, then smiled. It looked like an animal baring its teeth. He said, "If you think my reputation is bad here, Bianca, wait until we get to Kentucky. Then maybe you'll understand why I never wanted to go back."

He stood abruptly, ran a hand through his hair, went to the doorway, and hollered down the hall for Rayford. When he appeared, Jackson growled, "Take Bianca home. I have some things I need to take care of."

He stalked off and disappeared without saying good-bye.

Rayford and I looked at each other. I said, "Just give it to me straight. It's schizophrenia, isn't it? I've agreed to marry a schizophrenic."

"At least you won't be bored," answered Rayford with a shrug. "Crazy people are awful fun."

Awful being the operative word, I thought, reaching for the decanter of bourbon Jackson had left in the middle of the table.

I went to the restaurant and worked that night, though I remembered little of it afterward. I came home to cardboard boxes huddled on my back porch like burglars waiting to break in. With the boxes was a note.

Bring what you need, the rest goes into storage. Moving van coming at two p.m. tomorrow. Be ready to leave right after.

It wasn't signed, but it didn't need to be. I'd recognize that bossy tone anywhere, even on a piece of paper.

The amount of time it took me to pack my few belongings was pathetic. My books took up the most room by far. They were the only thing I collected. No porcelain figurines or needlepoint pillows for me. When I was finished packing I stood in the middle of my living room and looked around.

The squishy brown sofa I bought six years ago from Goodwill. The mirror with the crack in the upper right corner I found next to a dumpster in the alley behind the restaurant. The pair of mismatched guest chairs and the coffee table covered in mysterious stains had been left behind by the previous tenant. Except for pictures of my parents, my clothes, and my books, there was very little of me in this small house.

Which made my melancholy even more stark.

I'd been *happy* here.

With these simple, worn things and my books to keep me company, I'd enjoyed a good life. I'd wanted for nothing, except maybe someone to love. But tomorrow I'd move into an echoing mansion with a strange, lonely man who scowled more than he smiled, then fly to meet his spectacularly wealthy parents who had the power to undo this bargain we'd made with a flick of one of their pampered wrists.

By some miracle, I slept like the dead. I woke at the crack of dawn with the sense that a guillotine blade was poised over my outstretched neck. I showered and dressed, careful to tame my hair and apply makeup, ate a light breakfast, washed the plate and utensils and put them away. Then I made one last, slow trip around the house, poking through drawers and closets, thankful I'd long ago tossed all the sex toys Trace had bought me so I wouldn't have to put them out with the trash.

The movers came. It took four men less than an hour to clear everything out.

At three o'clock, the sleek black sedan with the obnoxious hood ornament pulled up in front of the curb. Rayford got out, smiling his carefree smile. "Miss Bianca," he said, loping up my front steps. He picked up my small suitcase. "You ready to visit Kentucky?"

I smiled so hard my cheeks hurt. "Ready as I'll ever be!"

He sent me a sympathetic look, opened the back door for me and helped me get settled, then went to the trunk to put my bag in.

Jackson was sitting on the seat beside me, wearing jeans and his old, scabby leather jacket, the one he'd been wearing the night we met. His greeting was curt. "We have to stop by my attorney's office on the way to the airport."

"Good morning to you, too."

He blew out a hard breath through his nose. The entire car vibrated with his tension. I didn't dare say anything else.

In a few minutes we arrived at a nondescript office building. When we went inside, a tall man in a suit was waiting for us with a folder of documents.

"Mr. Boudreaux," he said, enthusiastically pumping Jackson's hand and bowing so low he almost bent in half.

The man—whom Jackson did not introduce—showed us into an opulent office. We all sat around his desk. He opened the folder, flipped through a few pages of the stapled documents, turned the pages around to me, and pointed to a line at the bottom.

"Sign here, please."

From the top drawer of his desk he produced a stamp and a ledger book.

"What's this?" I asked Jackson, perplexed.

"The trust has to be notarized," he answered, as if it were obvious.

"Oh." I flipped to the front of the document and scanned the pages until I found the words *one million dollars*. Satisfied, I signed my name with a flourish on the line where the man in the blue suit had indicated. Then he presented me with his ledger book, which I also had to sign and affix my thumbprint to with ink that wiped off my skin without a trace.

Blue Suit Man stamped underneath where I had signed, closed his ledger, and put the stamp and ledger back in the desk drawer. He slid the documents into the folder.

Then he said something about a tax ID number and a certified copy for the bank and my attorney, and we were done.

Jackson ushered me out to the car with his hand under my elbow like he was leading an invalid. Once we were settled back in our seats, he seemed a bit less tense and even offered me a small smile.

He said, "You look beautiful."

I said, "I'm terrified."

"Of what?"

"What if your parents hate me?"

"Don't worry about it."

"Of course I'm worried about it!"

He ground his molars together. "No matter what happens, you're going to be fine," he said ominously, then closed his eyes and went to sleep.

He spent the rest of the ride to the airport sleeping, while I stared at his profile and wondered how many more layers I'd have to peel back before I uncovered the true heart of the walking contradiction that was Jackson Walker Boudreaux.

TWENTY-FIVE

BIANCA

At the airport we drove directly out to the jet waiting on the tarmac. While Rayford unloaded the luggage, we went through "security," which consisted of a cheerful woman in a sweater vest and a badge glancing at our IDs. We were seated on the plane in less time than it usually takes to find parking for a commercial flight.

This being rich business was certainly convenient.

Stroking my hands along the arms of my luxurious bisque-colored chair, I said to Jackson, "Is this leather made from a special kind of cow who got daily massages and deep conditioning for his coat and ate a diet of macrobiotic lettuces while being read poetry by beautiful young women?"

Sitting across from me in his own buttery soft chair, Jackson said, "I don't know, but I'd like to be that cow."

"Me, too. I've never felt leather like this."

"Wait until you go to the bathroom."

I grimaced. "Is the toilet seat leather? That sounds unhygienic."

"No, the toilet seat is *heated*. It can also be cooled, if you prefer your ass chilled while you take care of business. Then afterward, you have your choice of oscillating or pulsing spray wash, followed by a lovely air dry. It's very civilized."

I had other words for getting your butt treated like it was enjoying a spa day, but declined to share. "So how long is this flight, anyway?"

"Hour and forty-five, give or take."

"And are you going to spend it pretend sleeping, or are we going to talk?"

One corner of Jackson's mouth turned up. He hadn't shaved today, and the dark shadow on his jaw was masculine and appealing. The scruff also served to partially hide his scars. I wondered if that was its purpose.

"Are you going to be like this after we're married?"

"Like what?" I asked, the picture of innocence. "Charming and sociable? No, you're right, I should be surly and taciturn; it makes everything so much more fun."

He was trying to scowl at me and doing a poor job of it.

I sent him a coy smile, complete with batted lashes. He rolled his eyes and looked out the window.

I decided to take a different tack. "You're more prickly than a porcupine who wandered into barbed wire. Want to talk about it? Get it off your chest before you see mumsy and daddy?"

"No," he snapped.

As if that wasn't predictable.

I pouted and kicked off my heels. I'd worn a dress, one of the few I owned, and fiddled with the little gold buttons on the bodice, hoping they didn't look cheap.

"I already told you you look beautiful," said Jackson, still staring out the window. "Stop fussing."

I liked him telling me I looked beautiful. Every time he said it, I felt like a cat stroked down its back.

"Yes, but do I look *wifely*?" I was still worried about making a good impression on his parents. I wasn't thinking of me. I was thinking of him, and how he'd die of exposure from the elements within a week if he became homeless and had to live under a bridge.

Jackson sent me a searing sideways glance. His voice came out rough. "I told you not to worry."

I sighed. "Yes, you did. *So* helpful, by the way. So informative. Really settles my nerves." I sent him a pointed look.

"All right, Bianca, since you asked—no, you don't look wifely."

I stared at him, strangely hurt.

His voice softer, he said, "I've never seen anyone's wife who looks as good as you do. You're a fucking wet dream. Now stop fishing for compliments and buckle your lap belt, we're about to take off."

My heart was about to take off, too, blasting right out of my chest like a rocket. *You're a fucking wet dream.*

Dear Lord, I might have to take that pulsing spray-wash toilet for a spin.

Hyperventilating, I fumbled with the lap belt for far longer than it should have taken, until my fingers regained the ability to complete simple tasks and the buckle snapped into place. Then I sat back and expended a lot of energy trying to appear like a normal human being and not the mental patient bouncing off padded walls that I felt like.

A stewardess appeared from the front of the cabin. She looked like one of the girls who recited poetry to the cow my chair was made of. I'd never seen someone that pretty up close. She leaned over Jackson's chair, exposing acres of creamy cleavage.

"May I get you something to eat or drink, sir?"

Her husky voice indicated she was on the menu, too.

Without even looking in her direction, Jackson flicked his fingers dismissively at her. I wanted to punch the air and do a touchdown dance. Instead I smiled graciously when she turned to me, because it wasn't polite to gloat.

"Something for you, miss?"

"Water, please," I said.

She floated away, hips swaying, Miss Disney Princess circa 1952. I sighed, watching her and her eighteen-inch waist go.

"What was that wistful sigh for?" asked Jackson, glancing at the retreating stewardess.

I waved a hand in the air to dismiss the subject, but he said, "Nice try. Answer the question."

"Why do I have to answer questions, and you don't?"

He just stared at me, waiting.

"Ugh. Fine. I was just thinking that woman looks exactly how I've always wanted to look."

Jackson's brows pulled together. "What?"

"You know. All-American Malibu Barbie. Big boobs, blonde hair, lots of shiny teeth."

He looked at me like I was insane. "Why the fuck would you want to look like that when you look like this?" He waved an angry hand up and down, indicating my figure.

After a long time, I said, "Are you deliberately trying to butter me up so I'll feel more confident about meeting your parents?"

He looked at the ceiling, his jaw clenched, like he was asking for divine intervention in dealing with me. "No, Bianca. I am *not*. Trying. To butter you. Up."

So creamy, leggy blondes weren't his thing. Interesting.

"Well," I said, flustered. "Thank you. You're not half bad yourself."

I knew as soon as I uttered those words I was in for it. He leaned forward like a predator leaning over a fresh kill.

"Oh?"

"Yes," I said, aiming for disinterested cool. I lifted my hand and inspected my manicure. "I was just thinking the other day that you aren't entirely unfortunate looking."

Jackson opened his mouth to say something, but Malibu Barbie was back with my water.

"Here you are, miss." Her smile almost blinded me.

"Thank you."

The stewardess retreated with a lingering glance sent Jackson's way. That apparently reminded him of something, because he didn't press me for more details about our interrupted conversation and instead started patting his jacket.

I uncapped the plastic bottle of water and took a big swig.

"Before I forget," he said, "I have something for you." He pulled a black velvet ring box from his pocket and set it on my knee.

I spit out the water in my mouth in a spray that went halfway down the aisle. I started to cough, my eyes watering.

He said drily, "Remind me in the future that you don't react well to surprises."

I fanned a hand in front of my face, trying to catch my breath. "What's *this*?" I wheezed.

His expression was cloaked, revealing nothing. "Did you think I'd let my fiancée walk around without an engagement ring?"

I stared at the box like it was filled with anthrax or might burst into flames. "But . . . you . . . we . . ."

"Just open the damn box, Bianca."

Moving at the speed of a herd of turtles, I capped the water bottle and set it in the recessed cubby in the wall beside my seat. Then I picked up the box—holding it gingerly with both pinkies out—and opened it.

And immediately had a massive heart attack.

Through my choked gasps and garbled attempts at language, Jackson said calmly, "And I'm quoting, 'A five-carat flawless Tiffany brilliant-cut center stone with a pair of flawless one-carat stones flanking it, set in a platinum band.' No woman is that specific about the ring she wants unless she's spent a lot of time researching it."

I made a sound that was like, *"Grglefarbluhh."*

When it became apparent to him that I was in no state to govern my own bodily functions, he leaned over, took the box from my hands, removed the ring, and slipped it on my left ring finger, where it sparkled with the brilliance of a thousand suns.

Smiling, he snapped the ring box shut and leaned back in his chair.

The captain came over the intercom and advised us we'd be taking off shortly. I hoped they had a stretcher on board, because they'd need it to get me off this plane when we landed.

"Jax," I breathed. "Holy shit."

He threw his head back and laughed, deep, loud belly laughs that shook his chair and echoed through the cabin. "God, that right there made it worth the price! I made you curse!"

"Please don't talk to me about price." I groaned, still holding my hand out at arm's length and staring at the huge, glittering bauble. "Sweet baby Jesus. I'll get mugged wearing this thing. Some robber will cut off my hand with a machete. I can't cook without my left hand, Jax!"

"Ha ha ha!" he boomed, thoroughly enjoying my distress.

"Oh, I see," I said sourly. "Now I've discovered the secret. The way to make you happy is to freak out and swear like a sailor."

He stopped laughing and grinned at me. He was breathtakingly handsome when he smiled. How had I not noticed that before?

"You make me happy all the time," he blurted, then froze, a look of horror replacing his grin.

I think that was too much honesty for both of us, because I froze, too.

I made him happy? How was that possible? He spent most of the time we were together glaring at me and snapping like a crocodile. Except when we kissed. He definitely looked happy then.

Or something.

To cover for both our palpable discomfort, I said lightly, "That's because I'm so charming and sociable." I made a queenly hand wave like I was passing by in a royal carriage, greeting my subjects. "And have such good taste in jewelry."

He relaxed, though his grin was gone for good. He cleared his throat. "Obviously," he growled, and stared out the window, his arms folded over his chest.

The Beast was back. This man was going to give me whiplash.

The plane began to taxi away from the hangar and down the runway. We lapsed into silence as we prepared for takeoff, avoiding each other's eyes. By the time we were in the air, I'd managed to gain the upper hand over my pounding heart and fluttering nerves. I took a book from my handbag and settled in to read, knowing Jackson wouldn't soon be in the mood to talk.

The ring was heavy and cool on my finger, snickering at me that I was an impostor.

"Shakespeare?" murmured Jackson.

I glanced up. He was eyeing the title of the book in my hands. I said, "*Much Ado About Nothing.* Someone recently recommended it to me."

His blue eyes held mine in a grip that felt inescapable. Finally he released me, directing his gaze back out the window to watch the earth recede.

We spent the rest of the flight in silence. Because I was attuned to his moods now, I felt the tension grow in his body with each mile we flew nearer to Kentucky. By the time we began our descent, he was so taut I thought he might snap.

A limousine awaited us at the airport. A uniformed driver with a face like a slab of granite took our bags. It was close to sunset, the sky a spectacular orange and purple-blue. From the airport it was a short drive through the bustling city of Louisville to the countryside, where the houses kept getting larger and farther and farther apart. Finally we pulled up in front of a majestic stone gate, and the driver punched a code into a small silver box mounted on a pole beside the driveway.

Beside me, Jackson said, "Breathe, Bianca."

I hadn't even realized I'd been holding my breath. I released it in one big rush, smoothing my hands over my hair.

We pulled past the stone gate and started down a long, winding lane, shaded on both sides by enormous oak trees. Around a bend I spotted the house in the distance. It was beautiful, but nowhere near as large as I'd expected—maybe half the size of Jackson's home.

Jackson must have been watching my face. He said, "It's the guest house."

"Oh." Okay, that made sense. They were rich, of course they had a guest house.

He added, "There are seventeen on the property."

My mouth dropped open. I stared at him in disbelief. "*Seventeen* guest houses. Like *that?*"

"No. That's the small one."

When I made an inarticulate noise of shock, he smiled, only it was a dark smile, totally devoid of humor.

He said, "The estate comprises two hundred sixty acres, five lakes, seventeen guest cottages, botanical gardens, a deer park, a stable yard and coach house, and its own church. The main residence has thirty-seven bedrooms—by some counts it's thirty-nine, no one's really sure—thirty-two bathrooms, an entire wing dedicated to servants' quarters, a bowling alley, basketball and tennis courts, a fifty-seat theatre, a replica of an English pub, a thirty-thousand-bottle wine cellar, and a full arcade. And a bunch of other shit I'm forgetting."

We sped past more guest "cottages," set far back from the road on either side, partly hidden behind stands of trees and lush gardens. Then we crested a low hill, and the main estate came into view.

I gasped.

Jackson muttered, "Welcome to Moonstar Ranch."

Then he leaned over, put his head in his hands, and cursed.

TWENTY-SIX

BIANCA

Picture a castle—the biggest and most elaborate castle you've seen in a movie. But not a forbidding, fortress-type castle with dungeons and moats and weird smells. Something elegant and romantic. Something with crenellated towers and cascading fountains and flocks of doves soaring through misty vales. Or any castle from any fairy tale where a princess waits for Prince Charming to ride up on his trusty white steed.

Then triple the size, add in a herd of white-tailed deer prancing across a lush wilderness backdrop, a glittering lake filled with colored fountains and peacefully drifting swans, and an enormous orange moon cresting over the horizon in the distance, bathing everything in a warm amber glow, and you'll have a small glimpse of the magic, majesty, and soul-piercing beauty of the place called Moonstar Ranch.

I exhaled an awed breath that contained a lot of vowels. Then, panicked, I gripped Jackson's arm.

"Okay," I said, sounding slightly hysterical. "I've respected your privacy. I haven't pried into what happened that made you leave this place and never come back, but now you have to give me something. You can't let me walk in there blind. Just give it to me straight—murder?

Kidnapping? Sexual abuse? I swear I won't judge or repeat a word to another living soul. Just tell me why you would ever want to leave somewhere so beautiful. And also why it's called a ranch because *that* is like its own European country."

Jackson lifted his head and looked at me. He said cryptically, "Even the most beautiful things can be toxic."

I blinked. "That isn't helpful. At all."

He blew out a hard breath and leaned back into the seat. "You'll be happy to know that it's nothing as dramatic as what your imagination is conjuring. You ever think about giving up the chef gig and writing fiction?"

That made me feel a little better, though I still had nothing solid. I needed more. "So no sexual abuse? No bodies buried in the garden?"

He groaned. "For Christ's sake, Bianca!"

"What am I supposed to think?"

"Really? In a void of details, you go straight to murder and getting diddled by Daddy?"

"Well it had to be *something* major!"

He glowered at me. "It was. And *no*, it didn't involve murder, kidnapping, or inappropriate fondling on the part of my parents."

When I narrowed my eyes, he thundered, "Or anyone else, either!"

We glared at each other. Finally I thought of something. "Does it have to do with the man-eating shark?"

When he blanched, I thought, *Bingo*.

The limousine passed through a brick carriage house, then pulled to a smooth stop at the crest of a circular drive. Through gritted teeth, Jackson said, "Enough questions. Let's just get through this weekend, all right?"

He didn't wait for the limo driver to open his door. He burst from the car, rounded the rear, and yanked open my door. He stuck out his hand and impatiently wiggled his fingers.

So conversation time was over. Now it was face the music time. Meet the parents time. Try to act sweet and charming so the scary rich people don't hate me and set the dogs on me time.

I cursed myself for not slipping a hip flask into my handbag.

Jackson unloaded me from the car like a piece of luggage. When I was steady on my feet, I looked up into his grim face and poked him in the chest, which nearly broke my finger. Maybe he was wearing a bulletproof vest.

"Hey. Boudreaux. Down here."

His lips pressed to a thin, pale line, he looked down at me.

I said firmly, "I'm your friend. Don't forget that. No matter what you're dragging me into here, what psychotic ex-girlfriends or crazy relatives or dead bodies rotting under the rosebushes that you're not admitting to, I'm on your side. Got it?"

He swallowed. His eyes went all melty. He tried to cover up his emotion by scowling and looking away, but it was too late.

Mama was right about him. The man was crème brûlée. Tough on the outside, but on the inside all soft and gooey sweet. It made me feel good to know that secret, and also surprisingly protective.

These rich SOBs better watch out, because if one of them even looked at Jackson sideways, I'd go full Rambo mode and shoot their heads clean off. Only with my mouth.

"All right, then," I murmured, taking his arm. "Now pretend like you're madly in love with me and introduce me to your parents."

The inside of the house—and I'm using that word loosely—was exactly what you'd expect a castle would be. Hanging tapestries, oil paintings of grim-faced ancestors, lots of elaborate stonework and beveled windows. The herringbone inlaid wood floor was polished to a mirror sheen. Bouquets of flowers were arranged in delicate Chinese porcelain vases that were probably three thousand years old. The ceilings were cathedral. There was an overabundance of carved mahogany paneling on the walls, and I'd never seen so many branched candelabra outside of church. The entire effect was one of stately, distinguished elegance.

I said, "What a dump."

Standing beside me in the octagonal-shaped foyer, Jackson snorted. I took it as a win.

The limo driver followed us in with the luggage. "To your rooms, sir?" he said.

Jackson nodded, and the driver disappeared down a corridor to our right.

"You know that guy?" I asked, surprised.

"He's been on staff since I was . . . ten, I think. Charles."

"I thought he was a driver from a service. The two of you acted like you'd never met before!"

Jackson looked around with his mouth pinched. "Did you expect he'd throw his arms around me and give me a big hug?"

"But there wasn't even a 'nice to see you.' There wasn't even a hint he recognized you at all."

Jackson jabbed both hands through his hair and said roughly, "Rayford was the only one who ever liked me."

Oh boy. Minefield. I had a bad feeling the entire weekend would be filled with them. I quickly changed the subject. "So where's the lineup of servants?"

Jackson sent me a strange look.

"Just kidding. But . . ." I gazed around the empty room. "Um. Shouldn't there be someone here to meet us?"

At that moment, a sharp bark echoed off the walls. I turned to my left and froze in horror. Two enormous, muscular black dogs stood in the passageway, stock-still, staring at us.

My horror turned to relief when Jackson sank to his knees and opened his arms. "Zeus! Apollo! Come here, boys!"

The dogs leapt forward and crashed into Jackson's arms, a whirlwind of barking, licking, tail-wagging joy.

I took a step back, not completely convinced they wouldn't turn and rip me to shreds. They were bigger than a pair of wolves and had an equally formidable appearance.

"Don't worry, Bianca," said Jackson, roughhousing with the dogs, "wolfhounds aren't usually aggressive to strangers."

"*Usually* doesn't give me the greatest feeling of confidence, Jax."

"They're sweethearts." He stood. The top of the dogs' heads came up to his waist, which almost put them at eye level with me. He said, "Hold out your hand and let them sniff you."

Or eat me, I thought, but decided this was my first test at Moonstar Ranch, and I wasn't going to fail it. I gingerly stuck out my hand, then held perfectly still as two enormous heads swung around to inspect it.

"Nice doggies," I whispered, terrified. "Good doggies."

The dogs nosed my hand, then started to happily pant at me. Apparently I'd passed the smell test.

"You're early," said a deep male voice from across the room. Jackson went stiff.

In the arched doorway that led to the great room beyond the foyer stood a man. I'd never seen anyone in real life wearing an ascot with a smoking jacket, but now I had. He was Jackson's twin, except older and grayer, with laugh lines around his blue eyes.

"Father," said Jackson, confirming my guess.

They stared at each other. It wasn't unfriendly—more assessing than anything—but if I hadn't seen my mother in four years, you can bet our reunion would look nothing like this.

The elder Mr. Boudreaux turned his gaze to me. "And you must be Bianca," he said with much more robust enthusiasm than he'd addressed his son. "I've heard so much about you." His gaze flashed to my left hand. A faint smile lifted his lips.

Oh my stars. This was gonna get messy.

I mentally put my big girl panties on and sent my future father-in-law a smile that was so sweet it practically dripped honey. "Mr. Boudreaux. I'm so happy to meet you."

Then, just to shake off the general sense of doom, I went over and gave the man a hug.

Imagine throwing your arms around a marble statue, and you'll get the idea of how my friendly overture was met. Red-faced, I stepped back and tried to ignore the way Jackson's jaw was hanging all the way to the floor.

Mr. Boudreaux was red in the face, too. He said, "Oh. Dear. You'll have to excuse me, Bianca, I don't think I've been hugged by anyone in about fifty years."

But he kind of liked it, I could tell. Encouraged, I smiled at him again. "Sorry to be so forward, but we're big huggers in my family, Mr. Boudreaux. My mama always told me there are few things a good hug can't cure, and those things are what bourbon's for."

Mr. Boudreaux stared at me for a moment, then his face broke into a grin. "Call me Brig, Bianca. If you're gonna be family, we should be on a first-name basis, don't you think?"

Jackson made a soft choking noise that sounded like maybe he was going to faint.

And we're off to a rip-roaring start.

I said, "Thank you, Brig. That's awfully nice of you."

Brig looked back at his son. His grin faltered. "Well. You must be tired after your journey. I'll let you freshen up before dinner. It's at eight." With a nod in my direction, he turned and left. The dogs followed at his heels.

When he was gone, my relief was overwhelming. I said, "Whew! I think that went pretty well, don't you?" I turned to find Jackson staring at me like I was a stranger. "What?" I said, instantly worried I'd made some terrible gaffe.

But he only shook his head in wonder. "You *hugged* my *father*," he said softly, his eyes shining. "I can't decide if you're a genius or totally insane."

I beamed at him. "That's easy. I'm a genius."

"Yes," he murmured, "I'm beginning to think so."

Then, still shaking his head, he took my arm and led me away.

There wasn't enough time for a tour of the "house" before dinner, so we went straight up to Jackson's room via one of the elevators he informed me were scattered all over the place like gopher holes. Once inside the door, I stopped dead.

"I can see why you'd hate it so much here," I said, gazing around. "This is really beyond the limits of human tolerance."

More oil paintings, more soaring ceilings, more priceless antiques. But the thing that truly made this room so beautiful was the massive wall of windows that gave way to the view of the gardens and lake, and woodlands beyond. A fire crackled in the huge stone hearth on one end of the room. On the other end a door stood slightly open, giving a peek of what looked to be an Olympic-size bathtub in the en suite bathroom.

Jackson went straight to the enormous bed centered under the windows and flopped facedown onto the silk duvet cover, where he remained unmoving.

Which is when I realized we'd never had a talk about the sleeping arrangements for this weekend.

Big sofa over there, I thought, eyeing a tufted, peacock-blue couch in the corner, opposite a pair of straight-backed chairs. *Or whatever that thing is*, I thought, catching sight of a long piece of furniture against the wall. It had no back, only cigar-shaped pillows at each end, but was obviously designed for seating. A divan or some such that garnished wealthy people's homes. The pillows looked wicked uncomfortable, but Jackson would probably let me steal one from the bed—

"You're thinking again." Jackson's voice was muffled in the comforter. He raised his head and glared at me. "Stop it."

"Is this . . . are we . . ."

His glare intensified.

I sighed and spit it out. "Where will I be sleeping?"

Jackson rolled onto his back and put his hands under his head. That made his T-shirt ride up his abdomen a few inches, exposing a hard expanse of golden skin and a fine trail of dark hair that disappeared under the waistband of his jeans.

I hoped my gulp wasn't audible.

"Here," he said, looking at me with half-lidded eyes.

"You mean . . . on that bed?"

He nodded.

My pulse ticked up a notch. "As in . . . with you?"

When a corner of his mouth quirked, I blew out an irritated breath. He'd been baiting me.

"I'll take the sofa, you can have the bed," he said, muted laughter in his voice.

I tossed my handbag onto a chair by the door and wandered into the room. Ignoring him, I roamed around for a few minutes, touching things, being nosy. I poked my head into the bathroom and wondered how many people would fit into the tub. At least ten was my guess.

I knew he was watching me the way I always knew he was watching me, by the sense of having two hot irons poking into my back.

Finally, when I was done with my inspection, I turned to him and demanded, "Tell me about your mother."

He closed his eyes. "Christ, you're like a honey badger," he muttered.

I crossed my arms over my chest. "I don't know what that is, but it sounds extremely cute, so thank you."

His sigh was a tremendous gust of air. "It's like a large, ferocious weasel with impenetrable skin."

That was so ridiculous I wasn't even insulted. "Just give me a little something to prepare for. I assume I'll meet her at dinner?"

A long silence followed. Then a curt, "Yes. Unless she decides not to come down."

That sounded bad. "Are you on speaking terms with her?"

His jaw worked. He was silent for a long time before saying, "I haven't spoken to her since I left."

Well pick my peas. Dinner should be delightful.

I sat gingerly on the edge of the bed and looked down at him. He stubbornly refused to open his eyes, so I allowed my attention to wander to that exposed strip of skin above his waistband. My finger itched to reach out and lightly stroke that pretty trail of hair. It looked so soft and fine, like down. So inviting.

I bit my lip.

Jackson said softly, "What are you looking at, Bianca?"

My gaze flashed up to his. He was staring at me with so much heat in his eyes I was momentarily speechless. I ripped my gaze away and stared down at the ring on my hand, letting it blind me. "Nothing."

"Then why is your face the color of that chair in the corner?"

The scarlet chair, he meant. I closed my eyes. "Now who's the honey badger?" I muttered.

After a long, tense moment of silence, Jackson slowly reached out and took my hand. He gently placed it on his stomach, then flattened his hand over it so my palm rested against his warm, bare skin.

His voice a low, sandpaper rasp, he said, "Were you looking at this?"

I said, "Don't be silly," but we both knew I was lying.

He grasped my forefinger, touched the tip of it to the fine down of hair beneath his belly button, and whispered, "This?" Using my finger like a paintbrush, he traced it slowly downward until it hit the top button of his jeans.

A violent tremor rocked me, but I didn't open my eyes.

I didn't move my hand, either.

Jackson lay very still beside me, except for his breathing, which was rough. Radiating heat, his stomach rose and fell under my hand. My heart was like a pealing bell.

He whispered my name. It was so sweet on his lips, such a tender sound. I made a noise deep in my throat, a retort or a plea, I didn't know which. Big and slightly trembling, Jackson's other hand stroked up the inside of my wrist.

A loud throat clearing from the doorway, and I jumped from the bed like my butt had pneumatic springs.

"Excuse me, sir," said a uniformed male servant with a bland face and droopy hound dog eyes. He bowed. "Madam. Do you need anything before supper?"

Jackson sat up, rubbed his forehead, and growled, "No. And in the future your presence isn't required unless I ring for you."

The servant bowed again. "Very good, sir." He disappeared as quickly as he arrived, leaving Jackson and me alone in excruciating silence.

I said, "I'll just be hiding in the bathroom until dinner if you need me," and bolted, slamming the door shut behind me. I collapsed against it, fighting for air, wondering how far that little dalliance on the bed would have gone if we hadn't been interrupted.

Wondering how far I *wanted* it to go.

From behind the closed door, there might have been a muffled groan.

TWENTY-SEVEN

JACKSON

My cock had its own heartbeat. All the blood in my body had pooled in my groin. One lingering look from Bianca and I was twelve years old again, unable to control the sudden shocking flare of hormones that ignited a forest fire in my pants and left me speechless and sweating, and feeling guilty to boot.

Judging by her flight of terror into the bathroom, I was pretty sure I'd just made a fatal mistake.

"You fucking moron," I said to the carpet as I leaned over the bed with my head in my hands. "You complete, colossal fuckwit."

I couldn't even console myself with the memory that we'd already shared two kisses before I lost my mind and almost shoved her hand down my pants. Those kisses didn't count. They didn't mean anything, at least to her. The first was simply a ploy to make her ex jealous. The second was simply my infantile ego throwing a fit over being called nonsexual.

Though both kisses were scorching hot—I thought so, anyway—it wasn't like she *wanted* to kiss me in either instance. And now here I was again, mistaking what was probably a look of worry or concentration or something else altogether for a look of lust.

Could I be any more of a cliché? If a woman like Cricket couldn't love me, Bianca Hardwick was the last woman on earth who would.

My brain was scrambled eggs. I wasn't thinking straight. Bianca had told me not fifteen minutes ago that she was my friend. My *friend*. Not the girl who'd think it was a super great idea to play handsy with the aching, throbbing, twitching monster between my legs right before we went down to dinner with my estranged parents.

This was a disaster.

The water went on behind the bathroom door, followed by some faint gasping noises. That was probably Bianca puking into the sink. I had to make this right. I had to apologize.

I lumbered to my feet and went to the bathroom door. I rested my forehead against it and closed my eyes. When the sound of running water stopped, I said, "If you want to hit me with something, there's a very heavy bronze reproduction of the obelisk in Saint Peter's Square on the credenza. I can bring it to you. It has a conveniently pointy tip."

Her response was muffled by the door. "I don't want to hit you."

I didn't dare hope that meant anything other than she'd rather shoot me than clobber me over the head. I waited, my hands pressed flat against the wood, my heart pounding.

She moved closer to her side of the door, because her voice was clearer when she said, "Maybe we could just . . . forget that happened."

I was swamped by relief. Until she added softly, "For now."

I bolted upright and stared at the door. For now? *For now?* What the hell did that mean? Was she going to wait until after dinner to yell at me, or . . .

Or what?

Holy fuck. I was having a heart attack. No, I was letting my imagination run away with me again.

No. I was having a heart attack.

The doorknob turned. She cracked open the door and peeked out at me through a two-inch sliver. Only the left side of her face was visible, and all of it was flushed.

"You mentioned something about clothes," she said.

I nodded.

"Is the dress I'm wearing appropriate for dinner?"

"Yes. But there are things in the closet you can look through if you'd like to wear something else."

Her left eyebrow arched.

I said, "I had a few things brought in for you."

She swung the door open wide. "You shopped for me?"

I couldn't tell from her expression if she was pleased or thought that was creepy, so I just nodded again.

"How did you know my size?"

Now I knew it would be creepy if I said *I've spent a lot of time staring at your body*, so I went with, "I guessed."

Her expression soured. "Please tell me you didn't guess I'm a size two, because if you did, I'll be wearing this dress for the rest of the weekend."

Pressing the smile from my lips, I turned and went to the wardrobe. I opened the doors and stepped aside.

Bianca poked her head out the bathroom door and gazed at the wardrobe. It was a big hunk of carved oak, an antique from Italy, I think, and had enough drawers and hanging space for even the most dedicated clothes horse. Intrigued, she walked over and stopped by my side. She stared into the wardrobe for a while, then looked up at me, her face serious.

"There are a lot of clothes in there, Jax."

"They don't belong to someone else, if that's what you're thinking. I just wanted you to have choices."

She looked back at the wardrobe and kept looking at it without saying anything.

I wasn't sure what this reaction meant, but I was getting a little desperate. "You don't have to wear anything you don't like, of course. But anything you *do* like we'll take home . . . I mean, assuming you want to. Or we can leave it all," I finished lamely, looking at my shoes.

"This is all for me?" she asked.

"Yes," I said gruffly, trying not to vibrate with excitement because if I wasn't reading her tone wrong, she was happy.

Then I tried not to groan out loud because she turned to me, stood on her toes, put her arms around my shoulders, and hugged me.

"Thank you," she murmured against my neck.

Oh God. Sweet holy mother of God. I was going to buy her clothes every single day for the rest of her life. I wound my arms around her waist, pulled her closer against me, and closed my eyes. Breathing in the sweet scent of her skin, I whispered, "You're welcome."

A delicate shudder ran through her chest. I resisted the violent urge to run my hands all over her body, to take big, squeezing handfuls of her glorious ass, and stood there breathing raggedly, knowing nothing else except I wasn't going to be the first one to let go.

After a while, she said, "You're very tall."

I blurted, "I'll buy you platform boots."

Her laugh was muffled in my neck. Her perfume was in my nose. A soft curl of her hair was caught at the corner of my mouth, and I was in heaven.

She lifted her head and looked into my eyes. Could she see the stars there?

She teased, "I see *someone* in the family enjoys hugs."

There was a good possibility she was referring to the ten-inch steel pipe in my pants, but I didn't want to ruin the moment by mentioning it. Instead I said, "Lucky me."

My voice was so rough it sounded like I'd spent the last few days screaming.

She swallowed. Her lashes lowered, and then she was looking at my mouth. Her arms were still tight around my neck. She was so close I could see the pulse throbbing in the hollow of her throat, inviting me to touch it, kiss it, lick it gently with my tongue.

"What are you thinking right now?" she asked softly.

I closed my eyes. "You don't want to know."

"It's that dirty, huh?"

Fuck. Was she flirting with me or joking? I really needed to adjust my crotch but didn't risk moving my arms. I whispered, "Filthy."

Her breathing changed. I turned my head slightly, and the tip of my nose was touching her neck. My lips were so close to her skin, so fucking close . . .

In a voice so faint it was almost inaudible, she said, "Two years."

I was too far under her spell to speak, so I just gave a little shake of my head to indicate I didn't know what she meant.

She tucked her head down closer to my chest, like she was hiding again. "You asked me how long it had been since the last time . . . I had sex. The answer is two years."

My exhalation shuddered out of me. I fought with every ounce of self-control I had not to crush my mouth against hers, to stand motionless while the heat and tension built between us, while her heart pounded so jaggedly against my chest.

I wasn't going to make the same mistake again. I wasn't going to push myself on her. If—*if*—she wanted me, I had to let her come to that realization herself. Though I ached to throw her on the bed and bury myself in her, I had to let her be in control.

I couldn't live with myself if she ever felt obligated.

"That's nothing," I said, my voice faint. "I've got you beat by a mile."

When her arms loosened, I almost broke and kissed her, but I forced myself to stand still and allow her to pull away. She looked up at me with bright eyes and clasped her hands behind her back.

"Why don't you pick out what *you'd* like me to wear for dinner. Let's see what kind of taste you've got, Boudreaux. I'm going to fix my hair."

She went into the bathroom and gently closed the door behind her, leaving me standing alone, wishing there was something I could do to save myself from falling in love with another woman who would never love me back, but knowing it was already too late.

CREOLE OKRA GUMBO

Makes 6 servings

- 4 tablespoons butter
- kosher salt
- 1 tablespoon cayenne pepper
- 1½ pounds boneless chicken thighs, skin removed, cut into pieces
- 4 ounces tasso ham, cut into 1^2 cubes
- 3 cloves garlic, minced
- 2 teaspoons thyme, minced
- 1 bay leaf
- 1 yellow onion, minced
- 1 red bell pepper, minced
- 1 tablespoon fresh parsley, minced
- 6 large fresh tomatoes, skin, core, and seeds removed
- 2 tablespoons tomato paste
- 6 cups chicken stock
- 1 pound okra, trimmed, sliced ½ inch thick
- 6 cups cooked white rice

Preparation

1.   Melt butter in Dutch oven.

2. Season chicken with salt and cayenne on both sides, cook for 10 minutes or until browned.

3. Add tasso and garlic, cook for 5 minutes.

4. Add thyme, bay leaf, onion, and bell pepper. Cook until browned, 5–10 minutes.

5. Add parsley, tomatoes, and tomato paste. Cook 5 minutes or until softened.

6. Add chicken stock, bring to a boil. Reduce heat to low and simmer until chicken is cooked through and gumbo has thickened, about 1 hour.

7. Melt remaining butter in a nonstick skillet. Cook okra until slightly crisp, 8–10 minutes, then add to gumbo. Cook gumbo additional 15 minutes. Discard bay leaf.

8. Serve over hot white rice.

TWENTY-EIGHT

BIANCA

When I emerged from the bathroom, Jackson was gone. A twinge of disappointment flattened me, but I perked up again when I saw what he'd left.

A gorgeous red dress beckoned from the bed. It was sleeveless, with a belted waist and a flared skirt, the better to conceal my abominable childbearing hips and accentuate my waist. When I ran my fingers over the fabric, it shimmered like silk.

Because it *was* silk. I looked at the tag on the neckline and made a loud, unladylike honking sound. How much had this cost? Probably less than the hunk of ice on my finger, I decided. All in all, getting married was turning out to be quite expensive for my future husband.

Husband. My nerves went all catawampus.

"Keep it together, Bianca," I muttered, scooping up the dress. I headed into the bathroom to change and give myself a pep talk in front of the mirror. When finished with both, I had to admit I was looking rather well.

My eyes sparkled. The dress fit like a dream, and the color flattered my complexion. I was glad I'd worn strappy nude sandals instead of flats, because they were elegant enough to make the whole ensemble sing.

"Hair down."

I jumped. Jackson stood in the open doorway, eating me up with his eyes. He made a gesture to indicate my updo held in place with its usual clip.

"Oh. Um. Okay." I released the clip and shook my hair out. It fell around my shoulders in a swirling cloud.

Jackson looked like he'd been stabbed in the gut.

"Are you wearing that?" I asked, ignoring my thundering heartbeat.

"Yes." He didn't even glance at himself, he just kept staring at me with wild caveman eyes that did all sorts of unusual things to my body.

An idea started to gnaw at my brain, but I pushed it aside to concentrate on the situation at hand.

"Okay, I'm saying this only to be helpful, not judgy, but I think your old leather jacket and jeans might not be the most appropriate thing to wear to dinner with the parents you haven't seen in years. Who live in a castle. And probably dine on solid-gold plates."

When he didn't respond, I added, "Also you clash with my outfit. Which I love, by the way. It's beautiful. So . . ."

His gaze drifted slowly down my body, then back up again—one long, lingering sweep that was unabashedly lustful. I had to put a hand on the counter to steady myself.

He said, "Sure, I'll change."

Without moving from the doorway, he shrugged off the jacket and pulled his T-shirt over his head. Both slithered to the floor in a rustle of fabric and sat there, leaking air.

I sucked in a breath so loud it was almost a snort.

If I thought my silk dress was beautiful, it was a rag in a sewer compared to Jackson's body. The fine trail of down I'd found so bewitching led up from his abdomen to his chest, where it flared out between his nipples, a dusting of dark hair that was both erotic and exquisitely masculine. I was so used to seeing male models in magazines and online who were waxed to a neutered, eye-watering shine that this almost looked pornographic.

Then there were the muscles. Lord, the muscles. He had them in places I didn't know a person could have muscles, all sculpted and stacked and bulging, a pair of them shaped like a V from his hips to his crotch, like a neon sign advertising the way to his baby maker.

And don't get me started on his skin. Men should not be allowed to have skin that *glows*. Skin so golden and perfect it looks sprayed on, like something out of an artist's airbrush.

He was big, he was beautiful, and he was giving me a look like he was about to pull my dress up and bend me over the sink, and it was all too much for my poor little ovaries, who did the sensible thing and fainted.

"So this is what you do with all your free time," I said, my voice a kitchen mouse's squeak. "Work out."

His eyes burning blue fire, Jackson said softly, "Would you like to pick out my clothes for me? Since you're in the mood to be helpful?"

I tried to laugh but ended up sounding like I was attempting to expel a hairball from my throat. So attractive. "I'm sure you can manage." I turned away, not trusting myself to walk past him into the room, and started fussing over my hair like the giant coward that I was.

Our eyes met in the mirror. He didn't smile, but I got the sense he wanted to. I got the sense that he was pleased as punch with himself, so I sent him a frown.

He moved out of view. A moment later he returned holding one of the bags the driver had placed to the side of the wardrobe. He flipped it onto the bed, unzipped it, and rummaged around for a shirt, while I stared helplessly at all those spectacular muscles of his going to work.

Seriously, was it necessary to have so many hard, bulging places on a body?

Yes! roared my ovaries. *Yes, it absolutely is!*

"What was that great big sigh for?" Jackson looked over his shoulder, caught me ogling him, and smirked.

"Just a little gas," I said, and smirked back.

The smug bastard. He knew exactly what was going on. I bet my ovaries were on speed dial to his brain.

Jackson chuckled. He pulled a dark-blue dress shirt from the bag, tossed it over his shoulders, and turned to face me as he slowly buttoned it up, staring at me with bedroom eyes the whole time, like a striptease in reverse.

"Better," I said once the last button had been done. "Now tuck."

"You sound like a wife already," he protested mildly, but did as I said and tucked the ends of his shirt into his jeans. Of course this necessitated an unbuttoning of his fly, which revealed he was wearing white cotton briefs whose front seams were being tested by a muscle of a different kind, which looked huge and ready for business.

I made a peep like a startled baby bird and whipped my head around so fast I nearly broke my own neck. Confronted with my reflection in the mirror, there was no denying the obvious: I was turned on as all get-out. My pupils were huge, my color was high, and my bosom was heaving like a bodice-ripper cover model's.

Dear Lord. I was sexually attracted to my fake fiancé.

"Everything all right in there, Bianca?"

I heard the laughter in his tone and wondered where in the room that heavy bronze obelisk was. I kept my voice even by a miracle of self-control. "Peachy keen."

He rapped on the doorframe. I glanced over to find him leaning against it with one shoulder, his arms crossed over his chest, his shirt buttoned and tucked in, the picture of casual confidence. "Ready?" he said, his voice husky.

"For dinner," I clarified.

"Of course. What else would I be talking about?"

He blinked at me, innocent as a lamb, and I knew I was in serious trouble.

It's only a business deal, I told myself as he held out his hand in invitation. *Only a business deal,* I kept repeating as we walked hand in hand from the room. *Business, business, business.*

My lady bits were chiming in with some ideas of their own that were decidedly unbusinesslike, but after two years of practice it was easy to ignore them.

By the time we entered the dining room, Jackson's mood had gone from light to black as the bottom of the ocean during a hurricane.

The room was dominated by a double-sided fireplace and a chandelier so large it had its own atmosphere. The table looked exactly like what I imagined Count Dracula's dining table would be like. A long, coffin-black slab of wood dotted with silver candelabras, surrounded by black, elaborately carved chairs. Blood-red wine goblets lurked beside bone china place settings rimmed in gold. It was oddly terrifying.

The grandfather clock on the wall gonged solemnly eight times, and the haunted castle vibe was complete.

Maybe growing up here wasn't all sunshine and roses after all.

"Madam," said the droopy-eyed manservant, materializing from nowhere so soundlessly I jumped. At my startled little exclamation, he bowed. "Aperitif?" he inquired with a flourish.

My "Yes!" was so forceful he was taken aback. He blinked at me for a moment, then snapped his gloved fingers. Another servant glided soundlessly forward with a glass of champagne, which is when I realized the room was lined with uniformed servants, standing straight-backed and silent against the walls, gazing with blank expressions into space.

It was the creepiest thing I'd ever seen in my life.

"Sir?" said the head manservant to Jackson, who only scowled at him in response. The manservant bowed away and went to skulk in the corner.

Under my breath I said to Jackson, "What the unholy Christmas miracle is this?"

"My parents like to keep a full staff," he said, looking around in distaste.

I shrank a little closer to him. "I bet they're single-handedly propping up the state's unemployment rate."

"Bianca!"

At the sound of my name booming through the room, I nearly screamed. But it was only Jackson's father, appearing from the adjacent hallway with a big grin and his arms open wide like he was an emcee at a nightclub introducing the next act.

"Oh! Hello, Mr. Boudreaux. I mean Brig."

He stood in front of me and clasped my shoulders. Still grinning, he gave me a friendly little shake. "You look wonderful. Wonderful!"

Okay. This was really starting to get weird. I consoled myself that at least he hadn't set the dogs on me.

As if my thought had summoned them, Zeus and Apollo appeared in the doorway, then flopped on the floor in a mass of black fur, muscular limbs, and lolling tongues, effectively blocking that exit.

"Thank you." I smiled tentatively at Brig. He turned to Jackson, and his smile faltered exactly as it had when we'd first arrived.

"Jackson."

"Brig."

Brig's eyelid twitched at hearing his son using his first name. He struggled for a moment to find a topic of conversation. Jackson watched him do it with a ruthless slant to his lips.

Brig decided on, "Thank you for changing out of that dreadful leather jacket."

Jackson went stiff. "That was Christian's jacket," he snarled.

My ears perked up. Christian? His dead friend Christian? Cody's father Christian? I had a terrible suspicion that jacket might mean a lot more to Jackson than an item of clothing normally would and suffered a bout of guilt that I'd asked him to take it off. I thought of all the times I'd seen him wear it, thinking what a crappy old thing it was, and my heart sank.

"I made him put on a dress shirt for dinner," I said into the thundering silence. "But I think that jacket looks great on him. Not everyone can pull off the vintage look."

Brig stared at me for a hair longer than was comfortable. "Indeed." He cleared his throat.

Oozing fury, Jackson stood beside me, a plank of wood bristling with rusty nails. I squeezed his hand. He squeezed back so hard I thought he'd crush my bones.

"So. Bianca. Jackson tells me you're a chef?"

"That's right. I recently opened my first restaurant in New Orleans."

"How marvelous. I understand your mother was also in the restaurant business?"

I glanced at Jackson, wondering exactly how much he'd told his father about me, and nodded. "She had a spot in the Ninth Ward for about twenty years before Hurricane Katrina wiped it out. She retired after that."

Brig looked distressed. "I'm sorry to hear that. She didn't want to rebuild?"

"We didn't have the money to rebuild."

At the mention of money, Brig's eyes glazed over. "Well. It's wonderful that you're carrying on the family tradition. Your mother must be very proud."

If I thought Jackson was stiff before, now he became an icicle. But he didn't say a word. It was like he'd shut down all cylinders except the outrage one.

I knew I was in the middle of an ancient family drama and was ticked at Jackson for not giving me a compass to navigate my way. Judging by his silent performance so far, *I'd* have to float the conversation for the rest of the night.

But no matter how ticked at Jackson I was, I'd be damned if I'd let him get picked on. Especially by his own father. And there was no mistaking that last comment was a pointed jab.

I looked Brig dead in the eye. "Oh, she is. But she'd be proud of me even if I were unemployed and living on food stamps. She's not the kind of person who only loves her child unless she's following her own definition of success."

I know I didn't imagine the low intake of breath from the gathered servants or the way the room went electric. But I pretended I did, and so did Brig.

He said quietly, "Of course not. Parents always love their children, even when they make it hard for us to do so."

He and Jackson locked eyes.

Hello, giant squirming can of worms, please sit down and make yourself comfortable. If things got any more tense, I might shatter.

With a squeak of wheels, Jackson's mother rolled into the room.

She was pale, blonde, and fragile looking, with the exception of her blue eyes, which were lioness fierce. One side of her mouth pulled into a grimace, one hand curled to a claw on her lap. Her hair was scraped severely off her face into a low bun. Around her neck she wore a triple strand of pearls so tight it was probably cutting off her circulation. Pushing her wheelchair was a stout, middle-aged woman in a starched white nurse's uniform and rubber-soled shoes who looked like someone had threatened that everyone she ever knew would be murdered if she smiled.

Jackson's mother was even more terrifying than Dracula's dining room. I had to physically force myself to stand still and not turn and run screaming from the house.

"Ah!" said Brig. "Clemmy, come and meet Bianca." He acted as if Jackson weren't even in the room.

Clemmy cut her gaze to me. Her eyes were like ice in an ancient arctic lake that never thaws. A cat's hiss rose in the back of my throat, and I swallowed. Then she turned her eyes to Jackson. I glanced at him and found him white-faced and tight-lipped, in deep distress.

Jesus, Mary, and Joseph, what *was* it with these people? I decided I'd had enough of this nonsense.

"Mrs. Boudreaux. I'm so happy to meet you." I dropped Jackson's hand and marched resolutely over to Clemmy, a salesman's grin stretching my cheeks. The nurse looked on, alarmed, as I reached out and gently clasped Clemmy's good hand between my own. I said warmly, "Your home is so beautiful. Thank you so much for having me."

You could've heard a pin drop. For an eternity, no one moved a muscle.

Then the uncrooked side of Clemmy's mouth turned up, and her iceberg eyes thawed a few degrees. In a halting, slightly distorted voice, she said, "Thank you for coming."

I thought the manservant would collapse into a heap in his corner.

Deciding to push my luck, I said, "Your son has been giving me fits since the day I met him, but I know he must get his big heart from you and your husband. I'm so looking forward to getting to know you both better."

I'd astonished her. She stared at me with her lips parted, blinking rapidly, looking like she wasn't sure if she wanted to cry or put her good hand around my throat and crush my esophagus. After a moment she recovered her composure. "That's very kind."

Two of the servants against the opposite wall were now openly gaping at me.

This could actually be fun.

I released her hands and turned to Jackson with arched brows and a look he couldn't misunderstand. His gaze darted back and forth between his mother and me several times, then he lurched forward. He crossed to us, bent stiffly to kiss her cheek, then stood on my other side, using me as a buffer between them. He clasped my hand like it was a life vest.

Standing on the other side of the dining room, Brig beamed. He made emcee wide open arms again and boomed, "Let's eat!"

TWENTY-NINE

BIANCA

While Brig and I enjoyed a friendly chat about nothing of importance, Jackson spent the meal staring morosely down at his plate and guzzling goblet after bloody goblet of wine. I'd never seen him so miserable, which was saying something.

His parents were seated at opposite ends of the long dining table. Jackson and I sat across from each other, separated by a forest of food platters, wine carafes, and fruit bowls. The candelabra flickered and dripped wax. The servants stood vigilant guard against the walls. It was like something straight out of a *Pride and Prejudice* adaptation.

Not once did Jackson meet my eyes.

"So you two met at your restaurant?" Brig said as a footman or whatever he was called leaned over me with a platter of fish. It oozed a creamy yellow sauce that had a disturbing resemblance to phlegm. I politely declined.

"Yes, we did. Jackson came in to sample my spring menu, which was inspired by Boudreaux Bourbon. Didn't he mention it?" I said when Brig looked startled. "All the recipes are made with your family's bourbon."

Brig looked as astonished as his wife had when I'd taken her hand. "No," he said faintly, gazing at me with wide eyes. "No, he didn't mention it."

I glanced at Jackson, who was gloomily pushing a grape back and forth across his empty plate with a knife.

"It's true. In fact, he threatened to sue me for copyright infringement on the family's trademark."

Clemmy, in the middle of a swallow of soup, coughed. She dropped her spoon, and it clattered against the bowl.

"Oh! Are you all right?"

Her nurse scowled at me and began petting Clemmy's chest with a napkin, blotting at little splatters of soup. Clemmy waved her away impatiently. *"Sue?"* she repeated.

It came out like *Shoooe?* due to her disfigured lip, but she was perfectly comprehensible.

"Oh yes. He's very protective of the Boudreaux brand."

Flabbergasted, Brig and Clemmy stared at each other.

Shiitake mushroom, another minefield! I hurried on, trying to smooth things over.

"And then, uh, he hired me to cater the Wounded Warrior charity benefit he was hosting at his home when his chef quit at the last minute . . ." I faltered in the middle of my sentence when I saw how Jackson's parents both reared their heads back in surprise at the mention of a charity benefit, but I was too far in to stop. "Which turned out to be an incredibly successful event. You might have read about it in the papers?" No one said anything. I enjoyed a brief and crushing sense of terror. "He raised a few million dollars to help soldiers in need?"

By this time my voice was a pathetic, reedy thing, and I was ready to hide under the table. But then Jackson's father exhaled and he said, "Well that's . . . wonderful. That's really wonderful, son."

I felt like I'd just scored the winning touchdown. My terror evaporated, I looked to Jackson, grinning.

Glowering at his plate, he slowly pressed the sharp edge of the knife into the grape and sliced it in two.

I tried to kick him under the table, but my legs were too short. "Anyway," I said too brightly, willing him to look at me, which of course he refused to do. "That's how it all began. Now here we are!"

My attempt to weave a believable love story ended with a thud. I should've just said "Slap, slap kiss" and left it at that. We lapsed into awkward silence.

There were never any awkward silences in my parents' house during meals. Everyone talked over one another, laughing, ribbing, passing food and sharing stories, easy and happy in one another's company. What had happened to this family to make things so bad?

I could tell both of Jackson's parents had affection for him, though it didn't look anything like my definition of love. But mostly there seemed to be a chasm of silence no one was willing to be the first to reach across. And Jackson was visibly wilting with each passing minute. I didn't know how much longer he'd be able to sit in his chair before he slid onto the floor and expired.

Suddenly I missed Mama with such ferociousness it brought a stinging heat to my eyes. I dabbed at them with a corner of my napkin.

Sounding genuinely concerned, Brig said, "Bianca? Are you all right?"

Jackson finally looked at me. When his head jerked up, his narrowed eyes were a little too much to take, so I looked over at Brig and forced a smile.

"Don't mind me. I suppose I'm just homesick. A few hours away from New Orleans and I'm all out of sorts."

"Are you originally from New Orleans? Your accent is a little . . ."

He trailed off, not wanting to insult me, and I laughed. "I know. It's a mess. My mama's side of the family is Creole, but my daddy was from Alabama. I picked up so much of both their slang and twang my accent's all mixed up."

Brig said warmly, "It sounds just fine to me. What does your father do?"

I noticed that Brig didn't even bat an eye when I mentioned the word *Creole*. If there had been any doubt in his mind as to the origin of my dusky skin, now there could be none. I felt a twinge of shame at assuming he'd judge me, and scolded myself.

"He was an attorney. But he passed away years ago."

His face fell. "Oh dear. I'm sorry to hear that, Bianca."

I sighed. "It's all right. I miss him like crazy, but I have great memories of him. He was the kindest, most honorable and generous man I ever knew." After a short pause, I added honestly, "Aside from Jackson."

I took a bite of salad from my plate. It was only after a minute of chewing that I realized no one was saying anything, but they were all staring at me. Even the servants.

But it was Jackson's eyes that blazed.

The head manservant, Droopy Dog I was now calling him in my mind, leapt into action to save us from whatever new disaster I'd blundered into. "More wine?" he shouted, grabbing a carafe from the middle of the table. He loomed over me, perspiring, smiling so hard it looked painful.

"Yes. Thank you." *A loaded gun will do just fine, too*, I thought, miserably embarrassed without even the satisfaction of knowing why.

I was abruptly so mad at Jackson I could spit. How could he let me wander into the haunted forest without giving me any clues where all the ghosts and goblins were lying in wait? Did everyone in the room know about our little marriage bargain? Was everyone laughing at me? Was I sitting here in front of these insanely rich people and their gawking servants making a complete and utter fool of myself?

I chugged the glass of wine Droopy Dog poured me and motioned for another. He looked sympathetic as he poured.

I stabbed a chicken leg from one of the platters and deposited it onto my plate with an inelegant thunk. Then I started to saw through it, all angry elbows and flashing utensils, making a racket and a mess and a spectacle of myself.

But I didn't care anymore. I was fresh out of charm. If Brig and Clemmy decided to hate me because I was savaging a piece of poultry, they could go straight to the devil's doorstep and ring the bell.

I am my mother's daughter, I thought angrily, sawing away at the bone like an enthusiastic medical student with a fresh cadaver. *I was my father's pride and joy. I will NOT be the butt of anybody's joke!*

Across from me, Jackson darkly chuckled.

I pointed my knife in his face. "Not a *word* out of you, Boudreaux!" I hissed. Then I jammed a piece of chicken in my mouth and started chewing like a farm animal.

The servants were making googly eyes at one another like this was the greatest performance of theatre they'd seen in their lives.

Apparently Jackson had finally left me twisting in the wind long enough, because he stood, making a great display of noisily shoving back his chair, and announced, "Mother. Father. Please excuse us. I think Bianca and I need to talk."

"You're darn tootin'!" I muttered, prompting a hysterical cackle from a servant at the far end of the room, who quickly smothered it with a cough.

Not wanting to let Jackson outdo me, my chair flew back as I leapt to my feet, hitting Droopy Dog in the process. He let out a pained, "Oof!"

I apologized, then looked at Clemmy and Brig. "Thank you for the wonderful meal and your hospitality. I'm sorry if I'm being rude, and you both seem like lovely people, but now I have to go jerk a knot in someone's tail"—I glared at Jackson—"and depending on how that conversation goes, I may or may not require a bail bondsman. Have yourselves a wonderful evening."

I left with my chin high, smoke pouring from my ears, the sound of Brig's startled laughter ringing off the dining room walls.

I managed to make it all the way back to Jackson's room and get the door closed behind us before I let Jackson have it. I whirled on him and did my best impression of a banshee, while he made a beeline for the coffee table in the corner, which held several crystal decanters of liquor and a set of matching highball glasses.

"Do you have any idea how unfair it is, what you just did to me?" I said. "Leaving me totally clueless, acting like a gold star idiot in front of your parents? This agreement isn't only about *your* inheritance, Jackson, it's about my mother's situation, too! We're supposed to be in this deal together! Why aren't you helping me out *at all*?"

Jackson filled a glass, tossed it back, raked a hand through his hair, and poured another glass. Staring down at it, he said, "Because you're doing fine on your own." He chugged back the second glass of liquor, grimacing as he swallowed.

"Are you blind? Even the servants are laughing at me! What's the big secret here? What is it that you and everybody else knows that I don't? Just tell me what on earth is going—"

"I killed my brother," he said flatly.

My words died in my mouth. I stared at him in cold shock while my stomach made a slow, twisting roll and my heart tried painfully to reboot.

Jackson glanced at me. His face was hard, his eyes were dark, and his hand was white-knuckled around the empty glass. "Or at least they all think I did. They blame me for it."

All my outrage disappeared as quickly as it had appeared. I whispered, "Oh my God. What happened?"

Jackson went back to staring at his empty glass, like he was searching for answers in it. After a long time, his voice low and halting, he began to speak.

"Lincoln and I were twins. He was older by two minutes. Two minutes," he repeated bitterly. "You wouldn't think one hundred and twenty seconds could make such a difference, but it did."

He fell silent. I crept over to the bed and sat on the edge because I didn't think my legs could hold me up any longer. Jackson lowered himself to a chair and poured himself another drink. His energy was dark and electric, like thunderclouds before they disgorge their burden of lightning and rain.

"Linc was the golden child from the beginning. The heir and the spare, they jokingly called us, only it wasn't a joke. He could do no wrong. He was better than me at everything. Sports, school, girls . . . everything came easy for him. And I . . ."

Jackson closed his eyes. His voice a low rasp, he said, "I hated him for it. I hated my own brother. Which made me hate myself."

I covered my mouth with my hands. His pain was so palpable, his guilt so raw, I wanted to run and put my arms around him, but I stayed where I was and listened in horrified fascination as he continued his story.

"He looked like an angel. Literally, like a Raphael painting of an angel. Blond hair and dimpled cheeks, this smile everyone went crazy for. I was the dark one. The problematic one. The one with a learning disability and a temper so unpredictable they had to put me on medication when I was barely a teenager. I just . . . never . . . fit."

His Adam's apple bobbed up and down as he swallowed. His face was a grimace, full of anguish and bad memories, ruddy with alcohol, a sheen of sweat on his brow.

"Linc was being groomed to take over the company. It was the logical choice, him being eldest and so nice."

Jackson said the word *nice* like an accusation. His dark gaze flashed up to meet mine. "But the thing was, he *wasn't* so nice. He was like this perfect, shiny red apple that was riddled with worms and rot on the inside. Only no one could see it. No one could believe that something so pretty could be so corrupt. Except me."

Goosebumps erupted all over my arms. Jackson blew out a hard breath and downed the liquor in his glass. Between the wine he'd consumed at dinner and what he'd thrown back since we entered the bedroom, I didn't know how he was still standing.

He set his glass on the table with a *crack* and leapt to his feet. He began restlessly pacing back and forth, breathing erratically, his hands flexing, looking like he was on the verge of breaking something or having a serious cardiac event.

He said, "Linc used to tell me I was adopted, that I was abandoned by the side of the road by beggars and left to die because I was so ugly and stupid that not even my real parents wanted me. He said Brig and Clemmy were getting tax credits for taking care of a homeless runt. He said I should just kill myself and stop being such a burden." His voice broke. "Such a useless, stupid burden. But whenever I complained to my parents, they'd look at each other with sad eyes and sigh and talk about adjusting my meds."

I wanted to run downstairs and smack them both across the face. How could they treat Jackson that way? He was their *son*!

"On our fifteenth birthday, our parents threw us a party. Linc got all the attention, of course, and by then I was used to staying out of the way, so I went to the pool house and hid. I guess Linc decided I was embarrassing the family by hiding, because he came to look for me. We argued. It got heated. He called me names, I called him names. He took a swing at me but missed. I stepped out of the way too quickly. He stumbled and fell, cracked his head against the cement coping, and rolled into the pool."

Now Jackson was talking fast, the words pouring out in a cascade. His body movements were jerky, angry, and he was sweating, his hair sticking to his forehead in dark clumps. His eyes were bright and wild.

"I couldn't swim. I was terrified of the water because the one time I'd tried to learn, Linc held me under when no one was looking and I almost drowned. So I couldn't help him, I couldn't get to him, I couldn't—I didn't know what to do."

He broke off with a sob. I stood, helpless and horrified, already knowing where this was going.

"I ran to get my parents, but by the time they got there it was too late. They found him on the bottom of the pool. Later the doctors said he'd been unconscious when he went in, there was the mark on his face where he'd fallen, and they all thought . . . they thought I . . ."

I pressed a hand over my heart to try to stop its frantic pounding. "They thought you hit him and pushed him in the pool," I whispered.

He propped his hands on his hips and swallowed convulsively, looking at the floor, his face red and pinched. He was trying not to cry.

"No one ever said that directly, of course. But they never looked at me the same. People started avoiding me. Dozens of kids and their parents were at the party, and from that time on I was shunned. The word got out. You can't be alone with Jackson. Stay away from Jackson. He's capable of anything. Then my parents sent me away to boarding school. From there I went directly to college. Which is where I met Christian, by the way, the only real friend I've ever had. By the time I came home from college, my parents and I were basically strangers."

"Oh, Jackson," I said, my voice wavering. "I'm so sorry. That's terrible."

He laughed. It was dark and ugly, one of the most disturbing sounds I'd ever heard.

"It gets better," he said, and poured himself another drink.

THIRTY

BIANCA

A few minutes passed before Jackson spoke again, minutes in which my heart ached and I fought back tears, thinking how it must have been for him all those years growing up, and ever since. How lonely he must've been. I thought now I understood why he was the way he was, so surly and standoffish, but I hadn't heard the rest of his story.

"Her name was Cricket."

That's all he got out before he had to take another swallow of booze. He sank onto the sofa and stared blankly at the coffee table, his face white, his hands trembling, like a man suffering from shell shock.

"Cricket Montgomery. The most beautiful girl in Kentucky, by anyone's standards. We were in grade school together before I went away, so I'd known her for years. Known *of* her, I should say. Like everyone else, she adored my brother but never paid much attention to me, but a few years after I came back I ran into her at the public library in Louisville. I used to go there all the time to read and escape all the accusing eyes in this house. One day she was browsing for a book in the aisle near the chair I always sat in, and she recognized me and came over and said hello, even though I was trying to hide behind my book. She was really nice to me."

His voice gained an angry edge. "So fucking *nice*."

He finished his drink and looked over at me, his eyes glittering. "I should've known right then. But I was so starved for attention, for anyone to notice me or look at me like I wasn't a murdering freak, that I was completely fucking blind."

I didn't know what to do with my hands. They were fluttering around in my lap like frightened birds, so I sat on them and kept listening.

"We started dating. I couldn't believe my good luck. Here was this beautiful, popular girl, choosing *me*. I was so happy I was delirious. My parents were over the moon. My father started talking about having me take over the business. It was like a dream, everything I ever wanted falling into place. After a year, I proposed. And she said yes."

Nostrils flaring, he slowly inhaled. His voice shook with fury. "That evil, scheming, lying, soulless bitch said yes."

Now I was the one who needed a drink. I abandoned the bed, sat across from Jackson, and poured myself a stiff one.

He set his glass on the table and dragged his hands through his hair. Staring at the floor, his elbows propped on his knees, he continued to talk.

"It took another year to plan the wedding. Six hundred people were invited, including the governor. It was a zoo. All my parents' friends and business associates, all her friends and family, politicians, leaders in the liquor industry, a bunch of other people I didn't even know. We had it here at Moonstar Ranch, of course. Great location for a wedding. The church was too small for that many guests, so the event coordinator designed this whole fantasy fairy tale theme that ended up costing more than a million dollars."

He sighed. "I found out later the coordinator was one of Cricket's college friends. Cricket got a cut of her fee." He glanced up at me. He looked wrecked. He said quietly, "Because of course that's what it was about all along. Money."

I started to feel sick. Finishing my bourbon in one gulp didn't help.

Jackson stood and started pacing again, like it hurt to sit still. But there was a hitch in his walk now, a slight, unsteady weaving. Everything he'd had to drink was starting to catch up to him.

"The ceremony was ready to start. The guests were seated. The violinists had begun to play. But the bride was nowhere to be found. The coordinator was having a nervous breakdown. So I went looking for Cricket. I thought she was probably just taking a minute to herself, nerves and all that. I had a hunch she'd be in the stables because she loved to ride, so that's the first place I went. And I was right . . . she was there. And she *was* getting a ride."

The inflection in his voice left no doubt to his meaning.

I gasped. "Oh, no!"

He turned and stared at me with wild, black eyes. "Oh yes. Right there in the tack room, bent over the saddle stand with her thirty-thousand-dollar wedding dress that *I* paid for shoved up to her waist, her panties around her ankles. They didn't see me come in. They just kept fucking and talking, him grunting, 'You're always gonna be mine,' and her crying that she was, that it was all for him, she was doing it for him, for their future, they only had to pretend for a little while longer. Everything became very clear to me. Very clear."

His voice went dead. "And then I lost my mind."

I covered my mouth with my hands, terrified of what he was going to say next. He staggered over to the bed and collapsed onto it, his face crumbling. He gulped in lungfuls of air. When he could talk again, his voice was a hoarse whisper.

"My hands were around his throat. She was screaming. Screaming at me to stop, I was killing him, but of course that's exactly what I intended to do. Kill him. One of her so-called 'friends' that we hung out with who smiled at me and clapped me on the back every time I paid for dinner. I wanted to kill him with my bare hands. And I would have, I'm sure of it, but Cricket came at me with a big metal tool used to punch holes in leather and hit me in the face. She had to hit me three times before I let go.

"My blood was all over him. He was lying on the ground, bloody and unmoving, and she fell on him like Mary over the body of Jesus, weeping and wailing and begging him to say something. When he didn't, she turned on me. You've never seen anything so savage. And the things she said. God."

He broke off and covered his face with his hands.

"Jackson, you don't have to tell me," I said, but he shook his head.

"I do. I have to tell someone, because I've never told anyone else. Maybe if I get it out . . . maybe if I just . . ." He flopped onto his back and laid there, arms out, chest heaving.

Sick and helpless, I went to him, sat on the edge of the bed, and took his hand. It was clammy and trembling. With his eyes closed, he told me the rest in a broken whisper.

"She never loved me. We didn't meet in the library by accident. They'd planned the whole thing. I was just a . . . meal ticket. A patsy. Who could love me, the murderer, the freak, the awful lover? She fucked me for two years, and it was torture, she said. It was hell. She wished I was dead."

I squeezed his hand and vowed that the first thing I was going to do when I got back to New Orleans was have Eeny put a voodoo curse on this nightmare named Cricket Montgomery.

Jackson's head lolled sideways. His eyelids drifted open. His eyes were unfocused. He was very drunk.

He whispered, "I left. I didn't say anything to anyone. I went to my room and packed a bag, and left Kentucky, right then. I couldn't bear to see their faces. I drove until I found myself in New Orleans. I checked into a hotel and hid there for a week, trying to drink myself to death. I didn't have a gun and didn't want to leave a bloody corpse for anyone else to clean up after anyway, so I thought alcohol poisoning was the way to go.

"It was Rayford who found me. Credit cards leave a trail. After Linc died he was the only one who would talk to me. Anyway, Cricket and her 'friend' told everyone they were just talking in the tack room when I came in and went crazy with jealousy. Didn't matter, I had a death wish to take care of, who cared what story they made up? But that old bastard Rayford wouldn't leave me alone."

A faint smile crossed Jackson's face. "Stubborn son of a bitch."

"Oh Jax," I said, my heart breaking. I turned his hand over and traced my fingertip over the semicolon tattoo on his wrist. My eyes filled with water.

Jackson said, "The day after the wedding that never was, my mother had a stroke. I didn't know about it until later, but obviously it was my fault. The humiliation was too much for her. The disappointment." He heaved a great sigh. "Who could blame her? With a son like hers, it's a miracle she didn't die from shame."

He trailed off into silence. His breathing deepened, evened, and I realized he was close to passing out. But he had one final piece of horror to deliver first.

His voice slurred and faint, he said, "A week after I got to New Orleans, Christian had his legs blown off by a roadside bomb in a hellhole halfway around the world. He was my real brother. The brother who accepted me for who I was. He was the only one who ever did, aside from Rayford. He was my only real friend." A sweet smile drifted over his face. "And you."

I was crying openly now, but silently, tears running down my face, my free hand in a fist in my mouth to stifle the sobs.

Jackson murmured, "Christian had no family, so he came to live with me. He was in so much pain all the time, as much physical pain as I was in emotional pain. He started to drink. He'd go down to a bar on Bourbon Street and drink during the day, and I'd go with him . . . nothing better to do, either of us. He met this girl. I knew . . . what she was, of course . . . I knew what she did. But at least it was honest. They both understood. Not like me . . ."

His voice was getting more and more faint, the pauses between his words growing longer. He licked his lips and turned his head with a sigh, and his face looked heartbreakingly vulnerable without its usual armor of scowls.

"She got pregnant. Had a paternity test. It was Christian's. He died before Cody was born. Never got to meet his son. Trina signed over her parental rights to me and disappeared. I get a call every once in a while . . . bail money, rent money . . . everyone wanting money . . . all I was ever good for . . ."

Jackson fell asleep with his hand in mine. A lone tear leaked from his eye, tracking a zigzag path down his temple.

I leaned over him, hugged him as tightly as I could, and sobbed.

I cried for a long time, my ear pressed to his chest, listening to his slow and steady heartbeat. Finally when I had nothing left, I sat up, wiped my eyes, slipped off his shoes, and settled a blanket over him. I went into the bathroom and splashed cold water on my face. I called Mama and told her how much I loved her, how lucky I was to have her, how she and Daddy were the greatest parents in the world.

Then I marched my booty downstairs to have a nice, long talk with Clemmy and Brig.

THIRTY-ONE

JACKSON

I knew I was dreaming because the warm, soft, unmistakable curve under my left palm was a woman's hip.

Dream woman had an incredibly sexy hip.

She also smelled delicious and was warm as a little furnace against my chest.

All of that helped to distract from the odd fact that I had a headache and my mouth tasted like bourbon. This was a really vivid dream. At least I was lying down comfortably, my head resting on a nice, fluffy pillow, my legs curled up behind dream woman's legs.

She sighed in sleepy pleasure when I pulled her tighter against me and nuzzled my face into her hair. When I slid my hand over her hip and gently cupped her ass, she sighed again, arching her back and rubbing against my crotch.

This was a fucking awesome dream.

She smelled like strawberry shampoo and sunshine. Like goodness. Like something I wanted to soak in . . . or taste. I found the nape of her neck with my lips and stroked my tongue over the delicate bump of her spine. She breathed the softest, sexiest moan, which was even sexier because it was my name.

My dream boner was Godzilla. King Kong. Attila the Hun leading his army of savages to plunder the riches of foreign lands. I pressed it against her, curling my hand around her hip to draw her close. She made an appealing sound, a kitten's soft mew, which drew a growl from deep inside my chest.

I opened my mouth over the curve between her shoulder and neck. She tilted her head back, giving me better access to her throat. I trailed my lips up satin skin, gently bit down, felt her shiver. She made a restless noise and squirmed.

She put her hand over mine and dragged it slowly up her waist and over her rib cage, to her breast. It was full and heavy in my hand, the nipple peaked—and highly sensitive. When I pinched it, she jerked and moaned, this time louder. A thin layer of cotton separated her skin from mine, and I needed it gone. I needed her skin on my tongue. I needed that moan again.

I found the hem of her shirt and pushed it up impatiently. I cupped her bare breast and gently squeezed.

"Yes, Jax," she breathed, arching.

I rolled her under me, pinned her down, and sucked her taut nipple into my mouth. Her groan sent a shockwave of pure lust singing through me.

I rocked my hips into hers. She fisted her hands into my hair, urging me closer, scratching my scalp and softly crying out when I tested that hard bud with my teeth. Her thighs were open around my hips, her sweet smell was in my nose, the sound of her ragged breathing was in my ears. I pushed her breasts together and went slowly back and forth from nipple to nipple, sucking and licking, gently biting the fullness of the globes, then stroking my tongue over where I'd bitten to chase away the sting.

"Please," she panted. "Oh, please don't stop. More."

My cock was so hard it ached. I was in heaven. This was dream heaven, and I was never, ever leaving. "I need to be inside you, sweetheart," I murmured. She answered with a shudder.

My eyes drifted open.

Bianca lay panting softly beneath me with her eyes closed and her head thrown back, her pink T-shirt bunched up under her chin. Her gorgeous breasts jutted out from the cage of my hands, her nipples slick and darkest rose.

It hit me like a bucket of cold water poured over my head.

I wasn't dreaming. This wasn't heaven. This was *real*.

Fuck!

When I froze, Bianca opened her eyes. Then I was treated to the piercing anguish of watching her realize she wasn't dreaming, either. Her eyes widened. Her lips parted on a choked gasp.

"I'm sorry," I whispered hoarsely, disoriented and disgusted with myself. I'd mauled her in my sleep! I could probably be arrested for this! How was I even on the bed anyway—I was supposed to be on the couch! What a fucking disaster!

I made a move to pull away, rearing back on my elbows, but she threw her arms around my shoulders and yelped, "Wait!"

I froze again. We were eye to eye, nose to nose, staring at each other. The only sound in the room was our labored breathing.

Her gaze dropped to my mouth. My heart pounded so hard I was breathless.

She moistened her lips. Her hair was wild all around her face, a dark mass of curls, and she was so beautiful it hurt to look at her.

She said breathlessly, "So I had this idea yesterday. When you were prancing around showing off all your muscles."

My arms shook. I didn't dare speak. I just stared at her, waiting, burning up with naked lust.

"That maybe it would be a good idea if we . . ." Color rose in her cheeks. She hesitated for what felt like forever, until finally she worked up the courage to say, "If we got it out of our systems."

My entire body was so tense I was in danger of shattering like fractured glass. "*It?*" I repeated, my voice raw.

Her lashes lowered. She managed to look demure even though her bare breasts were exposed. Her tone was crisp. "Don't be intentionally obtuse, Jackson. You know exactly what I mean."

When I continued to stare at her, trembling with disbelief, she made her meaning perfectly clear by biting her full lower lip and rocking her pelvis against mine.

On a groan, I dropped my forehead to her chest. She was murdering me. I was going to die in this bed, lying on top of her, my heart exploded in my chest like a grenade.

She turned her lips to my ear. "It doesn't have to change anything. One time just so we can get past it and put it behind us. And since neither of us has gotten any in forever—"

"I won't be able to have you *once*," I growled, and took her mouth.

The kiss was hot and desperate, partly because I figured I had nothing to lose and partly because I was so turned on I was almost angry. She responded by arching up into me and digging her fingers into my shoulders, which made my already-throbbing cock so hard it was physically painful.

I broke away and cuffed her wrists over her head on the pillow. We were both panting. I was practically vibrating with frustration.

"Fuck. *Fuck*, Bianca!"

She wasn't done torturing me. She lifted her head, put her mouth against my throat, and bit me. Gently, but enough to sting. Against my skin she murmured, "Yes. That's exactly what you should do, Jax. Fuck Bianca."

I groaned. What the hell was going on? Hearing those words from that normally chaste mouth made it all the more carnal. I wanted nothing more than to rip off the little shorts she was wearing and bury my cock deep inside her, but I knew it would be a disaster. Everything would be awkward afterward. Everything would change.

There was no way I could have her only once. I knew I'd be addicted from the first taste and end up being obsessed, hounding her like a dog in heat, pestering her like her ex until eventually she hated me.

It was the thing I was most afraid of: Bianca hating me. My inheritance be damned, I couldn't lose her.

The little savage lifted her legs and hooked her ankles around my waist. She inhaled deeply against my neck and made a sound of pleasure. She started to wantonly rock her hips.

"You're killing me," I gasped.

"Why are you making me beg?" she protested, sliding her hands under my arms so she could reach down and squeeze my ass, which she did, with vigor.

"Why are you suddenly so horny?"

She lowered her head to the pillow and gazed up at me, her eyes half-lidded and hot. Her voice was a throaty whisper. "Because you're beautiful, Jackson Boudreaux. Inside and out. I'm an idiot for not realizing it sooner."

My heart stalled out, then took off like a rocket. Resting my weight on my elbows, I cupped her face in my hands and stared down at her, wanting to memorize every little thing, every aspect of this moment. Her eyes and chin and nose, the way her hairline dipped to a widow's peak at the top of her forehead. Her sexy red Cupid's bow mouth.

I said raggedly, "I can't. Not only once. I can't risk it being weird after. I couldn't live with myself if I fucked this up."

She drew in a slow breath, let it out through her nose. Then she cocked her head and considered me. "So it's a negotiation, then."

My brows shot up. "Excuse me?"

"Well if you can't do it only once, how many times do you think you *would* be able to do it?" She blinked lazily. One corner of her mouth lifted in a tiny, rogue grin that she quickly suppressed.

Speech was becoming difficult. "I . . . I'm so out of practice . . . I think the first ten or twenty times might just be getting me back up to speed."

"Ten or twenty? Hmm. Ambitious, aren't you?" She unhooked her ankles from around my waist and slid her foot down my leg, her toes curled around my calf. "And would that all be in one day, or . . ."

"No," I said forcefully. I took my tone down a notch and tried to look serious. My blood pressure was through the roof. "No, I think I'd need a lot more time than that." I cleared my throat of the rasp. "I mean, I don't want to wear you out or anything."

"Such a gentleman," she whispered. Looking into my eyes, she slowly rubbed her breasts against my chest.

Her nipples were hard. I felt them right through my shirt, two firm little peaks that needed my tongue. A growl built low in my belly and worked its way through my chest and out my mouth, but still I held back.

Suddenly all the teasing left her voice and her eyes. She said firmly, "Jackson. I'm in your bed. I'm wearing your ring. We're hot as two jalapeños for each other. Do me, dammit, and hurry up about it!"

A heartbeat of silence pounded between us. The moment stretched thin, then snapped, and the final shreds of my control curled up like burning paper and turned to ash.

I said, "You should write poetry," and crushed my mouth to hers.

THIRTY-TWO

BIANCA

I'd seen Jackson's scary side. I'd seen his hidden sweet side, too, and his suave side, and a dozen others.

But I'd never seen him dirty.

"Off!" he snarled, impatiently pulling my T-shirt over my head. He tossed it aside and it sailed across the room. He took a moment to stare down at me, his eyes black with lust, then he grabbed my sleep shorts and yanked them down my hips. Away they went, flung over to the dresser along with my panties. Kneeling between my spread legs, he made an animal noise as his gaze raked over me. Then his mouth was on my flesh.

There.

I cried out in shock. His mouth was so hot and wet, so unexpected. He dug his fingers into my hips and thrust his tongue deep inside me. I almost died from pleasure.

"So fucking sweet. I'd knew you'd taste sweet." He took a moment to growl, his breath fanning over my spread thighs. Then he went right back to business.

I threaded my shaking fingers into the thick, soft mess of his hair because I needed to feel it. I didn't realize how much I'd wanted to touch it until now. And now that I could, I took big, greedy handfuls of it and breathlessly laughed.

I sounded like I'd just robbed a bank and gotten away with it.

Jackson ignored my crazy laugh. His tongue—oh clever tongue— circled round and round that small rigid nub between my legs until it throbbed and I was gasping for air.

When I arched off the bed and cried out, Jackson turned his head and gently bit my thigh. "Close already?" he asked, laughter in his tone.

My hips rocking, I begged him not to stop in a garbled mess of words.

"You're so goddamn beautiful," he whispered. "I wish you could see yourself." He ran his palms up and down my thighs, testing the flesh, pinching it and stroking it, his big hands rough and warm. "This beautiful skin." He kissed my leg. "These perfect tits." He reached up and squeezed them, thumbing over my hard nipples so I shivered in delight.

His voice turned spine-chillingly dark. "And this gorgeous pussy. Look at you, spread open for me, all pink and soft. Christ. I can't decide if I want to eat you until you come and then fuck you, or if I should make you come on my hard cock first."

Sweet baby Jesus in the manger, Jackson Boudreaux is a dirty talker.

"Please," I pleaded brokenly. "Jax."

He gently pinched my clit between two fingers and blew on it. I moaned like a porn star.

"Tell me what you want," he demanded, lazily stroking me.

I blurted, "Anything. Everything. *You.*"

"Oh, sweetheart," he murmured, "you already have me."

Then he gifted me with his tongue again. I sighed in relief, my breath shuddering out of me, my body writhing under the expert movements of his hands and mouth.

He knew exactly how to take me to the edge and keep me there, teasing and gentling when I got too close, chuckling at my delirious implorings of *"More. Hurry. I'll kill you if you stop."* He took his time, though I knew he felt the same unbearable urgency I did. His fingers digging into my skin were just shy of painful. Every once in a while, he would catch his breath and curse.

I felt like I was riding a wave. A wave of heat and emotion, expanding from my body to fill the room, the house, the entire state. I wanted to laugh and cry and scream, I wanted to break apart and let him put me back together. I was sinking into the bed at the same time as I was floating over it, the feel of his stubble exquisitely rough on my inner thighs, the sound of his deep-chested grunts reverberating all the way through me.

"Oh God, Jax." I groaned, unable to hold it in. "I'm there, oh God I'm there I'm so—"

My orgasm stole the words right out of my mouth. I bucked and gasped. My body bowed. My fingers dug into his hair, and I exploded.

He hooked his forearm over my belly and held me down as I convulsed. He slid two fingers of his other hand inside me. Clenching hard around them, I screamed.

It lasted forever, or seemed to. Pulsing and heat and flashing lights behind my closed eyelids, the feel of his fingernails breaking my skin. Everything so crystalline clear, so achingly raw I felt exposed on every level, all my nerves on fire and the frantic hummingbird beat of my heart pounding like gunfire in my ears.

When I came back to myself, I was crying.

"Hush, sweetheart," Jackson crooned, climbing over me. He settled his weight between my legs and nuzzled my neck. I clung to him, overcome, shaking with the aftermath of acute pleasure and a sudden bottomless fear.

Whatever that was, it was something I'd never felt before. And it scared the bejeezus out of me.

"It's okay," he whispered, peppering soft kisses all over my cheeks. His heart pounded against my chest, as hard and erratically as mine did. He was so warm and big and comfortable, an enormous man pillow I could burrow into and get lost.

I loved his weight. I loved how he smelled. I loved how tender he was being, this giant of a human who could crush me in one fist but was stroking my face with the care of someone handling fine china. I loved how he made me feel so safe.

I did *not* love the strange terror that evoked.

When I finally managed to pull myself together, I sniffled in embarrassment and turned my face to the pillow. "Sorry. I'm not normally a weeper after sex. But that was . . ." I shivered and tightened my arms around his neck.

He whispered into my ear, "Don't apologize. I feel like a sex god right now."

I cracked open an eye. He was staring down at me, a big, goofy grin on his face. His dark hair was mussed, his blue eyes were alight, and he was so handsome it took my breath away.

Dazed, I said, "You *are* a sex god, Jax. You're the Michael Jordan of sex. You're the Warren Buffett of sex. You're the Steve Jobs of—"

"Okay," he interrupted drily. "No more other men's names out of your mouth while you're in my bed."

I smiled at him. "I'm sorry. That was just like . . ." I sighed dreamily. "Wow."

The light in his eyes grew hotter. He whispered, "And that was only act one."

Fingers crossed there were a dozen more to follow.

Jackson rose to his knees. Staring down at me, he slowly unbuttoned his shirt. It parted under his fingers, revealing his gorgeous hard chest, those abs of steel, that fine dark happy trail I found so enticing. He shrugged the shirt off his shoulders, and I sighed again, wiggling my toes in happiness.

"Goddamn, woman," he said, his voice husky. "You're gonna turn me into an egomaniac. You should see those eyes. Filthy."

I giggled. "You're very pretty, Jackson. This, especially, is my favorite." I propped myself up on one elbow and trailed my finger down the soft line of hair on his stomach. His abs quivered under my touch. I glanced up to find him gazing down at me in molten stillness, watching me with predatory eyes.

I had an idea.

I sat up, flattened my hands over his abdomen, and smiled up at him. I pressed a soft kiss to the square inch of warm skin right below his belly button.

He froze. "What're you doing?"

"Wouldn't you like to know?" I teased. Maintaining eye contact, I traced a circle around his belly button with my tongue, then dipped it in.

His sucked in breath made me grin. I was getting an inkling of how my unraveling made him feel, and I wanted more of it.

I wanted him *undone.*

My fingers found the fly of his jeans. The buttons slid open with the silkiness of melted butter. I pressed a kiss to the small strip of newly exposed skin above his briefs, and Jackson stopped breathing.

When I licked it, he softly moaned.

"Your little tongue," he whispered, staring at me in fascination. "Your little pink—"

His words were swallowed by another moan when I curled my hand around the enormous bulge straining the front of his briefs and gently squeezed.

Straight-faced, I said, "There seems to be something requiring attention in your underwear, Mr. Boudreaux. Judging by the size of engorgement, it could be a medical emergency. Shall I have a look?"

He looked like he was going to pass out. He said faintly, "Yes, nurse. Please do."

It took a geologic epoch for me to pull down his briefs because I was enjoying his expression too much to go any faster. When I finally tore my gaze away from his and looked down, I gasped.

"Holy guacamole," I breathed, floored by the sheer size and grandeur of Jackson's jutting erection. "Mr. Boudreaux. This is *life-threatening*."

In a strangled voice, he said, "Perhaps . . . you should administer . . . oral treatment?"

I nodded. "I concur. Excellent diagnosis."

Then I applied my mouth and thrilled to the sound of Jackson's hoarse gasp.

He was too big to fit more than a few inches into my mouth, but I made up for it with both my hands, which I wrapped around his shaft and stroked in tandem with my tongue. His shaking hands cupped my head. His breathing was labored. After I'd established a rhythm, Jackson matched it with gentle thrusts of his pelvis, each one working a soft groan from his chest.

He was ridiculously large, but I loved the way he tasted and smelled. All that masculine warmth and musk. Delicious. I opened my throat, testing my endurance, and was rewarded with Jackson barking, "*Fuck!*" His fingers twitched against my scalp.

So of course I had to do it again. And again.

And again.

He sucked in a breath like a hiss between his teeth. He warned, "Bianca."

I looked up at him. His eyes were barely open. His face was flushed. His chest was heaving. I felt like a superhero.

I said, "Hmm. I can't decide if I want to blow you until you come and then fu—"

In one swift move, Jackson had me on my back with my legs spread around his waist and my wrists pinned against the pillow. He kissed me, hard, holding nothing back.

I rocked my hips against the straining heat of his erection, and he bit my lower lip.

"Are you trying to drive me crazy?" he hissed, eyes blazing.

"Yes," I said. "I want the Beast unleashed. I want both of us unleashed. I want it to be wild."

His eyes closed briefly. He muttered to himself, "Thank God," then kissed me again, so hard it left me breathless and bruised.

A small table sat beside the bed. He reached over me, grabbed his wallet, pulled something out. A rip of foil and I knew we were covered.

"Good thinking, Mr. Boudreaux." I gasped as his heat and hardness slid into me. Then I couldn't talk anymore because he flexed his hips and drove himself deep inside.

My hips rose to meet his. My neck arched. My eyes slid shut. I heard his rough whisper against my ear like it was coming from somewhere very far away.

"Bianca. My Bianca. I knew we'd fit just right."

Then he dropped his mouth to my neck and started to fuck me.

It wasn't sweet. It wasn't gentle. It wasn't controlled, but it was everything I wanted and needed. I praised him with such loud, wanton moans I probably scared Droopy Dog half to death as he heard the echoes down the halls.

Jackson still had on his jeans, which somehow made everything even hotter. The waistband was bunched around his ass. I shoved it down farther so I could grip those gloriously firm globes as he pumped hard into me, grunting and swearing.

"So good so amazing oh God don't stop," I babbled, writhing beneath him.

He panted. "I can't—we have to—slow down—"

I hollered, "If you stop, you die!"

He groaned like he was in agony. I gripped his face and kissed him so hard I tasted blood. I wrapped my legs around his back and held on as he started to buck wildly, thrashing the bed. We were both sweating, panting, moaning, and kissing sloppily, out of our minds and loving it.

He reared up on his hands, threw his head back, and roared my name at the ceiling.

So this is what all those stupid love songs are about, I thought, just before I went supernova and exploded in a white-hot ball of fire into space.

THIRTY-THREE

JACKSON

We lay stunned and speechless, tangled in each other's arms on the demolished bed like victims of a bombing.

After a while, Bianca said in a tremulous voice, "Oh. My. That was . . ."

"Perfect." I stared at her in awe. "Incredible. Mind-blowing. We should get a trophy."

Blinking slowly, she smiled. It was a heartbreaking smile, a thing of such soul-lifting and astonishing beauty I felt like a man who'd just discovered religion.

She was my religion. My north and south, my heaven and earth, the axis of rightness around which everything had suddenly aligned. For the first time in my life, all my polarized parts worked as one, humming happily along in harmony with the universe, finally understanding their place.

I surrendered to the feeling completely and without hesitation, knowing that most people would never experience this. This blinding joy. This transcendent bliss. This seismic shift of focus from themselves to someone else that strangely and simultaneously gave birth to the freedom and bone-deep peace they'd been seeking all along.

I always thought love was a pair of shackles, but I was wrong. Love was the opened door of a cage.

"You certainly have a lot of *energy*, Mr. Boudreaux," my love said, prim as a librarian. It made me laugh so heartily it shook the bed.

I threw my leg over her, pulled her to me, and sighed in happiness. She burrowed against me, making soft growly sounds of pleasure, her little hands pawing my chest.

"Sex fiend," I whispered indulgently as she ran her hands all over my body.

"I can't help it," she protested. "You're built like a skyscraper, and your skin is like a unicorn's mane."

I frowned. "A unicorn's mane?"

"All silky and shiny and mystical."

She said it like, *Duh, what moron doesn't know what a unicorn's mane is like?* I laughed again, helplessly charmed.

"You're awfully jolly after sex," she said. "Me likey."

Oh God. My fucking heart was going to split open like an overripe piece of fruit. "And you're awfully chatty." I captured her lips and kissed her to shut her up.

When we finally came up for air, she stretched against me like a cat, supple and satisfied, lazily licking her lips. "You're a *dish*," she declared. "If you were food, you'd be the filet from that cow on your father's plane that was massaged and coddled into beefy, delicious perfection."

"That's disturbing," I said, kissing the tip of her nose. "But thank you. I think."

Her mood shifted like quicksilver, from gossamer light to guarded. She pursed her lips and contemplated my sternum. "Speaking of your father."

"What?" I was instantly on high alert.

She glanced up at me. "You need to talk to him."

There was something behind her eyes that worried me. "Why?"

She dropped her gaze to my chest and started toying with my chest hair. "Um. Well. I had a little chat with him last night after you passed out." Her pause was infinitesimal. "With your mother, too."

My blood pressure went from sleeping baby to day trader on the stock market on Black Monday. "*About?*"

Her eyes flashed up to mine. "Don't shout!"

"I'm not shouting, I'm asking!"

She glared at me.

I blew out a deliberate breath and lowered my voice. "I'm sorry. Talking about my parents when I'm naked in bed with you is . . . yuck."

She pouted for a second, then relented. "How much do you remember from last night?"

I opened my mouth to answer, then closed it. How much *did* I remember? Backtracking to before the amazing dream that turned out not to be a dream this morning, I recalled arriving at Moonstar yesterday evening, meeting my father in the foyer, coming up to my room to change, going back down to dinner to suffer through the screaming silence of all the family dinners I'd enjoyed growing up, and then . . .

Nothing.

"I drank too much," I pronounced. I slanted my eyes down at Bianca, hoping she'd fill in the blanks.

She knew I was bluffing but took pity on me. "You told me about Linc and Cricket," she said gently. "And about what happened after. Going to New Orleans. Christian. Cody. Everything."

Coldness sliced through me, freezing as an arctic wind. Then, worse, suspicion. *Did she sleep with me because she felt sorry for me?*

Examining my face, Bianca pounded her little fists on my chest. "If you ever look at me like that again," she said, seething, "you won't be a nice, tasty filet anymore, Jackson Boudreaux, you'll be ground beef!"

Her threat made me feel oddly relieved. "I love it when you threaten me with bodily harm," I said, and kissed her again.

She sighed contentedly against my lips. I was enamored by how quickly she could get over anger. It usually took me days.

She said, "Well, someone's got to keep you in line. Might as well be your wife."

It was a throwaway line, but it speared me right through the heart. It took a moment for my blood to start circulating again. "Wife," I repeated solemnly, gazing into her eyes.

She wrinkled her nose. "Lord, you make it sound like someone just told you Christmas was canceled."

I cupped her jaw in my hand. "No. It's like someone just told me I won the lottery."

"Do billionaires play the lottery?"

"They would if they knew you were the prize."

She squirmed a little, pleased but acting like she wasn't, and resumed toying with my chest hair like it was her new pet. I stroked her face, dazzled by all the little dancing hearts in my eyes.

"I need a shower," she pronounced, then looked at me from under her lashes.

"God, those filthy eyes. You could probably be arrested for that look. Pervert."

She said casually, "Well, since we're doing a sex weekend before we go back to real life, I might as well make the most of it, right?"

Inside my head was the sound a freight train makes when it slams on its brakes, then topples off the tracks, spilling its load of munitions and poison gas, which promptly explode in an enormous orange ball of flame, scorching the earth and destroying all life in a fifty-mile radius.

Clearly for Bianca, this wasn't the start of something deeper between us. This was the itch that needed to be scratched before it could be forgotten. This was the annoying, tickling pressure that had built to the point where it could only be relieved with a reflexive action, like a sneeze.

Bianca was going to sneeze me out of her system. She'd told me flat out, "it would be a good idea if we got it out of our systems."

And I'd gone and fallen in love with her. What a fool.

"Right," I said, shuttering my eyes.

She examined my expression for a moment. "What's that face you're making? I don't recognize that face."

This is what heartbreak looks like. "Nothing," I said flatly. "I'm fine."

She pushed me in the chest so hard I flopped onto my back. My eyes flew open in surprise. I grunted as she threw herself on top of me.

"No!" she shouted. "No, you don't get to do that after you were just inside me not even five minutes ago! You do *not* get to be all weird and withdrawn and noncommunicative, do you hear me? Talk!"

She jabbed me in the chest with her finger. Glaring down at me with her dark hair wild all around her face and her eyes blazing black fury, she was a little bit terrifying.

But I was madly in love with her, so I had to tell her the truth. "I told you once wouldn't be enough," I said gruffly. It sounded like an accusation.

"So? And?"

It was a challenge, which pissed me off.

"*So,*" I snapped, "you fucking seduced me!" Her eyes flared in outrage, but I was only getting started. "*And* now you're telling me this weekend is all I'm getting! *And* I already told you I didn't want to fuck this up! *So* now it's too late because it *is* fucked up because I won't be able to have you just once and I'm going to go fucking insane trying to keep my hands off you now, because to you this was only sex but to me it was a lot more, *and you told me I was beautiful!*"

I roared it into her face with so much force her hair fluttered back from her cheeks. I stared at her, panting, enraged, all the tendons standing out in my neck.

Then her eyes softened and she smiled. "Oh, Jax," she said tenderly. "We're going to have to do something about that temper."

She took my face in her hands and kissed me.

I was completely confused.

"Kiss me back!" she demanded when I remained frozen beneath her.

I sputtered, "Are you having some sort of psychotic break I should be aware of?"

She sighed and tucked her face into the space between my neck and shoulder, snuggling closer to my body. "You conveniently forgot about the 'ten or twenty times' part of our conversation, Beastie."

When I remained stiff and unresponsive, she sighed again. "And the part where I asked if that would all be in one day and you said you'd need a lot more time than that?"

When I still didn't say anything, she tapped me impatiently on my sternum. I turned my head and looked at her. She was smiling up at me indulgently, like I was a giant, fussing baby.

"I'll be very clear, since you seem to be having trouble processing what I'm trying to say." She cleared her throat, becoming businesslike. "Mr. Boudreaux. When I said we were having a sex weekend, I didn't mean we were *only* having a sex weekend."

All the breath left my body in an audible rush. I put my hand over my eyes to hide my relief.

More gently, she said, "I'm not putting any rules on this. When I said sex didn't have to change anything, that was the truth. I hope it doesn't make things awkward when we get home if—*if*—one of us decides it's better to remain friends. Seeing as how this is a business deal and all."

I couldn't help myself. I growled.

"I know," she whispered. "It's an odd situation. For us both, obviously. But if it even has a *chance* to work out, we have to promise to be completely honest with each other." There was a long pause. "And I was being honest when I said I thought you were beautiful. So. There's that."

After I corralled my stampeding emotions, I griped, "You're not so bad yourself."

She burst out laughing. "Such flowery, romantic words! Oh, I'm overcome!"

I rolled her onto her back, pinned her down, and kissed her all over her face as she laughed and laughed and my heart expanded like a balloon.

The problem with balloons is that at some point they have to either deflate or burst.

After I brushed my teeth and changed into clean clothes, I left Bianca dozing in my bed and went downstairs to find my parents.

They were eating breakfast in the solar off the kitchen, a large, sunny room with a glass ceiling to let in the light, the noisy chatter of my mother's caged songbirds coloring in the air. I stood outside the doorway for a moment, watching them, a band of steel tightening around my chest.

What had Bianca told them? And would it change anything?

My father looked up and saw me standing there before my mother did. His face transformed. "Jackson," he said, smiling. "Good morning."

My mother looked up, slowly set her fork down onto her plate, and blinked, gazing at me like she'd never seen me before.

All in all, it was unsettling.

I walked stiffly to the table. My father stood. I cleared my throat, awkward words of greeting on my tongue, but he canceled that plan when he opened his arms and grabbed me in a bear hug, squeezing tighter than a man in his seventies should be capable of.

"Son," he said, his voice choked. "Oh, son." He gave me a good, hard shake. "It's so good to have you home."

Wide-eyed, I looked over his shoulder at my mother. She was dabbing at her eyes with her napkin.

My father released me and clapped me so hard on the back I almost pitched forward. I caught myself in time and took refuge in a chair, where I sat looking between the two of them with trepidation. My mother reached over and grasped my hand. A miracle.

A servant deposited a glass of orange juice on the table in front of me. "Breakfast, sir?"

I waved my hand, and the servant melted away. I couldn't deal with food right now, but the orange juice was too great a temptation, so I chugged it.

"We owe you an apology," said my father, instantly prompting me to choke.

He had to pound me on the back several times before I was able to catch my breath, and even then I wasn't able to speak, only stare at him in watery-eyed, gasping disbelief.

"Oh, now don't gimme that face," he said, snapping his napkin over his lap. "You're not innocent in all of this, either! You never even told us we had a grandson!"

The sound that came out of me wasn't technically a word, but my father snorted like I'd disagreed with him.

"Yes, Bianca told me you adopted Christian's son, and I'm damned pissed off that you'd keep that from us! You know how much your mother wants grandbabies! And you could've told me what really happened with Cricket—it would've saved us years of grief!"

He looked at me, stricken. "Not that it was anything like what you probably went through, of course. I didn't mean that. Only . . . well, shit, Jackson. You never gave your mother and me a chance to be there for you. You just disappeared, and when Rayford found you, he wouldn't tell us anything, either, and we never saw either one of you again! It was like the two of you went into the witness protection program!"

It took a long time for me to recover from that. "But . . ." I looked at my mother. "I gave you a stroke."

She sighed like she was disappointed she'd given birth to such an idiot.

Exasperated, my father trumpeted, "You can't take credit for that, boy! Your mother's been on a blood thinner for twenty years because she'd had a minor stroke before you were born and the doctors were tryin' to prevent another one! Sticky blood runs in her side of the family! Jesus H. Christ on a crutch, what nonsense! And this is why you stayed away?"

My temper snapped. I stood, shoving back my chair. "I stayed away because you loved Linc more than you ever loved me!"

My mother gasped. My father gaped at me. The servant silently excused himself from the room and disappeared.

"Jackson Walker Boudreaux," said my mother in a halting, horrified whisper. She was white as a sheet. Her eyes filled with tears. "That is a terrible thing to say, and untrue!"

My father said crossly, "Well now you've done it. Congratulations, boy. You've made your mother cry."

He went to her, took her hand and held it, crooned soothing words to her as she wept and I looked on, convinced I was in a state of shock so severe I'd had a mental break with reality.

Finally when he'd calmed her down, he pulled himself to his full height, straightened his shoulders, and let me have it.

"Now you listen to me real good, son, because I'm only gonna say this once. We love you. We love you now, we loved you then, we'll love you until we die. *You're our son.* We know we weren't perfect parents, but you were a handful. Maybe we didn't always know the right way to deal with you, but we never loved you less than your brother. Never. And we never blamed you for his death, either, even though I know you think we did."

When I blinked in shock, he nodded. "That's right. I'm not stupid. You got my blood in your veins, you think I don't know what you're thinkin'? But you're a stubborn SOB—just like me. Once you get your mind set, that's it."

My mother made a placating noise, and he heaved a great sigh. "But it was my fault for leavin' it alone for so long. I shoulda . . . done something. I don't know. Made you talk to me. But gettin' you to talk is like pullin' teeth."

He waved a hand in the air like he wanted to dismiss that last part. "Anyway. The bottom line is that the past is past. We're gonna have a new daughter-in-law. It's time we started actin' like a family again. By the way, we love Bianca. What a firecracker. Hopefully we'll have another grandbaby or two by this time next year."

I stared at him. I stared at my mother. I opened my mouth and found I had no words.

"Well, look at that, Clemmy," said my father. "Ha! I've left him speechless. Score one for the old man."

I sank into the chair and put my head into my hands.

The servant reappeared, set a Bloody Dixie on the table in front of me, and murmured, "I hope you still like these, sir. Thought you might need it. Welcome home."

When he disappeared again it was to the sound of my soft, disbelieving laughter.

BLOODY DIXIE

Makes 4 servings

- 1 32-ounce bottle of tomato juice
- 2 ounces vodka
- 1 tablespoon freshly grated horseradish (or prepared)
- 1 tablespoon lemon juice
- 1 tablespoon hot sauce
- 1 tablespoon Worcestershire sauce
- dash of celery salt
- dash of pepper
- 4 slices cooked bacon
- 4 ribs celery

Preparation

1. Pour out ¼ cup tomato juice from bottle.
2. Mix horseradish, lemon juice, hot sauce, Worcestershire, celery salt, and pepper into the remaining tomato juice in bottle and shake vigorously.
3. Add ice to 4 highball glasses.
4. Pour 2 ounces vodka over ice in each glass (or to your taste).
5. Add tomato juice mix to fill.
6. Stir, then garnish with bacon and celery.

THIRTY-FOUR

BIANCA

I was singing loudly and badly in the shower when the glass door opened and Jackson stepped in.

"Don't stop," he said, amused. "I still have ten percent of my hearing left."

He was naked, calm, acting like we showered together every day of the week. He stepped in front of me, blocking the spray, and took the bar of soap from my limp hands as I ogled him.

Jackson naked was one thing. Jackson naked *and wet* was something else altogether. Water worshipped his muscles, making all those gorgeous, golden bulges gleam and sparkle like he'd been photoshopped by a mad, horny housewife. He tipped his head back to wet his hair, and it was in Technicolor slo-mo, a sexy soundtrack playing in the background. I watched with my mouth hanging open as he slowly began to soap his chest.

Even Trace hadn't reached this level of physical perfection. I was showering with a Greek god. With art. How had I been so blind?

Around the estrogen surge wreaking havoc in my nervous system, I said, "I'll have you know I won a talent contest once with my excellent rendition of 'You Are My Sunshine.'"

Jackson shook his head, spraying water droplets from his dark hair, and smiled down at me. He turned me around and started soaping my shoulders and back, gently digging his thumbs into the muscles. I groaned in pleasure. He said, "Really? How old were you? Seven?"

"Eight." I pouted. "Jerk."

He chuckled. "You don't think I'm a jerk." He bent down to kiss my ear. It brought his warm, wet skin in velvety contact with mine. He whispered, "In fact I think you *like* me." He slid an arm around my waist, pinning me against the wall of his hard body.

I trashed my previous position that heaven was a library with every book ever written. No. Heaven was showering with a big, naked, soapy man who had a husky voice and a gentle sense of humor and an erection that should have its own zip code. I relaxed into his embrace with a happy sigh.

"Maybe," I said, almost purring as he massaged my neck. "The jury's still out."

His big hand slid from my neck to my shoulder, then down my arm. He curved his fingers around my rib cage, reverently tracing each rib like it was a love story in braille, then palmed my breast.

He murmured, "You said you wouldn't lie to me, sweetheart," and tweaked my hard nipple with his thumb.

When I gasped and jumped like I'd had a mild electric shock, he chuckled again. "Any other lies you want to tell?"

"Um. I felt nothing when you did that?"

"Oh, that's a good one," he whispered, thumbing back and forth over my nipple as I shivered in delight. "You must be shivering because it's so cold in here."

Hot steam billowed all around us. I couldn't help myself, and laughed. "Definitely."

He gently bit my neck, which I was quickly realizing was one of my favorite things in the world. He was never rough, no matter where he pressed his teeth. It was like he was testing the firmness of my flesh, like he found me so delicious he wanted to eat me. Savor me, bite by bite. Hold my flavor on his tongue and enjoy it, like one would with bourbon or a fine wine.

My head resting on his shoulder, I reached up and wound my arms around his neck. That gave him access to all the girly real estate on my body, which he immediately claimed.

His lips still on my neck, he ran his hands down my sides, armpits to hips, his grip firm and possessive. His erection dug into my bottom. He flattened his hands over my stomach.

"I love this belly," he said faintly. He dragged his hands up to my breasts. "And these. So pretty. So perfect. Look how perfectly they fit in my hands."

He cupped them to prove his point. It was incredibly erotic, looking down at myself, his wet, soapy hands full of me. The way he touched me made me feel proud of my body, intensely feminine and powerful, though he could overpower me in a heartbeat if he wanted to.

His hands slid lower. Past my waist to the triangle between my legs. "And this," he breathed into my ear, slipping his soapy fingers into my folds as I gasped. "I love this. I want this in my mouth or my hands or on my cock every day for the rest of my life."

What was he saying? I was so dizzy I hardly knew. My head lolled to one side. He took my mouth in a kiss so intense it would have made me lose my footing if he hadn't held me up.

It was slow, hot, and deep. His fingers swirled in small, lazy circles between my legs. I trembled and shook, making desperate sounds in my throat.

"I love your sweet little noises, too," said Jackson, a hitch in his voice. "Bianca. You're so sweet."

I didn't feel sweet. I felt ravenous, a ferocious little animal who wanted to tear him to shreds with my sharp, tiny teeth. I was so hungry for him my stomach ached.

He turned us to the wall. I flattened my hands over the wet tiles. He spread his hands around my waist, measuring the span. Then he surprised me by kneeling behind me and biting my ass.

"God." He groaned, stroking my bottom, nipping it, grabbing big handfuls of it like he couldn't get enough. He put his hand between my legs and cupped me, slowly rubbing me as I ground myself against his palm and moaned. My eyes slid shut with pleasure. I leaned my forearms against the wall and dropped my head, canting my behind out because I loved what he was doing so much.

"You're the sexiest fucking woman I've ever seen in my life."

His voice had a harder edge now. A desperate edge, like he was unraveling. Then he stood and tilted my head back with his fingers clenched in my hair and kissed me.

I reached behind me and grasped his erection. He moaned into my mouth.

"Like this," I said, panting, stroking his length. I went up on my toes, guiding him where I wanted him, to that aching place between my legs. "Hurry."

When he slid inside, he dropped his head and bit me on the long muscle between my shoulder and my neck. He shuddered. His low groan went all the way through me.

We stayed like that, unmoving, breathing raggedly, until I couldn't stand it anymore. I flexed my hips. He jerked, driving deep into me, and I yelped in surprise.

"Sorry," he rasped.

My laugh echoed off the walls. "You're forgiven. Do it again."

Gripping my hips, he started a slow rhythm. I clung to the wall. He slid his hand along the back of my thigh and lifted my leg, setting my foot on the tile seat to my right. It changed the angle of everything, deepening it, forcing a low moan from my chest.

He reached around and slid his fingers between my legs. I moaned again, louder.

"She likes that," he said, softly laughing, reaching up with his other hand to caress my breasts.

No, I didn't like it. I loved it. I was obsessed by it. I never knew dirty, wet shower sex would turn out to be something I adored more than chocolate croissants fresh out of the oven, dripping in butter.

"I don't want this to stop," I gasped, headed toward that bright white peak too fast. "Jax. Don't ever stop."

"It won't stop," he said roughly into my ear. "I promise. Now quit holding back."

How did he know? I was beginning to think the man could read my mind. I leaned against him, reached around his neck with one hand, and pulled his head down. We kissed. He tested my lower lip with his teeth, explored my mouth with his tongue, took his time enjoying me. Time spun out and slowed until all the clocks stopped ticking and it was just the two of us, the water, our soft, shared moans and ragged breaths.

When I opened my eyes, he was staring down at me, a drop of water clinging to the tip of his nose, a look of adoration on his face.

Something in the center of my chest unlocked and broke free.

My orgasm slammed into me like a comet into earth. I stiffened and cried out, safe in the circle of his arms, gazing into his eyes as it happened. The bathroom echoed with the sounds of my undoing.

"You've ruined me for anyone else," he whispered hoarsely, beginning to lose himself. "Bianca. I'm ruined."

I convulsed around him, too overcome with emotion to speak.

He braced his arm against the wall to hold us up. He trembled, spasmed, made a sound like he was deeply in pain. "Fuck," he groaned, and withdrew from my body. Then he kissed me like his life depended on it as he spilled himself onto my skin.

By the time we came back to our senses, the water had started to turn cold.

Jax reached out and turned off the spray. He wrapped his arms around me and hid his face in my neck, hugging me hard, his chest heaving.

He said my name, but I shushed him. "Not yet. Let's not talk about it yet," I whispered.

I was afraid what might come out of my mouth if he asked me how I was feeling.

We dried off and dressed in silence, avoiding each other's eyes. We knew words would be too much, yet not enough. Something had changed between us in the shower. Something profound had taken root.

"You need food," Jackson said, looking pointedly at my abdomen after another alarmingly loud rumble. My stomach sounded like it was occupied by a large, carnivorous beast, roaming around and kicking over furniture.

"Food! Yes!" I said with the volume of a person shouting across a highway to her friend stranded on the other side.

Jackson looked at me askance.

He stood in the bathroom doorway, watching me wind my damp hair into a big, messy bun. I'd pulled on a white cashmere sweater he'd bought for me and a pair of lovely charcoal-gray slacks he must've had custom made because they fit perfectly in *both* the waist and hips, a statistical impossibility.

"And maybe a stiff drink," he added drily, examining my expression.

Stiff. Lord, don't talk to me about stiff! I met his gaze in the mirror and forced myself to sound like a sane person. "So did you talk to your parents?"

One side of his mouth quirked. "I did."

He let it hang there, torturing me. "And?"

A smile bloomed over his face. It was like watching the sun rise over mountains. "And they love you," he murmured, holding my gaze.

Love.

Green beans, there was that word again.

It had been popping up in my head and on his lips for the past hour like weeds through cracks in the sidewalk. I had to remind myself that this was a business deal. He was here for his inheritance, I was here for my mama. It wouldn't do to get ahead of myself and start attaching deeper meaning to things on account of hot shower sex.

Hot, emotional, vulnerable, soul-searing, life-changing shower sex.

"Uh-oh," said Jackson. "I smell smoke. You're thinking again."

"Ha ha. Can we please go get some food before I eat that bar of soap?"

He pushed away from the doorway and wrapped his arms around me, resting his chin on top of my head. "Yep. But you have to promise if this little breakdown you're having gets any worse, you'll talk to me, so I won't have to hold you down and tickle it out of you."

I gave him scary crazy-lady eyes. "You will *not* tickle me. Ever. Understood?"

He tilted his head and whispered in my ear, "Sorry, sweetheart, that's not in the contract." Then he dug his fingers into my ribs.

I screamed and tried to twist away, but he was too strong. He wrapped his arms around me and lifted me clear off my feet so we were nose to nose, my arms pinned to my side, my feet kicking uselessly around his shins.

"It isn't fair that you're so giant," I groused. "And freakishly strong."

"I'm not that strong, but thank you."

"Honey, you're holding up my entire weight like I'm a loaf of bread. One of the airy kinds, like sourdough."

He chuckled and kissed the tip of my nose. "Honey?" he drawled.

He lowered his lashes, smug as all get-out. I wondered with irritation why those kind of thick, silky, black eyelashes were always wasted on boys who didn't appreciate how lucky they were to have them.

I sniffed like a snooty aristocrat. "It was a slip of the tongue. I'm getting lightheaded from lack of food. I could faint at any moment."

He pressed a soft kiss to my lips and chuckled again. "I see. You're still in fibbing mode. All right, I'll let it go until"—he checked his watch, which meant he was now holding me up with *one* arm—"noon. Deal?"

I muttered, "Showoff."

He laughed and set me on my feet. "After breakfast," he said, leading me by my hand from the room, "you have your choice of horseback riding, bowling, tennis, fishing, boating, or touring the botanical gardens or rickhouse."

"Rickhouse?"

He looked over his shoulder at me and grinned. "It's where we house all the ricks, obviously."

I rolled my eyes. "Obviously."

The rest of the day was a fairy tale, and I was Cinderella.

We ate breakfast in a sun-filled room Jackson called the "solar," serenaded by songbirds flitting in dozens of large cages hung at various heights around the room. The hovering servants seemed friendlier today, even daring to smile pleasantly at us when they brought our food and cleared out plates. Even more surprising, Jackson smiled back.

He seemed like a different man than he was yesterday. Lighter. Less burdened by ghosts. His parents seemed different, too, though they didn't hover. They greeted us warmly when we came down to eat, made light conversation, and then took their leave with a promise to see us for dinner.

I got the feeling they were leaving us alone together and not avoiding us, which are two very different things.

Jackson gave me a tour of the estate on a golf cart emblazoned with a giant B on the front, rear, and roof, which I found hilarious. As if anyone could mistake who it belonged to. The botanical gardens were a marvel of engineering, designed by an anal-retentive botanist with a fetish for nude statuary and hedge mazes. Had I been there alone, I would've been hopelessly lost in five minutes.

We drove by the stables at top speed. Jackson pointed them out with a jerk of his thumb. I was glad I hadn't taken him up on his offer to go riding, because there were obviously still a few of his ghosts lurking in the tack room, waiting to shriek and rattle their chains.

Lakes. Trees. A beautiful white church topped by a steeple. Acres upon acres of wooded pathways and hidden putting greens and spectacular sweeping vistas dotted with wildlife. More than once we had to swerve to avoid a startled jackrabbit or white-tailed deer. Moonstar Ranch was a place steeped in magic, and my feeling of being immersed in a fairy tale grew as the day wore on.

All the while my engagement ring flashed and winked on my finger, sending prisms of light in starburst patterns everywhere like a promise of good things to come.

We talked, laughed, held hands shyly, smiled at each other with our eyes. In the rickhouse—a massive concrete rectangle where the family stored their private reserve—Jackson kissed me in a cool, shadowed corner behind a soaring wall of bourbon barrels stacked twenty high on metal racks. We ate a picnic lunch under the shade of an enormous willow tree on a hill overlooking a sparkling lake. We made plans to have dinner with his parents. I wanted to make them Mama's famous jambalaya with a blackberry-and-bourbon cobbler for dessert.

When we went back to Jackson's room to change for dinner, my cell phone was ringing. I'd left it on the dresser, too distracted from what had happened between us in the shower to remember to bring it along.

"Hello?" I swatted away Jackson's attempt to pinch my ass with a laugh.

"Bianca," said Eeny. Her voice caught on a sob.

The words fell down on me like bricks thrown from the top of a building.

So sorry.

She's gone.

There was nothing we could do.

I tried to inhale but couldn't. I tried to speak, but a gasp of anguish was all I could muster. My body went hot, then freezing cold. I began to violently shake.

"Bianca?" Jackson's voice rang sharp with concern as he looked at my face. "What is it?"

I dropped the phone and sank to my knees on the floor. "Mama," I rasped, choking on the word. "She's dead."

From that moment on, so was I.

The fairy tale was over.

THIRTY-FIVE

JACKSON

I've suffered through my share of painful moments. Before now, I thought I knew all pain's ugly faces, all the ways it can cripple and scar.

But with one phone call I discovered that there's no worse pain in the world than watching someone you love suffer and being powerless to make the suffering stop.

I kissed her and held her and rocked her, I promised I'd do everything I could to help. Words. All of them useless. None of them changed a thing or broke through the new encasing of ice swiftly crystallizing around her. From the moment Bianca took that phone call, she went cold. All the life was sucked out of her. All the fire was extinguished. What was left was a shell-shocked husk.

She didn't even cry, which somehow made everything worse.

"I need to get back as soon as possible," she said hollowly, sitting on the floor with her back against the side of the bed. I crouched beside her, holding her clammy, limp hand, fighting a terrible slipping feeling inside me, like a landslide in my chest.

"Of course. The plane can be ready within the hour. I'll make sure the bags get packed."

She closed her eyes. She didn't speak again until we got back to New Orleans, except to say good-bye to my parents, who were as distraught as I was when they heard the news. We left Moonstar Ranch the same way we came, by limo and private jet, but everything had changed.

I could tell by the way Bianca stared with flat eyes at the ring on her finger that what had happened between us was "before." This was "after," the new reality in which her mother was dead, taking Bianca's reason for us to be together to the grave with her.

So yes. I thought I knew Pain before. I thought I knew Loss.

But those two ruthless bitches were just getting started with me.

THIRTY-SIX

BIANCA

It was raining when we touched down in New Orleans, the sky the same ugly lead gray as my soul.

I didn't know why I felt so numb. Shock, I suppose. In any case, I was grateful for the way all my senses were dulled, because I knew there were a thousand invisible knives of anguish hovering all around me, hungry for their moment to slash and draw blood.

They'd get their moment, of that I was sure. But for now I was safe in a cocoon of soft white noise where nothing could reach me. Not even the torment in Jackson's eyes.

His engagement ring was a cold, heavy weight on my finger, a constant reminder of the bargain we'd made, and why.

I couldn't think about it. I couldn't face any more harsh realities today. All I could do was put one foot in front of the other and keep breathing.

When we arrived at Mama's house, I could barely even do that.

"I've got you," said Jackson when I stepped out of the car and almost fell. He put his arm around my waist and half dragged, half carried me up the steps and into the house. Eeny was there, her face streaked with dried tears, which got a fresh coat the minute she laid eyes on me.

"Boo!" she wailed, and crushed me into her embrace.

"It's okay," I whispered into her bosom. "We're going to be okay." I didn't know who I was trying to convince, her or myself.

A young redheaded woman in pale-blue scrubs stood by the sofa, wringing her hands. "Miss Hardwick," she murmured, moving closer. "I'm Jennifer Wright, from Home Angels Health Care. I'm so sorry for your loss."

Home Angels. I supposed they were the company Jackson hired. I struggled to focus on her voice as she continued to speak.

"I was assigned the afternoon shift. Gina, who was here in the morning, said your mother was resting comfortably when she left at noon. She had a little lunch, then went to take a nap. Then she must've . . ." Jennifer didn't know how to politely say it, so she skipped ahead. "Apparently Eeny arrived just before I did, at four."

Eeny clung to me, her tears wetting my neck. "She looked like she was sleepin'! So peaceful, like an angel—"

She dissolved into a fresh round of weeping. Jennifer chewed on her lower lip and increased the speed of her hand wringing.

Realizing he was the only capable person in the room, Jackson went into efficiency mode. "The paramedics were called?" he asked Jennifer, sounding like he might snap her in two if she answered incorrectly.

"Yes," she peeped, going pale. "They tried to resuscitate her. When that failed, they asked if we wanted to transfer Mrs. Hardwick to the hospital or make arrangements with a funeral home to pick up her remains here."

Her remains. I almost fainted, but held myself up through sheer strength of will, gritting my teeth against the sob rising in the back of my throat.

Jennifer hurried on. "Eeny and I thought it would be best if Mrs. Hardwick stayed where she was until her daughter arrived. I hope that was all right?"

"Yes," I said faintly. I pulled out of Eeny's embrace and nodded at Jennifer, who looked frightened that she might have done something wrong. "Thank you, Jennifer." I looked down the hallway at the closed door of Mama's bedroom.

Noticing the direction of my gaze, Jackson gently settled his hand on my shoulder. "Do you want me to . . . ?"

"No," I said. "I want a minute alone with her, if you don't mind."

"Of course not. Take all the time you need. I'll call Robertson's Funeral Home and get the arrangements started, unless there's somewhere else you'd rather—"

"That's fine," I whispered, already moving away. It didn't make a difference what company took Mama's body. The parts of her that mattered were already gone.

Steeling my nerves, I hesitated a moment with my hand on the door before going in. The only other dead person I'd ever seen was my father, and he'd died when I was young enough to understand death but not be terrified of it. I didn't know how I'd react to seeing Mama lying lifelessly in her bed, and I said a silent prayer I'd be able to withstand it.

The door creaked open. The room was dim, lit only with the lamp on the table beside the bed. The air was cool and still and smelled faintly of Mama's perfume.

I crept over to the bed with my heart pounding, terror closing around my throat like a hangman's noose. When I grew nearer and saw the serene expression on Mama's face, the terror faded away like a tide receding, and I could breathe again.

I knelt beside the bed and took her hand. Not even a hint of warmth still lingered in it.

"I can't believe you left me," I whispered, hearing the accusation in my voice. All of a sudden I was a child again, six years old, lost in the

Mardi Gras parade when Mama briefly let go of my hand. I had the same feeling now as I did then, raw disbelief mixed with rising hysteria, searching desperately for her face in a crowd of strangers.

Only this time the hysteria wouldn't be replaced with sweet relief when I was found. I'd remain lost forever, alone in a sea of unfamiliar faces, crying out her name.

I told her I loved her. I told her she was the best mother who ever lived. I told her I hoped one day to be half the woman she was, and that I'd always try to make her proud. Through it all she was silent and still the way only a corpse can be, that utter absence of life like a negative charge sucking the air from the room.

It wasn't until I whispered, "Tell Daddy I miss him," that I sensed a change in the atmosphere. Something shimmered briefly. The air gained a palpable spark.

Maybe it was my imagination, but I'd swear on the Bible I felt a gentle touch on my head.

Then it was gone, and I was alone in a cool, quiet room with the body of my mother, and all the pain I'd been holding off came rushing over me at once.

I threw my head back and howled like an animal, loud enough to scour every ghost within miles from its grave.

The bland-faced men from the funeral home spoke in soft, soothing tones and wore black suits with white carnations in the lapels. I picked out a casket from a catalog, one with a beautiful lavender lining I knew Mama would've liked. Arrangements were made. Paperwork was signed. Condolences were given.

Then they loaded Mama into a hearse and took her away.

Eeny sent her off with a teary cry of, "Safe travels, Miss Davina!" and the pain was so breathtaking I almost fell to my knees.

Through it all, Jackson was a rock. He kept his hand on my lower back, or my shoulder, or my arm, a constant, gentle touch of support. When I found it hard to stand, he held me up. When I found it impossible to speak, he spoke for me. He thanked Jennifer and told her to go home, then he asked Eeny if she could go to the restaurant and take care of things there, because we all could see that I was in no shape to handle it.

"Cancel all the reservations for the rest of the week," I told her in a dull voice. "Put a sign on the front door. CLOSED INDEFINITELY."

"Should I call anyone for you, boo? People will want to know Davina passed."

"Yes," I said, my head pounding. "Call everyone. I'll let you know as soon as I schedule the funeral service with the church. Thank you, Eeny."

When Jackson said, "Tell the restaurant employees they'll be paid for the days off," I didn't have the strength to argue. By then all I wanted to do was lie down and sleep for a few years.

Weeping, Eeny left. Then Jackson and I sat at the kitchen table, staring at each other like two people who've survived a plane crash only to find themselves stranded on a desert island with no food or shelter and a hurricane blowing in.

"I'm so sorry," he finally said. His eyes were fierce. "She was a lovely woman."

I looked at the table, its wood surface nicked and scratched from years of use, while grief swept through me like a raging river overflowing its banks. "Yes. Thank you. For everything you've done, thank you. You've been a great help."

I didn't mean for it to sound like a dismissal, like a decision had been made by a committee that he'd performed well under pressure but should now be on his way, but somehow it did. He flinched a little, slouched lower in his chair.

A minute passed in silence. Then Jackson cleared his throat. "You're staying here tonight?"

I hadn't thought about it, but the moment the words were out of his mouth I knew I wanted to do exactly that. "Yes," I said, strangely relieved.

He nodded. His jaw was set. My engagement ring caught a ray of light and reflected it around the kitchen in a million prism sparks. I couldn't imagine a more awkward moment had ever occurred.

He asked, "Is there anything I can do? Anything you need?"

When I said no, he visibly deflated.

"Okay," he answered quietly. "Then I'll just . . . I guess I'll just go."

I couldn't look at him. A chaos of wingbeats filled my chest. Did I want him to go? Did I want him to stay? I didn't know anything anymore, only that it was hard to catch my breath. I feared if I looked up into his face, I might shatter into a thousand tiny pieces.

He stood. "Call me if you need anything." His voice had an edge of sorrow, like he already knew I wouldn't.

He kissed the top of my head, his lips the barest brush of pressure, fleetingly there, then gone. Then he walked slowly to the front door, his shoulders slumped in a way I'd never seen before. When I heard the door open, my lungs filled with breath, as if I were about to shout, but then the door closed, and I was left alone in silence, the awful reality of the day settling into my bones.

Somewhere off in the distance, a dog howled. It exactly matched the sound inside my head.

That day passed. Heartless how the sun has the nerve to rise and set and rise again, witness to so much ruin.

I awoke in the morning with no idea where I was. I bolted upright on the sofa, staring around the small parlor in confusion, in my clothes from the day before, blinking against the glare of sun streaming through the curtains. Then I remembered, and felt a thousand years old.

Everything looked different without Mama in the world. Even my own face in the mirror. I looked older. Harder. Something had extinguished in my eyes.

I couldn't eat but desperately needed coffee. I made myself a cup and almost dropped it when the phone rang, my nerves were so shredded.

"Hello?"

"Bianca," said the Colonel, sobbing. "Oh, Bianca, tell me it isn't true!"

I closed my eyes and rested my forehead against the wall. "I can't believe it, either. It's impossible that she's gone."

Listening to a man cry is one of the most terrible things in the world. Their tears seem so much more devastating than female tears. Maybe because they so infrequently shed them.

"Was it a heart attack?" the Colonel asked, his voice choked with shock.

"I don't know. She didn't want an autopsy, so we won't know the exact cause of death, but the chemo was really hard on her system."

There was a stunned silence. "Chemo?"

"She had lung cancer," I whispered. "She's been on chemo for weeks. She was scheduled for surgery on Wednesday."

The Colonel's small cry of distress pierced me straight through my heart. "*Cancer?* My God! She never said a word—I thought she had the flu!"

"I know. I'm sorry. That's what she told everyone."

It was a minute or two before he composed himself enough to talk. "You know what I think?" he said in a ragged whisper.

"No. What?"

He drew in a long, shuddering breath. I imagined him on the other end of the phone, wiping his eyes and pulling himself up straight into that ramrod posture he was known for. He said, "I think she was just tired of bein' without your daddy, and now that you're settled, she decided it was time for her to be on her way."

A sob broke from my chest. Fighting tears, I clapped a hand over my mouth.

"I loved your mama, Bianca. She was a good woman, and I'll miss her somethin' fierce. But I always knew she'd given her heart away a long time ago. I knew she'd never stop loving your daddy, but I'm grateful for the time we spent together because she made me happy. She made the world a better place."

I didn't know how I was still standing. Strange, strangled noises gurgled up from deep in my throat.

The Colonel asked gently, "Is there anything you need, darlin'? Anything I can do for you?"

I managed to tell him no, but it was someone else's voice who answered. Someone with a whiskey-soaked growl and a broken heart. We said good-bye and hung up, but before my coffee got cold the phone rang again.

It didn't stop ringing for hours.

In between phone calls were the visitors.

They came in a constant stream, friends and neighbors and members of Mama's church, bearing casseroles and weeping into crumpled-up tissues. Everything became a blur. All the faces began to blend together. I was simultaneously exhausted and energized by all the people who came, their grief piling on top of my own, their voices like the angry buzz of wasps inside my head. I started to feel disconnected, numb again, and was grateful for it.

Numb was better than the alternative. With any luck, numb would get me through the rest of my life.

I spoke to the church and set Mama's funeral for Wednesday at noon. So the day she was supposed to have life-saving surgery was the day she'd be buried. I didn't want to examine the coincidence.

When Jackson called, I told him I needed to stay at Mama's house for now to deal with everything that had to be done. When he asked if he should come over to help, I said no. After the awkward pause that followed, he said he'd send some of my clothes over. I think he was hoping I'd say don't bother, I'll be coming to live at Rivendell soon, but I was so tired I just said, "That's fine."

When we hung up it felt like I'd been untethered. I was a little boat who'd lost her moorings and was drifting aimlessly out to sea.

For the next two days, I didn't eat. I barely slept. I survived on coffee and adrenaline, forgetting to shower until Eeny told me I smelled like a goat. By Wednesday morning I was a wreck. I didn't know how I'd make it through the funeral without collapsing.

But once again, Jackson's strength shored me up.

Then he gave my little boat a hard push into rough waters and set me free.

THIRTY-SEVEN

BIANCA

It was a bracing fifty-eight degrees, the sky a clear, brilliant blue above our heads. Eeny stood to my left, crying softly into a handkerchief. Jackson was to my right, stony as the inside of my heart.

The church service was beautiful, attended by almost four hundred people. A gospel choir raised the rafters in song. Hoyt arranged for a jazz funeral procession from Saint Augustine's to the cemetery. Two dozen musicians in black caps and white dress shirts slowly led the mourners on foot through the streets of New Orleans to the sound of hymns played on trumpets, drums, saxophones, and clarinets. At the grave site there were so many flower arrangements the bees came out in force, adding a gentle hum to underscore the priest's final blessing of farewell.

Then Mama's casket was lowered into the ground, and it was done.

Back at the house, the wake lasted for an eternity. Finally, well after nightfall, the house emptied, and I was left alone with my grief and a grim fiancé who looked exactly as wrecked as I felt.

His rough black beard was back. His hair had obviously only been finger combed. He was restless and edgy, a dark thundercloud of mood over his head. Though he wore a suit and tie, he seemed more of the Beast than I'd ever seen him.

"Let's sit down," he said gruffly, gesturing to the sofa. "We need to talk."

Surprised, I sat and folded my hands in my lap while I waited for him to sit, too. That moment never came. He stood looking at the floor, his hands hanging loose at his sides and slightly trembling.

"Jackson?"

He glanced up at me. His eyes were so dark. Something about the look in them made my skin crawl.

Spooked, I said, "What is it?"

He moistened his lips. From the inside pocket of his coat he slowly withdrew a set of folded papers. "We don't have to draw this out any longer than necessary. I wanted to wait until after . . ."

He swallowed, moistened his lips again, then started anew. "I knew you had so much on your plate. I wanted to wait until after the funeral to give you this."

He held out the papers. "It's my copy of our contract."

Taking the papers, I furrowed my brow in confusion. "I don't understand."

Jackson dragged a hand through his hair. He loosened his tie, then went to stand at the front window and gazed out at the night like he was no longer holding out hope of finding something he'd lost. His voice low and rough, he asked, "You didn't think I'd force you to go through with it now, did you?"

When I was silent, stunned because I thought I understood what he meant, he turned to me with a look so anguished it made my heart skip a beat. "Please tell me you don't think I'm the kind of man who would do that."

I slowly rose. The papers shook like mad in my hands. "We made an agreement," I said hoarsely, not recognizing my own voice. "Your inheritance—"

"It hasn't been about my inheritance for me for a while now, Bianca," he interrupted harshly, his eyes glittering. "Honestly, I'm not sure it ever was."

It hung there between us, breathtakingly raw. I whispered, "Jax."

Something in my expression caused him visible pain. He turned away, stuffed his hands into his pockets, and bowed his head. "I'll have all your things brought back here. I'm sorry you had to let go of your house. The timing was just"—his laugh was hollow—"shit."

I wanted to say something—anything—but words wouldn't come. Jackson was letting me out of our deal. I didn't have to marry him.

He was going to lose everything.

Finally I came to my senses. A deal was a deal after all, and I wasn't about to renege on my end of the bargain, no matter what circumstances had changed. "I can't let you do that," I said, and dropped the papers on the coffee table. They landed with a dull slap that seemed unnaturally loud in the quiet room.

Jackson turned from the window. He looked at the papers, then at my face. Then he crossed the room in a few long strides and picked up the contract. He ripped it in half with one abrupt, savage motion. "Don't you get it? You're not *obligated* to me anymore! You're free! Go live your life!"

His voice was choked with emotion. His eyes were wild like I'd never seen them. I put my hand over my thundering heart.

"I'm sorry," he rasped, instantly contrite, taking a step back. "Fuck. I'm so sorry. I'm an asshole. I know this is the worst day of your life. I didn't mean to—I can't—"

He cursed again, whirling away, and headed for the front door. "Keep the ring," he said over his shoulder. "Hock it. Throw it away. Whatever you want. I'll send all your things tomorrow. Let me know if there's anything else you need."

He opened the door and was gone before I could even decide if the words forming on my lips were "Thank you" or "Don't go."

The screen door slammed shut behind him.

True to his word, Jackson had all my things delivered to Mama's house the next day in the same boxes I'd packed them into a lifetime ago. I spent a few days in a weird kind of limbo, puttering around aimlessly, trying to decide if I wanted to sell the house or keep it, before I gave up pressuring myself to make any big decisions and retired to the sofa in the front parlor, where I stayed for several more days, rising only to scrounge from the casseroles and leftovers crammed in the fridge.

I didn't allow myself to think about Jackson. There was a dangerous ache under my breastbone when I got too close to even picturing his face, so I shoved the memory of him and our short, magical time at Moonstar Ranch down into a dark corner of my heart and concentrated on the business of being depressed.

Eeny didn't let that continue long before barging through the front door and scolding me to within an inch of my life.

"Get off your behind, girl, and get back to work! Who do you think you're honorin' with all this mopin' around? Because it sure ain't your mama! She'd be scandalized if she could see you right now, lyin' there wallowin' like a pig in shit!"

Eeny loomed over me, hands propped on her hips, scowling down at the pathetic picture I made in my dirty pajamas and unwashed hair on the couch.

I severely regretted giving her a key.

"You're right," I said tonelessly, staring at the ceiling. "I know you're right."

"Then get your ass in gear and get up!" She gave the sofa a frustrated little kick, jostling me.

"I'm in mourning. You shouldn't curse at people in mourning."

She snorted and crossed her arms over her chest. "You're in danger of gettin' on my bad side, boo."

She didn't have to say more than that. The last person who got on her bad side ended up with four slashed tires on his car, a headless rooster on his doorstep, and a strange, persistent rash.

"I'm up," I grumbled, rousing. "Terrorist."

"You're the terrorist, child. Have you looked in a mirror lately? You're so frightenin' I'd hire you to haunt a house! You're so scary lookin' you'd make a freight train take a dirt road! You look so bad—"

"I get it, I get it," I said, stumbling to my feet. "I look like crap."

Eeny nodded as if I'd said something remarkably intelligent for once. "Like you fell out the ugly tree and hit every damn branch on the way down."

I sighed heavily. Eeny grimaced and waved an offended hand in front of her face.

"*Lawd!* That breath of yours is nuclear, girl! Can't believe it hasn't melted the lips right off your face."

From somewhere deep inside me emerged a grudging chuckle, which made Eeny smile and nod her head.

"That's better. Now go take a shower and put on some clean clothes. We're goin' to the restaurant. You got people to feed, and I miss that ornery ol' billy goat Hoyt more than I ever woulda guessed. Don't gimme that stink eye!" she snapped when I raised my brows. "And if you repeat that to anyone, I'll mash your potatoes!"

"My lips are sealed."

I smiled for the first time in days as I headed off to the bathroom to wash away a week's worth of neglect. I stopped when I heard my cell phone ring from the kitchen counter. I didn't recognize the number when I picked up.

"Hello?"

"Miss Hardwick, it's Michael Roth."

He was the attorney I'd hired to review my contract with Jackson. "How can I help you, Mr. Roth?"

"I received a copy of the trust documents from Mr. Boudreaux's attorney."

"Oh. Yes, um, well Mr. Boudreaux and I . . . the contract you reviewed . . ." I sighed. "Mr. Boudreaux doesn't want to move forward with the marriage, so the contract is void at this point."

The attorney's pause was so loaded I imagined the phone gained weight in my hand. He said, "But the trust isn't."

I yawned, scratching my head. "Hmm?"

"Miss Hardwick, did you seek legal counsel before signing the trust documents?"

Oh dear. There was an accusation in his tone. I wasn't in the state of mind to deal with a peeved attorney. "Well . . . no," I admitted sheepishly. "The whole thing was a little rushed—"

"The trust isn't linked in any way to the marriage contract," he interrupted impatiently.

I rubbed my eyes with my fist, starting to get irritated with the conversation. "Mr. Roth, you'll have to speak English. I haven't had my coffee yet. What're you saying?"

Amusement warmed his voice. "I'm saying Mr. Boudreaux gifted you a million dollars."

I frowned. This didn't make any sense. Maybe I was understanding him wrong. "No, that can't be right. The trust is part of the marriage contract. The two go together. Without a marriage, there's no money."

Mr. Roth started to speak slowly and patiently, as you would to a child or someone mentally impaired. "There is *no mention* of establishing a trust in the marriage contract, Miss Hardwick. As far as the contract is concerned, the trust doesn't exist. There was only a stipulation that a payment in the amount of one million dollars would be conferred to you upon your marriage, but it never specifically spelled out *how* that payment would be made. This trust I've just reviewed"—I heard the sound of rustling paper in the background—"is ironclad. It's irre-vocable. You are the sole trustee. No one else has access to the money. That million dollars is yours, married or not."

I rolled my eyes. "Mr. Roth. Respectfully, you're talking out of your behind. I know you graduated from college, because I saw the framed degree on the wall behind your desk, but you've got this all wrong. Jackson Boudreaux would *never* make such a stupid mistake."

After a while Mr. Roth said, "I agree. He wouldn't. It was intentional."

My mouth opened. Nothing came out.

"Of course if you don't believe me, I advise you to get another opinion." He sniffed, his ego dinged by my disbelief. "But any attorney will tell you the same thing. Congratulations, Miss Hardwick. You're a millionaire."

I breathed, "I'm . . . whaaa . . ."

Mr. Roth kept talking, his voice a distant drone in my ear, but I heard nothing else he said. I stood in the kitchen, blank with shock, until the house phone rang and jolted me back into reality. I discon-nected the call with Mr. Holt, who was still talking, and picked up the phone on the wall.

"Hardwick residence," I said, completely disoriented.

Mr. Holt had to be wrong. He had to be. Why on earth would Jackson do a thing like that?

"Bianca," said Trace.

His mouth turned my name into a sneer. I stiffened, going from disoriented to teed off in two seconds flat. "You've got some nerve call-ing this house!" I said, hackles rising.

He chuckled. It was an ugly sound, full of malice. "What, I can't call to pay my respects?"

We both knew he wasn't calling to pay his respects. He had other business on his mind, which I had no intention of listening to.

"I'm only going to tell you this one more time, Trace. *Stay away from me.*"

"Or what?" he snarled. "You'll have Jackson Boudreaux buy up the whole block instead of just the one building?"

"What the heck are you talking about?" I hated myself for taking the bait but needed to know what he meant. Suddenly anything to do with Jackson was of paramount importance, even if it came from Trace's fanged mouth.

"You know *exactly* what I'm talking about!"

When I didn't answer, he shouted, "My restaurant? The building it was going to open in suddenly getting bought up even though it wasn't on the market? The new owner canceling my lease?"

The hairs on my arms rose in gooseflesh. My heart started to thump. Not daring to believe it, I said slowly, "Jackson bought the building where you were going to open your restaurant, and then canceled your lease?"

Trace's laugh was hard and a little scary. "You're a shitty actress, bumble bee," he said bitterly. "Don't think for a minute I don't know who asked him to do it."

For a moment I went totally blank. My mind was as snowy as a polar bear's backside.

Then a hysterical laugh broke from my chest.

Jackson bought the building where Trace was going to open his restaurant and canceled the lease! Filled with glee, I cackled madly again, stamping my foot on the floor.

Eeny came in from the parlor and looked at me like she was wondering if I needed to take a nice, long vacation in a place with barred windows and padded walls.

She wasn't the only one affected by it. Trace flipped his lid. He roared, "You're fucking stupid!"

I hooted, positively giddy. "And you're proof!"

Apoplectic, he sputtered, "You need me! You told me you'd always love me! 'I will always love you'—those were your exact goddamn words!"

Then it was like something inside me was just done with him, dusted off its hands, and turned tail without another look back.

I said calmly, "I'm not Whitney Houston, you silly goose. I need you like the word *knife* needs the letter *k*. The only thing you ever gave me was dick and a headache."

I hung up.

Eeny and I looked at each other.

"Who on earth was that?" she asked, wide-eyed.

"Snake oil salesman. I told him to find the nearest tall building and go stand out on a ledge."

She narrowed her eyes at me, leaning in to look closer. "You okay, boo?"

I stared at her as several things became clear all at once, like a light switch had been flipped on inside my brain and a thousand bulbs glowed white-hot, illuminating what had been standing there in the dark all along, waiting for me to open my eyes.

I was a damn fool. A stubborn, blind, hopeless fool.

The worst part was, it was *myself* I was fooling.

With wonder in my voice, I said, "Eeny. Jackson Boudreaux asked my mama for permission to marry me when he didn't have to. He gave me a seven-carat Tiffany diamond ring when I said I wanted a simple gold band. He gave me a million dollars in cash, for *nothing*. And bought an entire building so a man who'd hurt me couldn't hurt me again. And told me his deepest, darkest secrets—things he'd never told anyone before."

Eeny blinked at me, unimpressed. "What's your point?"

I inhaled a slow breath. My nerves tingled almost painfully, like they'd been frozen for years but were finally coming alive.

I whispered, "I think Jackson Boudreaux *is in love with me*."

Eeny made a face like I was the world's biggest moron. "Of course he's in love with you, dummy! A blind man could see that! Stars above, don't tell me you didn't *know?*"

When I just gaped at her silently, she threw her hands in the air. "How I'm supposed to deal with this kind of ignorance I surely don't know! Heavens to Betsy, Bianca, sometimes you can be *awful* dense!"

My throat raw with emotion, I said, "I thought love was supposed to be weak knees and butterflies in your stomach and a terrible longing that could never be quenched."

Eeny shook her head, chuckled, came over and embraced me. "No, child," she said gently, patting my back. "That's romance. Romance is built on doubt. Love is solid. Constant. If you're not careful, you might mistake it for bein' boring because it's so reliable. Love is warm and deep and comfortable, just right, so you float in it peacefully without ever being scalded or frozen, like a perfect, relaxing bubble bath.

"But it's also fierce and strong and demands all the best parts of you, the parts that are giving and honest and true. Love makes you a better person. It makes you *want* to be a better person. You know it's love when you feel comfortable just as you are, when you feel seen and understood, when you know you could tell all your darkest truths and they'd be accepted without judgement."

Eeny pulled away and gently smoothed a hand over my hair. "Love isn't butterflies, boo. It isn't weak knees. It's a pride of lions. It's a pack of wolves. It's 'I've got your back even if it costs me my own life,' because unlike romance that fizzles at the first sign of trouble, love will fight to the death. When it's love, you'll go to war to avenge even the slightest offense. And you'll be justified.

"Because of all the marvelous and terrible things we can experience in this life, love is the only one that will last beyond it."

A car with a bad muffler rumbled by on the street outside. I heard the distant hum of a jet plane flying somewhere far overhead. And deep, deep down inside my soul, a calm voice said *yes*.

"Oh God," I blurted, my eyes going wide. "I love him, Eeny! I love Jackson Boudreaux!"

Eeny sighed deeply, tilted back her head, and beseeched the ceiling. "Honestly, Jesus, how can you burden me with such stupidity?"

"I have to call him, I've got to call him right now, oh Lord what is the matter with me, I'm an A-plus idiot," I babbled, scrabbling wildly at the phone on the wall like it might launch itself into outer space to escape my insane clutches.

I punched in the number with frantic stabbing motions. I waited breathlessly for the line to connect, but his cell phone went straight to voice mail. Panicked, I called the house.

Rayford picked up with a smooth, "Good evening, Boudreaux residence."

I began to holler incoherently. "Rayford it's Bianca I need to speak with Jackson please put him on the phone!"

Rayford paused before answering. "Mr. Boudreaux is . . . occupied at the moment," he said in a strange, ominous tone. "May I take a message?"

My heart pounded so hard I was out of breath. "Occupied? No, Rayford, you don't understand, it's *very* important that I speak with him—"

"I'm sorry, but that's not possible," he said briskly. "Is there anything I can help you with?"

Rayford had never been remote like this with me before. He was acting like we'd never even met. This smelled to high heaven.

Something was seriously wrong.

"Rayford," I said, controlling the hysteria in my voice as best I could, "what's going on?"

Another pause, like he was considering whether or not to answer, then he made a little embarrassed cough. "Mr. Boudreaux has a guest. I'll be happy to tell him you called, however. Have a nice evening."

The phone went dead in my hand. I stared at it in amazement. Then, with a shock like I'd stuck my finger into a power outlet, I knew.

Eeny said, "Well?"

Cold with horror, I said, "What day is it, Eeny?"

She frowned at me. "It's Tuesday."

"No, the date!" I shouted, flailing my hands. "What's the *date*?"

"The sixteenth. Why?"

The sixteenth. Dear Lord. Today is Jackson's birthday.

He had to get married by his birthday or lose his inheritance. He couldn't come to the phone because he was occupied with a "guest."

I dropped the phone and left it dangling from its cord as I tore down the hall to the bedroom to get a pair of shoes, screaming at Eeny over my shoulder to call me a taxi and put it on super emergency rush.

I had to go stop a wedding.

THIRTY-EIGHT

JACKSON

Rayford quietly hung up the library phone. I didn't look up from the paperwork I'd been perusing when I asked, "Who was that?"

"Telemarketer," he said. "Annual fund-raising for the local police."

Now I did look up, surprised. "I wonder why the chief didn't call me himself? He knows I don't like to talk to telemarketers." I thought for a moment. "Didn't they just have the police fund-raiser a few months ago?"

Rayford's expression was bland. "You write so many checks for fund-raisers, sir, I can never remember which one's which." From the corner of my desk he picked up my crystal decanter, tilted it over my empty glass, and smiled. "Refill?"

I sighed heavily. I knew I'd been drinking too much lately, but it was the only thing getting me through the nights. "Yes. Thanks."

He poured me a generous measure, then turned to the young woman in a navy pantsuit and sensible shoes seated across the desk from me. "Miss Taylor, would you care for a drop?"

Her mouth pinched. Which was a feat, because her mouth was already so small it looked like a tiny puckered butthole.

Her choice of brown lipstick was an unfortunate one that only added to the effect. Every time I looked at her, I had to bite the inside of my cheek so I didn't laugh.

"No," she said, like she was offended by the question. "I don't drink."

Rayford and I shared a glance. My heavy sigh came again.

"Call me if you need anything else, sir," said Rayford. He nodded at Taylor, then excused himself, leaving the library doors open behind him.

Miss Taylor didn't waste a moment getting back to the subject at hand. "Section four D could be problematic. I think it's too vague."

My head pounded. We'd been reviewing the paperwork for almost two hours, and every time I thought we were close to finishing, she found something else she deemed problematic.

The crick in my neck was problematic. The cramp in my lower back was problematic. The raw ache in the place in my chest where my heart was supposed to be beating was also problematic, but I wasn't thinking about that.

It makes no sense to dwell on things that are out of your control.

I took another big swig of bourbon instead.

"Four D," I repeated, flipping through the document. "Right." I stared at the page. Legal terms swam up into my vision. I poured more booze down my throat.

How is she? What's she doing right now? Is she thinking about me?

Fuck. Who was I kidding? No amount of bourbon or denial could stop me from thinking about Bianca. I knew I'd be thinking of her for the rest of my life, which was part of the reason I was so depressed.

"Excuse me?"

I snapped my head up. Taylor was staring at me like I'd farted in church.

"What?" I asked apprehensively.

"You made an odd sound. Like you were trying to say something."

Oh, no, Taylor. That's only the sound of rampant despair. Please ignore me, I'm just over here dying. "Thinking out loud," I said with a straight face. "Sorry."

She looked like she had an itch somewhere indelicate that she really needed to scratch. She folded her hands over the contract in her lap and glared at me. "Mr. Boudreaux," she said, her pinched lips barely moving, "would you like to take a break?"

I almost groaned in relief. "Yes. I need to stretch my legs. Back in ten." I was already on my feet and headed toward the door.

"I'll be right here," she said, adding to my misery.

I had to get out of the house before I started throwing things.

Ignoring Rayford's startled glance when I passed him in the kitchen, I burst through the French doors and out into the cool evening air. Then I stood on the lawn in the backyard with my hands on my knees, gulping in deep breaths, wondering how long it would take before the taste of Bianca's skin would fade from my memory.

It had been six days since the funeral, and I was dying by degrees without her.

But the nights were the worst. The dreams, dear God. Torture. Every little moment I spent in her presence had somehow seared itself into my subconscious, so when I fell asleep I was treated to a Technicolor replay of everything she'd ever said to me, every look, every smile, every touch. They were nightmares of a sort. Especially the dreams about our time together at Moonstar Ranch.

Even in my dreams I could taste her.

"Fucking hell," I muttered. I straightened and ran a hand over my face. My beard, which grew like weeds, was almost as thick as it had been the night I met her. It was a scratchy mess, not unlike my brain.

I spent a few minutes just breathing, letting the fresh air clear my head. Then I wandered down to the lower lawn where the tent had been set up for the Wounded Warrior benefit, leaned against the rough bark of an ancient willow, and stared out at the lake. It glittered like a thousand stars under the light of the rising moon.

Being with Bianca had changed me in ways I didn't know I could change. They say it's better to have loved and lost than never to have loved at all, but that was a big, steaming pile of bullshit. It was infinitely worse for me now. I thought I'd loved Cricket, but that was nothing compared to the fire Bianca stoked in my heart.

I loved her so much it burned. It scorched and glowed white-hot in all the dark places inside me, like I'd swallowed the sun.

But this was reality now. Loneliness and longing and arms that ached to hold someone who was no longer there. Who would never be there.

Who would never love me.

My eyes stung. I realized when I swiped my fingers over my cheeks that they were wet. I laughed—a hoarse, ugly sound—and turned away from the lake. I couldn't stand to look at it suddenly. It made me sick. The moonlight reflected off its surface was too romantic, and I was in no mood for romance.

Let's get this over with. Glaring at the house, I took a moment to steel myself, then I trudged back inside, not ready to finish what I'd started with Taylor, but knowing it had to be done.

Rayford wasn't in the kitchen. From down the long hallway, I heard raised voices.

Someone was shouting in the library.

A woman.

I knew it was only my lovesick heart that made the voice sound like Bianca's, but I took off at a run anyway. My steps echoed like gunfire off the marble floor.

When I reached the open library doors, I skidded to a stop, blinking in astonishment.

Rayford lounged on the sofa, an amused smile lighting his face. Standing on opposite sides of the coffee table were Taylor and Bianca, squared off like pistoleros about to draw their guns. Bianca was dressed in rumpled pink pajamas with little blue bunny rabbits all over them, a beige raincoat, and a pair of those hideous clogs she wore to work. Her hair was sticking up in wild tufts all over her head.

She looked like an escapee from an insane asylum, and also the most beautiful thing I'd ever seen.

"And another thing!" she shouted at Taylor. "You really shouldn't wear brown lipstick!"

"Well hello there, sir," said Rayford calmly. "As you can see, Miss Bianca and Miss Taylor were just gettin' acquainted." His smile grew wider. "I tried to tell Miss Bianca you were busy, but she almost broke down the front door, so here we are."

"Bianca," I said, my voice raw. "What're you doing here?"

She turned to me with burning eyes and a heaving chest, the color high in her cheeks. She shouted, "I'm here to stop the man I love from marrying the wrong woman!"

Taylor's mouth dropped open.

Rayford giggled.

And my heart stopped dead in my chest.

I wheezed, "Love?" before Bianca cut me off.

"Yes, that's right. *I love you, Jackson Boudreaux!*"

It sounded like an accusation or a confession of something terrible and terminal, like you'd say, "The tumor is inoperable and I only have a week to live."

But she kept talking, and my heart rebooted and took flight like a phoenix rising from the ashes.

"I'm sorry I didn't realize it sooner, but I think I'm just about as stubborn as you are. You're the best man I've ever known, and I'll be damned if I'm gonna let you hitch your wagon to some cash-hungry bottom-feeder just to save your inheritance!"

She gestured to Taylor, who cried an offended, "Oh!"

I exhaled, and it was like fire.

Bianca stepped toward me. She squared her shoulders and looked up into my face.

She said, "My whole life I've been waiting for someone like you. Only I didn't know that someone would come with a caveman beard and a bossy streak and a scowl that could peel paint from the walls. And then you came at me with your ridiculous proposal, and then Mama died, and then I lost my mind, so it took me a minute to figure it out."

She swallowed. When she spoke next her voice was quieter.

"But I love you, Jackson. And I hope you know that I don't give a damn about your money, because I don't. In fact I think it would do you a world of good to flush that inheritance right down the toilet and live like a normal person for once."

She added drily, "I've recently been informed by my attorney that I'm a millionaire, anyway, so it's not like we'd be broke."

Taylor huffed. "Mr. Boudreaux, will you *please* tell this woman—"

"Shut up, Taylor," I said.

She threw her hands in the air and rolled her eyes.

Bianca took another step closer to me, then another, until she was so close I could see the flecks of gold in her beautiful brown eyes. She flattened her hands over my chest.

I thought my heart would explode it pounded so hard.

Bianca said softly, "We went about this whole thing ass backward. Marriage proposals are supposed to come *after* you've fallen in love, not before, but I have a feeling nothing we're ever going to do will be in the proper order. So what *I'm* proposing is that you tell this skinny little mercenary with the weird brown lips to go pound sand, and you and me get married."

Her lips curved into a shy smile.

I took her sweet face in my hands. She slid her arms around my waist and hugged me, and I wondered if it was possible for a person to die of happiness. I felt like I might float right off the floor.

I whispered, "That skinny little mercenary is my attorney, sweetheart."

Bianca blinked. Her brows pulled together into an adorable frown. "What?"

A rumble of laughter burbled up from somewhere deep inside me, shaking my whole body, loosening decades of anguish and pain.

"Taylor is my attorney. Has been for years. We're not getting married. We're working on the contract for the new division Boudreaux Bourbon's going to open in New Orleans. The one I'm going to run."

Bianca's eyes went wide. She squeaked, "Contract? *Division?*"

I nodded. "My father and I had a long talk after you and I left Kentucky. We agreed that opening a new distillery in Louisiana would be good for business. There's no wedding going on here."

Bianca's gaze turned to the paperwork on my desk, then to Taylor. She paled. Then she whispered, "Oh, shit."

From the sofa, Rayford cackled and clapped his hands.

Bianca whirled around and glared at him. "Rayford! You did that on purpose!"

He shrugged. "Sometimes you gotta give the blind a helping hand."

Bianca turned to Taylor. She put her hand over her chest and said, "I am so, *so* sorry. Oh my goodness. I take back what I said. You're not a mercenary. I'm sure you're a wonderful woman. You look very . . . smart. And you're not skinny, that was just me being jealous. You have a lovely figure."

Taylor crossed her arms over her chest. "And the brown lipstick?"

Bianca grimaced. "Well . . ."

"Enough apologies. Come here."

I grabbed Bianca by the arm and kissed her. She took big handfuls of my shirt and kissed me back like she was starving.

At some point Rayford and Taylor must've left the room, but I didn't hear them go. I was too busy drowning in Bianca.

"What about your inheritance?" she asked breathlessly, breaking away.

"It was get married *or* work for the company, remember? Not that I care about the money anymore. It was just time for me to let go of the past and grow up." I stroked her satin cheek. "You're responsible for that, you know. I never would've reconnected with my parents if it weren't for you."

Bianca rested her forehead on my chest. "So you don't need to get married after all."

A little tremor went through her. It made me smile.

"Technically, no," I whispered. "But I want to."

She lifted her head and stared at me. Her eyes glimmered with moisture.

"And I noticed you're still wearing your engagement ring, so I think you still want to, too."

A tear crested her lower lid and slid down her cheek. In a broken voice she said, "I just want you. Rich, poor, smiling, growling, bearded or clean-shaven, I just want *you*, Jax. There's nothing in the world I want more than you."

My happy sigh slipped past my lips, barely audible. "Be careful what you wish for, sweetheart," I murmured, my heart singing. "If you think *I'm* a beast, you haven't seen this beard when it really gets going."

Bianca's eyes were dreamy. She went up on her toes, wound her arms tightly around my neck, and whispered into my ear, "I can hardly wait."

SLAP, SLAP, KISS COCKTAIL

Makes 2 servings

- 1 ounce cognac
- 3 ounces vodka
- 2 ounces absinthe
- 1½ ounces gin
- 1 ounce blackberry liqueur

Preparation

1. Put all ingredients into a cocktail shaker with ice.
2. Shake vigorously.
3. Strain into two chilled cocktail glasses.
4. Down the hatch, kiss your beloved, enjoy a very potent happily ever after.

ACKNOWLEDGMENTS

This is the fourteenth novel I've published in five years. For some writers that number isn't so remarkable, but for me it's staggering because I've never sustained that kind of interest in anything except reading, napping, and a bath before bed.

There are many people who have helped this slothful writer produce fourteen books in five years, and they deserve more than just a few flowery words in the back matter, but this is all you're getting, guys. Maybe when I hit twenty I'll send you a plaque or something, but probably not. (You could always frame this page and hang it on the wall?)

In no particular order, here are the people who've helped me birth fourteen novels, and to whom I'd like to say THANK YOU:

Jeff Bezos

Amazon Publishing/Montlake Romance

Maria Gomez, my current editor at Montlake

Kelli Martin, my editor-between-editors at Montlake

Eleni Caminis, my first editor at Montlake

Melody Guy, my developmental editor who I would literally die without, who flagged the word *literally* during her last editorial pass, which makes me love her even more

Jessica Poore, my Montlake author liaison

Tara Gonzales, PR guru

InkSlinger PR

Najla Qamber, cover artist extraordinaire

Marie Force, NYT bestselling author

Teri Clark Linden, audiobook narrator

Sebastian York, audiobook narrator

Melissa Moran, audiobook narrator

Geissinger's Gang, my Facebook readers' group

My readers everywhere

Jay, my husband and my heart, without whom nothing is possible

Also I'd like to acknowledge the Wounded Warrior Project for their amazing dedication and service to the injured men and women of the US armed forces. To learn more about their mission, please visit www.woundedwarriorproject.org.

ABOUT THE AUTHOR

 J.T. Geissinger is the author of more than a dozen novels of contemporary romance, paranormal romance, and romantic suspense. She is the recipient of the Prism Award for Best First Book and the Golden Quill Award for Best Paranormal/Urban Fantasy. She's a two-time finalist for the RITA Award from the Romance Writers of America, and her works have been finalists in the Booksellers' Best, National Readers' Choice, and Daphne du Maurier Awards.

Join her Facebook reader's group—Geissinger's Gang—to take part in weekly live chats and giveaways, find out more information about works in progress, get access to exclusive excerpts and contests, and receive advance reader copies of her upcoming releases. You can also check out her website, www.jtgeissinger.com, or follow her on Instagram @JTGeissingerauthor and on Twitter @JTGeissinger.

Made in the USA
Columbia, SC
04 August 2023